Crombie Hill
By G. M. Donley

Crombie Hill
Published by Miscagon, Cleveland Heights, Ohio

ISBN (print paperback): 979-8-9876725-2-5
Library of Congress Control Number: 2023921262

Design by Miscagon
Printed in USA
First edition December 2023

For Carol, EB, Karen, and Gwen

Stacked inside an orange milk crate in a dim attic wing are old papers from college days. Among these is a typed manuscript in a slim black three-ring binder. Sheets of handwritten notes, torn from a journal, are interleaved throughout.

Primary Sources: Retracing an American Journey

Eleanor Webster
December 1988

1.

I hadn't even known I was looking for Emma Crombie's letters when I found them. History works like that sometimes.

When Aunt Cordelia died—she wasn't actually my aunt, but my father's mom's aunt—there was a general invitation to visit the property on Middle Ridge Road in Madison, Ohio, to give family members a chance to take any items they might want out of the house.

It's an old place, one of the oldest in the area, dating to the early- to mid-1800s. Madison isn't exactly a metropolis now, but back then it was just a name on a forest that somebody planned to make into a town. When this house was built, there were no other buildings nearby. Today, if you noticed the house at all, you might see how its windows are small and narrow and the dimensions of the building don't match up with the newer houses along this road. Now the little windows and the nonstandard proportions make the place easy to spot if you're looking for it, up on a rise, big trees in front that partially obscure the house from the road. Behind it is a mostly open field stretching along the edge of a hill, scattered with a few decrepit fruit trees. The house's flaking blue paint and gray wood beneath only add to the impression of a place being slowly forgotten right before your eyes.

I had not been close to Aunt Cordelia, nor had my dad, so I'd only been in the house a few times. I didn't have anything in mind to take home when we visited that Saturday morning during spring break in April. We wandered around the place, noting the sagging floorboards, marveling at the charmingly antiquated kitchen, negotiating the steep and narrow stairs to the second floor. Up there were a few small rooms, one of which had windows looking out over the back yard. In the distance, you could see a tiny little strip of Lake Erie on the horizon, so that would be north, more or less. The walls were painted the color of brown-shelled eggs, over wallpaper whose vertical stripe and floral pattern was slightly embossed so you could see it faintly. A small oval mirror hung beside a closet. My tanned face and pointy cheekbones startled me, the unkempt swirl of wavy dark blonde hair a reminder not only that I had not braided it today, but also that I had driven here with the car window open. My expression looked kind of wild and lost, so I smiled and then stepped away so the smile would stick.

Two other things caught my eye in that room: one was a small painting depicting a white house on a grassy hill with a forest rising behind it, and the other was a wooden box sitting on a side table with a piece of paper sitting on top that said "Emma Crombie." Emma Crombie? I had never heard that name.

I opened the box and found inside a stack of handwritten letters. Carefully pulling one of them partway out so I could unfold it a bit, I saw that it had been dated 1818. I read a few lines. "When we get to the top of a ridge and look out ahead there is a wide valley. We go downhill into that valley and cross the bottom of it, then we work hard up a big long hill on the other side until we get to the top, and then there is another valley. All the ridges go crosswise to the way we are going. Uz said it would be more convenient if we could just get in a valley and travel along in the same direction that the valley goes, but the Problem is that would not take us to Ohio. I am trying to save on paper so I am writing as small as I can. I think I am getting better at it. I took a knife and made a different edge and slot on the quill and now the ink comes off of it better. Please tell Mama how I did that, and it was not even Papa or Uz who told me how, I just Figured it out."

I'm taking this box, I thought. I slid the folded sheet back in place. I lifted the little painting off its hook and picked up the box and went back down. Having no free hand to balance, I leaned and slid my shoulder down one wall of the narrow stairwell. The worn-shiny/grimy strip on the paint suggested this was standard procedure.

My grandma was downstairs and I showed her the two things I wished to take. Her eyes lit up and she burst out in her low husky voice "Oh, that funny little painting. I'd completely forgotten about that. Maybe you can figure out where that place is. If it's anywhere." She muttered those last few words more quietly. "Please do take it, though. And that box—you might find this interesting with that literary-historical type of mind you've got, Ellie—that box contains letters written by a young girl named Emma Crombie as she emigrated out here from New Hampshire in the early 1800s. For generations ever since, someone or other has had the presence of mind to save that box. Or at least never got around to really cleaning out the house." She placed the box on the kitchen table and opened it, carefully thumbing across the tops of the letters without removing any.

"That's awesome," I said. "So I can take it?"

"You just have to promise to keep it alive, pass it along, Ellie. It's not just some grubby old thing to forget about."

"Of course I will." I pulled the box across the table and closed it again. "But . . . who's Emma Crombie? And how come I haven't ever heard of her?"

"Oh, well you may have noticed," she looked up to see who else was nearby, "that this family pays a bit more notice to the grandpas and uncles than to the ladies they married. That's a natural enough thing. If the last name isn't Webster, then it's—well, not a footnote, but . . . peripheral, that's the word I was looking for."

I laughed. I had picked up on that annoying dynamic.

"But of course," she whispered, "that important-looking framed Sons of the American Revolution certificate in your papa's office doesn't trace through the Websters, it traces through Emma Crombie."

"What? I thought we were related to Daniel Webster."

"Mmmm-hmmm, maybe just ask yourself have you ever heard anybody specifically affirm that, or do they just not say no? You know, people just jump to an assumption. Don't even think to ask the question."

"So how is she related?"

"Emma is . . . let's see . . . my mother's mother's . . . mother's mother, so my great-great-grandmother, and your whatever-that-is. Aunt Cordelia and I worked out a chart one time. Maybe I can find it for you. I was born in 1914, my mom in 1882, and her sister Cordelia a few years later, and their mom in the 1850s, her mom in the 1830s, and her mom was Emma. It all traces through women, mind you, and as I said, you know we're kind of peripheral to the family story, all those forgotten maiden names." She winked at me. "Except when you're needed for your patriot credentials!"

"Typical," I shook my head. "Anyway, if it's really okay, then I will definitely take this box. Keep it safe. Pass it on."

My grandma handed me the box and raised her hand in a mock toast. "Here's to the patriot women, whoever the hell they were!"

"Hear, hear!" I said. I love my grandma. She's a hoot.

2.

I took the box and the picture home and that night I read through the letters. It was a fascinating, sometimes harrowing account of a journey into what at that time was barely charted wilderness, all written from the perspective of a girl who turned 12 along the way. As a historian, it struck me not only as an interesting personal story, but a glimpse into a formative time in our country's evolution, an iconic journey that could stand for many similar migrations taken by many other pioneering families.

That in itself was interesting enough, but even more intriguing was Aunt Cordelia's map. In blue pen on plain white paper, it showed a series of circles with labels that read, left to right: Madison, North East (?), Lake Trail, Wales (?), Geneseo, S. Livonia, btw. Geneva/Seneca Falls, Cazenovia, past Cherry Valley, Altamont, Hoosick, before Brattleboro, Crombie Hill. I went out to the driveway and fished around in my dad's car and found an eastern United States road map. It didn't have enough detail to find half the places. But his 1984 New York

State road map had nearly everything, and since it had been published only four years ago, I decided it should be pretty accurate. I lined up Aunt Cordelia's map and plotted her circles against the road map, locating each with red marker.

In that moment, the concept for this honors thesis formed in my mind. I could retrace the journey of Emma Crombie and document it from my own perspective as a young, educated woman in 1988. This would not be another dry tome droning on with that patronizing air of unassailable authority that characterizes every history book I've ever read, but rather, in effect, another primary source text, matched to the late 1980s version of the same landscape Emma had traversed in the early 1800s. But because I would be undertaking this effort with the knowledge and skills of a trained historian, my account could bring a level of informed insight to the project. In short: a new way to do history. Finally, an honors project idea that I could get excited about.

The other element of the concept that came to me instantly was that it would be ideal not only to follow Emma's path, but to do so at the same speed and closeness to the land that Emma had. Walking, however, would be impossible given the time constraints of the coming summer. That was where I could play my other ace: the bike. As a fit and experienced bike racer, it would certainly be within my capability to do this on a bicycle. I checked the map again. Overall, the distances looked totally feasible—it would take one day on the bike between letters for most of them, a couple instances where I could cover two letters in one day. The roads were much better now, and traveling back then by mule-drawn carriage and/or walking would certainly have been much slower.

The next afternoon, as my dad drove me the two hours back to campus, my bike lying across my clean laundry in the back of the wagon, I asked if I could borrow the New York road map to plan out a possible summer project.

"Summer project that requires a New York state road map?"

"Grandma let me take this box of letters from Aunt Cordelia's house that are from when Emma Crombie came out to Ohio from New Hampshire, and I want to retrace that trip, or do it backwards, actually, here to there. Back in time."

"That? Oh yeah, Cordelia used to go on and on about those letters. It's not like they're a draft of the Constitution or anything, just a girl scribbling in her diary."

"No, they're more than that. Have you read them?"

"I don't know. Does it matter?"

My blood was hot but not yet boiling. My dad could be dismissive like that, but I knew the conversation wouldn't go to a useful place if I got into my feelings about how the women in the family seemed to get kind of second-fiddled. That was something to do more subtly, over a longer time—by making this journey and documenting it and showing in a way that anyone could see that Emma Crombie was a hero of this family even if none of the men were championing that idea. I don't think it was an intentional, overt relegation of women to supporting-actress roles as just habits of talking about the family. We were the Websters. So I changed tactics. "Anyway, letters or no letters, this summer might be my last opportunity to get out and see some of the country up close, and I want to take a couple weeks and do a bike tour. Next year I will probably be off to grad school and who knows what happens after that."

"Well, that does sound like a good use of a couple weeks, but you've never done anything like that, have you?"

"We've been backpacking a lot and I ride my bike all the time. This just combines those two things."

"I know you're an adult," he turned his head with a skeptical look, "but you're planning to do this all by yourself?"

"Yeah."

He paused. "Look, it's not that I don't have basic faith in my fellow human beings, but I'd be a lot more comfortable if you had somebody with you."

"So you want to ride with me? Just like Emma and her dad?"

He laughed. "Good one. I can barely climb two flights of stairs. I'd volunteer your brother, but . . . "

"Med school wins." I finished his sentence.

"Med school always wins," my dad nodded.

"Plus Kevin is in Boston and has a wife," I noted, "who already never sees her husband."

Then he looked over. "Your mom might be up to it. She's still got that bike. On the other hand, I can't remember the last time she had it out. But really, there must be some-body among all those rough-and-tumble bike racer friends of yours who would think this would be a fun way to spend the summer vacation."

"They'd be missing real races."

He nodded. "Well . . . I just had to say it."

I had not thought of this beforehand, but an idea took shape. I was pretty sure I could convince my biking buddy and former and now kind-of-again-boyfriend Axel to come along. That would accomplish three goals at once: one, give me a riding companion so they couldn't say I was doing something foolish (and plus, it really would be a good idea to have a bud-dy on an excursion like this, for a number of sensible reasons); two, finesse my parents into approving an adventure that I knew would be stretching their comfort (in a necessary way); and three, show Axel that he could do well to follow my exam-ple and get his act together life-direction-wise. That's a lot of boxes checked. "I think I would be okay going alone, but I see what you mean. What if I ask Axel?"

"Axel?" he sighed. "Of course, Axel. Are you two formally 'dating' now, if that's what you call it? Well I guess he's harm-less enough, even if he isn't exactly setting himself up for the corner office." I'd heard this insinuation before. I think it was less a criticism of Axel than a questioning of my judgment. I was ready for it.

"We're kind of together, but I'm not sure people do 'dat-ing' anymore. He's a very decent and capable person, and I trust him. He's just a little bit unfocused right now, like a lot of men are at his age. I think you were, if I'm recalling some of Mom's comments accurately. I actually think this could help him."

"That's very magnanimous of you." He paused for a few seconds. "Look, you're 20 years old. I'm sure half the men who fought in the Revolution were under 20. You can do what you want. I'll be the enlightened modern dad. And your mom will have doubts but she'll bite her lip. I'm sure Axel will agree because what red-blooded American boy would say no to an opportunity like that?"

"Come on, Dad, he's a good friend."

"I'm sure he is, and no ambitions beyond that, right? When I was his age, no girl would have . . ."

"Dad . . ."

"All right all right, I said all right. If you're gonna go, you're gonna go. It's not like you all haven't been off at college doing whatever you wanted for three years anyway. And I really am more comfortable knowing you'd have a teammate to watch your back, so to speak. You can even borrow my New York road map. Maybe get me a new one while you're out there."

So that went okay. I don't know what I'd do as a parent of me, to be honest. Not my problem, fortunately.

$$3.$$

In every bike race, Axel somehow always managed to look like he was terribly out of position with three laps to go, and then he'd miraculously get himself into the right place when it came to the finish, but this time it didn't work out that way. A big crash on corner three before the bell lap took him out just as he was moving up to the front, and he ended his day flipping over some hay bales into a clump of flowering azaleas. He and his bike emerged only a little bit scathed, and also decorated with pink and white blossoms: a nice, pretty wipe-out, as these things go.

I was able to see the whole lovely vignette unfold because the women's race had finished an hour before, with our collegiate team putting in a good showing of three girls in the top ten, including first place. We had worked well together getting our sprinter Nonie into position and me leading her out into the final 300 meters, and she took it from there. I hung on for eighth. That might sound impressive, but the women's fields are smaller and the whole group was only about 30 racers.

The main-event men's race (the men's race was always the main event) started out with 120, reduced by attrition to maybe 80 or 90 by the end, but that's still a lot of bikes to run through the corners at 30 miles an hour, especially toward the end when everybody who thinks they can win takes more chances to try to be at the front when the sprinting begins. The rarity is for there not to be a crash in the final laps. So Axel shrugged it off.

"On the wrong wheel at the wrong time," he said, picking some petals out of his helmet. "No teammates left up there so I had to try to freelance it. Those orange jersey dudes were setting up some kinda leadout train so I jumped on that, but then somebody crossed wheels and boom chakka boom!" He yanked a twisted brake lever back into position. "At least the girls won."

"Women," I said.

Our collegiate team was made up mostly of people who raced outside of college already, and would get on the college team in order to scrounge a little bit more free food and maybe a water bottle or two in addition to the team jersey. There wasn't any team bus or anything—everybody had to make their own way to the race. Some of the races were collegiate-only, but most were just regular amateur races, and the college teams would participate just like any other team.

In his car on the way back, a cassette of the Replacements blasting on the stereo, I broached my idea with Axel. "Hey Ax. What would you think of taking a break from the summer racing circuit to take a little touring trip with me? On bikes?"

"Now? How about when I'm 50?"

"No really, it's a cool project." I explained about Emma Crombie's letters and Aunt Cordelia's map and how it would still be training even if it weren't racing if we retraced the trip on bikes. Plus it would be awesome to trace back to my family's colonial roots.

"I'm adopted, what the hell do I care about colonial roots?"

That was a point. Agency regulations forbade the disclosure of where adopted kids had come from, so all Axel knew was that his physical features seemed to imply some Asian lineage. He wasn't sensitive about that or anything. It was just a fact.

"Yeah, you're right," I said. Then I kind of oversold it. "Look, one thing is that they don't take me seriously and they don't think I should do this, and they don't take you seriously because they would never take any boyfriend of mine seriously, and they don't treat this Emma Crombie or any of the women in the family seriously because they're not named Webster. See what I'm saying? I have to prove them wrong. And we have to prove them wrong about you. Plus, why not? You don't have the freedom to do something like this too many times in life, right? Come back to my room and I'll show you the map and letters. Then you can decide."

But really, I knew that seeing the map would be the clincher. He couldn't resist that.

5-26-88

Taking notes, duh. No big journal or anything, just scribbles to remind me what happened on what days and who said what so I don't forget. Assume I'll be able to read my terrible hand-writing or somehow remember what the words must be. Later on when I write the whole thing up, refer to notes/fill in the rest from memory, add some history and [illegible], etc. That should work. I figure this story really begins before I will actu-ally start the ride, so background notes today to get it going. On the road I'll sit down for 15 min. in eve. when I get off the bike and scribble down what happened that day.

Or maybe I should try to write the whole thing as I go. That would be a real primary source. But Emma Too's letters, she didn't write about all those events and her brother getting killed and all that right when it happened. She did it later, when she had time. Still a primary source. So that's how I'm gonna do it, like Emma Too did. Except I'm not gonna write it out longhand except for my notes. Type and retype [illeg-

ible]. Honors thesis ought to look good. So anyway, notes for today—

Asked Ax to do the ride. Told me he's adopted, why should he care, and go fuck myself. In a friendly way though. Told him careful what you wish for, wink wink. In the back of my mind I thought Chrissy might not be back yet and we might get a little private time, since that never happens. But no, we walk up, knock-knock. Chirpy Chrissy voice calls "Hi, I'm decent!" through the door. So much for my little storyline. But I was right about the other thing: Ax saw map and said he was in. I said cool but just be aware my dad thinks you want to get in my pants, and he goes Yeah right, we both know who the dangerous one is Ellie, and so much for [illegible].

4.

Primary source materials sometime digress into esoterica related to the occupation and interests of the scribe, thus establishing for the reader that the author has a certain level of experience and expertise in certain areas.

Mom's 1971 Raleigh International was still a sweet ride even if it was 17 years old now. Goldish-green with beautiful chrome lugs and Campagnolo cranks, pedals, and derailleurs, it was a thing of beauty. Designed for fast touring, the frame was made of Reynolds 531 steel tubing, just like many racing bikes, but it also had fittings for attaching racks, and bigger wheel clearance so you could put fenders on it if needed—it was a little bit heavier than a racing bike, and its handling leaned toward stability rather than twitchy-fast, but it was still plenty fun to ride.

She had gotten the bike when I was a kid so she and her older sister could participate in a two-week tour in Vermont during the height of the "bike boom," as they called the early-1970s time when European-style bikes and cycling culture experienced a popularity surge in the U.S. They made that Vermont trip and then, to my knowledge, never made another, though mom used to like to take the bike out for a spin on a sunny Sunday afternoon from time to time. But mostly, the International gathered dust.

She and I are about the same height, and I had borrowed the bike before, so I already knew it would fit with a little bit of adjustment. In fact, one time for fun we put mom on my Eddy Merckx so she could get the full racing-bike experience, but after a few spins around the neighborhood, she came back and declared that it required too much attention.

I figured Mom would probably be glad to see the old steed get a new adventure, so I lifted it down off the hook in the basement and cleaned it all up. Axel's bike-shop job made it easy to replace the chain and freewheel and run new brake and shifter cables, so Mom got all that out of the bargain too, even if she didn't know it yet.

As for Axel's ride, at first he said he could just ride his 3Rensho sprinter-basher bike and wear a backpack. Fortunately, the shop owner Jerry was within earshot and said "Are you out of your mind? By the time you rode that bone-rattler two days on bumpy back roads all your teeth would fall out and your ass would be filing charges for assault. We can figure out something better."

It did not take too long for them to cobble together a better option. First, there was a touring bike that had been gathering dust in the back of the shop for a couple years—a Univega whose frame had been damaged in a repair-stand mishap. Though the damage did not affect anything functionally, it rendered the bike unsellable, so the machine had been partially cannibalized for parts. The dented top tube of the Japanese bicycle was "repaired" with a French componentry sticker, the scratches in the paint touched up with clear nail polish to stop the rust. A saddle and a pair of pedals came from boxes of take-off components that people had replaced when setting up new bikes with non-standard stuff. Axel built up a new front wheel using a hub rescued from the trash and an aluminum rim nobody would buy because silver rims were out of fashion. A rear rack came from a junked bike and a couple cargo carriers got attached to that. The resulting vehicle was a hodge-podge and nothing too fancy, but it would serve the purpose. Upon our return, the official plan was that it would become the shop's grocery store bike, which was how the shop owner justified doing it all for free so Axel could have a reasonably practical bike to ride.

5.

The semester ended at the end of May. I knew my advisor, Dr. Hendrickson, the unofficial grand-poobah of the academic patriarchy, would be skeptical of my idea, so when I showed up for my appointment, I was ready for the questions.

"So let me see if I've got this right," he said. "The girl wants to write a report on 'What I did on my summer vacation' and get college honors credit for it."

"Well," I said, "I'm not really taking a vacation this year. This is a working project."

"That just happens to be on a bicycle?" He glowered at me over the half-glasses.

"The original journey was on foot and by mule-drawn wagon. I can't really do that, but driving it in a car would insulate me so much from the details of the land and the people. Doing the same route on a bike is slow enough to really get connected to the landscape and meet folks along the way, while also being fast enough that I could do it this summer."

"And the idea is to retrace the route taken by this little girl at the beginning of the last century."

"Exactly, but in the reverse direction, from the end point to the start. I would intersperse transcriptions of her letters in my own detailed account, so her letters would appear in reverse order, matched up with the places where they were written."

"Why?"

"Because her journey stands for the journeys so many others took in the generations after the Revolution, and because her perspective as a young female is unique. We don't get that point of view in the history books."

"With good reason." He smirked. "History is not made by young girls, is it? Marie Antoinette notwithstanding."

"History as written by middle-aged men is not made by anyone but middle-aged men," I retorted. "It's a limited picture. We need more. History is fascinating, but every history book I've ever read is a drudge, just some tweedy guy standing up there telling you what everything is supposed to mean. I want to reinvent how history is told."

He sighed and rolled his eyes. "Do you want to be taken seriously as a historian or not? This isn't even a confirmed primary source. How do you know it's authentic? How do you know it wasn't dreamt up and faked by some dreamy-eyed coed in 1950?"

He had me there. "I did take the letters by the historical society and they said the paper was the right age and the language was appropriate and there was nothing to suggest they were not created around 1820, but you're right, it's not possible to verify that 100 percent. They could be more recent writing on old paper, for example. But we do know that a lot of families migrated along this pathway during those decades in the early 1800s, and my objective would be to compare what I can learn of the experience of those people to my experience today, and take from that some lessons about this country and what makes it tick. Why do certain narratives rise to the top while others are closed out?"

"The letters alone are pretty thin, and I take it you don't really know much else about this person or even her offspring. Why not skip the bike ride and the letters and just do a research paper on early 19th-century migration from New England to Ohio? Oh wait, I remember why—books have already been written about that. And besides, you're going to show everybody how to do it better because all the historians who came before you are a bunch of old crushing bores."

"We have so little from that time that gives us the experience of a young female, I was hoping I could shed some light on what their experience may have been."

"You were hoping. That's not very scholarly. You need more than a sweet story and a big smile."

I bit my tongue. I was pretty sure he was talking in this incredibly sexist way to test my resolve, to try to provoke me into an emotional reaction. Not going to get sucked into that game when we both knew he had all the power. "Retracing the letters and doing the journey by bicycle is the closest I can get, within the limits of practicality, to what her trip would have been like. The history we tell ourselves about this country is built up from a whole suite of mythologies that leave out the stories of a lot of people: native Americans, slaves, women. Small-town people, out-of-the way people. Young girls who drive wagons. There's more to it than what a few old white guys in New York and Boston and Chicago and LA decide to pay attention to. I'm not going to accuse anybody or try to put motivations in their heads, but I think this project—by combining the letters that show the perspective of a young girl in the early part of the last century, and my own account that will show the perspective of a young woman in the last part of this century, and tracing along this landscape that is so rich with the early history of the United States as it expanded to the west—I think all that will add something worthwhile to the discourse."

"I'm sorry, Miss Webster, this just doesn't have the rigor I require for an honors project in history. One could complete this little exercise without even setting foot in a library. You can go ahead and have your adventure, of course, but I am not prepared to say that honors will be in the offing. And there's another matter. I'm sure you are aware that proposals for honors projects were due in March. Now, if there were some very recent historical event that had prompted this concept, I might bend the rules a bit, but in this case I'm afraid it's simply that you missed the deadline. Of course, I will be glad to read whatever you produce, and depending on the quality of that product, perhaps some credit might be awarded. But if not, this is your gamble. You'll have your degree, but no honors. That might affect your graduate school aspirations."

Once again, I didn't take the bait. I simply said, "All right. I can live with that. Thank you." And I left.

5-31-88

The thing with Hendrickson went about like I expected. I hoped he might see my logic, but I think it was just too far out of the norm, plus I [illegible] history with him already. And he was right about my missing the deadline by a couple months. I still think it's a solid idea—you have a general history of America that everybody kind of agrees on, but if you start to dig deeper you find out that same story means different things to different people. Stuffy academics vs. 12-year-old-colonial girls. Adopted kids from who knows where vs. black people. They're all American, right? Same story, but different story.

Anyway after walking out of there all proud of myself for not blowing my cool but kinda depressed because maybe I won't get honors, I went home and packed: camping stuff, two pairs of bike shorts, red team jersey, white one from last year, 2X bike socks, warm-ups, running shorts, lightest bra, those 2 little silk bikinis Gma gave me for Christmas ([illegible] but thrill for Ax maybe), t-shirt, tank top, long-sleeve base layer, thin rain jacket, flip-flops, soap, shamp, toothbrush, little towel. Got my BC pills, just finished my period, no worries. Bathing suit? Don't forget to pack this little notebook and a couple pencils.

While Axel went home briefly to stash college stuff in his old room, I got other things in order. First I found my mom's panniers she had used on her Tour de Vermont. Then I rummaged through all the family backpacking stuff to find the most compact cookstove, the smallest and lightest tent, a couple warm-weather sleeping bags, two ponchos. I grabbed a couple of little daypacks but they were too bulky so I decided we could use the panniers for shopping. Then I went up to my room and packed a small selection of light and fast-drying clothes, assuming we'd rinse or wash stuff every evening. Then I went to the camp store and picked up a dozen freeze-dried meals, figuring we could alternate those with real food. On the way back I got $200 cash and a couple traveler's cheques from the bank. The banks keep offering me free credit cards just for being a college student, but I haven't gotten sucked in yet. But it would have been handy right about now. Last, I stopped at the Amtrak station to pick up schedules and fares for the Lake Shore Limited, which we knew we could pick up in Albany or Springfield, Mass., to get back to Cleveland if we ran out of time to ride the bikes both ways.

Back at home in Shaker Heights, I called my grandmother to tell her about our adventure and to see if I could make another visit to Aunt Cordelia's house—more specifically, could Axel and I stay there overnight before we began our trip. Axel's parents lived down south of Cleveland in Medina, so it would be most convenient and save us at least 60 miles if we could just get up and go from Madison. Plus, Madison was where they had ended up in 1818, so starting there made sense anyway if the idea was to literally retrace Emma's route backwards.

"What, are you going to marry that boy?" She responded.

In general, she was suspicious of boys I dated, and she didn't really know Axel. Over the phone I could not read her face, so I wasn't sure if she was kidding or not. Probably at least seventy-five percent kidding, I decided. "What if I'm not the marrying type?" I dodged.

"Then you keep your name Ellie Webster," she answered. "What if Emma Crombie and that line of ladies after her had all kept Crombie? You'd be a Crombie."

"Well, I guess I am really. Mathematically, I'm as much Crombie as Webster, which is to say not much. It gets diluted by half every generation, right? Before long you're splitting atoms."

"Which is dangerous, I think," she said.

"So I hear. Never done it myself." I paused and waited for her to say something. When she didn't after a few seconds, I resumed. "So my plan is to use this as the basis for my senior honors project. I think between Emma's letters, which are an amazing primary source, and our contemporary view of the same migratory path, so to speak, it will be a very interesting way to creatively explore a bit of American history." I did not relate how my advisor had seemed to think that all I wanted to do was get college credit for taking my summer vacation, and that creating this narrative was not actually approved as my honors project.

"I should say so," she said, affirming that there was nothing wrong with the phone line. "It's got America written all over it. I'm a little bit surprised your university is willing to support it, though, I must say. In my day the old boys would not have been so enlightened. Is this history or creative writing, this senior project?"

"Well," I said, "they say history is written by the victors, and I think that writing can get pretty creative."

She snorted. "Well anyway," she said, "the front door is always open, doesn't even have a lock. So nothing is stopping you from staying there."

"Thank you." That wasn't quite a yes as much as a not-no, but I guessed I would take it.

"Be careful, honey." She actually was worried.

"Thanks, Grandma. I think if Emma Crombie could do what she did a hundred seventy years ago, I can do this. And don't worry, I'll keep Axel safe, too."

She laughed. "Just like a Crombie girl."

6.

Axel planned to arrive at my house at 4:00 in the afternoon on Sunday, June 12, 1988. He and his gold Ford Escort wagon showed up early. We loaded up all the camping gear and put the International up on the roof rack next to the Gran Turismo. My dad came out to the driveway and handed me a little envelope. "Just in case you need it."

My mom appeared next, wearing her light blue gardening hat. "So you're off?" She looked at me, then and Axel, then at the wagon. "That looks like my bicycle."

"Yeah," I said. "All set for a new adventure."

"You may borrow it," she gestured mock-beneficently with both hands. "Nothing wrong with asking."

"Sorry." I really had meant to formally ask. "Guess I got wrapped up in all the planning and I didn't make sure with you. Sorry, and thank you. It's really okay, right?"

"The brakes don't work for shit in the rain." Mom used profanity rarely, like a carefully chosen spice.

"Oh—is there a story?"

"Another time," she said. "You two had best be off before I change my mind." I knew she was my ally in this adventure as far as the sticking it to the patriarchy part went, but I also knew she was dubious about Axel (or probably any other male) being trustworthy enough to be alone with me over such an extended time. She leaned close to my ear. "If you ever feel even a little bit uncomfortable being alone with him, don't be proud. Get out of there and call us."

"I know what you're saying," I said, "but I wouldn't do this with just anybody. Axel's always been a solid friend and an honorable guy no matter what kind of relationship we've been in. Of course I'll ask for help if I'm wrong, but I'm not wrong about this. You don't have to worry."

"I'm a mom. I worry." She looked over at Axel and caught his eye. He smiled awkwardly and nodded.

"Thanks, guys. Love you both." I slipped the envelope into a zippered inner pocket of my pannier. "We'll call you from about halfway, somewhere around Syracuse."

"Call collect or use that," my dad said, pointing to the pannier where I had put the envelope.

My mom stepped back over towards Dad. "And you think it will take you about a week and a half one-way?"

"Yeah," I said. "It's 580 miles or so and we should be able to average 80 or 90 miles a day. We ride 65 every Saturday morning just on training rides, so we ought to be able to manage that. Then add some time for the extra baggage and unplanned stops or terrible weather. Coming back should be about week without extra stops, or we just take the train."

"Okay sweetie." She gave us both hugs, to my surprise. "Watch out for each other."

We backed out of the drive, waved, and were off.

Madison is just a township, not even incorporated. It's about 30 miles east of Cleveland, situated on a ridge that runs parallel to the Lake Erie shore about three miles inland. Some of the earliest European settlers in the region started out here after crossing New York state and then following the old Indian trail that ran along this ridge all the way from up near Buffalo. The elevation, a few hundred feet above the lake water level, meant the area was relatively immune from the malaria that plagued lower-lying parts, but it also helped make this part of northeast Ohio—and on to the northeast through Pennsylvania and New York—locally famous as the "snow belt." When cold winter winds come across the lake before it freezes or after it thaws, the moisture-laden air hits the higher elevation and dumps snow in copious amounts. It's not uncommon for Cleveland to have an inch or two of snow on a given night and Madison to have a foot on the same night.

Local farmers tell themselves, and maybe it's true, that the snow is good for agriculture, especially things like fruit trees and the cool-tolerant grapes that are cultivated in the area. Aunt Cordelia's farm still showed the remnants of hav-.ing once been an orchard, with scattered century-old apple tress still standing here and there behind the house. These are easiest to see as one approaches along Middle Ridge Road from the west, as I noted now. We pulled into the drive and left the car out front rather than putting it around back where people usually parked, because there were some low-hanging wires that the bikes might snag.

We walked in the unlocked front door and set our take-out Chinese food on the kitchen table.

"Hi kids," came my grandma's voice from the living room. "I decided to keep you company tonight."

7.

After we ate (Grandma had her own sandwich but also shared a bit of our hot and sour soup), I spread out the New York road map and described our general plan. These days it would be easy to drive from northern Ohio to central New Hampshire in a single day, and while riding bikes would not replicate the experience of a three-and-a-half month trek by foot and mule-drawn wagon in the era before pavement, the slower pace and physical effort and just being out in the air and the elements might put us more in the mind space of those pioneers.

"Well, that seems substantial," she nodded. "I can't imagine riding a bicycle all that way, but I guess you two know what you're doing."

"I can't imagine walking all that way," I said, "and that's pretty much what they did."

"That's true," she said. "And Axel—that's it, right? Axel not Alex?—what do you think of this?"

"Well," he said, "My full name is Alexander, but when I was a kid I would always write 'Axel,' and it kind of stuck."

I hadn't known that, but then I had never thought to ask.

"But, yeah, sure. We can do this. We're both in racing shape already, and this is easier than racing, so yeah."

"What are you studying?" she asked.

"Studying?" He looked at the map to try to discern what she was referring to.

"In school."

"Oh, school. Yeah, it's looking like I'll end up as a geology major."

"What brought you to that?

"Geology rocks." He paused. "Ha ha. No, seriously I was kinda aimless my first two years and me and my advisor looked at what classes I had to that point and what majors would be in reach, and geology worked out. Plus I like being outside, and you can do a lot of field work with geology. Now when I do bike races out in the country I can identify the rock formations I'm trying not to crash into."

"I've never heard of an aimless college student." She deadpanned, glancing over at me.

"No such thing," I said. "It may just not be obvious until later. You know, liberal arts."

"Mmmm-hmmm. And your parents, please tell me about them."

"You know all about my parents," I pointed out.

"Don't be annoying," my grandmother said.

"They—well, I'm adopted, first of all, but of course I do consider them my parents," said Axel. "They both work. Mom manages a craft store and dad travels a lot—he's like a city planning consultant."

"Well, that's interesting," she said. "My husband was an engineer, building bridges and such."

"Has he passed away?"

"No, he just took off. Midlife crisis, right? What's interesting is that he went on to work in a hardware store."

"Oh, I'm sorry," said Axel. "But that is interesting. Not your typical career path they tell you to shoot for."

"Not exactly," she said. "And how did you and Ellie meet? The bicycles?"

"I guess that's right," he said, looking over at me. "Was it at that Athens thing?"

"Probably I guess," I said, though I knew exactly the moment.

"Is that a solid basis for a relationship, the bicycles?"

"The faster it goes, the more stable it is," said Axel.

We all laughed, though I'm not sure it quite made sense.

"Do you have brothers or sisters?"

"No, just me. I was enough to handle, I guess! My mom had a very dangerous miscarriage and the doc said she should not try again, especially since she was already older, so they decided to adopt. The agency connected them up with me when I was about two years old. I don't know my story before that—they don't release that information."

"Oh, well it's wonderful that you found a loving family," she smiled.

Axel nodded. "I'm very grateful."

"Well, I guess you kids know what you're doing, and it looks to me like you'll take care of each other," Grandma said. "Enjoy your search for America!"

Axel chuckled. "Thanks, but what if I'm not even American? I'm just in it for the bike ride."

I chimed in "What even is an American?"

She squinted at us back and forth. "Well, maybe you'll find that out. And if you do, please tell me—good news or bad!"

I got out my camera, checked that the aperture and shutter speed (set for the Tri-X 400 film I always used for the school paper), and asked her to take a picture of Axel and me.

I had thought at first that Grandma was planning to spend the night, but after we got done talking and set up the sleeping bags in the living room, she came in and said she was headed back home. For her that was a 20-minute drive to the west, to the little town of Fairport Harbor where the Grand River empties into the lake. "I love you Ellie," she said. "You be safe. Both of you." Then her car engine started behind the house and the sound passed around the side and we went to the front window and watched the orange blinker go on, and the red tail lights pause then converge and move off to the right.

6-12-88

Surprise, Gma at the house! Had dinner, talked about trip. I think she was vetting Ax to make sure I'll be safe w/ him. Shoulda been vetting me [illegible]! She knew Ax kinda from when we dated before a couple years ago, but that never got serious, just turned into biking buddies. Then lately turned more back into a little more than biking buddies, but how much more? She doesn't know we never slept together or anything, not even now. Wonder what old people assume about "kids today"?

Not sure exactly where in Madison that first house was, but probably Middle Ridge—according to everything I could find that was the main way through here, old Indian path. So I'd call Aunt Cordelia's house a good a bet for our starting point (i.e. E2 ending point), esp. since it's pretty old. Don't know if THAT old, but it could be the actual house E2's dad built and they lived in. Funny how it's not that long ago, but that brand-new house they lived in that was one of the first ones around is old and worn out now, maybe long gone.

Did they build it big enough for the rest of family to come out and stay there from NH? Why are we sleeping on the living room floor when there's beds upstairs? I guess I know, so Gma would see the 2 separate sleeping bags for what that's worth. Just teammates resting up before the big adventure, right? And now he's asleep [illegible], so I guess that's gonna be true for one more night at least. Isn't he supposed to be the horny one? How much of history comes down to who was horny at what moments? Another honors project.

8.

May 15, 1818
Eliza Crombie, Crombie Hill, New Hampshire

My dearest sister Eliza,

I puzzled out what day it is, May 15, which is a Friday. Uncle Nathan told Papa where his cabin was good enough that we found it this morning. This is a place called Madison, the same as the President, but Papa says they should name it Adams because that President never owned a slave and Ohio is a Free state. There was happiness that we have arrived and sadness when Papa told about Uz, and about Hester. Uncle Nathan put his hand on Papa's shoulder and told him that we can meet the rider on the post road which is also the ridge road on Monday morning and send the letters.

Aunt Eleanor made a fine supper with some Rabbits and Carrots. Papa and Uncle Nathan talked about the land company and made a plan to visit two places where Uncle Nathan thought it might be good for the Saw Mill.

Papa says that thanks to Uncle Nathan and Aunt Polly, we will stay at Uncle Nathan's farm until we pick out the land, and then first the Saw Mill will be built, then a Frame House near to it. He said we will save the time of building a cabin that way, and then after Papa and I get settled into the house, we will build a Frame House for Uncle Nathan and Aunt Eleanor. Papa said how with so many fine, tall hardwood trees here, you could make a whole House with just two trees and make the beams as long and broad as you like and make the boards as wide as you like.

Uncle Nathan says we should have fine weather all through October, and he and Papa think that will be enough time to build the Saw Mill and our House at least. By next summer Uncle Nathan and Aunt Eleanor would get their House built and be able to move into it.

Aunt Eleanor took me aside and said two things to keep in mind for my safety were that a lot of Wolves are out in these woods so I should stay close and not go out alone. They are shy of people near a cabin, but not so much in the forest. We heard them howling in the night and I could not tell how close or far they were but I am going to stay close. The other things is that there are some rattle Snakes about and they like to lie coiled up next to a fallen log or a fence and sometimes under the cabin, so always watch where I am stepping. Uncle Nathan is trying to kill all of them, and the other farmers are too, but there are more Snakes than farmers and it might take some time for them all to get Killed.

I asked her if she remembered from Crombie Hill when the men set all of Rattles Snake Ledge on fire to try to burn them all out and stood around there with guns and axes to get the ones that didn't get killed in the fire, and she said yes it was a miracle that nobody got bit because those Snakes were mad. These ones here are big and fat and with a strong poison, she said, so you are not likely to get a second chance at life if you get bit. A few Bears live here, too, but not so many like in New Hampshire.

So I promised to be careful about those things, and you can believe that I will. Please tell Mama that I will be Careful.

Papa worried about Indians, too, but we have not seen any at all and Uncle Nathan says that they have all gone off West. Papa said he was not sure to be worried anyway, since the only Indians we ever met were always agreeable. Even the British are gone, and the French who used to come here sometimes.

Uncle Nathan told us a story how some of the folks who got here a few years ago during the last war with the Redcoats, they said they could hear cannon booms across the Lake from when Commodore Perry won the Battle of Lake Erie in 1813. Uncle Nathan said that glorious victory, even though it was just nine small American boats against five big British ones, and even though only a few score of men fought against each other, and even though it happened out in a wilderness where nobody lived yet, that battle chased the Redcoats off once and for all, and that made it the real end of the War for Independence. Aunt Eleanor said they were telling tall tales, though, no way you could hear that from so far away.

Your loving sister,

Emma Too

9.

Madison/Ashtabula/Erie/Barcelona/Park. Still dark for breakfast and a note for Gma, set off. Brr! Set sights for where I think E2 stopped, just past the PA/NY line. Place with a good lake view based per her letters, but who knows now with trees and bldgs and everything. Add some bikey banter, set tone.

Got on 5 in PA, met other riders. Asshole in BMW, etc. Barcelona then LE State Park, camped there. Dinner and to-morrow food from camp store. Hoping for nice romantic eve but Ax kept talking about bike racing. I got annoyed and said Can't you think about anything else and winked suggestively and he said What am I supposed to be thinking about? and I shrug and crawl in the tent and take off bike clothes and he follows me in and we fool around a little bit but he seems dis-tracted. Then he says maybe we should get some dinner ready, don't know when [illegible]. I'm like goddamn, torture me why don't you? And he's like I know and laughs and gets up to his knees and pulls his running shorts [illegible] boner. And I [illegible]. Are you blowing me off? And he says just [illegi-

ble] right now, you know what I mean? And I say no, I don't. I don't want to mess things up, he says. And I say what would get messed up? And he says [illegible] in that kind of relationship with me right now. And I say it's just sex, right? What's the big deal? (As if I had actually done it before, with another person.) And he says maybe you're right. But I gotta go with my gut and my gut [illegible] desirable and even though one head wants to get right in the other head says wait a minute. And I say I thought it was your gut not your head, which ever head. [Illegible], there's nothing to worry about. And then I lay back. And he looks at me for a long time and then pulls his shorts back down but [illegible] says I'm sorry and I say I bet I can fix that and he says I'm sure you could but we gotta make dinner and I say Fuck dinner and he says No really and I say why don't you just tell me Go fuck yourself [illegible] says If that would help and laughs and steps out of the tent and says [illegible] 10 minutes and that should give me time and he laughs again, and I say Fuck you [illegible] but then he's gone and it seems like the only thing to do. More like 10 seconds.

It's total dark now and I'm at the picnic table writing this [illegible] reasonable and take a deep breath [illegible] historical context and primary source account. I got to go to bed it's too dark to write.

In the morning, after we took the bikes off the roof and unloaded the rest of the gear from the back of Axel's wagon, we moved the car around back and locked it up. I don't know what time it was. Maybe a half-hour after dawn. It was chilly enough that we started out with long sleeves on. We rolled out the drive to Middle Ridge Road and then turned left, to the east—going back in time, I remember thinking, from where Emma ended up to where she started out.

"Oops, sun glare." I fished around in my jersey's rear pockets for the cheap sunglasses I had picked up during last summer's family trip to the beach in North Carolina. "How did people live without sunglasses?"

Axel already had his pair of fancy Oakley Factory Pilots on. "Blindly?" he responded. Those glasses cost as much as a department store bicycle, but he had gotten them through a team sponsorship. "It's not just the sun, it's the bugs and the dust and dirt."

I slid on the glasses with one hand while still holding the bars. I was not comfortable no-handing this bike quite yet. "There, now I'm stylin'."

"Not like me though."

"You ever feel guilty about having all that high-end equipment for free and other people are skipping going out to dinner to pay for it?"

"No." He laughed. "I'm legit broke otherwise."

Cycling is one of those sports where you can carry on extended conversations as you're training. Try having a deep philosophical discussion while swimming. I'm sure that social aspect is one of the attractions of bicycling, even though the athletes rarely mention it. To be honest, Axel and I hardly ever just sit around and talk. Most of our deepest conversations have been while riding.

"Hey, don't fart on me," Axel called from behind me, speaking of deep philosophical discussions.

"It wasn't me, it was that cow."

"Cows have four stomachs, right?"

"More fart power."

"Reagan says cow farts cause global warming."

"So nuke 'em."

Primary source details.

We hadn't actually test-ridden the loaded bikes before this morning. This could have been a major strategic error, but proved not to be anything more than a little extra excitement in our morning.

First, when one is used to flying around on an unloaded racing bike that weighs 20 pounds or less, the experience of plodding along on a loaded touring bike is like having gone from a Fiat Spyder to a U-Haul truck. Second, the balance of weight is much different, and requires a bit more care especially at slow speeds where momentum and gyroscopic action don't do so much to hold you upright. And third, since these bikes were much heavier, they not only took longer to go uphill, they took a longer time to stop. Axel's bike at least had powerful cantilever brakes brazed directly onto the frame, but the International had old-fashioned center-pulls that were spongy and unconvincing even without the extra cargo weight.

So we rapidly adapted our jumpy bike racer riding styles to more of a long-range planning attitude. For example, if I see a stop sign two hundred yards away, I better start braking now. And if the road is wet, double the distance.

Axel had actually foreseen this situation, and at our lunch stop just across the PA border, he opened an inner pouch of his bag and pulled out four sets of brand-new brake pads. "Could be needing these!" He laughed, and carefully put them back.

It will be helpful, I think, if I explain some regional historical background. As preparation for this endeavor, I had made an afternoon visit to the Western Reserve Historical Society in Cleveland. I took notes from a few sources about how and when this area of Ohio had been settled. A couple of those sources were first-person accounts (recalled and written down decades later) from people who had settled here in the early 1800s. I hoped to discover how typical or atypical Emma's journey had been, and to get some background information that might help Axel and me make our own journey with "open eyes," so to speak. I found nothing about any specific New Hampshire towns there, but of course this historical society is in Cleveland, Ohio, so naturally it would focus on Ohio. My plan was to pick up a detailed New Hampshire road map once we got to that state and then locate a library or local historical society once I got to Crombie Hill.

Ohio became a state in 1803. Prior to that, the area that would become Ohio was part of the Northwest Territory, ceded to the United States from Britain at the end of the American Revolution. The Northwest Territory had been divided in 1800 to allow portions of it to be defined as states. The Ohio territory had become a British colonial possession after the French and Indian War in 1756. Prior to that, it seems likely that the only Europeans to visit the region were French fur traders.

The history of native people in the area seems to date back thousands of years. By the time Europeans began filtering into the area, the predominant tribes were Iroquois and related off-shoots. The Iroquois, in turn, had displaced people speaking Algonquin languages, including the Erie, in the mid-1600s. Long before them, people including the Adena and Hopewell and "mound-builders" had been present, leaving behind their distinctive earthen works. None of the later populations had ever been dense, but rather small numbers of people ranging widely over the territory. However, some of the mound-building societies supported cities of thousands of residents around 2,000 years ago. The name "Ohio" comes from the river the Iroquois called O-y-o, and was used to describe the territory north of that river and south of Lake Erie.

The latest 1980s thinking suggests that the native peoples of the Americas had gotten here by way of Asia when, during the last ice age, sea levels were enough lower that people could walk across a land bridge to cross what is now the Bering Strait between Alaska and the far eastern shores of the Soviet Union. Those people had gotten to Asia by migrating eastward from North Africa and the Mediterranean. Europeans had also come by way of North Africa and the Mediterranean, so when the French fur traders first encountered the Algonquin and Iroquois, it was, in a way, family reunion.

But families sometimes have enigmatic internal relations, and the same proved to be true in this case. First, trading arrangements and various battles ended up with the British formally allying with the Iroquois Confederacy (the "Five Nations") against the French and against Indian tribes who had affiliated with the French. Armed with British firearms, the

Five Nations quickly extinguished the competing tribes who had been occupying the Ohio territory. But not long after that, other tribes began to migrate into the area, having been forced out of where they had been further to the east. By the time of the French and Indian War in the 1750s, there was constant turmoil in the region. George Washington came out (working for Britain at that time of course) and lost two battles against the French and their Indian allies, but eventually the British prevailed. Just before the onset of the American Revolution, Britain formally made the Ohio territory part of its province of Quebec. In the 1780s the area of Ohio was formally ceded to the United States.

Indian tribes in Ohio were divided in their affiliations during the American Revolution, with some siding with colonials and others with the British. Unfortunately, the colonials often did not differentiate among Indian tribes and in more than one case massacred people who considered themselves allies of the colonials, resulting in reprisals that further poisoned relations. By the early 1800s, many of the Indian populations had been forced out.

In the years after the Revolution, the Northwest Ordinance stipulated that these lands west of the Appalachians, newly acquired by the fledgling United States, would be available for settlement, especially by war veterans, and that slavery would be prohibited in these new territories. The authors of the ordinance came from Puritan descendants and they believed slavery was immoral. With the conclusion of the battle of 1812 after which the United States and Britain finally ceased their hostilities, the territory was steadily opened up to settlement. Ohio was at first settled by easterners from two regions: in the northeast, New Englanders migrated to what had been the Connecticut Western Reserve; and in southern Ohio, new settlement came primarily from Virginia. As a result, though Ohio was always a free state, attitudes about slavery were notably different in the northern and south parts of the state. These initial patterns were reinforced by the geographical fact that the best way to get to southern Ohio was from the south by way of the Ohio and Mississippi rivers, and the best way to get to northern Ohio was by way of the Great Lakes and waterways through upstate New York. Follow the water and you find the source of the attitudes.

Emma's migration fit right in with a pattern that took place throughout the early 1800s. New England families would send a sort of advance party out west to find a good place to settle. These first arrivals would build a cabin and get a farm up and running, then additional people from the home back east would move out to join the western settlers. In the early years, there were even crews of men who specialized in clearing land and building cabins that they would then sell to an incoming family who could thus make the move without having to start from scratch in a remote forest.

Early on, this migration took place along old Indian trails that had been improved for wagon travel. By the late 1820s, the Erie Canal had connected the Mohawk and Hudson rivers to Lake Erie, and that spurred much faster settlement of the parts of New York along that artery and opened up the upper Great Lakes (Niagara Falls prevented boat travel between Lake Ontario and Lake Erie). But Emma's move had taken place before the canal existed. I knew it would not be possible to literally recreate that journey since so much development had taken place in the intervening 175 years, but retracing the route by bicycle would give a more intimate sense of the landscape at least, and traveling under our own power would give some appreciation of the effort that had been required to make the journey. Meanwhile, bike travel would be fast enough that the trip could be made during a reasonable time over summer break. And I'd get back home in great shape if not in racing form specifically. That was my vision, setting out.

I am pretty sure the old Lake Trail would correspond with what is now Route 20 in Pennsylvania, but that seemed trafficky and not very attractive, so we opted for Route 5, a smaller road that clung to the lake shore and was marked by little green "scenic dots" on the map. I had also learned from my visit to the Western Reserve Historical Society that there were some parallel routes along some sections between Cleveland and Buffalo and travelers might opt for one or another depending on the weather or other factors, so it's possible we followed the exact path of Emma Crombie. There certainly were some very old houses along Route 5, we observed.

In any case, it was pleasant to follow along close to the lake. We rode single-file most of the time, taking turns at the front while the other would roll along in the slipstream behind. The winds were southwesterly anyway, so we were getting a helpful push, and that combined with first-day enthusiasm added up to our making very good time. Route 5 seemed to be a popular bikeway, as we encountered a number of other cyclists riding in groups. We sat on the back of one pack of eight or so and let them pull us for a good while. They were serious road riders, all dressed in bike shorts and real cycling jerseys with the pockets in back, the whole group taking turns in the lead, rotating counter-clockwise. As we came through a narrow wooded section, a couple cars gathered behind until it was safe to pass. When the road opened up a little bit, a big old boat car rumbled past, dark brown with a vinyl top and looking about seventeen feet wide. On the back I read Mercury Marquis and a faded bumper sticker that said Buy American. Just as that car got clear of our group and pulled back over to the right, a loud horn and revving engine signaled the likely presence of a driver who was about to take out his life stresses on us. Sure enough, a silver BMW roared by very close, then cut in hard, forcing the first two riders in our informal group to hit the brakes hard and swerve to the right. The third bike in line was forced off the road but somehow managed not to fall at the edge of the grassy ditch. A burly left arm with middle finger extended stuck up from the driver's side window, then he gunned it and peeled a bit of rubber.

Axel immediately jumped on the pedals and began a ferocious pursuit, heavy panniers and all, followed by a couple others in our group and me. The guy right in front of me couldn't hold the speed and came off the group. I surged around him and muscled myself into the slipstream. The International was enjoying this. Seconds later we heard the car horn blasting again ahead and saw brake lights. The bimmer guy was stuck behind the boat car. Not only that, the dark brown Marquis was half out into the road and gradually slowing. Our group presently caught up and surrounded the silver car as the boat car came to a complete stop in front. While a chorus of profanity directed at the driver might have been perfectly appropriate, this time Axel arrived at the driver's window first, and Axel had his own strategy in these situations. "I'm sure you didn't realize what you were risking back there, sir," he intoned in his most level and reasonable voice. "A respectable gentleman with such a fine automobile would never intend to hurt or kill an innocent person—and certainly would not have been thinking of his indisputable criminal liability in such a situation." The driver said nothing, but the window rolled up.

"You folks okay?" The driver of the Marquis, a white-haired gentleman in overalls, was standing by his open door.

"Yes sir," Axel called. "Thank you."

"Brave fella there, huh?" The man replied, shaking his head. "You want me to report anything?"

"No thanks," Axel said. "I think maybe he understands a little better now."

"I wouldn't count on that, but it's nice to see you kids so optimistic." He turned back toward the car. "Look, I'll move on real slow and you all let Mr. Grumpy here be on his way and I'll then I'll let him pass and get on to abusing his employees or yelling at his wife or whatever he's in such a hurry to do."

Axel waved and nodded. The BMW driver never said a word, but drove off behind the Marquis, which pulled to the right after half a minute and allowed the silver car to pass.

"Helluva sprint, dude," one of our temporary companions high-fived Axel. "You got booster rockets in those bags?"

"Adrenaline," he replied.

"And her too."

"I just know when to jump on a wheel," I said. "Speaking of which," I pushed off. "Let's roll."

Our companions took a turn inland after another 20 minutes during which we related our adventure plan and they noted a couple other good riding routes in this area should we ever find ourselves around here again. "May the road rise with you," one of them sang, quoting a Public Image Limited song that was on the radio a lot lately. I think the phrase is very old. Maybe somebody said it to Emma Too and her dad when they set off from New Hampshire.

We crossed the PA/New York border, 80 miles already according to my little Avocet bike computer (which Axel had cleverly thought to procure from the shop), at about 3:00 and started thinking about finding our first campsite. Emma's letters suggested they stayed right around this place, maybe a mile or two behind us, but we weren't ready to stop quite yet. Before long, we came into the little town of Barcelona, which had a tiny village park around a beautiful stone lighthouse—this would be a very cool place to stop for the night, but unfortunately it didn't appear there was any way we could unobtrusively set up our little tent. So we forged on. The map noted a Lake Erie State Park with camping about 20 miles up the road, so we decided to be official for our first night and pay for a real campsite.

It was a lovely spot, on high bluffs overlooking the lake. I could imagine weary travelers gazing out there in centuries past, glad for the day's progress and also glad to sit down. Maybe Emma went right along this bluff and had the same view but going in the other direction.

"Hey, can't you imagine a race that finished up here?" Axel was standing on the picnic table. "If it started back from the lake and finished here, the riders would get this great view just as everything was winding up, and for the spectators and everybody it would be a great place to just hang out."

"Can't you think about anything besides bike races?" I teased.

"Why, what should I be thinking about?"

I shrugged.

Rather than get into our freeze-dried delicacies, we bought enough food at the park's camp store to make dinner and breakfast and the next day's lunch. I snapped a couple pictures of the lingering sunset under wispy pink clouds. I had packed three 36-exposure rolls of Kodachrome and my not-too-heavy Pentax school camera that had a light meter built in so hopefully I would not waste much film on guessed exposures. Axel thought of propping it on the picnic table and using the automatic timer to get a shot of both of us with the lake behind, but we decided to wait until the morning when the light would be from the east instead of behind us. Then we forgot to take the picture in the morning.

10.

May 3, 1818
Miss Eliza Crombie, Crombie Hill, New Hampshire

My dearest sister Eliza,
We have had some fine days and some rainy days. Artemisia is tired and we are not pushing her too much, because she has done so much for us already without Hester to help her pull the wagon.

Papa thinks we finally got out of New York state today and we are in Pennsylvania. It feels as if we have been traveling across New York for 10 years, so that is a relief to be in Pennsylvania. However, the land and sky and forest appear exactly the same. The trail is a mire of muddy ruts and it follows along the ridge line. From time to time, when the trees allow, we see that water over to our right side and you can't see the other side of it and to our left side is the forest and you can't see the other side of that either. Papa says he looked at a map and Pennsylvania has a short coastline on Lake Erie between

New York and Ohio. New Hampshire has a short coastline on the Ocean, at Portsmouth. You don't need to have the whole shore to yourself as long as you can stick your toe into the water, Papa says. So that is why Pennsylvania has a small coastline on Lake Erie.

I have been thinking about Uz and whether he will stay where he is. I asked Papa again and he said he had not settled his mind on that yet, it was too soon. He said Mama might want Uz to be with her, or she might want him to rest where he is. He said he is troubled that the burying grounds in New Hampshire are too small and might not be taken care of forever since it is not part of the town cemetery. I said I cannot picture the town cemetery and he said it was just getting started.

After mostly my whole life in Crombie Hill, I can tell you some things that are different here. First of all, I don't see rocks. The only fences I see are made of wood, not stone. Some leaves are just coming out on the trees now, and there are a lot of pretty blossoms. Some of the trees are pines, but Papa says most of them look to be oaks and maples and beech and cherry, with sycamores and cottonwoods in the bottomlands and dogwoods underneath. They are very tall trees except for the dogwoods. I am sure I have never seen so many trees so tall and big around.

The hills are gentle, but with steep valleys when we cross a river. When the wind comes off the lake, it is a much cooler breeze than when it comes from the other side.

It was my birthday last week but I forgot. Papa remembered, though, and he gave me a little packet with a bear that Uz carved for me, and he said that getting to be 12 years old in this hard life is an accomplishment and he was glad to be my Papa, that I was growing up strong and smart and pretty like Mama, so please tell her that!

I hope I can be useful to Papa in building the cabin, and I am also wondering what other folks we might meet here. The first thing we will do, says Papa, is find Uncle Nathan and Aunt Eleanor. Then we will find a proper parcel of land to buy for making the Sawmill and maybe put up our new house there, too.

Your loving sister,

Emma Too

<h1 style="text-align:center">11.</h1>

We awoke to clouds and spitting drizzle. Comparing our map and Emma's letters, it seemed like we should continue along the lake to somewhere around Ellicott, where we would find Route 20A and head east. Route 5 merged temporarily with Route 20 along the way, then they split apart, but again it appeared that Route 20 was often a busy commercial thoroughfare, so again we opted for the parallel Route 5 closer to the lake shore. At Athol Springs, we would find Big Tree Road and that would take us a couple miles inland where we ought to find 20 and a turn-off for 20A. Right near this place would be where Emma had written when they reached the Lake Trail.

But that spot looked to us like only 45 miles or so from our starting place, so we decided to shoot for somewhere around Wales Center, a bit farther along, where Emma had also written.

Our bellies fueled with instant oatmeal and raisins, we set off. In was only later in the day that I realized we had not gotten a photo of ourselves near the lake. Well, maybe on the way back.

We ascertained presently that the clouds and drizzle had been accompanied by a wind shift to the northeast, so our progress today was more labored from the outset. It never poured rain, but there were intervals of heavy sprinkles—enough dampen everything we were wearing to the degree that stops turned quickly into shivers. So we made a point to keep rolling. That agenda was helped by the fact that today's gray mist eliminated the expansive views we had enjoyed yesterday and we focused instead on plodding our way into the headwind. You kind of get in a trance.

"Hey Ellie," Axel jarred my attention from just staring at his freewheel spinning and the water droplets spitting off it. "Look at that." He pointed at a sign we were approaching. It read "Cattaraugus" and then a long word, undecipherable to me, followed by "Seneca Nation." We quickly passed it.

"Well, that was cool," I said.

"We're trespassing, man," he replied.

We both laughed.

"I wonder if they were still here when Emma came through?" I called ahead.

With no cars in sight ahead or behind, Axel pulled off to the left and coasted back to ride beside me. "Seems like they would have been, if you figure the reservation was made around where they were already living."

"Nothing about that in the letters."

"Guess they must not have been too dangerous."

"Isn't there a Mark Twain story about frogs and Cattaraugus County?"

"I don't know. Good frog weather now."

That was just like Axel. If he was being led into an area of knowledge or experience with which he was unfamiliar, he could deftly deflect the conversation. I gave him a little primer on Mark Twain and then went through some of the history I had learned about migration along these pathways and what I could recall about the history of the Indians in this area. I was pretty sure he could hear me because he would nod occasionally, but as he was in front pulling us into the wind as I talked, it was hard to tell. But I knew he didn't mind my talking because if you want to get somebody to shut up on a bike, all you have to do is crank up the pace hard enough that they have to choose between talking and breathing. Most people choose the latter. Axel was certainly capable of putting me in gasp-for-breath mode but he wasn't doing that. So I educated him about the land bridge and the mound builders and the fur traders and the Five Nations and the Connecticut Western Reserve and the Erie Canal, and how those morally steadfast New Englanders had set that standard against slavery as they settled to the west, and how I was proud that my own ancestors had been part of that tradition and I felt like that thread of righteousness carried through to the present day, like it was in my blood.

Axel paused my monologue by pulling off to the side and then getting behind me to let me pull into the wind for a while. It seemed to be shifting from northeast until now it was coming from straight north, so we were riding into a left-crossing headwind. We continued on for another hour or so, trading pulls every few minutes. Just around midday, we stopped at a town park in Hamburg and had our packed lunch. I was glad for the invention of lycra clothing. A few years ago, we'd have been wearing wool shorts and jerseys, and that would be miserable today. These new fabrics hold their shape better and dry a lot faster.

12.

April 26, 1818
Miss Eliza Crombie, Crombie Hill, New Hampshire

My dearest sister Eliza,

I am writing to you on a Sunday again, and that is because today we finally got to the Lake. You should see it. We were walking and walking and walking, because I was walking too on account of wanting to give Artemisia some assistance and because I got tired of Papa and me being too far apart so we could not talk very much, and this way I could walk next to him. We went over top of a little hill and up ahead between the trees I saw a piece of blue down past the end of the road. After a time we came out on an open field at the top of a bluff and that blue water was stretching as far as you could see to both sides. Papa decided to put our camp right there.

We were delayed in getting here because it went cold for more than a week and we had a very big Snow Storm. It was up past my waist. We could not get the wagon going anywhere and even if we could put the runners back on, the snow was too deep. Papa said we should be only about one day from the Lake, maybe closer, but we were stuck there for eight days. On the sixth day it got warm again and rained and that made the snow melt away but I told Papa I want to get to higher ground so we don't get in a freshet and he looked around and said he don't think we need to worry but just in case let's move over there, so in the pouring rain we walked Artemesia and the wagon up onto a hillock that was a little higher than the hillock we started out on.

Right about sunset on the first or second day of the snow-storm, we got bright sun shining on us while the snow was still snowing heavy. When it stopped for just a minute Papa pointed out over toward the sun and you wouldn't believe it but the sky was pure blue over there and then there was a solid line of gray and white clouds. It looked like the shore of a lake in the winter, except upside-down. The sky was the water and the clouds were the snowy land. Especially it looked like that when I laid down and looked at it upside-down.

The snow got heavy on the wagon and Artemesia was getting stuck in it, so even though we weren't going anywhere we still had to work all day to keep the snow from piling up too high on the wagon and to keep digging out Artemesia. It got so it looked like we carved out a cabin floor on the ground with walls of snow around it and us and the mule safe inside. It snowed like that for two days and then it was still Cold for some more days, and there was still no way to get anywhere on the trail which you could not even see, so we had to wait.

After the snow melted enough, we got on our way but it was slow on account of the mud. This morning Papa said let's take a Day of Rest after all of our hard work of staying in one place. It turned out that it was a Sunday but Papa said that was just a happenstance. He says if I want to go to church all my life, I am welcome to do it, but as for Papa, he says if it was

God's will to kill the people we loved, then God can keep his Heaven and Hell and Papa will be satisfied to just live and die here on Earth. Thank you for telling Mama everything except maybe don't tell her that part about no Church on Sunday.

Your loving sister,

Emma Too

P.s. I am writing this extra on Monday because today we got on the Lake Trail, which Papa says the Indians made a long time ago, and as we rested under a big tree where our path ran into the Lake Trail, we saw a stagecoach go by. It had four horses and a big fancy carriage. No way could we go that fast even with eight Artemesias. Papa says that stage is going from Buffalo to Cleveland and they will switch out the horses for new ones over and over again the whole way there. Poor Artemesia, she has to pull our wagon by herself with no help.

13.

We blew right past Big Tree Road and only noticed our oversight a couple miles later, and in the meantime Route 5 turned from a meandering coastal road into a highway. Must have been getting close to Buffalo. We took the next little road to the right and that hunch was correct because it connected us back to Big Tree.

The wind was letting up a bit now and the skies even brightened as we moved inland. Big Tree merged onto 20 for a brief time—and 20 was a 4- to 6-lane commercial artery at this point, then we saw 20A branching off to the right and thankfully got off the big road. Presently we passed the stadium for the Buffalo Bills, with various entry drives marked for different parking areas. Route 20A wasn't a small road either, but it calmed down after we got past 219, the Pittsburgh-Buffalo Highway. At this point, Big Tree Road turned into Quaker Street, which seemed to point toward simpler times and, hopefully, less traffic.

Getting to that ideal was postponed as we immediately went through a busy little downtown in Orchard Park, but as we continued east beyond that, rolling countryside began to take over. With no formal campgrounds noted on the map, this would be our first night roughing it in the wilderness—provided we could find some wilderness. After passing through another main street downtown in East Aurora, we finally hit some more rural country and started looking for some place to unobtrusively set up. I noticed it had turned back into Big Tree Road.

Just after crossing a small river as we passed through Wales Center, which I thought I remembered as a place noted on Aunt Cordelia's map, I spotted a post office to the right and motioned that way to Axel. The open field behind it backed up against some woods, and maybe behind that the woods might overlook the creek we had just crossed. We pulled off the road and scoped it out. From behind the building, it seemed like it would work—the field was firm and the woods beyond looked fairly open so we could wheel the bikes back into the trees pretty easily.

"I don't know how to do this," Axel said. "Do we ask somebody?"

"Ask who?"

"Well," he looked around, "I guess the PO always closes at 5 or 6, so we could go get a bite someplace, then just roll on back there and see if it works. Can't really see it from the road and our tent is green anyway."

So we got some takeout from a little hotel restaurant (and used its bathroom), sat on the riverbank next to the bridge and ate our meal. We weren't the first to sit there, judging from the beer cans and food wrappers down by the water and the cigarette butts scattered about. It wasn't the most photogenic spot, but I actually thought to take a picture.

6-14-88 (6-15)

Orchard Park, Ellicot, Cauturagus, Warsaw, Wales Center. Our itinerary will be a little off from E2 because they got stuck in that snowstorm and didn't move for a week. That still happens around here! I wonder if they knew it snowed like that out here? Lake effect. Seems almost too good of a coincidence that they run into a big lake effect storm. Maybe E2 embellished that a little bit. Wonder if maybe she wrote the letters later, after realizing it would have been an amazing document to [illegible] 18 or 20 or 22, would be same old paper.

I'm actually writing this the evening of the 15th, while some chicken is cooking on a grill, about what happened the 14th. Didn't have time to write up the 14th last night, but no worries I'll remember it well for a long time.

Got up and rode on 6-14, drizzly morning. A little tense with Ax but that went away with miles on the road. Followed 5/20 until we got onto 20 east away from the lake, just getting close to Buffalo. Ellicot, Cauturagus, heading for Wales Center where E2 stayed. Set up behind PO. Almost got killed or worse by NY redneck stoner drunks, did some damage, hid out that night, got away clean in the morning, though I kept worrying all the next day that they would track us down and run us off the road or something. I think Ax and me made a good team that night for sure.

6-15 was going to be a big day anyway because we would be getting to where E2 brother Uz got killed, Genessee River, and that was weighing on me the whole way even while I kept thinking I was hearing their car rumbling. Or was it the river? Like Talking Heads, it's only the river, it's only the river. I smell home cooking. Oh, that's Natalie's chicken. Ha ha, I'm so funny. Feeling the beer, better pick this up later.

14.

April 13, 1818
Miss Eliza Crombie, Crombie Hill, New Hampshire

My dearest sister Eliza,

Papa said the weather was fine so we traveled right through Sunday. I did not notice that because I was not paying attention to the days so much. He says that he wants to be careful with Artemesia because she is by herself now and she might get too tired, so Papa never rides, always walks. I sit on the wagon with the reins, or sometimes I walk too, beside Papa. Today we are having a cold supper, so I have some time to write you a letter. I am sorry it is late. I do not know when the next post office is coming anyhow.

I did not think of it when we left off from Geneseo, but to go on our road we had to go right past the place where the Flood was. The river was low now and I could see it twisting and winding real lazy and slow back and forth across the whole bottom of a big wide flat valley. I could not even recognize the place from what it looked like in the freshet, but then I saw some of those big jaggedy blocks of ice that were still not melted yet, way up away from the river banks, stuck in some trees on a little hill, and then partway down the hill I saw that half-knocked-over tree where Artemesia was tied up, and then I got a picture in my eyes where I saw Uz and Hester in the blue light and the tumbled up white ice like a rockslide going by and then they were gone.

When we got down to that river, Papa did not even stop, he just walked right into the water pulling Artemisia behind him and we forded it and kept on without looking back.

Everything got thawed lately, and there is only a little bit of snow left in the ditches on the shady side of the hills. Papa says if we make good time we can get to the Lake Trail in the coming week. He says maybe we can get a boat instead of the Lake Trail because Uncle Nathan said the Lake Trail is all mud. We should be able to find a postman on the Lake Trail. It goes from two towns, Buffalo to Cleveland.

It is getting dark now and we have to pack up, so I am going to stop this letter. Please tell Mama. I will write again when we get to the Lake next week. I miss your company, my dear Eliza.

Your affectionate sister,

Emma Too

15.

It was getting close to the longest days of the year, so there was plenty of light after we ate. We rolled the bikes back into the woods and found an open patch inside a curve of the brook. That seemed pretty idyllic, so we set up the tent there. Axel produced a little can of WD-40 and sprayed both chains, then we spread one of our ponchos over the bikes.

"You're so prepared," I marveled.

"In some ways," he said.

"Even when you don't look prepared you actually are pre-pared. Like when you suddenly go from lost in the field to fourth wheel coming into the sprint."

"Maybe I just suddenly realize I better get my shit together."

"But then you do it, which means you were prepared."

"Maybe." He picked up a couple of branches. "Hey, I was thinking we could make a campfire but now I think we shouldn't because it might call attention to us and get us kicked out or arrested or something."

"Probably right," I said.

"I guess we just mellow out in the tent. Starting to get buggy." We climbed in. "Also, I'm gonna change," he said. "Don't mind me." He pulled off his jersey and looked through his pannier for street clothes.

I found running shorts and underwear and a t-shirt and quickly changed out of the bike clothes as well. "Hey did you see any water so we can rinse things out?"

"No. Not using that river," he said. "Maybe there's a hose thing on the back of the PO building. It's still early. We can check in a bit."

"Okay. Meanwhile, you know I made those xeroxes of the letters and Aunt Cordelia's map to bring along. I'm going to see if I can figure out where she was and if we have hit any of those exact places." We read through the few letters from the end of Emma's trip, and decided that it was possible that the "big tree" she described might be the current town of Big Tree, namesake of Big Tree Road. Maybe the big tree was a landmark for travelers seeking to get on the Lake Trail, or to get off it heading back east.

"She probably slept here behind the post office," Axel said.

"Hey I have an idea," I said.

"Uh oh," replied Axel.

"Let's walk over to that hotel and get a beer."

"That is an idea," he affirmed.

"Since we're still dressed and everything. It will be like a toast to our first night on the trail."

"Except it's the second night and it's not a trail."

"Yeah except for that," I answered, unzipping the tent door.

There was still plenty of light in the sky as we walked back across the bridge, and I thought maybe that was why there seemed to be no lights on behind the hotel restaurant windows, but we soon discovered that the place was now closed.

I looked up the street and saw that a gas station seemed to have a convenience store attached that was still open. I started walking, Axel paused, then followed.

Inside, the slim choices were 6-packs of Lite in cans or large single bottles of Olde English. I picked up one of the latter and carried it to the counter. Outside, a dark green car pulled up, stereo blasting some song by Journey. The glum clerk took the bottle without looking up. "ID?"

I fished out my driver's license and handed it over. "Sorry," she said, "gotta be 21."

"What? New York was always 18."

"That's been a few years, sweetie. Twenty-one."

I looked at Axel, but knew he wasn't 21 for another few months.

"And he can't buy it for you either," the clerk said. "Not like Ohio where you're allowed to drink at home if you're supervised. In New York, unless you're over 21, no dice."

"Oh," I said. "Well, that's okay." I turned to put it back and a guy who had lined up behind us reached out and took the bottle from my hand. He was quite tall, so most of what I saw was a yellow Foghat t-shirt and some long dark brown hair.

"Heeeey," he said. "Just what I was looking for." His red eyes and distinct aroma suggested he was pretty stoned.

"Oh, okay," I said, a little taken aback. "Glad to help."

Axel and I walked back outside and started back down the little hill toward the bridge. The driver-side door of the green car was open and three or four other people were sitting inside. A female voice called out unintelligibly from in there as we passed by. It was getting dark now so we crossed the street so we'd be facing traffic, even though that put us on the other side from the post office and our tent. About halfway down, the green car pulled up beside us, driving on the wrong side of the road, and the driver's window rolled down. "Heeey, you forgot something baby!" He handed the bottle of Olde English out and dropped it into my hands, which I had reflexively raised toward the car when it pulled alongside. Uproarious laughter came from inside and the car sped ahead a couple hundred feet, then pulled into the empty gravel parking lot between the hotel and the bridge. The stereo cut off in the middle of a Styx song. As we approached, the occupants all got out and stood waiting for us. It wasn't like we were going to turn around and walk back up the hill, so we kept going and waved when we got across the street from them. "Thanks, we owe you one!" Axel called over.

"Come on, man," the driver said. "Party party." He was wearing jeans with a wallet chain, which reminded me of going to the local amusement park when I was a kid ten years ago. Three women stood beside him, two dark-haired, one blonde. One of the dark-haired ones, short and round, had a big perm and a red sleeveless shirt. The other brunette was tall and skinny and wore a black tank top that said TEAM JESUS. Beside them stood another guy, shorter and plumper than the driver, with blonde hair and a bit of a beard and a tight floral print shirt unbuttoned to the middle.

"What?" I pretended not to understand as we kept walking.

"Come party with us!" The driver yelled.

"Yeah," said the blonde woman.

"We gotta hit the sack," Axel said. "But thanks."

"You got time for a beer, come on," the driver said. "You were gonna do that anyway."

Then the pudgy blonde guy added, "Plus you said you owe us one, so come on over and we call it even."

They had us on those counts. I looked at Axel and he shrugged. "Okay," I called. "Half an hour, then we gotta go." We crossed the street.

We sat on the riverbank in almost exactly the same spot where Axel and I had eaten our dinner. The blonde guy immediately fired up a joint and began passing it. I really did not want to get stoned out here in this situation so I did my best to fake a short toke when the perm girl handed it to me, then declared I was really more in the mood for the beer. I passed the joint on to Axel who without a word passed it to the other brunette, who was sitting beside him. She wasn't looking so he tapped her on the shoulder and she took it. I have wondered occasionally if any of them ever noticed we hadn't really smoked any, or if they were too long gone already. In any case, it would seem clear not much later that there was something in it more than just your run-of-the-mill weed. I opened the screwtop and took a deep swig. I'd never actually had Olde English, only seen the bottles in stores and discarded by the roadside, but it wasn't too bad. Strong. Axel and I traded swigs a few times, then he held up the bottle. "Anybody?"

"No man, we don't drink that nigger piss," the driver said. He produced a 12-pack of Coors that he had evidently procured somewhere other than at the gas station, unless I had missed it. In the dimming light, I could see down the line past Axel to where the driver was sitting at the end. The blonde girl laughed at his quip and repeated the last two words. Her blue halter top said "Cutie" in script letters. She was wearing white shorts that couldn't possibly still be white after sitting on this scrungy grass.

"Hey!" Perm girl tugged at my elbow.

"What?" I turned. She handed me the joint again and I shook my head. "All yours."

She drew deeply, wobbling slightly, and handed it back to blonde guy. I turned my eyes back to the river and Axel handed me the bottle. I took a swing and handed it back to him. I felt bad for not raising an objection about "nigger piss," but I couldn't think of what to say.

"Shit," said Team Jesus. "I am so fucked up."

Everyone laughed uproariously. She made a show of keeling over and leaned into Axel, who had the bottle in his mouth at that moment and thus spilled on himself and on her hair. I stood up.

"Hey!" She yelled. "Get that offa me!"

"You fuckin with her?" The driver stood up.

"Hey asshole I'm your girl, remember?" said the blonde next to him, also standing.

"You wish," he growled and shoved her. She slipped down the slope a little bit then steadied herself.

I felt myself grabbed from behind, hands on my breasts. Instinct kicked in and I elbowed hard and upward, catching blonde guy on the chin and apparently dazing him enough that he keeled over sideways and slid face down until he hit a shrub at the edge of the water. I felt something tickly against my leg and realized that it was the hair of perm girl, who was lying there passed out.

Axel had gone from trying to wipe the beer off the girl's hair one second to grabbing my arm the next. "Let's get the fuck out of here."

Blonde Cutie had picked up a rock with the apparent intention of assaulting the driver, but now turned her attention our way. "Hey bitch, you crossed the line!" she yelled, I think at me, and took a step my way before stumbling, which caused the driver also to stumble over her and end up at the edge of the water next to the other guy, who had gotten up to his knees and was screaming unintelligibly at us. There was enough light from the lamp in the parking lot to see there was lot of blood was pouring out of his mouth onto the floral shirt.

"Jason!" The driver yelled, tugging on the other man's arm. "Get the fuck up, we gotta beat some ass."

"Muh fugga dug!" yelled bloody floral shirt guy, holding both hands up to his mouth.

Seemed he'd bitten his tongue. Maybe off.

Axel heaved the mostly-empty bottle straight up into the air and we scrambled back up toward the road. We heard the glass shatter below a second later, and heard some yelled commotion in response. "Not to the tents yet," he whispered and started running back up the hill toward the gas station. I followed and we ducked into a side street and hid behind a hedge in a yard that seemed to offer a couple routes of departure. It was super dark, just a sliver of moon. We heard yelling down the hill and some disordered footsteps. I distinctly heard the driver yell, "Come on Tammy, get up! Help me get her up!" And I heard bloody shirt guy yell something, and then blonde cutie screamed at him to quit bleeding on her.

Axel whispered, "They don't know anything about us—they don't know we're on bikes, don't know where we're headed, don't know about the tent or where it is. All they know is we're not 21 yet and maybe they know we're from Ohio. Once we get clear of this town, we never see them again."

"So we just have to be sure," I said, "that they don't find out we're on bikes or headed east. Sneak out of town early?"

"Yeah. Tonight?"

"It's tempting, but what if they keep looking for us tonight? We'd have to get back out on the main road to get out of here."

"First thing in the morning. They won't be early risers."

A light went on behind us and I saw a guy at the front window of the house behind whose hedge we were hiding, wearing just his tighty-whities, peering out into the dark, phone in his hand with the cord trailing off behind. "We better move along," I said. Axel nodded and we gradually made our way through yards and woods back down the hill until we heard the green car's engine start up, the stereo resuming "You're Fooling Yourself" at full blast. Someone found the volume knob and reduced it after half a minute, but by that time we could see a hint of blue flashing lights coming from the left, beyond the bridge. The green car rumbled up the hill past us and continued until we couldn't hear it anymore. The police lights stopped across the street from us, at the gravel parking lot. We saw a flashlight scanning the river bank. The officer returned carrying the remnants of the 12-pack of Coors, which he deposited in the trunk. Then he drove slowly up the hill and turned into the gas station.

We made our way through the woods and a couple of back lots until we were opposite the post office, made sure we heard no cars from any direction, then crossed the street. I really had to pee, so I made a quick detour at the edge of the woods.

I kept thinking I heard the rumble of that green car. In fact, even as I fell asleep not too much later, I still kept thinking I heard it. And "Slow Ride" by Foghat playing on the car's stereo.

In the darkest part of the middle of the night we were awakened by a ferocious screeching commotion. Dim light was casting shadows of branches on the tent walls. I had not yet managed to remember where I was but I immediately thought of the green car and its cast of characters. Foghat/driver. Blonde Cutie. Pudgy boob-grabber. Perm girl. Team Jesus beer-in-the hair. Axel unzipped the tent and stuck his head out the tent door. "Oh, crap."

"What?" I asked.

'Racoons fighting over something. Probably our food. They're over by the bikes."

"Oh, crap." Now I knew where we were.

We were not eager to be bitten by rabid raccoons, but on the other hand we needed our food, so we got dressed and put shoes on and went out to try to shoo them off. We also didn't want to make a huge amount of noise and thereby call attention to our unauthorized presence.

They were not much intimidated by our silent jumping up and down and throwing sticks at them. On the other hand, we perceived that they had not actually found our food supplies, but were fighting over the empty take-out containers from our dinner. We decided to take a chance, and quickly moved the bikes out of the woods and leaned them on the back of the post office building. Then we un-staked the tent and dragged it, sleeping bags and all, out of the woods and re-staked it in the grassy field right beside the bikes. We left the takeout containers to the combatants.

"Whew," I said.

"Just like home," said Axel.

I laughed.

"Like my parents."

I took a few seconds to process.

"I shouldn't have said anything, sorry." He brushed some dew off the rain fly.

"No, you can tell me. You should."

"They've kinda been at it for a while. I'm not sure where it's headed."

"Oh, Jeez," I said. "Is this a good time for you to be gone?"

"A very good time for me to be gone, yes."

"Oh, Ax. I'm sorry."

"Nothing you can do. But thanks."

He put his hand on my shoulder and just let it rest there. I reached my arm around his waist and did the same. It was actually quite a lovely night, despite the intermittent screeching in the woods. Despite how it had started out. I decided that all of our recent party companions were likely to be deeply unconscious at this moment.

I didn't sleep much the rest of the night because I kept thinking I heard the green car, and because I was afraid that the raccoons would lose interest in our dinner trash and come looking for more goodies, or that some authority like the Postmaster General would show up with glaring spotlights outside our tent and rouse us up and take us to jail. How did those pioneers just travel at will and stop wherever they wanted to? With the first bird chirp my eyes popped wide open and I sat up.

"Ready to go?" asked Axel.

"Let's go."

We put on bike clothes, rolled up and stuffed the bags, and collapsed and packed the tent in about five minutes and loaded everything back onto the bikes. Axel noticed that there was indeed a spigot on the back of the building, so we quickly rinsed yesterday's bike clothes and our things from last night and stashed them in the netting on the outsides of the panniers. Most of it would be dry in a couple hours. Unless it rained. After a quick scan to be sure we hadn't left anything here, Axel trotted back to the woods to check there as well. He returned after a couple minutes carrying the shredded remains of our take-out bag. "No need to litter," he whispered.

As we wheeled the bikes around the side of the post office and into its front lot, I noticed with a chill in my belly that a police car was pulling in off the main road. The black-and-white Ford LTD stopped in front of us and the window rolled down. "Everything okay folks?" The dawn sun was right behind him so I couldn't see in.

"Yes, thanks."

"Sleep tight?" came the voice.

"Not really," said Axel.

The officer laughed. "There's a nice hotel a hundred yards from here."

"We know. We got takeout from there." Axel held up the bag. "But we're on a no-hotels adventure."

"Pioneer spirit," I said.

"I see. Not sure how you slept through all that ruckus last night, but it doesn't appear that you caused it, anyhow."

Axel and I looked at each other and shrugged.

"Well, thanks for not leaving that trash in the woods. Good to see the taxpayers taking good care of their own property. You be safe, folks." He rolled up the window and the car went back to the left in the direction from which it had come. My own personal opinion was that maybe this episode might not have gone the same way if one of the protagonists hadn't been a cute blonde girl. But I didn't say that out loud.

We looked at each other for a second, exchanged shrugs, then mounted up and turned right, heading east on Big Tree Road, straight into the rising sun.

16.

April 5, 1818

Miss Eliza Crombie, Crombie Hill, New Hampshire

My dearest sister Eliza,

Please forgive my poor words. Papa is writing a letter too. I am sorry I did not write one last Sunday.

It is hard to write because my hand shakes whenever I set down to put any words on the paper. But I will just say it. Uz got caught in a freshet of ice and he Died. I am sorry my writing is so ugly. He was trying to get Hester out from the flood and then he was washed under, and Hester too. Do you remember from the reading book, Xerxes the great did die And so must you and I? I did not know that book was about us.

We gave the letters to the postman in Geneseo, who said a rider was heading back east first thing in the morning. It was raining and raining all day. Papa said let's get a little bit out of town and set camp, and maybe the rain will stop tomorrow. It was already getting dark. We went out from the town and down a hill partway until we found a good spot on a high place in a clearing near some trees, but by that time it was so dark and raining so much we just had to make do with a cold supper. Uz tied up Hester to one tree and Artemisia to another one and we got inside went to sleep like usual, all three of us lined up like we do with the blankets.

Then I heard a big crashing sound like when a rock falls off the north cliff. Uz and Papa were already outside. There was moonlight and the rain stopped and I looked out the back of the wagon and I could see it looked like the whole ground was moving, except all the snow was broken up into pieces, and then I could see that it was pieces of ice floating. Papa hitched up Artemisia to the wagon and yelled at me to stay inside and yelled at Uz to leave Hester, but just when he said that, the little tree that Uz was trying to get Hester untied from tipped over and both Uz and Hester washed away with it. Papa yelled at Artemisia to get up and she pulled us up higher onto the hill. Then Papa yelled at me to stay here and look after Artemisia and he ran back down to where we were before.

I just stood next to Artemisia patting her muzzle and looking down that way, where the white flat chunks of ice were coming from the left side and going to the right side where I last saw Uz and Hester. The high place we found for our campsite was all under the crashing ice now. I saw the tree where Artemisia was tied up, a bigger tree than the other one, and it got tipped sideways but did not get washed away. I kept looking there and then after a while the sun came up.

Some folks came down the road from up the hill and asked me if everybody was all right and I said my Papa went to look for Uz and Hester who got washed away. A nice lady stood there next to me and put her hand on my shoulder and she didn't take her hand away until we saw Papa walking back up to us from down that white hill with the ice still sliding by. He fell on his knees and then just laid on the ground.

Papa and I stayed there in Geneseo for a time. After two days, some men found Uz and Hester up in some woods by the river. Uz had the lead wrapped around his arm and he got hurt real bad on his head, and a man said God was merciful that this poor man did not suffer. Papa had some other words for God that he said real quiet, words that I will not write down here. Papa talked with the pastor at the Presbyterian church, who allowed that Uz could be buried there in Geneseo at the town cemetery on Temple Hill. There were not many other graves there because the town was young. Papa used his tools to carve into a plain stone that said

Uz Crombie

1797–1818

Taken by a freshet

The pastor and some of the town people stood there with us and said some Prayers and Papa and I threw some handfuls of dirt in there before they buried him up. They were crying some of them even though they never knew him. I asked Papa if Uz would stay there forever, and he said he did not know. I said Is it in God's hands and he said Nothing is in God's hands.

For many days Papa lay down in the wagon and never got up. The people were asking was Papa ill, and I said his heart is ill because of who he lost. But he ain't going to lose me. So I shook him on the shoulder and I said Papa we got to go. I can't figure a way where it makes sense to turn back to New Hampshire since before Uz died he said we are more than halfway to Ohio, and now we have only Artemisia and we have lost Uz. I want to see everybody so badly, but I know we got to go. When you all come out later when we have made the cabin, then we can have time together. I will help Papa build the cabin.

I do not want to ask you to do it, but please tell Mama. The postman said the rider will take our letters tomorrow. It pains me that I know about Uz and you all won't know for a long time. If I was a hawk I would fly to you right now, but when I got there, I would not want to say the words that I flew there to say.

With Sincere Regard,

Emma Too Crombie

17.

I couldn't help but wonder if some of the unsavory characters we'd encountered last night were descended from the kind people Emma had met in this area. Or from bands of ruffians? Or from wandering Puritans? Or maybe the cop? Or the lady in the convenience store? How did people end up here? Why did they stay if they stayed? Why did they leave if they left? Did they pass down stories? Did they tell the sad one about the pioneers coming through who camped by the river and one of them was taken away when the ice broke upstream and the river swelled and scoured its banks in the middle of the night? Or did that kind of thing happen so often that nobody would even make a story of it? Unless it was her own brother. Was life really so much cheaper? It was not so long ago. People could not have changed very much in so little time. The loss of a son or a brother must have been just as crushing then as it would be now, even if such tragedies were a more common- place occurrence. Commonplace and tragedy: those two words often came together in those days in our young country—probably in all days, probably in every country. Maybe our own time is the exception. How quickly we adjust our normal.

It looked to be only about 40 miles from the post office campground to Geneseo, but we had decided before departing from Madison that we would stop overnight in Geneseo because that was where Emma's older brother Uz had died in 1818, and we hoped to find the grave.

The road headed straight east, with occasional jogs one way or the other. The approach to Varysburg involved going down a significant hill, and the road swept through a couple of curves to reduce the grade. After crossing a river at the bottom, the pavement curved up the other side.

"Ugh," said Axel. "These hills."

"Making us stronger, right?" I puffed behind him.

Ten miles later as we approached Warsaw, the brakes got another test with a couple of ten-percent pitches cut into the hill so there were walls of shale either side of us (Axel pointed out that the flaky loose layers were shale) . . . and we knew what that would mean on the other side as we had to climb back out of the same valley. We passed the local public school as we approached the commercial district, then rolled through a downtown that mixed some surviving 19th-century buildings with gas stations and convenience stores.

Sure enough, moments after flanking a large brick church, the road pitched steeply upward through a narrow passage reinforced by a tall concrete wall on the right side, virtually eliminating any shoulder. "This is gonna be fun," Axel quipped from behind me as we began to labor our way up the cattle chute as a small convoy of cars, trucks, and a gigantic RV backed up behind us.

I was already standing up in my lowest gear and torquing the pedals as mightily as I could, but the International, being set up for "fast touring," didn't have any truly low gears—in jargon, the "bail-out" gear the bike had as standard equipment was 42 teeth in the front and 24 in the rear, and we had changed the freewheel to get a 26 (the maximum that derailleur could handle) to get at least a slightly lower gear, but Axel's more modern "real" touring bike for comparison had a triple crankset and a low gear of 36x28. He was carrying a bit more of our shared cargo weight than I was, but I was still lifting plenty of load. It quickly became a battle for me not just to get up the hill, but to avoid falling over. To further complicate matters, cinching up the toe straps was necessary to get up a hill like this, but it made getting one's foot out a precarious maneuver that required reaching down with one hand, successfully loosening the strap on the first grab, and yanking your cleated shoe straight up off the pedal and putting it on the ground, all in the space of half a pedal stroke. Plus taking one hand off the bars meant needing to sit back down momentarily and losing some leverage and control. Also, plus the bottoms of the cleated shoes could be pretty slippery on pavement. And, of course there were steady lines of vehicles both following and oncoming, any of which could potentially run you over if they didn't understand what was going on. All of this made it extremely desirable to somehow avoid stopping.

Axel of course understood all of this perfectly and was riding behind me slightly toward the middle of the road to try to give at least a little protection. The road did a jog left-right with the speed limit posted at 10 mph as the road squeezed its way under a sharply angled railroad trestle. I almost lost it when my front wheel got diverted by some gouges in the pavement that had no doubt been caused by some previous car wreck or train crash, but I stuck out my right elbow and pushed against the edge of the trestle and thus managed to stay upright. "Damn, good save," I heard Axel say. Immediately after that, mercifully, a climbing lane appeared on the right side and the traffic behind us was able to pass, except for one heavily laden truck we could hear grunting and gasping behind us almost as loudly as we were. As one car came by I heard some yelling that I half-expected to be abusive taunts from the green car of last night, but it turned out the car was blue and they were cheering me on. "She's a beast! Go! Go!

Go!" I could not wave or speak, but I gave a quick smile and acknowledging nod. My full-effort leg muscles always look pretty impressive, Axel reminded me later. And the blonde braid swinging back and forth probably helped the she-beast/Viking warrior effect.

Not long after the extra right lane finally ended about a mile later, we noticed a big sign across the road on the other side, facing the oncoming lane; when we got past it, I turned around to read it: trucks, busses, and cars with trailers must exit. It was bright red with white lettering. I imagined poor Artemesia hauling the wagon up that even steeper hill we'd come down on the other side into Warsaw, with Emma and her dad pushing. At least the railroads didn't exist yet at that time, so there would have been one less hazard to negotiate.

Axel said, still catching his breath, "Too much of that . . . and shit is going to . . . start to break."

The road became straight and level, the shoulder wide. Traffic was very light, so we began to ride two abreast. "Tell you what," I said, "I was worried that I might get out of shape doing this instead of racing, but now I think I changed my mind."

"Ditto. Might lose some speed, but definitely not strength."

'Isn't it funny to think that a couple of centuries ago, what you and I are doing now would have been almost incomprehensible?"

"What do you mean?"

"I mean there was no pavement almost anywhere. The bicycle hadn't been invented. As a woman in the 1780s I probably would have been at home and working on my second or third kid. You would have been either off at the war or fresh home from it."

"Depending which side I was on," he chuckled.

"Ha ha. I mean even on a more basic level, the idea of two 20-year-olds, one male, one female, not married, just going on a trip together so that one of them could get some material to write a senior project for college—"

"Oh, that's why we're doing this? I thought it was to get in touch with your patriot ancestors."

"Well, that too."

"So can I also get some college credit for this?"

"Hey, worth a try. But you may not have patriot ancestors."

"I'm still American."

"I guess so," I said, half joking. But of course he was right.

"Anybody who doesn't know who his great-great-great grandparents were or where they came from and never will, but who was born here and lives here . . . I mean, that's me, but it could also be descendants of slaves, or people who escaped to here from the Holocaust, or Indians who got cut off from their tribes and their lands. You find yourself in a certain position and improvise. That's really a more common story of America than yours, isn't it?"

"That sounds like you in a bike race—find yourself in a position and improvise."

"Hey, don't mess with success."

"Not that much success," I pointed out.

"Working on that," he said. "Anyway, I don't see a lot of patriot pioneers on the podium."

"How would you even know?"

"Those hats?"

"Okay, so maybe there's more than one American people story," I said, fully planning to recreate this entire conversation in my paper. "What's the geology angle?"

He adopted a haughty mock-professorial voice. "It appears that we have a landscape that was scoured flat by ice sheets and has been eroded through by rivers ever since the glaciers melted. There also seems to be some kind of north/south process going on with all these ridges. I don't know if that's glacial leftovers or rippling related to the fact that we're on the eastern flank of the Appalachians. I do know that it adds up to one ahss-kicking hill after another if you're heading east-west."

"Can you imagine poor Artemesia?"

"Who?"

"The mule."

"Oh, the patriot wagon-puller. Yeah, rough going for her. But she would have her Donkey of the American Revolution certificate at least."

"Traced through her mother's side."

"I like your grandma. She's a trip."

"I think she had to check you out before she'd be able not to worry too much about me on this adventure. You passed."

"It's nice to have somebody looking out for you that way."

"It is. I'm sure yours are looking out for you."

"How would I know?"

"Because you're adopted?"

"No, because my parents don't stay much in touch with theirs. I don't really know them. Well, a couple of them have passed away, to be fair. But they don't live anywhere close by and haven't felt the need to visit much, I guess. So even if I was their biological kid, I wouldn't know much about where my grandparents came from."

"Oh, that's too bad."

"Hard to say that for sure. They could be assholes."

"Yeah, but still . . ." A hawk suddenly glided past us and ahead over the roadside ditch. "Yeeks, startled me."

"Big one."

"Looking for lunch."

"Kinda hungry myself," he said. "Wanna stop soon or try to make Geneseo first?"

"It shouldn't be more than another half-hour. Let's keep rolling."

Route 20A veered to the left and ran along with 39 for a bit. We saw signs for Letchworth State Park and I made a mental note to look more closely at what that was later today when we stopped. After a broad right turn, we meandered through Cuylerville, keeping an eye out for the Route 20A signs as the highway route seemed to merge and unmerge with other routes every minute or two. Shortly we emerged among cornfields and catalpa trees as the road gradually descended for a couple of miles, crossed a muddy creek, then bore to the left and climbed somewhat more steeply on the other side. Our road merged again with another and then branched off to the right where a sign said Geneseo was one mile away.

"Wait a sec," I said and pulled over. Axel, who had been ahead, waited for a car to pass and looped back around. I pulled the map out from my handlebar bag.

"What is it?" He asked.

"That river we just crossed," I said. That was the Genesee River, and right around there would be where that flood was where they lost Emma's brother Uz and the other donkey."

"I didn't even notice a river," said Axel. "Although it did seem like we were crossing a big wide flood plain."

"Exactly. It wasn't anything. I pictured something more dangerous-looking."

"Want to go back?"

"No, I don't think so. Or if we do, we could stash the gear up in town here and ride back unloaded."

The road continued on, after about 10 minutes passing some collegiate-looking red brick buildings with a big parking lot on a sweeping right curve, then we were in the village. That caused the hunger pangs to kick in, so we sat and ate on a low stone wall in front of a palatial, rambling white building described as a "Homestead." My idea of homestead was more log-cabin-style, but I guess some people are more ambitious. Or maybe the title was ironic.

After eating, we sought out the historical society that was marked on the map, thinking it would probably be open on a Wednesday early afternoon. You never expect such things to be easy to find, but there was a clear sign on 20A and the cobblestone building a couple blocks away was obvious and the front door was open. We leaned the bikes outside, took off our cleats, and walked in.

"Oh hello," came a voice from behind some bookshelves. "One moment."

"No hurry," I said.

A young woman who did not fit my stereotype of a small-town historical society employee stepped out. She was wearing rollerblades and cutoff shorts and a tank top. "Sorry," she said. "We're not actually open today, but I just stopped in to get my kneepads." She looked us up and down. "Where did you ride from?"

"Ohio," Axel said.

"Well, not today," I clarified. "Just from Wales Center today."

"Oh, my." She put the kneepads on the desk and rolled herself around to sit on the front of it. "Well maybe I can help you with something. I'm just a volunteer anyway, and I can take off a little early some slow days. Which is pretty much every day. Sorry, I'm so rude—my name is Natalie." The rollerblades made her about my height, five-seven, which would make her five-three or so, plus a wavy tangle on top of thick reddish-brown hair.

"Wow, thanks. I'm Ellie. Just looking for a gravestone actually. Maybe this isn't even the right place to check." I explained briefly about Emma's letters and the deaths of Uz Crombie and Hester the mule, and our bike ride to retrace their route.

She perked up. "You have letters from 1818? That's awesome!"

"I have xeroxes with me. Not the real ones." I stepped outside for a minute and brought back the plastic freezer bag with the letters. "Here's the one she wrote in Geneseo. Is that how you say it, like the beer plus oh?"

"Yep, that's right." She read over the letter. "That's incredible. And incredibly sad. Well let's see. We do have a register from Temple Hill Cemetery. It's a bit spotty in the early years, but maybe . . ."

She skated across to a set of file cabinets, knelt, and opened a lower one. "Ow. This is why I have the kneepads in here. This floor is hard." She rose and skated back over holding a dark green a spiral-bound volume and placed it on the desk.

"Okay, here—well, no. No Uz Crombie or Uz anybody or anybody Crombie on the register for 1818. But that doesn't mean much, especially for the early years. They didn't start thinking much about record-keeping until there were too many graves to remember, and by that time some of the old soft stone ones were crumbled or the names worn away. And lots of remains would get moved to another site."

"Another site?" I asked.

"For example, maybe the family retrieved a dead soldier later and buried him along with other family. Or part of the land would prove too prone to erosion or too swampy. Happens sometimes. A lot, actually. In the big cities, whole cemeteries get moved to make room for progress." She leafed through and checked a couple of other places in the book, then closed it. "Sorry, that's all that's there. If you want to look at the cemetery, it's just up the hill on the way out of town on 20A to the east. If you're heading east you'll go right past it."

"Thank you, that's so helpful," I said.

"And I can enlighten you a little bit more about the river and floods as well," she said as she re-closed the filing cabinet. "You would have crossed the Genesee before coming into town from the west. Out there it meanders along a big wide flood plain, and pretty much does that all the way downriver to Rochester, but these days it doesn't flood much anymore. There's a dam in the park, Mount Morris dam in Letchworth, and that has controlled it pretty well. Earlier there were some devastating early spring floods in Rochester—one on St. Patrick's day at the end of the Civil War, another on Easter in the early part of this century. Evidently it used to flood pretty severely every 10 or 15 years. This town was only founded in the 1790s, so not that long before your people came through here, so that may have been the first time anybody knew about it. Though the Indians knew for sure, and a geologist or anyone who spent much time living near a meandering river could take a look at the shape of the land down there and guess that it must flood pretty often. Anyway, what made it worse is that just a couple miles upstream is the gorge where the state park is now, really narrow with steep walls, so what would happen is things would get jammed up in there and then let loose all at once. They built the Mount Morris dam maybe 40-50 years ago to try to mitigate that and so far, it has worked. In fact, this whole area got its name, Big Tree, from a tree that used to be on the banks of the Genesee, but it got taken out in one of those floods."

"Wow. Gives you the chills," I said. "At least it gives me the chills."

"Not camping down there," said Axel.

"So that's her family," Natalie turned to Axel. "How about you? Seneca, right?"

"What?"

"Oh my God, I'm so sorry, that's so rude, I should never guess. I was just wondering what your story was, or are you just following hers?"

"That's pretty much what I'm doing. Riding support, you might say."

"And you're camping the whole way?"

"Pretty much. In fact," he said, "after checking in with the historical center which ended up being not open but kinda open anyway, we were going to look for a campground."

"Mmmm, no campground in this town. There are a few bed and breakfast-type places, and SUNY has a few rooms you can rent, you know, for families visiting. You would have come by the campus, on the left side on the way into town."

"No biggie," I said. "We'll just roll out of town a little ways and find a nice meadow by a woods and stream."

"With screaming raccoons and local cops spying on us," Axel added.

"Exactly."

"Hey listen," Natalie said. "If you're gonna do that, what you ought to do is just set up your tent in my back yard. You'd get a shower and a bathroom out of the deal, too."

"You sure?" I asked. "Camping out is really no trouble for us."

"Yeah, for sure. I wouldn't have offered. Plus you're still camping out."

"I guess the thought of a hot shower does appeal," said Axel.

"Okay, settled," said Natalie. "We can pick up some stuff to grill out and make an evening of it." She skated over to the door and inserted a key into the lock. "But now we gotta get out of here before any more riffraff wanders in."

Skating on a series of side streets, she led us a few blocks uphill to a dead-end at the terminus of which she turned into a gravel drive leading to a white cottage with black trim. She skate/walked over the gravel around to the back, squeezing past a long-parked old gray Volvo station wagon, and declared "Here we are! It ain't the Homestead, but it's mine."

A small concrete patio in the with a round table in the middle and a half-dozen chairs scattered around it backed up on a grassy lawn flanked by large oaks. "You can set up on the high place over there by the edge, and you're welcome to use my clothesline if you need to wash or dry anything," pointing to a rope strung between two oaks where a bathing suit and a couple days' worth of assorted shorts and tops and underwear were clipped up. She opened the back screen door. "Now come inside and I'll show you the bathroom and shower—uh, excuse the mess. It's usually just me and the frozen burritos and the ramen."

The doorway entered into a kitchen whose dish-filled sink was centered under a window that looked out on the back, and past that sink was a short hallway. "The bathroom is down here." She reached into some recessed shelves in the hall. "And here's a couple extra towels," which she handed to me. She turned on the bathroom light and scooped up some clothes off the floor, pointed out her bedroom and tossed the clothes into that room as she walked back out the hall, then led us back through the kitchen and through a doorway to the right, where a living room/dining room and front door completed the floor plan.

"No washer or dryer, so I either go to the laundromat or just hand-wash stuff while I'm taking a shower and hang it to dry wherever. Usually the latter cuz I'm lazy."

"You sure you're not a bike racer?" said Axel. "You have the lifestyle."

She laughed. "No bike, sorry."

We partially unloaded and Axel and I ran inside to change into street clothes, then the three of us together rolled a couple of blocks to pick up food for dinner (and for Axel and me, breakfast and a road lunch tomorrow): pound of coffee, loaf of bread, peanut butter and jelly, chicken, barbecue sauce, potato salad, and a case of Genesee Cream Ale in 16 oz. bottles ("Genny Pounders," according to Natalie) in honor of the river. We walked the bikes back with the beer balanced on Axel's rear rack. I commented on Natalie's impressive ability to negotiate uneven terrain on rollerblades while carrying varied items, and she laughed. "It's that or fix the car."

We each opened a beer and Natalie finally took her skates off and then got a charcoal fire going in a little hibachi on the back patio while Axel and I set up the tent—and none too soon because it was still damp from last night's dew and might start getting mildewy soon. I draped the sleeping bags on the clothesline to let them air out alongside our bike clothes and Natalie's things. I saw the camera and was reminded to take a picture, so we set it up on the table and used the self-timer to get a shot of the three of us.

Soon the chicken was on and the second beers underway, with a light breeze dispersing the delicious smoke and the long late afternoon of June gradually shifting to the long orange dusk. As Natalie crouched over the grill and flipped the pieces and moved them around to hotter and cooler spots, I noted that we'd had our much more rudimentary lunch in front of the huge white mansion. "Kind of a switch—from squashed day-old sandwiches in front of a palace, to a gourmet spread behind a cottage. I guess it all evens out!"

"Yeah, maybe." She took a swallow of beer. "That's my distant relatives down there who put up that modest little homestead."

"Really?" I imagined some version of Natalie among the people who would have met Emma and her dad. "That's cool."

"Well, it is impressive, that's to be sure, but how they came by all of that is not the most uplifting story. Start with tons of money from back east, add in a couple centuries of elimination of the tribes who had always lived here, and wrap it up with a bogus treaty that permanently stole the land and gave it to the white settlers except for a few reservations. Then go ahead and steal big parts of those reservations."

"Harsh," said Axel.

"But true," said Natalie.

"What, and now you're on the other side?" I asked.

"Other side?" She flipped a chicken breast. "I'm not sure what the sides are now. I mean you have white folks here who are descended from early settlers, and they're barely squeaking out a living, so I'm not sure you can pin it on them. And you can blame just the rich folks, but not every rich person is bad."

"So do you think it's possible to get rich," said Axel, "without exploiting anybody?"

"Does it have to be intentional?" I asked.

"Intentional or not, it's still exploitation, right?" he replied. "I mean if you benefit because of someone else's deprivation, that's not fair, is it?"

"Well, the race can only have one winner, and only a few on the podium," I said. "You of all people know that!"

"It's the difference between winning because you're faster versus winning because you do harm to somebody else," he said. "Just play fair, man."

"We have exploited this chicken to the degree that we can eat it now," Natalie said. "Plates!"

"So what do you do," Axel looked at Natalie, "for a living, to make money? You can't just volunteer at the historical center."

"Well . . . to be determined," she replied. "For now, I can go for a bit without anything regular. I had a chunk of money from my grandma and I used that to buy this place, and there's still a little bit to live on. I do some freelance tree work, forestry stuff."

"College?" I asked.

"Mostly done. Taking a year or two off, but I'll finish up. You?"

"We're both going into our senior year," I said. "Geology for him, history and writing for me."

"Between you both, you could do cave paintings."

"So those ancestors of yours," I said, "some of them must have been in the Revolution."

"Oh, yeah, for sure," she laughed. "All sides. I mean a lot of the wealthy folks were allied with the Brits, so I know some of our people took off for Canada and only came back after. This would have been back in Connecticut before they came out here. And others were very invested in what would become assets of the colonial side, so they naturally were patriots and we're all very proud of them."

"Beer?" Axel opened another and asked if anyone else was interested. "These are pretty good."

"Yeah, I'll have one," I said. "Pretty good but not sure how we'll feel about it on the road tomorrow."

"We're young and strong," he replied, handing an open bottle to me and another to Natalie, who had not responded but not said no.

"When we get to this little town in New Hampshire," I said, "I'm going to try to find out what my ancestors used to do there. As far as I can tell, the people there were farmers and lumber people, but I'm not sure what that means."

"Sounds honest enough," said Natalie. "But you never know. Those plantation owners down south with all the slaves called themselves farmers."

"There wasn't slavery up north, right?" said Axel. "Just like poisonous snakes, some things can't survive up here."

"Yeah, well you read Emma's letters," I said. "I always thought rattlesnakes didn't range this far north, but turns out Ohio was crawling with them, and New Hampshire had plenty, too. They just methodically killed them all off."

"Seems like they must have missed a few," Axel replied.

"There were slaves up here," Natalie said. "Especially in those early colonial days. Even after the Revolution it was still grandfathered as legal for decades in Connecticut, you know. Domestic servants and such. It just didn't happen at the same scale as down south. My theory is it was because the land in New England is too rocky to make big plantations. Then they spun it later as something more noble."

"Jeez, Negative Natalie," Axel said.

"Sorry, can't help it. I have access to historical materials."

"This chicken is delicious," I said. "We can't thank you enough."

"What she said," said Axel.

"I feel like we're only talking about our two families," Natalie looked at Axel. "What about you?"

"Not much to talk about . . . or at least not until after I've had a couple more beers," Axel laughed.

"They're in a bit of stormy weather," I said.

"Oh, sorry," Natalie said. "Just trying to be fair."

"Appreciated," Axel said. "I don't really know where they came from anyway. They're both kind of loners, self-made types."

"Like anybody's really self-made," I said.

"Well, people make their own mythologies, and that's self-making, right?" said Natalie.

"They both would tell you they worked very hard to get where they are," he said.

"Probably true," said Natalie. "Lots of people work very hard."

"That doesn't mean they didn't also get a lot of help," I said.

"Well, I'm afraid what's happening is their paths are spreading apart and neither one of them wants to follow behind in the other one's path and meanwhile I'm not there anymore to force them into one lane."

"That's not your job," I said. "They are supposed to lead you out."

"If you get into the bicycling metaphors," he said, "it seems like two people ought to be able to take turns at the front and that way they give each other a break. But maybe that's not real life. Maybe it's really a solo effort with a little cooperation, every once in a while, just to thin out the competition."

I lost count of the exact number of Genny Pounders, but long after the sun went down, we collectively determined that it was time to stop. Axel wanted to shower before going to sleep, but I elected to postpone my clean-up to the morning.

The only fragment I remember of the dream I had was of cold muddy water flowing around a small hill with a huge tree in the middle of it, and standing under the tree were my parents and all my grandparents, Axel and his parents, Natalie, about a dozen other people dressed up in play-acting costumes of Indians and colonials, and the comedian Richard Pryor. They were motioning at me to paddle faster, but I was slowly being pulled away by the current.

The cheeping birds woke me up. It took me a minute to register that I was in my sleeping bag, and that Axel was snoring lightly beside me.

18.

March 22, 1818
Miss Eliza Crombie
Crombie Hill, New Hampshire

My dearest sister Eliza,

The postman charges according to how many pages and how far the distance, so Papa wants to mail the letters as we go, to make the distance is as short as it can be, and also not write on more than one sheet. One of my letters went two sheets before, but I will make this one fit on one. Uncle Nathan remembered to Papa that there is a post office in a town called Geneseo, and we should get there on Tuesday, Papa says, so we will post this letter and the one I wrote before it from that place.

I believe it is going to thaw out soon. Two days last week was snow mixed with rain. Not enough to melt the ground, but we took it as a sign that we might be putting the Winter behind us soon. Speaking for myself, I will be ready for it.

We passed more skinny lakes all lined up like the other ones. To me I decided it was like a giant Bear scratched its claws down the land, and then the rain came and filled up the scratches. If I was a hawk soaring up there, it would look like that, and I would be worried to meet a bear that big even if I was a hawk. You could try to scare it away by making a lot of noise and trying to make yourself look big, but I would want to have a different plan too, just in case.

Now it is starting to rain again so I will finish this letter. Please tell Mama that we saw a robin red breast, which means Spring is coming soon, Uz says.

Your loving sister,

Emma Too

19.

I kind of zoned out in Natalie's shower, counting the tiles and the rows, looking down at my extreme biker tan of dark arms starting at the bicep and dark legs starting lower thigh, and everything else like midwinter. There was no fan so the place started to steam up and I didn't even see the door open when Axel stuck his head in to say hurry up. He half-whispered, so I figured Natalie was still sprawled half-dressed on her bed like she had been when I tiptoed past her door to the bathroom.

I got out and dried off and pulled on my bike shorts and jersey. When I passed her room this time, she was no longer on the bed, though it still showed her imprint. She and Axel were sitting at the little table outside sipping at white ceramic cups, looking at the map. "Coffee's on the stove," she said. She had put on a long gray SUNY Geneseo t-shirt. "PBJs for breakfast."

"And lunch," I said.

"You guys should take the beer," she said.

You're nuts, take a half case of Genny Pounders on bikes?" Axel responded reasonably.

"It's much less than a half a case now," she pointed out.

"Even so . . . well, maybe one each, for our end-of-the-day refreshment," I said.

"It will probably get warm by then," he said.

"Still refreshing," I said.

"The bottles are returnable," he said.

"Twenty cents for you," Natalie said.

"Okay, two bottles," he relented.

Natalie pulled two from the case and placed them on the table. "Actually, they're warm already after sitting out all night. So, no suspense."

"They were probably warm by the end of last night," said Axel. "I just didn't notice."

I got out my journal and spent 15 minutes finishing up my notes about yesterday and we ate our peanut butter and jelly sandwiches and made four more for the road, leaving the rest with Natalie, who protested but then acknowledged the silliness of our taking two mostly empty jars in our space-and weight-sensitive situation. She handed me a slip of paper with her address and phone number, and I wrote both of ours on a sheet for her and promised we'd send her a note after everything to let her know how the rest of the adventure had gone.

Axel pumped the tires and strapped on the tent and bags while I helped Natalie gather up last night's bottles and plates, then we quickly washed and dried the dishes.

"Looks better than when you got here," she said as we headed back out the door. "Thank you!"

"No, we owe you for the hospitality," I said.

"Please, a patch of grass and space on my clothesline?"

"Hey, no raccoons, no police, no effed-up New York hill-billies. That's worth a lot," Axel said, meeting us on the patio. "Not to mention a shower and a memorable cookout."

'Yeah, well . . .' she shrugged. "Hey give me a sec to get my skates on, since I accidentally left them out here all night anyway, and I'll run you out to the road." She looked down. "I think I'm dressed enough."

"Thanks, but I think we can get there," he said, glancing from Natalie to me with a skeptical look.

"I wouldn't want to you take a wrong turn and get into dangerous territory," she said as she squeezed a foot into one boot.

"Out here on the wild frontier," I said, shrugging back at Axel. If she wanted to go skating around the neighborhood like that, well okay.

Natalie laced up and we walked the bikes out to the road behind her as she picked her way down the gravel drive. We coasted back to a cross street, then turned left and rolled through a leafy neighborhood for a few blocks.

"Here we are," Natalie stopped and held to a signpost. "Left is east."

"Thanks for everything," Axel said.

"Do we hug goodbye or something?" I asked.

"Worth a try," she said and skated around between us then somewhat precariously put an arm around each of our shoulders. "Okay, now I'm stuck."

"How about we just roll off and you try to not fall?" Axel suggested.

"Right," she said. "You first."

Axel pushed off, then Natalie stepped sideways and skated a little loop while I got going. We turned left onto 20A, waved, and started pedaling.

"When we were checking the map," Axel said after a few minutes, once we were clear of town, "it looked like we could save some time in a couple places by getting off 20A to take a better angle."

"Okay, sure. Who knows where Emma's trail actually went but for sure it had to go north of all those lakes."

"Right," he said. "So it looked like we follow the 20A signs and stay on it until we got to a T at 64 and turn left where 20A runs with 64 for a while. Shortly after that something branches off to the right at an angle, and after a few miles that thing ends at another thing where you would bear right, and then that runs into 32, where you would go left and re-join 20 in Canandaigua. It looked like 20A ends in an intersection with 20 a few miles west of Canandaigua, but that's less direct and bigger roads, probably more traffic."

"Okay," I said. "Let's make a call when we get there, but a little shortcut on smaller roads seems fine."

It was obvious the Route 20A designation had been laid over a series of pre-existing roads that probably never were a continuous route across upstate New York, but 20A was our best guess as to Emma's route based on what she had mentioned in the letters. So in places where 20A followed a larger road, we did not take that to mean necessarily that the old trail had followed that route, only that later development encouraged the official route to hit the larger settlements. Sometimes the most direct route followed smaller roads, and this was such a case.

Shortly after we passed the Bristol Valley Mobile Home Park, we came to the merger with Route 64, turned north, then came to the branch-off. Vincent Hill Road, it was called, and it was not paved. However, as dirt roads go, it looked to be pretty firmly packed and with minimal gravel, and so—in the spirit of trying to empathize with Emma's transportation experience of 1818—we took that road less traveled, or at least less traveled recently.

Part of the reason it was called what it was called was that it went up a hill, and presently we began said ascent, picking our way among the rocks and taking us much of the road as we liked since there were no cars at all. I imagined a mule pulling a wagon up this track, snorting at the effort but enjoying the pastoral scenery. I always figure animals like scenery, but really, who knows?

A nagging question popped into my mind. "Hey, do you think Natalie really was descended from those founders of Geneseo?"

"Sure, why not?" Axel responded.

"It just seemed a little too perfect, you know?"

"Maybe that whole night a was a set-up."

"That's not what I mean. It's just that if you wanted to talk about the moral compromises the white settlers bought into when they came out from New England—and even when they came to New England in the first place—then it would lend credibility if you could say that it was your own ancestors who partook of those compromises."

"Yeah, I see what you mean. But really, what American hasn't benefited from those compromises? I mean besides the Indians. Hey, look out, I think that's a black snake on the right side up there."

"How do you know that's a black snake?"

"I just know what they look like, real long and skinny like that. Not poisonous or anything. I think they eat mice and chipmunks and stuff like that. He'll probably zip off into the grass before get there."

Indeed, the snake went from looking like a stationary bent stick lying in the road to gone in a second or two as we approached. I kept my eye out for more, but that one was it. Aside from a couple of very old farmsteads (always perched on the top of a rise) and a rustic private home or two, the road was unpopulated. The dirt surface had its hazards, but the lack of traffic meant we could avoid them for the most part, that is until the last half-mile or so when the grade steepened downward and the gravel, doing what gravity inspires it to do, collected toward the bottom. The heavy bikes and higher speed made it impossible to avoid the gathered rocks, and just as the road leveled as we approached a diagonal merger, I heard the telltale punctuated hissing of a puncture. In a few seconds, my back tire was flat.

I removed the panniers and got the wheel out. It looked like the tire itself was okay and had no rips or cuts, so I got one of our spare tubes in and stashed the flat one so I could fix it tonight and then we'd have that as a spare. Axel pumped it up because he really has a way with that Zéfal frame pump.

"And anyway," Axel said while pumping, "isn't the whole discussion kind of weird? Who is the rightful owner of the country? I mean, name me one country that wasn't created by somebody taking over land that used to be somebody else's."

"I don't know. My knowledge of geopolitical history isn't what it should be."

"Well, speaking as a geologist, it's just land: dirt, rocks, water, plants, animals. Why wouldn't you say the mosquitoes own it? Or the oldest rocks? They have as much claim as anyone."

"Well, it's not just the land. Isn't it the idea of a certain form of government? Self-government, we the people, all that."

He replaced the pump on his frame. "The rocks have been governing themselves for a few billion years. You wonder sometimes why you need any government at all."

"Well, somebody had to build this road you're using," I pointed down.

"Yeah, and look at the condition of it. Nice job, government."

"Oh, come on. It still is a big expensive project to build even a dirt road," I said as I pushed off and started rolling again. "And to make a road good enough for us to ride bikes on is even a bigger deal."

"Not to mention smooth enough for rollerblades."

"Damn right," I said, "Natalie couldn't go skating around in her underwear without those taxpayers."

"Three cheers for them," he laughed.

"Ha-ha," I said. I had set myself up for that. I coasted for a second and tightened up my toe strap.

"I was thinking," Axel said, catching up to me, "back on that Lake Trail. The Indians made that trail long before anybody thought they owned anything. They just wore a path, and everybody who used it probably brought along a hatchet to clear out overhanging branches and to take out any saplings that might try to grow in the middle of the trail. That was it: the people who used the trail made the trail and maintained the trail."

"And they didn't have horses before the Europeans came, so it was just walking. You wouldn't need to clear that much of a path. But to get something smooth and consistent enough to drive a car on or ride a bike, that takes a whole nother level."

"Just like people to go and have to make everything complicated."

6-15-88 morning

As I write this, we're sitting around Natalie's table getting a quick bite before Ax and I head off. Her giant boobs are wobbling around like crazy and stretching out the word Geneseo and I'm trying not to laugh and also watching Ax try keep his eyes elsewhere. Yesterday too, bursting out all over the place.

One thing I became concerned about while she was going through the cemetery files was the lack of any record of Uz ever being buried here. Emma's account made it seem like a big deal, described the stone, a lot of people at the funeral, everything—yet no record. This seems like one more gap, one more thing that can't be verified, one more reason to think that Hendrickson's [illegible] some "coed" in the 1950s might not be so wrong. Not as late as 1950, probably, but maybe in the mid-1800s. Maybe recreating a real journey [illegible] details wrong because the author was making shit up. Fake record of a real trip?

Last night I crawled into the tent, got half undressed, forgot sleeping bag still hanging on line outside. [illegible] out half-dressed, I decided to wait for Axel to return from his shower so he could get it for me. Meantime, guess I fell asleep. I had some weird dreams about a river and a flood, cold muddy water flowing around a hill with a huge tree in the middle, and standing under the tree were my parents and all my grandparents, Axel and his parents, Natalie, about a dozen other people dressed up like Indians and colonials, and Richard Pryor. They were motioning at me to paddle faster, but I was being pulled away by the current and like often [illegible]

I realized at some point that I was naked. But it was hard to cover myself because I was trying to paddle as well, but Ax said don't worry about it and smiled but I didn't know which thing he meant not to worry about.

When I woke up I was in my bag and covered up so I guess he must have got me into it, so I asked him and he said Don't you remember? You were a wild woman, and I said What? and he said Joking, joking, but then he said You sure looked damn hot, I was proud of myself for not taking advantage of you and I said You should have, that's what I had in mind if I could have stayed awake and he just nodded.

20.

March 15, 1818
Miss Eliza Crombie, Crombie Hill, New Hampshire

My dear sister Eliza,
One thing I noticed is that the date Numbers on my letters from March are just the same as the date Numbers from my letters I wrote in February, and that keeps making me think we haven't got anywhere. Papa left a bundle of letters on Monday at the Cazenovia post office. The man there thought the packet could cross the Connecticut by the middle of April. Papa said Goffstown was the closest stop on the third post road and that was where the family had agreed we would send letters. According to Uncle Nathan, the best chance of successfully sending a letter to where we are destined in Ohio is to address it to Chardon, Ohio, which is the capitol of the county where we are going to build our cabin. When we get there, we will try to find that place, but we might have to build our cabin first, Papa says.

Papa told me his plan, which is to build that cabin to live in for one season while he gets his sawmill built. We have three blades in the bottom of the wagon. Then when that sawmill is ready, we can build a frame house, and when the people there see the frame house, they will come to Papa to buy the milled lumber so they can also build a frame house, because everybody wants a frame house. So we will have to find a place near a good River or Brook to build the sawmill. Uz already knows how to run the saw from back home, and also we will need to make a farm because like as not there is not a general store built yet close to where we will settle. That's what Uncle Nathan said.

I think this week has been the prettiest part of our trip. Every day, the road comes to the end of a big long lake. The first one was on Tuesday afternoon, it was little skinny lake that looked like a river almost, then Wednesday morning was a bigger one but still skinny. Then on Thursday we came to one that was so big that we had to go up around the end of it and it took most all day and part of the next. Yesterday we finally got past that one and camped up above ANOTHER big lake. They are all long skinny lakes like a garden bean and Uz says they all run North and South and we are going past the top end of all of them, looking down where on the big ones you can't even see the other end of it.

Uz says a lot of the folks who are building up these towns here by these lakes are using their war bounty or their daddy's, where in exchange for going and fighting off the Redcoats they got paid something or got some land given to them so they could come out here and build a town. He heard tell of families from Connecticut that got their whole town burned down by the Redcoats, and then rather than try to build up again where those sad things happened, they set out for these parts. And he says Connecticut goes all the way to Ohio, but it skips over Pennsylvania. I can't figure what he's talking about, and I have never been to Connecticut anyhow even though I crossed that river with its name on it. But Uz says because of that, even though Ohio is a long ways away, when people get out there they find other people who also came from where they came from, and that makes it easier to make a good town.

Papa says Uz is right, and I can't believe I heard that, but that's what he said. And he also said that he heard the timber out in Ohio is Majestic, that's the word he said. And there's a lake so big it's like the ocean but the water is fresh and with that lake and that timber you could probably make a shipyard right there. And he also said there's a Waterfall bigger than anything anybody has ever seen, and because of that, any ships you might make will just have to stay in there because they couldn't get past the Niagara Falls without getting crushed to bits. Uz said a French man either Cartier or Champlain discovered it by exploring up the river from the Ocean and then the river came to that big waterfall that he could hear from far away and see the mist and that was as far as they could go.

Papa said one other thing folks will want to build with milled lumber will be Churches, and he did not want to bring up the sore spot with the Church we got kicked out of, but folks would still want to make a nice Church and we would be glad to make the boards and beams and rafters for it. And also wasn't it curious how all them Crombies came to America back in the 1630s because they were Puritans and did not want folks in England telling them what to believe and how to worship the Lord and then what do they do but turn around and tell other folks what to believe and how to worship the Lord. And Uz said Papa sure was right and I can't believe I heard that either. You can tell mama that or not. I am not sure if she would like to hear that.

Your loving sister,

Emma Too

21.

Vincent Hill Road ended at paved Fisher Hill Road, and we bore to the right on that, then left on Country Road 32, which we followed until we hit Route 20 just outside of Canandaigua. We rode that into town, even though it was a fast 55mph highway. At least the shoulder was adequately wide. If we were to do this again, it might be worth identifying smaller roads that hugged closer to the lake shore, as we had only fleeting glimpses of Canandaigua Lake and it would be worth a little extra distance to get close to the water avoid some of the traffic. It's a bit of a Catch-22 because the best way to identify the optimal cycling roads in any place is to be shown them by cyclists who live there, but of course if you have never been to a place, how do you know its cyclists? Sometimes local people publish maps of their area that identify the best roads for bicycles, but getting one's hands on them from far away can be a challenge, beginning with determining whether they exist at all.

From the map it appeared we would be going through a series of towns all day, each of them situated at or near the north end of a finger lake. Route 20 connected the dots of all these towns. We decided to take a lunch break somewhere around Geneva, at the tip of Seneca Lake, and begin looking for a place to camp after Skaneateles Lake and its eponymous village, the last of these lake-tip towns.

In the town of Geneva, Route 20 did skirt the lakeshore, and we found a nice park—adjacent to a Finger Lakes welcome center—where we ate our sandwiches while gazing south over the water. At the other end of this lake, the map told us, was Watkins Glen, a racetrack and sometime home for outdoor music festivals, and at the bottom of the next lake, Cayuga, was the town of Ithaca, with Cornell University. Those would be nice places to visit, but a very long detour, so perhaps another time.

Back on the road, we rode through Waterloo, Seneca Falls, and Auburn, and finally left behind us the little village of Skaneateles. We were well past where Emma Too had stopped, which she had been between Geneva and Seneca Falls, according to Cordelia's map, but making good progress was worth that disconnection.

At this point I remembered that I had told my parents we would call them from somewhere near Syracuse, and we were just beginning to pass to the south of that city, so in addition to looking for a place to camp, we started looking out for a payphone as well. We ended up finding both in one stop at the Finger Lakes Kart Track.

Axel first noticed that payphone against the wall of an old house that was set back from the road behind a gravel parking lot. A little hatchback car was parked at one edge. Only when we pulled in and leaned the bikes against the side of the building did we notice the paved track behind, a serpentine path of sharp curves and straight sections built into the hillside.

As I fished for a quarter to begin the collect call, a skinny blonde-headed man walked out from the back and greeted us in an accent I could not quite place. "Hello. Good afternoon." He was wearing jeans and a black Metallica t-shirt.

"Hi," said Axel.

"Do you need help? Is there any kind of trouble?"

"No, no trouble," Axel replied. "We promised to call home from somewhere around here and we noticed your payphone."

"Ah, I see."

I found a quarter but decided to postpone the call since it seemed a conversation might be forming. "Is it okay to use the phone?" I asked.

"Yes, certainly. That belongs to the phone company." He motioned with his hand toward the track. "We are completing our tasks for the end of the day and I noticed you riding your bicycles in. I thought you might have a problem. There is not much around here, no one to help."

"Thanks," I said. "We're going to make our call, then look for a place to camp and make some dinner."

"Ah," he said. He was not unfriendly, but his demeanor was cool, undemonstrative. "My brother and I will continue our work, then." He walked off.

Axel and I exchanged bemused glances. I checked the bike computer to see what time it was. "Hmmm, 4:30 on a— what is this, Thursday?—probably a little too early to call. They won't be home quite yet."

"Oh yeah. Want to have the other sandwich to kill some time?"

"Good plan. I'm starving anyway."

We sat against the wall and began to eat.

"Excuse me," the man returned, now alongside a slightly taller but equally skinny gentleman dressed in a mechanic's coverall.

"Welcome to our track," said the taller one. "I am Mikko Toivonen, and my brother is Pekka. There is no camping area anywhere near this place, but you are welcome to camp here beside the track. There is a toilet and water. It would be no trouble for us."

"Wow," I stood up. "We were just planning to find a spot off the road some place."

"Surely, as you wish. It is quite safe. There have not been too many bears recently," said Mikko.

"Only the one," said Pekka.

"Bears?" Axel said.

Both men stood silent for a couple of seconds. Pekka looked at the bikes. "I think you could ride faster than a bear, if you could get on the bicycle quickly enough."

"Yes," said Mikko. "That is the critical point."

They stood silent again, but then Pekka's face slowly showed a grin as he looked back and forth at Axel and me. "They look fast enough."

Both men burst out laughing.

"So," I said after they caught their breath. "No bears?"

"Very likely there is a bear," said Mikko. "But I have never seen one."

"Except in Kuopio," said Pekka.

"Where's that," Axel asked, "in the Adirondacks?"

"In Suomi," said Mikko. "In Finland."

The Toivonen brothers had emigrated to the United States in the late 1970s. "We helped some Russians disappear from Leningrad and reappear in California, so the state department was agreeable to our plan to come to the United States and convert America to rally car driving," Pekka said.

"But that idea failed," said Mikko. "I tried to explain to the officer, but he was not so interested."

"So instead we started this track," said Pekka. "We copied the one we used to go to in Kuopio."

"Wait," Axel broke in, "you got defectors out of Russia?"

"Only a few. I had a Mercedes station wagon with a false deck in the back. Two very thin defectors would fit in there under the spare tire," said Pekka.

"And we put some illegal beer in a corner and act very upset when they confiscate it," said Mikko. "Then they wink and let us go."

"Kuopio is far north of Helsinki or Leningrad, well into the lakes district, and the Soviet border only 80 kilometers, and there is nothing to do at the border outpost except drink beer and smoke," said Pekka.

"We sell reindeer meat and import some vodka and special gin," said Mikko. "We are a small multinational trading unit."

"Unbelievable!" Axel said.

Pekka got that grin again. "You are correct. All made up."

"Except the rally cars," said Mikko. "Americans are such terrible drivers that would never work here."

"You should see them putt-putt-putt around this track like they are mowing the lawn on a garden tractor, and they still overshoot the corners," said Pekka.

"Hey!" I interrupted. "We're not all bad drivers." Let Axel and me ride our bikes on there."

"Yeah, we can take a corner fast," Axel said.

"Bicycles? On our track?" Mikko seemed incredulous.

"Yeah, these aren't racing bikes, but if we take all the bags off it could be a blast," I said.

"Okay, on one condition," Mikko said. "We time you. Warm up three laps, then we time you one lap."

"Then you go on our hall of fame board," said Pekka.

"Deal," said Axel and I simultaneously.

Touring bikes or not, without their loads of baggage our rides felt like racing bikes already. We warmed up together, gauging the tight corners. There was one super-tight 180-degree hairpin but it was on a sharp uphill so the slope would slow you down; then a couple other wider 180s, a few snake-squiggles and a couple straights including a long start/finish. And little whoop-de-do hills throughout. We figured out you could take the banked uphill hairpin at just about as fast as you could go if you took a really high line around the outside, but most of the other turns were standard: start at the outside, dive into the apex, and hit the pedals a split-second later. Axel pulled off in the pit and made me start first.

"Rolling start, right?" I asked Pekka, who was standing at the S/F with a stopwatch. "Either that or somebody holds me up so I can strap in ahead of time."

Mikko trotted up. "I hold you up, standing start."

"Okay, just get my rear wheel between your knees and hold my shoulders, and give me a countdown."

Pekka counted down. "Five, Four, Three, Two, One, Go!"

Starting with the chain on the big chainring, I torqued hard out of the saddle, sat down, and shifted into a higher gear. I blasted down the straight and swooped through the hairpin without touching the brakes, but carried so much speed out of it that I had to brake hard into the next turn and skidded the rear tire a little, but kept it upright and danced through the rest of the course, accelerating with leg speed alone without ever shifting gears again.

Pekka jumped up and down "53:12! Under a minute on a freaking bicycle!"

Axel took his lap, almost lost it in the same place I had almost lost it—maybe there was a little oil on the track in that turn—and came in a little faster. "50:43!" Pekka yelled.

"Ain't gonna be no rematch!" Axel declared.

"You drive rally cars?" Mikko asked. "You should drive rally cars. You understand turning and braking and accelerating."

"No," I said. "Just race bikes. Do they race bikes in Finland?"

"Not so much," said Pekka. "We ride a bike for transportation if there isn't enough snow to ski."

"But in Kuopio that is only a few months," said Mikko. "Usually plenty of snow."

"More than here?" I asked. "Isn't this part of the New York snow belt?"

"Yes, not the heaviest part of it, but plenty," Mikko said. "But often it gets warmer in between snowing here. Back at home, as long as you are away from the Baltic, it stays cold all winter. No thawing. Same snow November to April."

"That is why you can skate on the lakes and ski everywhere," said Pekka. "Much better than summer."

"Whatever you say," Axel said. "Anyway, thanks for letting us play on your racetrack."

"You went faster than some of the kart drivers," Pekka said. "With no motor."

"I have a motor," said Axel.

"Me too," I said.

"Now what you need," said Mikko, "is sauna and beer."

"I wish," I said.

"Okay, let's go," said Pekka. "Bring bikes this way." He started walking up a path into the woods to the right of the track.

The trail curved uphill for a hundred yards or so, then leveled and descended to a small lake. On the left shore was a wooden building with a dock. Smoke wafted out of a metal chimney and a couple of clotheslines hung with white towels stretched to nearby trees. Pekka stopped at the door. "You can lean the bicycles on a tree, then come in quickly and close the door so the heat doesn't go out." We complied with that request and found ourselves in a small foyer with a couple of benches and hooks on the wall. A high shelf was stacked with folded white towels. "Have you done sauna before?"

We shook our heads.

"Okay, you will have a treat. Traditionally, you disrobe, rinse off, and take a towel," said Mikko, who had already disrobed and wrapped himself in a towel. He was lean but well-muscled. "We do not have a rinsing shower here, so either we rinse off in the lake, or use a towel and some water from here." He pointed to a small basin and demonstrated, quickly wiping down his skin, and then tossing the towel in a bin by the door. "All the clothes stay in here, nothing goes into the sauna room. When you are rinsed, then come into the next room and sit on the bench. After you get very warm and the pores open, then you go out the other door onto the dock and swim in the lake. Once you get cool in the lake, then climb back on the dock and re-enter the sauna. Repeat repeat repeat."

"Uh, okay," I said. "Swimsuit or anything?"

"If you wish, of course," said Pekka. "But traditionally, no. It is not the same. It is more healthy without swimsuit.

This is a big sauna, built for 12 people, so with only four nobody needs to sit too close. Excuse me." He turned away and unzipped and stepped out of his pants and took off his Metallica t-shirt, and quickly rinsed himself down and donned a towel. "We will wait for you before the steam. If you want to stay wrapped, take an extra towel to sit on."

I looked at Axel, thought very briefly about going back outside to rummage through the pannier to try to find the swimsuit I may or may not have packed at the bottom, then quickly pulled off my bike clothes, wiped off the road grime, and knotted a fresh towel around myself. He did the same. We opened the door and stepped tentatively into the next room, first me, then Axel.

"Good," said Mikko, a smile setting us at ease. "No need to be nervous—Pekka is happily married and you don't need to worry about me lusting for a woman," he winked. Axel gave me a side-eye and a shrug. The room had the same unfinished pine walls as the outer, but at one side was a raised bed of rocks from which intense heat radiated. On the adjacent wall was door with a window through which the dock and lake were visible. Opposite the fire were built-in benches, one at floor level and another behind it and a couple of feet higher, like bleachers. Mikko took a ladle from a bucket and drizzled water on the rocks, causing a cloud of steam to fill the room. "Heat rises, so it is more intense up top. Coolest down here off to the side."

I had forgotten to get a spare towel, so I climbed to the higher tier, unwrapped and sat on the towel. I leaned back on the pine wall and let the heat permeate. I could feel my muscles relaxing already.

"How was this fire going already?" Axel inquired.

"Important task for the end of the day. I was finishing when Pekka told me about visitors," said Mikko. "It takes only 30 minutes. Logs go in from the outside, cast iron and the rocks on it heats up and stays hot for an hour, perfect! Bonus when bicycle adventurers visit us!"

"Oh damn, I forgot to call my parents," I said. "Remind me when we're done."

"Maybe tomorrow," Axel said. "I can't move."

"You will need to move," said Pekka. "When you become too warm, then go to the lake. You are not used to the sauna, so this might be soon."

I was in fact already getting to that point. "So, I just go out that door and jump in the lake?"

"Take your towel," Pekka said. "Walk outside and leave the towel on the dock, then either jump in the water or climb in. It is deep, taller than a person. There is a ladder. Then when you get cool, climb back out, get the towel, and come back in."

"Okay. Back soon." I walked out the door and quickly closed it behind me. Leaving the towel next to the ladder, I jumped in and treaded water for a few minutes until the heat had dissipated into the water. Then, as instructed, I climbed out, re-donned the towel, and went back into the sauna just as Axel was headed the other way. "You're going to enjoy that," I said.

Pekka and Mikko were still leaned back, eyes closed. "Steam?" Mikko asked as I sat back down.

"Sure," I said. Another cloud enveloped us.

"A fine young man, Axel," said Mikko. "You are lucky."

"He's a keeper," I replied, saying the first inane thing that popped into my head.

After a while, Pekka finally got up and went outside. After the door closed, Mikko reached for the ladle and made some more steam.

"This is paradise," I said.

Mikko nodded. "The sauna is where all of the problems of the world are solved."

"Oh really?" I responded. "I happen to know that on bike rides is where all the problems of the world are solved. For example, earlier today Axel and I discussed issues of taxation and infrastructure spending."

"Did you solve the problems?"

"Almost," I laughed. "We got stuck on that transition from where everyone who uses a road helps build and maintain it, to everybody pays taxes and the government builds and maintains the road, and the problems with that."

"This road, our address for the track, is 'Cherry Valley Turnpike.' I thought this was a very strange name when we first came here. Then it was explained to me that the path was improved to a road by people who would charge a fee to anyone who would use the road. This is in early 1800s. The word 'turnpike' means a kind of gate they have so they can let your horse and carriage through after you pay the toll. But this turnpike road is only a certain distance, and after it and before it are some parts of road with no fee and no improvement, and it was totally unpredictable or travelers. So the state takes over and you pay taxes."

"Is Finland like that?"

"More like that than here." He still had his eyes closed. "But it is a much smaller country, easier to organize it. Except for the Sami in the north."

"The what?"

"The Sami people, maybe a little bit like Eskimo people who live in the arctic places in North America. They have their own life, starting long before there was a Finland or Sweden or Russia, and they herd reindeer and move across the far north as if the border lines do not even exist."

"Can you see the border lines?"

"No, not over land and water. On the roads, yes, but nowhere else. And there are only three roads."

"Did you really help defectors?"

"Maybe a little."

Axel came back in, then I got warm again and went back out to get in the water again. Pekka came in, Mikko went out. Axel went out again. After I don't remember how many repetitions of that, each of us on his or her own schedule, Mikko announced that the fire was cooling and we would be done soon. I got back in the lake one more time and I think I can confidently say I have never felt so clean or so relaxed. I seriously came close to dozing off while floating in the water.

Axel roused me up, speaking from the dock. "Hey El, I'll go get a change of clothes," he said. "What do you want?"

"To stay here, I laughed." I scissor-kicked and coasted a little further out on my back.

"Now beer," Pekka called from the dock. He led us back down the path. "Mikko will wash towels and join us soon."

"Hey, the Pounders," Axel blurted out.

I was still in a blissful daze but after a few seconds I decoded what he had said and remembered the two beers we had packed away so long ago this morning. Pekka motioned us to lean the bikes on the back wall of the building and went inside, emerging shortly after with four cans. "Utica Club," he pronounced. "The Karjala of America." He placed them one of the four picnic tables that occupied the patio.

"What does that mean?" I asked.

"It tastes like Karjala beer from Finland, that's all. No political message about the Russians and where the border should really be or anything like that."

"Okay. Well, we have uncontroversial beer, too," said Axel, placing the two bottles on the table. "Imported exclusively from historic Geneseo, New York. Maybe not so cold anymore. And maybe open carefully because of all the shaking all day. And some people were probably exploited during its manufacture."

Mikko walked down and joined us. "Welcome to America," Pekka raised his can. "Kippis!"

Opening a beer, Mikko pointed up the hill toward the woods. "If you set a tent on that level place, you will be protected and not visible from the road. Inside this door is a refrigerator and a sink, and a toilet next room. No need to lock. We will come back Saturday."

Pekka added "We have no plans for supper except to get a sandwich to eat in the car, and there is not store or restaurant unless we go all the way to I-81, and that's only McDonald's."

"We can share some of our elegant freeze-dried backpack dinners," I said. "Just add boiling water and eat out of your own pouch. No dishes."

"Hey, Mikko, like our lake treks, remember? Those terrible instant suppers." said Pekka. "Are you sure you have enough of this to share terrible camping food?"

"Absolutely," I said.

So we set up the camp stove and boiled water and chose among packets beef stew and chicken alfredo. We described our adventure retracing Emma's trek, what had happened so far, what our plans were for the next few days, talked a little bit about bike racing. The Toivonen brothers, it turned out, actually lived near Ithaca, but they would come open the track summer weekends and sometimes other days for special events. Earlier today they had hosted a qualifying session for a youth cart meet that would be held on Saturday. They would go back home tonight and come back Saturday. Mikko taught design classes at the small college there and Pekka and his American wife ran a bakery and coffee shop. We exchanged contact information. As dusk approached, they climbed into the Honda Civic hatchback that was parked out front, wished us well, and drove off. As we got back around to the rear of the building, I heard another car rumble by and its familiar sound prompted me to take a quick and apprehensive look over my shoulder. Light blue station wagon.

I put the beer from Natalie in their fridge and left them for the next thirsty throats that came along. We quickly set up the tent in the spot Mikko had suggested and crawled into our bags. The moon was notably brighter than just a couple of nights ago. I fell asleep right away, but woke up a little later.

"Hey Axel," I whispered. "I forgot to call my parents." He made an unintelligible sound. Mikko and Pekka, I mused— their story was American, too. Something like the sauna could be the center of life, literally, and the people who grew up that way could come here and bring a version of it with them. And gradually, that thing might become part of a new culture, layered on top of every culture that left traces of itself before. When Emma Too came across here, stayed overnight somewhere very near this place, and shared a meal with her father and her brother that reflected the traditions of their imported culture, would they suspect that, a century-and-a-half later, another imported culture would leave its mark? Before Emma Too, had others stayed just where they had camped that night? Other European settlers headed west? Fur trappers? Soldiers? Indians? Each new culture that brought its own flavors, would it welcome the new smells and sounds that came with the people after them? Would the Puritans relax in the nude with the Finns in the sauna? Had some of them gone for a swim in that clear, cold pond? My mind went back to that afternoon, floating on my back, looking up at the patch of sky through the trees. The same sky they would have seen before they looked back down and went on to other things.

I decided we would get going early, probably stop at the McDonald's by the highway for breakfast, and call my parents from there.

22.

March 8, 1818

Miss Eliza Crombie, Crombie Hill, New Hampshire

My dearest sister Eliza,

We do not see other people very much, and talk to them even less, but two days ago we went alongside a man and his son who were going the same way as us. I think the boy was a little bit older than me. His name was Nathan he said, and that got me to talking about how our family has so many people all with the same name. I can think of seven or eight or nine Nathans, some of them Crombies, some Dows, some Baileys, and other names, and most of them are cousins or uncles of each other and all different ages so you can't even keep track. You could switch a boy into one family and out of another and nobody would notice. Same with girl names. When I said my name was Emma Too, he thought at first that was one word and I said no and then he said Oh number two, and I said not really, and then I explained how when I was just a small child named after my mama and somebody asked my name, then before anybody could say it, I yelled out My name is Emma too, and that stuck. Emma Too. I like that better than Junior, but they never call girls a Junior anyway.

That boy Nathan said they were headed to his cousin's house to help them fix a sheep shed, and I asked if his cousin's name was Nathan, too, and he laughed and said, No, just Nathan. Then I said I bet you don't have Uz, and he said, nope. They parted off in the afternoon and then it was quiet again except for ourselves.

We set up camp this time by a Lake. There is a great big white house up on the hill looking down on everything. We are right between. Right now I am looking west because the morning sun is behind me, and the big house is up to the left and the lake is to the right. The water is frozen all across, but I think the air feels a little bit warmer so maybe it will melt soon. I know it is easier to go on the hard pack snow, but I am ready to have some warm air around me.

The land goes up and down in big Waves it looks like to me, how Uncle Robert said about being on the ship. When we get to the top of a ridge and look out ahead there is a wide valley. We go downhill into that valley and cross the bottom of it, then we go up a big long hill on the other side until we get to the top, and then there is another valley. All the ridges go crosswise to the way we are going. Uz said it would be more convenient if we could just get in a valley and travel along in the same direction that the valley goes, but the Problem is that would not take us to Ohio.

I am trying to save on paper so I am writing as small as I can. I think I am getting better at it. I took a knife and made a different edge on the quill and now the ink comes off of it better. Please tell Mama how I did that, and it was not even Papa or Uz who told me how, I just Figured it out.

The most exciting news I have to share is that the people we met who were going to fix the sheep shed told us that there is a post office in Cazenovia, and Cazenovia is the Town where we are today. We think the post office is in the big house. Papa says we will put all of my letters so far into one bundle and take them to the postman tomorrow, Monday, before we go on our way to the west, although it will probably cost too much money. But since he will be paying the money anyhow, he will put his own letter too, and one from Uz if he wants to. They both did want to, but Papa asked me to write his for him since I can write so pretty. Then Uz wanted to write his own so I let them use my quill but he wrecked the point from pushing too hard so I had to cut it out nice and clean again. That's why the writing in this last part of my letter looks not the same as the other part.

Your loving sister,

Emma Too

23.

6-16-88 morning

Didn't have the occasion to write last night. Left Natalie and her negligée and rollerblades and made for Geneva or beyond. Made great time, wind assisted (made us feel really strong!). Spotted a black snake on a dirt road, then [illegible]. Fixed a flat, first one so far, [illegible].

Ended up stopping at a go-kart track run by 2 Finnish guys, Pekka and Mikko, did a little demo race with bikes on their track, had a beer with them, [illegible] sauna. Ain't that America. Alternate between hot sauna cabin and jumping in the cold lake. The Finns do it nude, so okay. Didn't want to do it wrong. Nervous at first but it ended up fine. You readjust. Even with just me and 3 men, I wasn't worried. Maybe I'm stupid. When [illegible] I went back out and got in the lake one last time and I was scissor-kicking on my back and Ax was standing up on the dock holding a towel, but not wrapped. "You are some sight, Ellie," he said, just as the same thought passed through my mind about him. We shared some backpacking food with Pekka and Mikko, and then they headed of for home, near Ithaca [illegible]. One of them teaches at a college over there. Other one runs a bakery/coffee shop with his wife. Came over here maybe 10 years ago. Talked about smuggling defectors and I [illegible] different world, I'll say!

Fell asleep fast, but then woke up sweaty sometime later. The air was close and still [illegible] unzipped the bag and flipped it off me. I could see from the moonlight that came through the tent that Axel had already done the same thing and [illegible] tent in his boxer shorts, but I heard men just sleep that way. A little while later I removed my damp t-shirt and got right next to him. I was trembling, surprised how nervous I was. I watched our bare breathing chests glistening side-by-side in that blue moonlight and that calmed me down, just focusing on the breathing, and then I reached out and got his hand and put it on me. That hand woke up (maybe was already) and slid along my damp hot skin and explored me all over and me him too and pretty soon we were finally doing it, and I know some people have a bad first experience, or [illegible] but not me. Pretty sweaty but two thumbs up. I'm getting worked up all over again writing this, but we gotta go.

Our breakfast stop at the McDonald's at the I-81 exit worked as planned: McMuffins and biscuits and coffee and OJ. It was a little after 8:00 when we were done eating, a good time to call my parents. My dad picked up and accepted the collect call.

I quickly recapped our progress and assured him all was good. He put my mom on briefly so I could say hi, then we agreed that I'd call again after we reached our destination and we'd finalize plans for our return. As we were rolling off, I thought to ask Axel if he wanted to call his parents also, but he waved it off. "Maybe tonight or tomorrow." Also I realized we had forgotten to take a picture at the race track. So far, I had lugged this camera and three rolls of film along and taken only three or four photos.

Our plan for the day was ambitious—to make it all the way to the little town of Esperance, just west of Schenectady. There were two reasons: one, Emma had mentioned the town in a letter, and two, my high-school French had been good enough that I remembered that "esperance" meant hope, and it was a place we hoped to get to. But it would be somewhere around 110 miles, with a lot of up and down, so we were prepared to stop earlier if necessary.

Fortunately, the prevailing westerly winds were quite brisk this day, and we were able to make very good time getting pushed all the way. Around an hour after crossing I-81 we came to the town of Cazenovia, where Emma had posted some letters. It was a quaint town, but way too early for a lunch stop, so we just sort of took in a general impression as we passed through, but didn't stop.

The route was getting hillier, which was challenging, but the scenery was terrific and the tailwind lessened the pain of the climbs. Our New York State map included a short text which was largely devoted to promoting how efficient the highway network was. The drive times between places at opposite corners of the state, east, west, north, south, had been dramatically reduced as the interstate highway system had been completed between the 1950s and today. Sure enough, everywhere along the way were indications that this road, Route 20, had once been—but no longer was—the main east-west route through this region. Well-worn downtowns featured a hodgepodge of shops that, with their handmade (and obviously not professionally handmade) signs, seemed improvised to fill vacated spaces: second-hand stores, DIY china-painting studios, sole-proprietor insurance agents, or sometimes nothing. On the outskirts of many towns were often small motels or groups of tiny cabins, about half of them out of business. Just looking at the map we could see how the New York Thruway, which ran north of and roughly parallel to Route 20, and according to the map had been completed in the 1950s, would logically have taken over most of the though traffic as soon as it was finished, especially since it also hit all the big cities. So that was maybe 30 years of nobody building anything new along here, of old stuff being repurposed or just abandoned, and probably of people gradually moving away to places that seemed to have more of a future. But to us, riding our bicycles today on this well-appointed but sparsely traveled road, it was like we had hit the jackpot.

The town of Madison was still too early for lunch, so we rolled through there and eventually stopped after 1:00 in Richfield Springs, where we sat on an open green across from the post office and split a whole box of granola bars. Axel went to replenish our water at a municipal drinking fountain. "Do you think we'll make Esperance?" he asked as he returned with the full bottles.

"It looks like maybe another four hours, right?" I answered. "So probably, as long as we don't hit any delays."

"Ugh, I'm feeling sluggish today. Like it's the hangover I should have had yesterday."

"Too much swimming?" I winked.

"Or something," he laughed. "You feel okay?"

"So far," I said. "No complaints."

We continued on and, after about an hour, the reason for the brisk wind became apparent as the sky clouded up and it began to spit rain and get generally blustery. The temperature dropped from ideal to a little bit cooler than ideal. The wind was still behind us, so we kept making good time—even a little better as we picked up the effort to fend off the cold. We traded pulls, cranking as hard as we could sustain in high gears we couldn't have pushed without the wind. I paid no attention to the surroundings, focusing only on the white line of the shoulder or on Axel's rear wheel, whichever was in front of me at the time.

The skies really let loose as we descended a long hill and closely bypassed the town of Cherry Valley, which must have at some point been important enough to name an entire turnpike after it. I barely saw the sign as we streaked past in the deluge: "Cherry Valley 1" with an arrow to the right. Meanwhile, a caravan of pickups towing wind-buffeted camp trailers splashed past on the left, leaving no room to maneuver. My brakes were virtually useless between the rain and the momentum and I could feel the tires losing their grip in the bigger puddles, so I strongly hoped there was not a stop sign or light at the bottom. That hope was fulfilled. Esperance. Axel, who had been behind me absorbing all my road spray, came around to lead us up the hill on the other side, which was coming just in time to get us warmed up after the chilling descent. "That was a little dicey," he observed on the way by. We flew up the hill and barreled along the flats that came after, still gambling that nothing would come up that would put us at the mercy of my wet rims and weak brakes.

The wind gusts abated and the rain lightened up to a sprinkle, then stopped altogether. We were tempted to pull off at a soft-serve ice cream place on the left, but that option was quickly discarded in the face of an oncoming oil truck and our desire to reach our destination. Soon after that, we noticed that the road had come alongside a river, a few hundred feet to our right. Suddenly, we passed a little sign that said "Village of Esperance, Incorporated 1818," and only three and a half hours since leaving our lunch spot. Funny what a little adrenaline will do.

Just as we got to the other side of town—about two minutes later—the river swung in from the right and ducked under a bridge as Route 20 continued on east. We stopped at a little supermarket a short way up the road and stocked up for the night plus breakfast and lunch for tomorrow. Behind that building looked like it might be a viable camping spot, but the store didn't close until 9:00 and it was only 6:00. So we elected to explore a little further, continuing east on 20.

"Little League," Axel said after another mile or so.

"Little League?" I asked.

He pointed at a sign and a small paved drive on the right. "Probably have bathrooms and water, open space, away from the road. As long as there's not a game tonight." We ventured down that path and found five baseball diamonds and, sure enough, a central concession building with outdoor water and bathrooms. And picnic tables. And the place was deserted. Unfortunately, though, the bathrooms were locked.

There was a stand of tall oaks along the third base line on one of the fields, so we set the tent up in there—you almost couldn't see it from the main drive—then changed into street clothes and set up to make sandwiches on a nearby picnic table. Then the cars started streaming in.

At this point we were more or less trapped in here, and besides it seemed that everyone was going to the first field, which happened to be the furthest from our position. Lights came on over that field and we noticed then that only the first two fields had lights. A small gray car pulled up alongside the concessions building. The metal blinds over the sales counter rolled up. A person opened each of the bathrooms.

We finished our dinner and packed up the next day's road food, then walked over to the concession building. I made a needed stop in the bathroom and washed up, then we bought a couple cokes and some chips and walked over to watch the game. "Better late than never, huh?" said the teenage girl behind the counter. "Seems like a rain delay every week."

"Every time, it seems like," I said.

"For sure," said Axel.

There were sets of bleachers for each side, but no seating that seemed neutral. And everybody seemed to know everybody, and we didn't know anybody. One of the teams seemed to have been sponsored by the grocery store where we had shopped, though, so we sat with them. They lost 14 to 3.

Toward the end, as the score was getting out of hand, a couple behind us turned their attention to us. "Not sure we've met," said a slim, dark-haired woman in jeans and a flouncy floral top.

"No, probably not," I said. "Just visiting."

"Independent observers," Axel chimed in.

"Oh, from the league," said her companion, a short, muscular guy wearing tan cargo shorts and a Mets t-shirt.

"Northern Ohio," I clarified.

"Oh, strong district," the guy said. "And how about them Indians?"

I rolled my eyes.

"At least we're not the Red Sox," said Axel. "We won the series only 40 years ago."

The couple laughed.

"So are the Mets really the home team for you folks around here?" Axel asked. "Why not the Yankees? And isn't Boston closer?"

They laughed even harder.

"Hey really," I said, "you ought to be Indians fans. Seems like folks around here have more in common with northern Ohio than New York City or Boston."

"How do you mean?" asked the lady.

"Well," I said, "the people look the same, the houses look the same, the foliage looks the same, the people's accents sound the same. You guys don't sound at all like Boston or New Yorkers, you sound like you're from my neighborhood back home."

"Still no way I'm rooting for the Indians," said the man.

"Yeah, it's funny," said Axel. "We can come hundreds of miles east from Cleveland and the accents sound just the same, but if you start in the same place and go south for an hour, it sounds like you're in Kentucky, and if you go west for 20 minutes it's that nasal Detroit thing."

"Sorry, still a Mets fan," the guy repeated.

"But on the other hand," the lady said, "fuck the Yankees." Then she caught herself and looked around. "Sorry, I should watch my mouth with kids around. But still . . ." she lowered her voice to a loud whisper, "fuck the Yankees."

"We can agree on that much," Axel said. He looked out at the game. "Looks like there's a gnat problem in right field." The kid out there was sitting down, swatting away, not paying the slightest attention to the game.

"I'm not supposed to yell at him," said the guy. "But I'm tempted." He sighed. "Just pray the ball doesn't go that way."

"Sometimes your kids don't automatically have the same interests as their parents, you know?" said the lady.

We all laughed. The batter dribbled a ground ball toward the pitcher, who grabbed it and threw it over the first baseman's head into the woods. The right fielder sprung up and, after 30 seconds and all the baserunners having scored, emerged from the trees with the ball, jumping up and down with glee.

Baseball, of course, is known as "America's pastime," and it seems like a lot of writers present the game it as somehow metaphorical to the American condition. The boredom, the waiting, the tension, the bursts of action, the mental chess game where pitcher and batter try to anticipate each other's anticipations, the unpredictable bounce that can turn the game one way or another—it's a game of inches, they always say. Today's game, however, was not of inches, or even feet. If this was a metaphor for the American condition, the implication was that a lot of people can be playing the game at any given time, but often only a few of them are playing it well. Most of us are standing out there alone, paying attention only occasionally, with only modest capability to respond effectively if the ball happens to come our way. Nobody is born with this strange skill set. Maybe you can't even get good at this without being bad at it for a long while first. So I guess they're right. Good metaphor.

We ducked in the bathrooms again before everything was closed up. Axel had the brilliant idea that he stole from a movie of hiding in the men's room by standing on the toilet seat. When the concessions girl called in to make sure no one was there, he said nothing. When she stuck her head in to be sure, he stayed still. Then she locked the door, got in her car, and drove off.

I just stayed quietly behind the building and nobody noticed me. It was almost dark by then. After I didn't hear anything for a few minutes, I walked up to the men's room door and found it still locked. Then I had that spine-chill moment when it occurred to me that maybe the door didn't have a deadbolt knob on the inside—that you would need a key to get out as well as to get in. I couldn't remember how the ladies room was. I knocked on the door. "Axel?"

"Just a minute," he called out.

"What are you doing"" I called in.

"What do you think I'm doing?" He responded. Then I heard the toilet flush, the faucet go on, the towel dispenser clunk, and the knob turn. Axel stepped out. "Geez, give a person some privacy."

We made our way back to the tent in the dwindling light and settled in. The orange dusk light turned to gray through the tent walls. "Hey Ax," I whispered. I don't know why, but when it's dark, I always whisper. "Thank you for doing this. Today would have been a death march without you." But he didn't answer. Asleep? Just quiet? I stared at the tent ceiling. Then I got out my journal while there was still a little light.

6-17-88

Rolled out early, called my folks from McDs. Cazenovia, Richmond Springs (lunch) then made Esperance thanks to massive tailwind. That was caused by a cold front that [illegible] showers, but all pushing us in the right direction at least. Drenched to the bone, white jersey=Ellie wins wet t-shirt contest.

Found good place to camp, but a little league game cropped up so we watched it and talked with locals. People here sound more like Cleve than NY or Boston. [illegible] the game. Wonder what people sounded like when E2 came across here? Were NY and Bos. accents the same then? Everybody drove away and we brushed our teeth and got in the tent. [illegible] Got out my photocopies of E2 letters to try to synch us up with her. One thing I just notice, reading the one she supposedly wrote from here—if they way you send letters back then was to write on as much of the paper as you could, then fold it up and use one of the exterior panels of that folded-up letter to put the address and everything, then why don't these letters have that? Where are the envelopes? I'm thinking more and more that these were not actually mailed. Maybe she wrote them en route and stashed them away, or maybe she wrote them all later. Maybe she kept some kind of journal, like me, and then wrote the letters from those journal notes. Or maybe the whole thing was made up, just inspired by the migrations people made, but not documenting any one true journey. If that's the case, then why are we out here? To find Crombie Hill, I guess. [illegible] is historical fiction, that's a real place. They had to come from somewhere.

Okay now it's too dark to read what I'm writing. Looks like he's definitely asleep. Wake him up? No, let him sleep. Long day, I'm tired too. Night night Ax.

24.

March 1, 1818

Miss Eliza Crombie, Crombie Hill, New Hampshire

My dearest sister Eliza,

My feather pen just wrote March 1 but I can tell you it is not spring here. The ink runs thick on account of the cold, even when I hold the inkwell inside my arm against my side like Uz told me to do. We traveled all this week on hard packed snow, but with the wheels instead of the runners it is a lot more disrupting. I think my eyes are going to fall out. If you come along later and see some eyes on the ground, pick them up and bring them along to me.

I am not sure if you all will come the same way, but the Road was not too rough for a while. On some parts of it, they have what they call a turnpike where you pay some coins and then they let you into a section of road, and the turnpike is the big long pole they swing around so you can get through. In exchange for that Money, which Papa said was too much, they take some care of the road and it is easier to travel on it. However, we are past that now, and the wheels buck like we are riding on a river rapid. I saw a little sign one place that said Cherry Valley and that made me hungry for some cherries, but all I see is barren branches and more snow. Sometimes I think they name a place just to make you disappointed.

Two days in a row it snowed, but not so much that we wanted the runners back on. Uz said how the snow did make the road smoother, so there was one good effect from it.

I am sorry, I got started writing late today and now I will help with the chores. Tell Mama though that we snared two Rabbits this morning and we will have a fine supper. Uz noticed a lot of tracks at the edge of the meadow and set up a snare and the two rabbits obliged by getting caught. They should have gone to church instead! We will say a blessing over the stew-pot tonight.

Your loving sister,

Emma Too

<h1 style="text-align:center">25.</h1>

The road map had an inset for Albany, and it didn't look like we should stay on Route 20 much longer. "There's no way to tell from the letters exactly where they crossed the river," I said, pointing out the heavily urbanized street tangle on the map, "so I don't see any reason we have to stay on this all the way through Albany."

Axel pointed north of the city on the inset map. "See how the river is narrower up here. If I was me in 1818 I would cross at a narrow place—like this town called Waterford. Sounds like a place people would cross a river anyway." He found the same place on the big map and spread the map wider on the picnic table. "And we're here, so we'd want to get off 20 before it goes too far south. It bends way down to the south and into Massachusetts." Why was he suddenly in charge of navigation? Whose trip was this anyway? I reasserted myself.

"At this side of Vermont," I said, "we want to pick up 7 which turns into 9 in order go across the state from Bennington to Brattleboro, and you can see 7 shows up in New York a little north of Albany by Hoosick."

"In fact," Axel pointed out, "that same Route 7 crosses the Hudson at Waterford and goes all the way through Schenectady and intersects 20 not far from where we are now. It looks like a big road, but pretty direct. I don't see any way to avoid city riding through here without going a day or two out of our way either north or south."

"I can deal with the city," I said.

"Oh, wait," he pointed out. "It turns into a superhighway for a stretch here."

"Maybe we could continue straight on Route 2 at this point where 7 goes north and turns into superhighway, we cross the river on 2, then angle northeast on this Mud Turnpike thing. Whatever that is, it's smallish and it runs into 7 again before it gets to Hoosick. Then if we survive that far, we stay somewhere between there and Bennington. It seems like the trickiest thing will be finding a bridge over the Hudson where bikes are allowed, but Route 2 looks smaller than a lot of them, so maybe."

"I guess we just have to get to the river and find out," he said.

I said "So let's go."

Leaning the bikes on the concession building wall, we both went into the men's room. I hoped the kid wouldn't get in trouble if the door was discovered unlocked. But then maybe she'd be the one to open it again anyway.

The intersection with Route 7 was only a few miles down the road. We bore left at the "Y" and said goodbye to the road we'd been on most of the week. "Damn," said Axel. "Meant to find a phone booth."

"I didn't see one at the ballfield."

"Me neither." He resumed his silent mode.

Route 7 steadily got wider as we approached the city, but the shoulder also got wider—until we got into Schenectady proper, at which time it got very trafficky, multi-laned, fast, and narrow. We pulled aside for one more look at the map. If

Route 7 was going to be like this, or worse, all the way to that split-off with Route 2, then we would be wanting another plan.

That Plan B was to go right through downtown Schenectady (at least the roads would be slower, if still full of traffic), find something called 146 heading north that we could use to cross the Mohawk River, then turn right and follow River View Road, which looked like it would be pretty, following the north shore of the Mohawk. We'd make our way from that to something called Middletown Road that would angle down to the southeast for a couple miles before hitting Broad Street, where we could turn left and cross the Hudson on a nice, small, non-superhighway bridge. From there we could make our way over to Route 7 this side of Hoosick, which was right on the Vermont border.

So we got off Route 7 at Broadway and made our way through downtown Schenectady, rolling downhill past a smelly garbage-processing facility and then at one point coming alongside railroad tracks as an Amtrak train rolled slowly by, heading west. Axel stuck out his thumb as if to hitch a ride, and I pointed out it was going the wrong way—but it probably was the very train we would ride if we were to get back to Ohio that way. Eventually we found ourselves on Aqueduct Road, which headed in the right general northeasterly direction and sounded like it might lead to a river. That took us to a nice, peaceful crossing of the Mohawk, after which we followed the north side of the river according to plan. This "Plan B" route proved to be a very good decision, and perhaps even would be a preferred means of getting across to Vermont for a cyclist who lived around here and knew what they were doing. The roads through downtown were slow, safe traffic, with plenty of space for a bike, and the parkways were lightly traveled and pretty. We encountered a few other bikes.

After crossing the Hudson, we stopped to eat a sandwich on the other side, then found our way to Northern Drive and then Plank Road, which changed its name a few times but ultimately deposited us back on Route 7, which had turned back into a winding country road. It was all uphill, but we were making pretty good time. We decided we'd had enough of New York and therefore would not look for a place to camp until after we got into Vermont, which proved to be not a very long wait. At the crest of a rise, a little green sign welcomed us to Vermont and the NY 7 signs stopped and VT 9 signs began.

As we rolled into the college town of Bennington—which was pretty sleepy presumably because it was summer and the students were gone—we passed a couple cars parked windows down in a driveway, a stereo thumping "Godzilla" by Blue Oyster Cult, an unmistakable skunky smell wafting out into the road. Maybe cousins of our friends from a few days ago, I thought. On the other side of Bennington, just after crossing Route 7, we passed a sign that said Woodford State Park was 12 miles in the direction we were headed and a little tent symbol implied we might camp there. "It's a Saturday," Axel called back. "That would be a nice stopping point but I hope they're not booked up."

"It's early, too, though. Maybe that will help."

We picked up the pace, as if that would make any difference, and arrived at the campground in about 40 minutes. The tent spaces were indeed all booked up, but someone had just cancelled a lean-to reservation, so we splurged and took that. The ranger suggested we just set up our tent inside the lean-to because of the bugs. Black fly season, he noted. Mosquitoes too. And make sure to put any food in the bear box at the campsite.

Spotting a payphone on the outer deck of the camp office, Axel wheeled his bike over there and began to fish in his bag for change. "I didn't say I would call collect, so I'm just going to burn a couple bucks on a short long-distance call." He found eight quarters, good for two or three minutes on the weekend, and pushed them into the coin slot. After he dialed, he stood there as it rang a few times, and was just putting his hand on the receiver to hang up and get the quarters back when a voice came on the other end. "Got the damn machine," he muttered away from the phone. After the voice stopped, he spoke. "Hi it's Axel. We're in Vermont, everything's cool and going good. This uses up my quarters so if I call again it will have to be collect. Hope that's okay. I'll call when—" then a voice came on the other side. "Oh, you're there! I was leaving a message. Look I only have a minute since I'm out of quarters. Yeah, sure I can. Yeah, I'll hang up and call in a sec. Bye." The phone did not return any change.

He turned to me. "Hey, sorry, can I bum one quarter to call my dad back collect?" I found the same one in my bag that I had used earlier and handed it to him. "Thanks," he said and slid it into the coin slot.

"Hello, yes. I'd like to place a collect call from Axel. Yes, thank you."

I didn't want to snoop but it seemed weird to take my bike and walk away, so I just leaned on the railing nearby. From that distance I could not hear anything from the other side, and only bits of what Axel said because he was leaning down into the phone unit away from me. But the grim tone of the conversation was unmistakable. I could tell Axel was holding back. His jaw was tense and he was rapping on the phone shelf with his free hand. He turned around and faced toward me. "Yeah, a few more days. Then I'll probably take the train back either from Springfield or Albany. Right, I'll let you know. Yeah, she's good. We're good. Okay. Yeah. Talk to you soon. Bye." He handed the quarter back to me.

"So . . ." I broke the silence as we walked the bikes on winding lanes toward our lean-to site.

"The short version," he replied. "is he's moving out, going to stay with this new person who has come into his life. After he's out, my mom stays in the house. But I should get my stuff fairly soon in case they sell the place."

"Oh Ax," I said. "I'm so sorry."

"Not like I couldn't see something coming," he said, "but I didn't expect this other person. Shari."

"Shari?"

"Met her out on some consulting gig, I guess. Soulmates."

"And your mom?"

"I think she was in the house, but didn't come to the phone. I'll talk to her when I get back."

"Amtrak?"

"Yeah, I think I have to. Back before we left, I did some figuring and I can either ride back to Albany and get it there, or I could get a Greyhound in Brattleboro, ride that down to Springfield Mass, and catch it there. That probably makes more sense."

"Tomorrow?"

"What? No. Finish the ride, then get to a train."

"You don't have to finish the ride," I said. "I'll be okay."

"I know, but I want to," he replied. "Came this far."

I wanted to hug him but I was getting a not-too-close vibe and so I just reached over and put my hand on his for a few seconds where he was guiding the handlebars.

"Okay," he said when we got to the lean-to. "Let's think about something else."

6-18-88

Esperance/Schenectady/Albany/Waterford/Hoosick/Bennington/Woodford S. park. Rolled out of little league hotel after scoping the map to figure out how to get through/around Albany. Least fun riding of the whole trip, lots of traffic, shitty roads. One good parkway along Mohawk R. Crossed Hudson R. at Waterville, then started long climb up past Hoosick and into VT. Finally out of f-ing NY.

We got a lean-to at a state park campground, only available spot, and the ranger said we should put the tent inside it for bugs. Good call, there's swarms of them. We got some pork n beans at the camp store, special fancy dinner. Ax made a call home and it sounds like his folks are separating. Sucks. I don't know what to do for him. My parents are so boring and predictable. Not complaining this time. Will take train home.

26.

February 22, 1818

Miss Eliza Crombie, Crombie Hill, New Hampshire

My dearest sister Eliza,

The cold weather has held just as cold, and that means we have been able to travel past Albany with the runners still on the wagon, but I will tell you we almost had to take them off. Close to Albany when we got near the Ferry across the Hudson River the snow was packed so much and worn so thin from all the wagons and stagecoaches that the rocks were sticking up through the snow and we nearly got stopped. Lucky for us Hester and Artemisia are strong girls and between us all getting behind for pushing and them pulling, we got on down there. Papa said there is a bridge across the Hudson but it is too far north and we want to go more southerly to follow what he heard say from uncle Nathan. The ferryman was happy to see the runners on the wagon because he said that would keep her from rollin off into the Hudson.

Hester and Artemisia are calm by nature, but they did not take to the Ferry. The men had a big long cable run all the way across the river, and the Ferry had some clips onto that so it would not get carried downstream, but somewhere close to the other side, the current got strong and the Ferry started bucking a little bit and Artemisia started her braying and that got Hester to braying and bucking a little bit and pretty quick everybody was shouting and trying to hold them down and calm them. I looked down at that loud gray water with chunks of ice in it that were banging against the wood as they came down the river and I think I would agree with Hester and Artemisia that let's get back on that cold snowy ground. They were both steaming when we got off and we started to walking right away so they would not get chilled. Once we got up the long hill and put that river out of sight behind us, they settled down better.

That was two days ago. Yesterday we got to a village called Esperance, and Uz said that is French and it means "Hope" maybe because French people were here before us, and Papa said he did not know about that, sometimes folks just like to use a French word. But he said a town with a name like that would be a good place to stop for the night, so we set camp just this side of it.

I will not describe all that again because it is just the same every time. First we get the fire going with some dry wood from inside the wagon, then we go gather up some more firewood to keep it going and to have some more dry in the wagon. I could also tell you about the snow. There is a lot of snow, every place you look. I don't think it has got one whit warmer, but Papa says the thaw will come along sometime, and because of that we will pull off the runners today and have the wagon roll on Wheels from here on because it would be much difficulter to get the runners off in the mud compared to in the snow. Uz looked a little sad at that idea but then we undid the lashings that went through the holes in the runners and that laid in the valleys that Uz had dug for them in the bottom with an awl so they would not stick out, and then we undid the other lashings that kept the wheels from turning, then we three of us rolled the wagon backwards off the ends of the runners. Uz wrapped up the runners with their special ropes and tied them alongside the wagon.

Uz said he learned in school how General Lafayette had come from France to lead American troops against the British and help secure the victory for us, and then he went back to France and started a revolution there. Some folks in New Hampshire want to rename the Big Haystack mountain in honor of him.

Papa said Lafayette had the right idea because the natural rights of man should make the slaves all free and why did France get that right and get rid of Slavery and the United States got it wrong and kept it? A man is a man, Uz agreed. What about a girl, I asked. And Papa laughed and said a man is a man. I don't mind telling you this because I know Papa won't read my letters especially because I seal them up good with wax, but if he lets me drive the team, then why can't I have as much rights as a slave who got set free? I never saw a slave in my life, but I have seen ladies who have a cruel husband, like Mr. Nichols. I can't abide either one, and nobody else ought to either. You can tell Mama that or not, I don't care.

Your loving sister,

Emma Too

27.

Sometime not long before the sun came up, Axel crawled out of his bag and unzipped the tent. "Gotta pee, be right back," he said. "Where's my damn flip-flops?" The next thing I heard was an oof and a loud snap. A couple minutes later, Axel came back in. "Took a header off the platform."

"Oops," I said.

"Landed on a rock."

"You all right?"

"Think so. Kinda hurts though." He crawled gingerly back into his sleeping back. "Ow. Just lie still for a bit."

"Where is it?"

"Shoulder."

"Oh, damn." He had broken his left collarbone the previous year. "Same side?"

"Yep. Nothing displaced, so that's good. Maybe I cracked it though, or bruised it at least."

We lay there not sleeping for another hour, then got up to eat something and see how he was doing. I examined the shoulder and there was nothing that looked out of alignment, no surface bruising or anything—a broken and displaced clavicle is fairly obvious, and also extremely painful. It's a fairly standard bike-racing injury: you get launched from your bike for whatever reason and hit the pavement with your shoulder, and sometimes the skinny little collarbone can't take that. If it's badly displaced, the emergency room may recommend surgery to bolt and plate it back together; if it's only slightly displaced or just cracked, they usually just give you a sling and some painkillers and tell you to be careful.

Axel thought it was probably cracked but not broken all the way through and insisted on trying to ride. So we ate a little something, he took a couple of the ibuprofens we'd brought along, wrapped the shoulder in an ace bandage he'd stuffed into our gear, and we did a little test-spin in the park. He said it was okay.

"Are you sure you don't want to see a doc? We can ask the ranger I'm sure."

"No, I think I'm good. If it gets worse, then maybe."

Route 9 through southern Vermont is a lovely road, with a lot of up and down, but pretty good road surface. Our progress was slowed compared to previous days because Axel could not really get out of the saddle on hills and had to ride essentially with just his right arm, the left hand resting tenderly on the handlebar but not doing anything. He put the chain on the middle ring and just left it there so he would not need to shift the front derailleur with that left hand. Potholes and bumpy sections became major, potentially traumatic events. But despite all that, we covered the 35 miles or so to Brattleboro that morning and stopped for lunch at a roadside bakery and deli just before crossing I-91.

Axel sat himself down carefully at a picnic table while I went in to get some food. I brought back a couple of bodacious sandwiches and a giant cookie to split, plus some drinks. He looked a little pale, and held the arm close to his side.

"Ellie," he said halfway through the sandwich. "I think I better stop."

"Okay," I said. "I think that's smart. I'm sure there's a hospital in Brattleboro and that's only a couple miles."

"Nah, no hospital. All they'll do is make us sit around, take some x-rays, tell me to keep my arm by my side in a sling for 6 weeks, and charge me 500 dollars. I already know what the treatment is."

"But that's what health insurance is for."

"Yeah, that's true."

"So?"

"Well, I don't have any right now."

"What do you mean, your school policy covers this. I checked it out before we left."

"It would," he said, "if I were still in school. But if, for example, I didn't pass enough classes last semester to come back, then I would not be enrolled as a student, and I would not have any insurance right now."

"Oh, Ax," I sighed. "Why didn't you tell me?"

"Because I didn't know until last night. Well, that's not exactly right. I knew there was a pretty good chance that I wiped out the semester, but I didn't have the official word yet. That was more good news from my dad—a nice note from the registrar informing him that I was un-enrolled." He shook his head. "Good timing."

I contemplated for a few seconds. "Okay, well then let's go back. But I still think we should go to the hospital. If we just tell them your situation, maybe they skip the x-rays or something and the bill is manageable."

"I'm serious, I've had this injury before and I know other people who have, and I know they'll just tell me to keep it in a sling and don't lift any heavy weights for a month," he said. "I thought it might be okay to ride, and for the most part it is, but if anything goes wrong it could turn into a much more serious injury. Whereas the way it is now, if I just cool it for 6 weeks, I can be back on the bike and racing before the end of the summer. So that's why I think I should stop now. Just too risky."

"I still don't like that, but I guess it makes sense. Plus, I could help you carry stuff."

"That's the other thing," he said. "I was thinking about it as we rolled over here this morning, and I think you could continue and finish up the trip yourself. It's less than a day away, 50 miles or so. If you took the tent and one bag and just ate cold food or restaurant stuff, you could do it on your own, no problem. You might not even need the tent. Stay in a B&B or something. Then ride back here and get the Greyhound to Springfield and take the Amtrak back home."

Considering my original plan had been to do the trip myself, this idea did not seem too far-fetched.

"All we'd have to do," he said, "is go to a bike shop and pick up a couple leftover bike boxes for the bus and train. If they're like our shop, they'll just give them away and let us borrow a pedal wrench and a couple other tools, maybe charge us a few bucks."

"Okay, how do we find a bike shop?"

He held up the paper placemat I had brought out with our sandwiches, wincing because he had temporarily forgotten about his shoulder. The sheet had a map in the middle and was ringed with little display ads for local businesses, including one called Green Mountain Velo. "Keep in mind today is Sunday. They may not be open."

We finished eating and coasted down into Brattleboro.

On Depot Street we discovered that an Amtrak line, the Montrealer, actually stopped in Brattleboro, but then we discerned that this train had been suspended in 1987, maybe to resume, maybe not. That would have been too convenient. But Greyhound ran a few daily buses that way, and we knew the Lake Shore Limited departed Springfield westbound at 3:20 in the afternoon, so we booked a seat for Axel and made sure of cargo space for the bike for a departure at 9:15 Monday morning. Springfield would be an hour away without stops, so that seemed safe. Since we had no credit card, we could not reserve the Amtrak ahead of time, but we were assured by the Greyhound office that there would be no problem getting a ticket on that train on a Monday.

Green Mountain Velo proved to be three blocks away, and also proved to be open on a Sunday afternoon. We'd been warned about New England "blue laws" that tended to keep places closed on Sundays, but also that these had been loosening up and it might not be an issue, except for buying alcohol.

It was a slow afternoon in the shop, so the request for a bike box, along with the two loaded-down, road-dusty bikes, of course prompted a conversation about our adventure. We recapped the whole thing. They especially liked the Finns and the go-cart track.

"You know there's a steady stream," said a scruffy blond guy whose work shirt was embroidered with the name Steve, "of people coming through here on cross-country treks. Route 9 across Vermont seems to be a kind of preferred route."

"Just yesterday," said a slight, red-haired woman whose work shirt also said Steve, "we had a Jamaican couple on a Santana tandem. The thighs on them, damn!"

"She was offering the lady a lot of useful advice," said scruffy guy Steve.

"We're all about customer service," said redhead woman Steve.

Axel explained the current situation, that he had taken a fall and had a bad shoulder, so we figured he'd better cut it short and head home—but that I was going to continue. I got good props for that. I said that if all went well, I would be back in a few days to pick up another bike box and catch another Greyhound to Springfield and another Lake Shore Limited to Cleveland.

Redhead woman Steve went into the back and reappeared with a cardboard box in which a large Trek mountain bike had been shipped—not only was the box a bit more spacious than a typical road bike box, but the cardboard was also thicker. "And

I set aside another one for that bike. I would put your name on it, but I don't know your name."

"Oh, sorry. Ellie. Eleanor Webster. Thanks, Steve."

"Sure, no problem," she replied with a wink.

The reality of it began to set in when we actually started packing his bike up in the box: front wheel off, handlebars loosened and turned, seat down, left pedal removed. Then we took everything out of all our bags and figured out the bare minimum for me to take: my clothes, the tent, one sleeping bag, some of the freeze-dried food, a couple of tools. The rest we stuffed in and around the bike in the box, except for the daypack, where Axel packed some clothes and a bit of food and the ibuprofen.

"And your name, sir?" asked scruffy guy Steve. "Do you want to just swing by in the morning and pick this up? We open at 9:00."

"Ah, that's probably too late, so I guess we better take it with us. Bus is at 9:15. And I'm Axel."

"Like Eddy Merckx's kid?" replied scruffy guy Steve, referring to the son of the world's most famous bicycle racer.

"Yeah. Just coincidence, though."

"Well, where are you staying?" asked redhead woman Steve.

"Um," I said, "not figured out yet. Any recommendations that are in the bike hobo price range?"

"The best place I can think of would be in the apartment upstairs," said redhead woman Steve. "Old timey retail building with the store at street level and the owner lives upstairs. Except the owner doesn't live upstairs."

"Who does live upstairs?" Axel asked.

"Nobody," said scruffy guy Steve. "Just office and storage. But the couch in the office is one of those futon deals that folds out."

"Well, we wouldn't say no to that," I said, "especially with his bad shoulder. Not sure how it would go sleeping on the ground."

"Okay it's a deal then," said redhead woman Steve. "Now I'm gonna go get us some beers."

"Good luck on Sunday," said scruffy guy Steve.

"From home," said redhead woman Steve.

"I'll order a couple pizzas," said scruffy guy Steve.

"You guys are the best," I said. "Let us know what we owe you. We have cash. I even have traveler's cheques."

"Forget about it," said scruffy guy Steve. "Cycling solidarity."

I said okay but had already decided to sign over a $50 traveler's cheque and leave it next to their cash register. We went upstairs and changed out of bike clothes.

The Steves spread out the pizza and an assortment of Mooseheads, Anchor Steams, and Narragansetts on the sales counter, and we spent an hour or so eating, drinking, and playing darts, which was something Axel could do pretty well one-handed. Nobody was keeping score but I think he won. All the while, he and the Steves traded notes on bike shop life and found their experiences to be largely similar, except that Vermont was a cycling destination for the tourist crowd in a way that northern Ohio was not. "But I have to point out," Axel said, "that the cycling there is great, with nice rolling countryside especially east and south of Cleveland, and quiet country roads."

"No mountains, though," said scruffy guy Steve.

"No, but plenty of steep hills seven, eight, ten percent or more," said Axel. "They just don't go on more than a mile or two."

"So it's Belgium," said scruffy guy Steve.

"Yeah," said Axel. "Belgium weather, too."

"So where's this town you're going to?" asked redhead woman Steve, stepping up next to me at the counter.

I pulled out Aunt Cordelia's map and said my plan was to get a New Hampshire state map once I crossed the river.

"Huh," she said, pressing against my shoulder to get a closer look. "Past Keene and north of Jaffry, but not all the way to Concord. I never heard of Crombie Hill, but that doesn't mean anything. Wicked lots of little towns over that way."

"How hilly is it?" I asked.

"Hilly, but it's not mountains like up in the Whites," she said. "About like around here, maybe a little flatter."

"And traffic?"

"Not much once you're away from the big highways. But sometimes there's only one road through a narrow valley and that's the highway, no way to avoid it. You just go."

"I have a New England map," said scruffy guy Steve. "Might have your town on it." He fished around under the counter and produced a map, which he unfolded to the portion showing southern New Hampshire. "Nah, no luck. Sometimes they just give a town name to an intersection or something. But your plan should be good, just get a map over there, probably get one in Keene or Jaffrey or wherever you go."

"Is she really going to be safe over there all alone?" Axel asked. "I mean Ellie can hold her own just fine, but you don't want to get into some dumb situation."

"Totally safe," said redhead woman Steve. "But I tell ya what. Monday is my day off anyways and I was going to take a long ride anyways, so I'll keep you company for 30 miles then turn around. Get me my 4-hour ride and probably get you nearly there."

"Wow, you don't have to do that," I said.

"Like I said, I'm riding anyway. One benefit of working Sundays is I get another weekday off, right? Might as well go find a little town I never heard of."

"Thanks," Axel said. "Makes me feel a little less guilty about bailing."

"Okay," said scruffy guy Steve, "I'm gonna cut out now, but I'll be back in the morning a quarter to nine. If you have to leave earlier, just leave the front door unlocked. Steve, you lock up?"

"Sure, Steve."

She showed us the back stairs up to the office/apartment, then trotted back down and turned off all the shop lights. "There's a bathroom and shower in the back corner. If you need to get out, the front door has a knob so you can unlock it without a key. For the back you need a key, so I'm going out that way since I need to lock it anyway. The front is locked already. I'm leaving the alarm turned off tonight, so no worries about that. See you in the morning." With a little wave she disappeared into a dark hall behind the parts counter, then I heard the sound of a metal door closing and the lock being turned.

6-19-88

Woodford/Brattleboro. Ax broke his collarbone this AM. Not riding the bike, no, that would make too much sense—falling off the f-ing lean-to platform. Rode across Rt9 to Brattleboro. He doesn't want to go to hosp. cost a lot they won't do anything.

Found a bike shop so we can pack his bike up in a box to bring on the train. Need to get bus from here down to Springfield. He says I should continue, and I guess I will. I don't have the heart or the nerve to tell him I'm not sure anymore what we're doing is real, I mean that E2 letters may not be real.

Anyway the great folks at the bike shop are letting us stay in the upstairs apartment they never use, so that's a big help esp. with Ax shoulder. He's laying back on the futon now while I'm writing this. Luxury sleeping 2nite! He has just boxers on because why bother to put a shirt on. So I do the same. F-ing bra is getting really annoying. Skip the thing tomorrow, not like I need a lot anyway. He says Hey El and I say What and He says Never mind and shakes his head. No, seriously what? I ask. I was just thinking how nice it is to have a bed for tonight. He says, and I go Oh, is that all you were thinking? I walk over to stand beside him. And he says No, not just that, but I feel bad. I want to talk about . . .and I interrupt him Your shoulder? and he goes No, not that, about— and I cut him off and I

*say Be quiet and stay right where you are, and I kneel over him
and ask Will your shoulder be okay?, and he nods and gives me
a funny little half-smile. So as soon as I get this written out I'm
putting the notebook down . . . now.*

28.

February 15, 1818
To Miss Eliza Crombie, Crombie Hill, New Hampshire

My dear sister Eliza,

We made our camp last night in the State of New York! Papa was set to stop in Bennington, Vermont because it was so cloudy it would get dark early, even though it was not too much past midday, but me and Uz convinced him that we should go into a different State so that we could say we got all the way across Vermont in less than one week. It was almost dark when we stopped but the Mountains are flatting out to hills here and that made it lighter.

When it comes to going into Vermont, well that was not so dangerous as Papa afcared it might be. Except there was a man there collecting some coins to let us cross the bridge. That was dangerous for him because Papa said it was too much Money. Then I saw Uz roll his eyes at the man but Papa did not see that.

While we were tying off Hester and Artemisia to a tree and making the fire, Papa and Uz went on about the Revolution days. Uz said Papa should be proud that his mama's brother and her daddy and his daddy's mama's daddy's daddy all marched off to fight against the redcoats to secure the Founding of our Nation. And Papa said none of them was named Crombie and so he would not take credit for them. And Uz said well he was going to take pride in that even if Papa would not, and then Papa said they weren't fighting for any big fancy idea, they only wanted to be able to sell their own Timber for their own profit and not have to give all the best trees to the King. And Uz said so that's why great Uncle Thomas got his arm knocked off in Boston, just so he could sell a tree and now he didn't have an arm to even pick up a twig? And Papa said that's right.

Papa said his own Daddy came out this direction to New York with part of a plan to take Fort Ticonderoga, but by the time they got there, everything was done, so they walked home. Papa said some men might call it three months of service but his daddy never wanted to call it that. Nothing to shoot at the whole way except a few Indians they thought they saw up on a ridge one time but why waste a musket ball on anything so far away? Ammunition was hard to come by. So his daddy came back to the hill and what should happen but not soon after he got his leg broke cutting timber and it never healed right. When Papa's daddy was older he said everybody would always figure he got injured in the war because of the limping and the cane, and he got tired of telling them about how he really broke his leg so he just would turn the conversation to crops or mud or bears.

And Uz said well that is still three generations in one family who went over to the War and that should count for something. Any how, cutting timber was needed for the War effort so that was honorable. And Papa said of course it's honorable, now let us be honorable and go take down a couple of those dry stands over there to keep this fire going.

I think there might be even more snow here, but we are lucky the road has been used a lot ahead of us so it is packed down hard. Uz says as soon as it gets close to melting, we will unlash the wheels and remove the runners and the wagon will turn back into a wagon from a sled. He said we could even use the wheels now, or could have used them the whole way, since everything was so hard-packed, but if we ran into some new snow we would be happy for the runners. I think also he is proud of his idea for making a wagon into a sled.

It is Sunday but there is no church. Papa said some prayers, more like just saying Grace at supper I would say, and then Papa and Uz spend the day cutting some more wood and feeding the girls and repairing things I think. Papa said we might move along a few more hours in the direction of Albany but we decided to keep the day of rest.

Thank you for reading this to Mama. I hope the weather is fine for you. By the time I write next Sunday, Papa said Lord Willing we will be well the other side of Albany.

Your loving sister,

Emma Too

29.

6-20-88

Brattleboro/into NH/Winchester/Peterborough/park. Almost dark, writing in tent no idea if I'll be able to read much of this but whatever.

Ax up before me. Remember thinking that I hoped that sex last night hadn't made shoulder worse, but it was so gentle. Beautiful really. So that makes twice, here and at Mikko/Pekka place. Haven't told Ax he was my first. Maybe someday.

Not sure how to explain where I am now except to say that I been planning to hold back personal details from this stuff when I write it up because inappropriate to an academic paper [illegible] that happened today, and effect it's having on how my story is going, I saw a crossroads—one path = just go to the end just facts on the ground [illegible] historical [illegible] but unclear [illegible], the other = [illegible] honesty and enough detail but also respect the people involved not disclose too much. Maybe like E2 writing about Uz—what happened to him affected [illegible] the account = primary source. So I think I better get it all down Ax/Kelley not just E. Toomey and Peterborough lib. Guess I'll still turn this in to Hendrickson, but maybe better Eng. dept /cr. writing. Seniors aren't supposed to change their mind. Too late for that anyway.

Not sure what notes to write about this AM. Fresh in my mind for a long time. Even though it's super personal, I think it's critical to get it down. Not that historical [illegible] but first-person impressions [illegible]. Long story short, [illegible]. After Ax on train, rode with K, made a pass at me. Maybe I encouraged a little bit. K flirting a little I think. First I joke she should gain 30 pounds so I could draft her better, she said okay but then she might need to wear a bra. Then a next stop she unzipped jersey to show chest no bra and my bra has got so stinky and itchy chafing so I took it off right there, stuffed in jersey pocket. [illegible] in the first place, but force of habit. She wasn't watching (slid off under jersey pulled out sleeve) but she noticed, saw her looking, guess I was looking too. Hey our eyes are up here. Even comment Penobscot frigid water and nipples sticking up. Then later she said likes women, was getting a vibe from me like I was interested. I'm like no, you know I'm with Axel, and she says sorry, thought you might want company tonight, I go no thanks etc. Apology, no hard feelings. K rode back to Bboro, I went to PB library. So [illegible] pseudonym for Kelly or maybe not needed. Unlikely contact ever. Anyway [illegible] will find a way to tell enough [illegible] sexual preference, not trying to hide. Ashamed? [illegible] 20 years ago. Write and see how it comes out, can always edit. Primary source?

PB library and E Toomey—this part of NH disputed w/ Mass before rev, settlers to establish towns. Pine tree riot before Bos. tea party. Crombie Hill maybe place name informal not actual town. No comp data about cemeteries etc, working on it maybe 15 yrs. be computerized, come back in a few decades ha ha. Young lady should be careful out her alone, yeah I know

Ax I miss U right now.

Axel was up before I was. Maybe his shoulder woke him up. He was dressed, looking out the window at the street below. The early sun itself was out of sight, but its glow was filtering in from the left through the morning mist.

"Hey Ax," I sat beside him.

"Hey," he said.

"Pensive today," I observed.

"Or just not awake yet."

"Wanna get a coffee or something?"

"I'll just grab something at the station I guess," he said. "Listen Ellie, I've been thinking."

"Thinking. Uh-oh."

"Yeah, really." He laughed. "I've been thinking that, um, I'm at a place where I have to take some time and figure out what the hell I'm doing. Figure out what my parents are doing. Figure out school or not school. Figure it all out."

"Yeah, I can see that," I said. "It's kind of a moment of many decisions."

Outside, the sun was rising fast and now lit up the tops of the buildings down the street.

"It is," he said. "And the thing is I think I have to do all that on my own. Like it's not fair to drag anybody else through it with me."

"Yeah, I get that," I said. "Wait—what are you saying?"

"I don't know," he shook his head. "I feel like my brain is so full of crap to figure out that I don't have anything left for you. And it's not fair, to like drag you along with that. Plus, I was never exactly sure if we were dating or whatever anyway."

"Well not dating like in a 1950s movie, but yeah, we're together. Come on, you know that."

"Yeah, you're right. Dating 1988 style." Now he looked right at me instead of out the window. "But do you see what I mean?"

"Well maybe, but I hate it. Why can't we just go on?"

"Because I'm already not all here. And besides, next year you'd get out of college and go off to grad school somewhere and that probably pushes us apart, or I follow you or something and that's weird because we were never that serious anyway—"

"Not serious?" I interrupted. "Not serious? I asked you along on this trip with me, didn't I? That wasn't just to have a strong man along to keep me safe."

"I know and I totally appreciate that. If anything, you're keeping me safe. And as for me, I wouldn't do this with just anybody. I did it because I wanted to go with you. And I—I'll always remember it."

"But after all this, you just walk away?"

"I don't mean it that way. Step back for now, I mean. Until I get myself figured out. It's not a reflection on you at all. It's me."

"Like I'm supposed to believe that," I said. "Would you believe that if I said it to you?"

"I don't know. I mean, I think this is just kind of a natural re-set point. If it's meant to be that we get back together, then we'll get back together."

"We both know you don't believe in 'meant to be,' so let's not pretend."

"I'm not pretending. Look, I'm scared, okay? You have so much ahead of you, what if I crash and take you down with me?"

"I can watch out for myself. It's you I'm worried about."

"That's what's scary. It's not a time for you to attach yourself to me."

"You didn't just think this up this morning, did you?"

"No, like I said, I been thinking about it."

"The whole trip?"

"Since before the trip."

"So why did you even come along? Just to get into my pants? Is that what last night was all about? Maybe my dad was right."

"Damn, Ellie. I was trying to tell you."

"I'm sorry, that wasn't fair. I got into your pants too. I'm a grown-up."

"Because you asked me and I wanted to go. And I mean, it's been really special for me. But maybe it was stupid to go if I could have guessed the experience would have this kind of effect."

"What effect?"

"Being so close to you and sharing this with you, it's like it's felt more and more natural just to be with you, share decisions with you, you lean on me, I lean on you . . . well it's at a place where it could get more serious and then break really painfully, and that makes it the right time for a pause. Or maybe it's already too . . . "

"All this time," I said, "I was . . ." I couldn't think of the words, or maybe I just couldn't get myself to say them out loud.

"Shit, this hurts even more that I was afraid it would," he said.

"Do you need more ibuprofen?" I touched his chest on the injured side.

He smiled and shook his head put his other arm around my back, pulling me close. I looked over his bad shoulder. A few birds were taking turns perching on the wires outside, silhouetted against the brightening light.

"Ellie." That was all he said. I stood there, arms around him, my chin against his sparse whiskers. He was right—it had become very familiar, very comfortable to count on each other, just to be together. And to think that I had set out on this project thinking I would help him get his act together. Ellie, I said to myself in my head, look what you've let happen.

I gave him a little squeeze and stepped back a little. "Axel, it wasn't stupid."

"No?"

I shook my head. "If anything, I was stupid. Or at least I didn't think it through."

"You had the whole project on your mind. I had more time to think about the other stuff."

"Yeah, maybe," I said. "But you always look like you aren't thinking ahead when you actually are."

"Yeah, maybe." He paused. "Sorry."

"That's okay, I can still read you."

"Then you know what I'm saying, right? It makes sense to step away a little bit?"

My throat didn't want to make any words, so I just nodded. Inside I disagreed.

"I hope this is right," he said.

I nodded again. My throat finally loosened up. The problem was that what he was proposing made complete rational sense. It even made emotional sense. "There's no one right or wrong thing, right?" Moments like this, they can affect your whole life. They affect history. Every life affects history.

"If it's a mistake," he said after a minute. "We can always fix it."

"So is this a clean break?" I asked. "Or just on hold for a while?"

He didn't say anything.

"I'm not sure I can handle the limbo thing, not knowing," I said. "Either we're together or not." My own words hit me in the gut.

"Yeah," he paused, his voice breaking a little. "If the idea is that you're free to head off to grad school and I'm trying to get my own self figured out, then it only makes sense to make a clean break. It's hard to be completely rational about this, but that feels right, you know?" He looked down. "And meanwhile the other part of me says 'you idiot, how could you even think of splitting up with her?'"

"We're singing in harmony on that one," I mumbled. "But again, trying to be rational, if we get to the end of this apart time and we feel like we want to reconnect, we would just do it."

"Right. Since I won't be in school, I can't be exactly sure where I'll be if you wanted to get back in touch, but I'll leave that to you. I know how to get hold of you, at least, through your parents."

"Yeah, well what if they get divorced too?"

"Right, except for that." He put his hand on mine. "Give me some time, maybe 6 months, then if you want, get back a hold of me. If you never do, I'll understand. I'll be sad, but I'll understand. This is all on me."

"Are you saying you won't get in touch with me?"

"Well, I don't want to think that you're just waiting around for me to call you or whatever."

"That's a little presumptuous isn't it?"

"Good, I mean I didn't want to think you would just kinda put your life on hold while I got my shit together."

"What, like a ship captain's wife gazing out at the horizon waiting for him to come home? Not a chance. And meanwhile, how am I supposed to know how to get hold of you?"

"If you just sent a letter to the house, I'm sure that would get to me eventually."

"Sure."

"I'm really glad you're not riding alone today."

"Shut up, okay? I'll be fine."

I would like to say that the rest of that morning was a wistfully romantic interlude, both of us at peace with the reality of parting and at the same time grateful for the time together, but it wasn't really like that. I craved human touch and would have been content to just snuggle together for an hour, and I got the sense he felt similarly, but our conversation had kind of ruled that out and besides time was wasting. We didn't talk much, showered separately (too late it dawned on me that I could have offered to help him on account of the bad shoulder, but he managed somehow), went through the motions of getting ready, everything practical.

I'd been worried that the Steves wouldn't actually show up when they said they would, but I was wrong. We helped Axel haul the box down to the bus station—good, because I was worried about how he might do that alone—and when the bus arrived, we loaded it carefully into the cargo bay. Of course, Axel and I had not talked to the Steves this morning about our personal relationship situation, and that was just as well, but I was worried that we might make some kind of awkward impression upon parting. Then the bus driver helped us out with that by telling the passengers to board sooner than we expected, so there was only a minute or so between loading the bike box and Axel climbing up the stairs to take his seat.

That minute allowed for quick spoken goodbyes all around, a tight hug where Axel again forgot about his shoulder but continued anyway, and a good kiss. I'm sure it looked great. Honestly, it felt good too. Emotions were intense. Many people would have got caught up in the moment and said the "L" word, but we were strong.

He slid open the window and called "Be safe. Good luck!" as the bus rolled off. The three of us waved. I was crying a little bit, not for dramatic effect.

My planned treatment for the vacant feeling in my gut was—surprise, surprise—to get on the road. Redhead woman Steve was wearing regular bike gear now: black shorts, short-sleeve jersey with "Green Mountain Velo" printed across the back. The snug clothing showed a classic racer's build: muscular thighs and calves and glutes and everything else wiry and lean. She was straddling a Bianchi road bike in the company's trademark celeste color, a light bluish green that clashed mightily with her forest green color-of-Vermont top. But the red ponytail looked pretty good against the dark green, so all in all, the impression was favorable. She had two baggies containing slices of pizza uneaten from last night stowed in her back jersey pockets, the crusty edges sticking out the top. We mounted and set off and Scruffy guy Steve saw us off with a wave. "See you shortly."

We rolled down to Bridge Street, turned left over the Connecticut River, and were in New Hampshire. My body was feeling the accumulation of long days in the saddle: sluggish legs, achy neck—but no saddle problems, fortunately. She stopped at the far end of the bridge. "We got two choices," said my companion. "Either go left here on Mountain Road and get on 9, which takes us to Keene, but it's a pretty big road with trucks and all that, and a long uphill grind--or we go south a bit then east on 119, then 202 north through Jaffrey. That's a little longer distance but probably a lot less traffic."

"I guess I'd go for the smaller roads," I said, "as long as we can get a map someplace."

"Yeah, either way it's probably a good half-hour before we get to a place to pick up a map. I know there's a couple gas stations in Winchester and 119 takes us right through there, so let's go that way. Nice ride."

"Okay, lead on," I said. The way she said "half" was more like "hahf," the first significant change in accent I'd encountered so far in a week and a half of travel.

The red ponytail still draped between her shoulder blades, though if it was like mine, gravity would soon enough have it curling around her neck and dangling in front. Her upper body was still even as her legs spun, and I could see under the jersey the vertebrae tracking straight from her neck to her waist in a smooth line, back muscles rippling just the tiniest bit as she pedaled. It was one thing that I was carrying considerably more cargo than my companion. It was another that she was one of those narrow people with skinny shoulders and hips and so flexible that her back was just about flat as she rode. This meant that I couldn't get a whole lot of draft off her, and that in the default arrangement where two riders assume they would evenly split the time breaking the wind for the other, I was doing more work. It was nice to have the company, though, and I felt pretty strong and the steady effort had occupied my mind.

She was aware of the mismatch and commented to that point as she came alongside when I eased off to the left after a couple minutes pulling. "Much as I enjoy staring at your butt, I'm glad to take more time in front. Though I know I'm not much to draft."

"Yeah it would really help me out if you could put on 30 pounds and grow five inches," I suggested.

She made a joke, then got on the front and began taking longer pulls, maybe 3 minutes for every minute I would do, and together we moved along briskly.

The road followed the river to the south for a little while, then turned left and uphill, where it began following a smaller river that I soon figured out was called the Ashuelot. "We're gonna take a left up here," she said. "Shortcut." We followed that narrow street up and down a hill and into a residential neighborhood before it emerged in the center of the little town. At the intersection where 119 continued off to the east was a Mobil station, and we stopped there so I could get a map. I paid my $1.95 and walked back out to where she had found a picnic table behind the air pump.

I opened the map and she pointed out where we were now. I got out my xerox of Aunt Cordelia's map so we could compare. "It's not like I trust this hand-sketched map to be accurate to scale or anything," I said, "but I still don't see any Crombie Hill on here."

"Ellie," she said, wiping some sweat off her forehead, "you may be out of luck. I mean who knows how much has changed in the last almost two centuries? Best we can do is ride to where this looks like it might be and see what's around there."

"Yeah," I said, "It may come to that for me, but it's not like you need to go riding all over New England too, though I appreciate the help, uh— okay, what is your actual name?"

"Why not Steve?"

"I don't know, I just had a hunch . . ."

"Who doesn't like a name that comes with a shirt?"

"Or a shirt that comes with a name."

"Kept ya going pretty good there, eh? Me and Steve got those at the thrift store, six of 'em. Keeps everything simple in the shop: just talk to Steve." She laughed. "It's Kelly. Good to meetcha." She reached out and shook my hand. "Sorry I'm so sweaty, sticky day plus I admit I was working pretty hard back there." She unzipped her jersey a bit to fan her chest. "Ahh, that's better," she said, returning her gaze to the map.

"Let's try this," she said, looking back up. "We take 119 over through Fitzwilliam and get 202 north on the other side of town. That'll take us up past Monadnock. Now 202 goes all the way to Concord, and I'm sure your little town or used-to-be town isn't that far, but I wager one of the older roads over in that direction ought to be a pretty fair bet."

"Where do you turn back, then?"

"Ah, good question." She examined the map. "I think if I get 101 in Peterborough and take that back through Keene, then I can pick up Route 9 there and roll from there all the way back to north Brattleboro. The last part is downhill. Maybe 80 miles, 85 for the day. That's do-able. And, look, I see a history center marked here in Peterborough." She looked up. "That's gonna be your best bet. Go in there with your map and letters. I ride with you to that history center, we chow the pizza, then I head back. Unless you want company tonight."

"Appreciate the offer," I said. "You've done way too much already, really above and beyond—putting us up last night and then towing me over here."

"Been my pleasure," she said. "And it would continue to be. Woman alone has to be careful, and besides it gets cold out here at night."

"Don't tempt me," I laughed. "Really, I'll be fine. I may be ready for some alone time, to tell you the truth."

She took off the glasses, then nodded. "Yeah, I hear you. Just being sure." She replaced the glasses. Kelly seemed to be having a hard time feeling comfortable about leaving a woman alone in an unfamiliar place, reasonably enough.

We zig-zagged our way through the town of Fitzwilliam and then about 25 minutes later arrived at 202, a wider road with some more traffic, but still a reasonably comfortable ride. After a right-left jog in Jaffrey, 202 was labeled as Peterborough Street. I took a few pulls, but much of the time Kelly was in front as I kept my eyes mostly on the slices of pizza sticking out of her jersey pockets. As we entered town, 202 made a jog to the right, but a sign indicated that downtown, including the history center, were straight ahead via Grove Street. Within minutes we were dismounting in front of the history center. Closed Mondays.

"Well that's a pissah," said Kelly.

Further examination of the signs out front also revealed that appointments were required to use the library and talk to a researcher. I would reformulate my plans around these factors. But first, Kelly produced the pizza, which had been warmed up a bit by being in the pocket of a heat-producing body and with the sun shining on it. We sat on a low brick wall in front of the history center and began to eat.

"Okay one thing to know," she said, "is in New Hampshire you can always camp in the state forest or a state park as long as you're out of sight of the trail and not too close to a stream. So one thing you could do is go to this little state park here that's a little ways out of town to the east on 101. Even though there's no camping marked there, you can set up a tent, and there'll at least be drinking water and latrines by the parking lot."

"Yeah, no problem there," I said.

"Or maybe you can find a B&B in town."

"Nah, the park is good."

She handed me a card. "Before I forget, here's the phone number for the shop. If you call us up tomorrow and let us know when you're on your way, you should just plan to come back to the shop and stay in the office again. That way we can pack up the bike the day before so it's easy to get up and get to the bus in time."

"That's so nice of you," I said.

"And I guess you would probably be getting back tomorrow evening, but it might be Wednesday depending what else you find out here, so just make that call and let us know. It's not that expensive a call from here, maybe a couple quarters. And since I will have just ridden the same route, I'll know how long it should take you, adding on a bit for the touring gear. Though I won't add that much because you're a beast woman."

"Thanks, I think."

"It was a compliment." Kelly finished off the first of her two slices and smiled. "Mmmm. I don't often make it this far. I'm from Maine, but I went to school in Vermont and just stayed over here. So I drive back and forth sometimes between Brattleboro and Belfast, but hardly ever stop in between. Nice to come out this way, though that 202 is pretty busy. I'm sure there's smaller roads we could ride, but it would take some research to find them."

"I thought I saw a rail trail also, running alongside us back there."

"Yeah, those are gravel mostly so it might be a little iffy on a loaded touring bike. They keep talking about paving them. That would be nice, get off the big highway. Get chased by bears instead."

"Where's Belfast?"

"Up the coast, Penobscot Bay. Shipyards all around."

"Maybe another trip I will get up that way. I've never seen the ocean up in New England."

"Oh, yeah, you gotta see it. We could meet up and I show you around. But you better like rocks and frigid water."

I changed the subject. "Hey, thanks for looking after us," I said. "Even without him having to cut it short and go home, I would have had a hard time getting here without all your help."

"Well, that's some adventure you got going there. I mean my people got to America during the 1800s and that seems like a long time ago. Sounds like yours already been here and gone by then."

"Yeah, one thing I'm curious to know is why they moved."

"Folks just like to move sometimes."

"Could be simple as that."

"Our family mostly came over here in the first place to work in the shipyards. As bike-y as I am, they're boat-y, you know? Both my brothers work with boats. My dad works with boats. Even my mom works with boats. I'm the rebel I guess."

"Are you the only girl?"

"Yup."

We sat silent for a minute.

"Okay," Kelly said, "I think I better make my way back. Gonna fill up my bottles over there," she pointed down the street to the end of the block where a horse-head sculpture spouted water into a round basin. "Always scoping out the water sources, right?"

"And thanks for offering to keep me company tonight, too," I said. "That's very generous." It actually would have been quite sensible to accept the offer, I thought. It wasn't so much that I wanted to be alone but that I wanted to project an independent persona to anyone who was looking, mainly myself.

"Not a completely selfless gesture," she laughed. "But seriously, call the shop if you have any kind of worry about anything. Even in the middle of the night. We could drive over here in an hour and I know just where that park is."

"Appreciate." I walked my bike over behind her and filled my bottles too.

She turned toward me, pulling her jersey zipper up to the collar. "If you're not gonna change your mind, then I'm off."

I smiled and leaned over the bike to give her a quick thank-you hug. "Ride safe," I said.

"See ya in a day or two," she said. "To get to 101," she pointed back in the direction from which we had come. "I noticed a sign for it right when we got on Grove Street a few blocks back, so go back there and turn right and follow 101 to Keene and pick up 9 and that takes you back to Brattleboro, more or less. Should be a lot quicker than just backtracking the way we came, plus you get a wicked screaming downhill all the way to the river on a nice wide road. Good luck!" She pushed off, coasted as she reached down to snug up her toe straps, and pedaled away.

The clock said 1:47.

I had known already that I would need to spend the night here or somewhere nearby, so my revised plan was now to come back at 9:00 the next morning, hoping that I could get a research appointment that same day. At the very least, I could walk around the place and learn something about the area. The state park outside of town seemed like a good plan for spending the night, and a state forest was adjacent, so there ought to be ample good places to camp. But I would need some food. The state map was not very helpful in that regard, so I just rolled one block up to where Grove Street ended in a T, and turned right on Main Street, figuring a street so named might be a good bet to find some groceries. Indeed there was a local market on the right side one block up, but what caught my eye just as I was turning in there was on the other side, across a short bridge: The Peterborough Town Library. I postponed the grocery stop in favor of visiting the library before it might close at some early hour.

We had chosen to forego bringing bike locks on the trip because of their prohibitive weight, and indeed would not have needed one until this moment, but now I had to figure out how to keep the bike safe. There was a rack out front, but it was very exposed, so I opted to roll the bike in behind some shrubbery against the building. Swapping my bike shoes for flip-flops, I retrieved the New Hampshire map and Aunt Cordelia's map and the copies of the letters and went in. I could not help noticing a sign at the entry: "The oldest tax-supported public library in the world, founded 1833."

The air conditioning was a welcome relief from the sticky humidity. I poked around on my own a little bit, then made a visit to the reference desk, where I noticed there a sign for the Monadnock History Center. A thin gentleman with salt-and-pepper hair met me at the counter. "Afternoon. What can I do for you?" His name tag said E. Toomey.

"This is going to sound far-fetched," I said, "but I'm at the end of a bicycle ride from Ohio, retracing the path of an ancestor who migrated from somewhere around here to Madison, Ohio, in 1818. I went by the history center over there, but they're not open today, and besides it says you need an appointment. I was going on the state road map that showed the history center, but of course it doesn't have those other details."

"Sounds about right," he said.

"Anyway, I'm prepared to go back there tomorrow, but in the mean time I thought I might get a head start on my research in here."

"Closed tomorrow too."

"What?"

"Are you traveling alone?"

"Only since today. Then I have friends I'm going back to stay with in Brattleboro."

"All right. Don't like to see a young lady taking too many chances out there."

"Appreciate it, thanks. I'm being careful."

"I'm glad to hear that," he eyed me and my bike shorts and jersey and flip-flops with raised eyebrows, then turned his attention to the materials I brought. "What have we got here?"

I handed them over. "New Hampshire road map. A hand-drawn map made by my great aunt, who we believe may have planned a project similar to mine—without the bikes—maybe 30, 40 years ago. And xeroxes I made of my ancestor's letters written over the course of her journey."

"Ah. May I read?"

"Please do."

He leafed through the letters. "Take me about 15 minutes. Have a seat over there if you would, and I'll come get you when I've finished."

"All right, thanks," I said. I headed to the couch he had pointed out and sat down. A recent issue of *Rolling Stone* was on the table, with Martin Luther King Jr. on the cover. I picked it up and opened it to a random place and read about the latest Talking Heads record, which the reviewer thought was better than the last one, but still showed a band that seemed tired of what it was doing. That confirmed my impression from the couple of tracks I'd heard. They should have stopped after *Remain in Light*.

"Miss?"

"Yes," I stood up.

"Come on over to the desk and I'll see what blanks I may be able to fill in for you."

"Wow, thank you!"

"The reason the history center is closed today and tomorrow is that I am here instead of there," he chuckled. "What's there is mostly primary source materials, which are terrific of course, but I think perhaps not so relevant to your inquiry."

"Wait a moment, could I take some notes?"

He gave a little unsmiling nod and handed me a pad and pencil. "I could go on and on. What are the main things you would like to know?"

"Well, first of all, where is the town of Crombie Hill? And two, can I find out anything about these specific people, or at least about what life would have been like for them? I also wonder why she's writing the letters to Eliza but not directly to her mother, but that's probably impossible to figure out."

"Last question first," he said. "The history of this part of New Hampshire is interesting. The first settlers in the area, as anyone would guess, were close to the coast. Towns like Essex and Portsmouth. This is in the early 1600s. They were Puritans, for the most part. Which is to say they thought that even after the Reformation, the Church of England was still far too much like the Church of Rome. England in the late 1500s and early 1600s was inhospitable to such views, and that's what drove these people here—so named for the purity of their views." He added air quotes around "purity." Funny, I thought, how some of my own people had first come to this continent driven by religious fervor, and how they were all proud secular humanists now.

"So that was part of the early colonial population. Also represented were much wealthier folks who were here to set up business interests. That could be anything from the fur trade to shipbuilding to moving sugar up from the Caribbean. Everybody is a British subject, remember, at least after they kicked the Dutch out of New York. And north and west of here is all France.

"Now this is a curious situation because even though these lands are claimed by Holland and England and France, there are already people living here. But there's what you might call a difference in world view. All the Indian tribes are very different from each other, but one thing they have in common is this general idea that nobody owns the land. They feel that they are part of the land, but that it's not their right to divide it up and say this is mine, this is yours. Not so with the Europeans. So they get here and they say, Do you own this land, and the tribes say No, nobody owns this land, and then the Europeans say, Okay, if it's up for grabs, then we'll take it. It helps this logic that many of these Europeans believe that God says Christians have dominion over all the earth. The Indians aren't Christians so they don't have dominion. That's a great oversimplification, of course, but you get the idea.

"Naturally, this leads to a lot of conflict with the Indians, who do feel a deep connection to and a right to live on the land, just not the legalistic European conception of property ownership. But the Indians lose most of those conflicts because they're decimated by European diseases and overwhelmed by European weapons, and so on. Again, oversimplified. But they are steadily either killed or forced out to the west. There were bounties offered for Indian scalps and many bounties were collected. All pretty gruesome. So if you had an idyllic picture of life out here for those pious and hard-working settlers and their young families carving out a life in the wilderness, part of that rosy tinge was blood stains. Try as you might, those don't wash out so easily. Not to be harsh, but that's human history for you, isn't it? Show me a nation and I'll show you how it was both fertilized and tainted by the blood of who was there before.

"So as to this part of New Hampshire, in the middle 1700s, the colony of Massachusetts is looking to get itself kind of a buffer to the north and west and they send out this call to people to create new towns across what is now southern New Hampshire, with the idea that establishing these towns will effectively move the Mass border to the north. You can still see this behavior today. In order for one of these towns to earn its official charter, it had to attract a certain number of permanent settlers. This was not a large number, but they still had an awful lot of trouble. No sane rich person would move out here, so it was mostly folks of Puritan stock coming inland from the coast. The French and Indian War in 1754 earned some of the planned towns a kind of reprieve, but after that was over it turned out that some of these intended towns never did make it to real town status.

"Life out here would have been very difficult. There's almost no land that you could farm without first clearing tons of rocks. The winters are harsh. There are very few roads. One pattern would be to send a small advance party to build a couple of cabins and set up a water mill that could be used to power saws. When I read the description in your letter, the account of the father aiming to set up a mill rang true as something a person who had been around here would set out to do.

"There's a lesser-known event more than a year before the Boston Tea Party called the Pine Tree Riot. People who had come out here and lived the hard life setting themselves up in the timber trade found themselves, as British subjects, having to send all the tallest and best trees to the crown for very low prices, and so at one point they said enough is enough, we're selling our own timber to whom we want for the prices we want, and to hell with the King. Most people don't know that a wooden ship would typically last only 10 or 15 years before it burned up or was lost in a storm or hit a reef. The ones that lasted long enough to begin rotting out would just be run aground in the mud somewhere upstream and left to decay. So there was a constant need for new lumber, especially perfectly straight white pines for the making of masts. The Pine Tree Riot didn't go over awfully well with the British, and their reaction I think helped prime residents of this area to get behind the Revolution when things got going a couple years later. As usual for New Hampshire, it might be an overriding sense of national duty that is motivating them, but more likely they just want to be left alone to try to bash out a living amid the rocks and pines and with no interference from some muckity-mucks who are always trying to tell you what to do and how to live.

"So one possibility is that Crombie Hill was one of these towns that was sort of pre-chartered during the mid-1700s, but they never got the official status. But I am bit skeptical of that because I have heard of most of these failed non-towns and I think I would have heard of Crombie Hill if there'd been an official petition to charter the town.

"That leaves, in my mind, the likelier possibility, that your young protagonist here is using the term Crombie Hill to describe a place referred to as such by local folks of the time, but that never acquired an official title. For example, the Turner family's farm is at the top of a well-known local hill on the road from here to there, and everyone around calls that Turner Hill though it never makes any official register as such. She says that she has never written a letter before and so, even though she is trying to use the formal template taught to her in school, if she doesn't know what actual name of her town is, if it is a town at all, this might be what she would do. I also note that this was before the invention of or at least the general use of envelopes, so the equivalent of the modern mailing panel would have been the back of this actual sheet of paper with the sheet folded a few times to form a sort of self-envelope which was then sealed with wax. Some of your copies look like that, some don't. Not sure why that would be. It does appear that the address she wrote was the same every time, so it seems that must have been good enough to get them delivered (either that or she never mailed them and just stashed them away)—or else we would not have them today. That is not too surprising, because she writes at one point that the family planned to pick up letters at Goffstown, and thus the street address would not matter nearly so much as the name of the addressee.

"Her descriptions of the trip and her references to some specific landmarks—there are a couple of places known locally as rattlesnake hill or rattlesnake ledge, though one would be hard-pressed to find a rattlesnake around here these days. I believe there's a so-called Rattlesnake Hill up in Weare, and there's one in North Conway, and there's an island in Winnipesaukee. You don't just name things like that out of nowhere, so there must have been those snakes around. These clues suggest to me that she did indeed come from a place quite close to here." He unfolded the New Hampshire map. "If we look at places that would be about a week from Brattleboro by wagon, say 60 miles or so, and also look at if the journey from the place to Brattleboro would take you close to Monadnock, then you get places like Wilton or Lyndeborough or Greenfield or Francestown, maybe Hancock if you go more northerly. Maybe somewhat further away than those, but let's be conservative.

"Now as to the name, Crombie, this name was known around here as well as on the coast. The state library system and the universities are working on a comprehensive database that would allow a person to trace specific names to specific cemeteries and specific legal records. All of this data exists already in microfilm, but the big project is to transcribe all of the microfilm records into text in computer databases so that one could perform sophisticated global searches according various filtering criteria—name, age, dates, parcel number, and so on. But you're about 10 or 15 years too early for that, I'm afraid. In the meantime, if you had a few weeks to make your way through microfiche records, you might stumble across something.

"But if you're just going to be stumbling around, I would suggest doing so outside rather than huddled over a microfiche machine. Visit some of these towns that fit the pro-file, talk to some folks, take some notes, and see if anything clicks. And if you discover anything, please let me know.

"Finally, the simple explanation for the reason she's writing to the sister is that you need to remember this is a time when some people are not literate—by 1820 all boys and girls in these parts knew how to read and write so they could do their Bible verses like the good little post-Puritans they were, but in previous generations, the women especially may not have been taught. If the mother can't read, then you write to someone who can.

"Now, may I ask you a favor?" he paused. "I wonder if I might make photocopies of your letters."

"Absolutely, yes. My gosh, thank you for all the informa-tion. Do they look authentic to you?"

"Hard to know for sure, of course. The paper looks right. No doubt the writer is awfully eloquent for an 11-year-old turning 12—that does give me a little bit of pause—but it's not unheard of. I wouldn't ask if I could make copies if I weren't awfully confident the letters were at least contempora-neous. For one thing, why would anyone else write anything like this?"

"If you could fill out this card with your name and contact information and brief description of the items—letters writ-ten during 1818 migration from New Hampshire to Madison, Ohio, something like that—it would be most helpful. We have lots of material from people who came here or stayed here, but not much from people who left. That stuff tends to end up at the destination, not surprisingly."

I did so and handed him the filled-out card. "I can't thank you enough."

"Not at all. Safe travels to you. Have you got proper warm clothes or only that bicyclist's costume?"

I had forgotten about the cycling attire. "I change at night." I laughed, quietly because we were in a library.

"Are you staying in town?"

"I have a place just outside of town," I replied. I was a little uneasy about disclosing too much of my plans to this older man I didn't know.

"I see," he gave me a skeptical look. "I can't think of any establishments just outside of town, but you must know what you're about." He handed me back the originals. "Thank you, this will be a nice addition to the archive. Always make your copies on acid-free paper, you know."

I took back the letters and maps. "Thank you again Mr.— Toomey, is it?"

"That's right, Edgar Toomey. Good luck to you."

Outside, I felt a tiny blip of relief to see that the bike was still behind the shrubbery. The heat felt good now as I shook out the chill that had set in after 45 minutes of air-conditioning in damp bike clothes. I took one more look at the map before packing it away. I could go east from the state park, then head north and hit all of the towns he had listed in a single arc, then from Hancock make my way over to Keene and get back to Brattleboro by tomorrow evening. It would be a long day, 65 or 70 miles, but do-able. Give my friends at Green Mountain Velo a call from Keene.

I stopped in the grocery store and picked up cold snacks for the night's dinner and the next day's breakfast and lunch, then headed out to the state park. There's not much to report about that. I found a well packed bridle trail, veered off of it after getting out of sight of the parking lot, and set up the tent behind a large boulder, where I also leaned the bike. I took a photo of the campsite. It was clear people had made campfires here against the boulder. It was getting dusky out, a bright quarter-moon visible now through a gap in the trees. Changing into a t-shirt and the nylon warm-ups, I grabbed the flashlight, and walked to the parking lot to get some water and use the bathroom. I rinsed out my bike shorts and otehr clothes. One item in particular still stank, but mixed with latrine soap scent now. Back behind my boulder, I draped the damp things over the handlebars, as we had done every night, and climbed into the tent and took off the warm-up pants to get in the sleeping bag. A lot had happened today. I wrote down notes before it go too dark.

When I have thought about this night later, it strikes me that it was needlessly risky, a young woman being out there all alone in a remote place, especially since I had plenty of cash to get a hotel room for the night. And even this boulder was close enough to the road that it was the kind of place a carload of teenagers might visit from time to time to do things they wanted to do out of sight. I knew at the time that it might be dangerous for a woman, alone or not. But I also resented feeling that way, so I resolved to do it. And I'm not sure staying in a small-town motel all alone would have been any safer anyway. I've seen *Psycho*. I reminded myself that I hadn't let anyone know my plans, and no car had passed me between the grocery store and the park entrance. It was like Axel had reasoned back in Wales Center: nobody knew anything about me. Except Mr. Toomey. He knew a lot. I had even given him contact information for back home. But he did not know where I was tonight. Nobody knew that.

Well, Kelly—she could guess because she had suggested camping here and had even offered to come with me, whatever her motivations might have been. Anyway, she should be back in Brattleboro by this time.

Not even Axel knew where I was. He would be somewhere in upstate New York at this hour, train rolling toward Buffalo, trying to sleep if the pain would let him. Maybe thinking about me.

That left only me and the ghosts of the ancestors who had been here and left so long ago. It was a comfortable night, not cold, a little breezy. I lay on the sleeping bag listening to my own breathing.

The woods made their usual nighttime noises: owls, wind in leaves, the snappings and rustlings of various unseen critters moving around—plus the occasional vehicle going by in the distance. Once there was a rumble that conjured the green car back in Wales Center, but it faded off. At one point I picked up a sound like a bike's freewheel ratcheting, but listening further, I heard it no more. Your ears can get overly sharp in the woods in the dark and the sounds you've been hearing all day for weeks might creep into your head. A creaky branch could sound like that.

Somewhere near here, Emma Crombie stayed the night, too, just beginning a journey to a destination that must have seemed almost mythical. Ohio. What was Ohio? A place where the land is gentle and the trees are hardwood and they go on forever and the water is fresh and it goes on forever. Nobody lives there yet. Almost nobody. Why not? Why don't lots of Indians live there? Maybe they do. Maybe "nobody" means "nobody like us." But if nobody like us lives there yet, how do you know it will be a place where people like us even can live? It was like those Puritans setting off from England for a harsh and unknown wilderness to try to make a life according to their own rules, sleeping like sardines in a tin to try to somehow survive the winters. If people have a natural gift for anything, it's self-delusion. I heard a clicking sound again. Some kind of cricket?

After lying there for a long time, I decided I'd better stick my head out the tent and make sure my bike wasn't being wheeled away by a raccoon or something. My eyes were adjusted to the dark so I didn't turn the flashlight on. I slowly unzipped the fly. In the light of the quarter-moon I could see the International leaned up against the rock, the chrome pieces glinting blue-white. The clothes still hung from the bars.

The "what-ifs" started running through my mind. What if somebody or something was out there? Some local kids? A moose? A mutant bear thing like in that movie *Prophecy*? Maybe that Mr. Toomey had followed me. No, I would have noticed. Your ears are hyper-attuned to car sounds when you're riding a bike. Besides, that wouldn't explain the clicking sound. Kelly and her bike's freewheel would explain the clicking sound.

What if Kelly decided not to go back to Brattleboro and instead was here? That seemed possible. If she were here, what would I do? I would invite her in the tent, of course. I couldn't let her stay outside. Would she take that to mean something? Did it mean something?

What if Axel were here? That would explain a bicycle-ish sound also. But he was injured, and also I had watched him get on the train, his bike half-taken apart and crammed into a cardboard box. But if he were here, then what? Make love? Lie here hip to hip and look at shadows on the tent wall? Fall asleep thinking about the road tomorrow? This trip had not been very long, but already it seemed wrong to be sleeping alone. Did I chase him away? Or is he right, is this about him, and our separate circumstances, and was it not ever really about what I should have done or not done or said or not said? Why am I lying here thinking like this? I'm not sure what this story is about.

Oh, Emma Too, what should I do?

What did you hear in the night? You didn't know what was coming as you lay here awaiting sleep, that you would lose your brother, that you would be the one who would get your distraught father moving again so you could continue your journey, if for no other reason than that—to continue. Because continuing was the only option that led anywhere. Maybe that's how this loops back to history, to this country. People set out for something, maybe not even knowing what it is, and once on the road, they just keep going. Until they don't or can't keep going, and they settle for a bit. Maybe for a long time. And then they think about their story and come up with reasons and meanings after the fact so that it all makes some kind of sense. This is America. The American story. Me lying here, maybe that's the American story, too. Looking for something and not finding it. Something in the past. Something in the future. This vast landscape can handle as many metaphors as we want to pile onto it; it just absorbs them into itself like melting snow or spent coffee grounds or pee or even whole bodies. Yet the looking for that elusive something is what drives everything, even blinding you to what's right beside you. Is there anything particularly American about that restless drive? Seems instead like a more general human motivation, although one that people back in the "old country" might not have had the opportunity to pursue. Maybe what's particularly American is assuming we're so special.

But you wouldn't have been thinking about that, Emma Too, not yet. You were just a girl. Would you have wondered, staring into the dark and the moonlight, what your life would turn out to be? Of course. Everyone wonders that. Did you assume at age 11 that you would someday have children? Probably. Could you even suspect that a distant descendant of a child that you would bear in that life ahead of you would be sleeping here now, and that the end point of that story in the future would be the same rocky ground (or at least ground something like this, somewhere around here) as starting point of your story that was just beginning? Would it occur to you that anyone would ever try to retrace your steps? Or would that seem outlandish, pointless? Did you think about any of that? Or were you just lying there in the dark listening for something . . . a distant rock fall, a nearby twig snap, a closer hint of the breath of life.

30.

February 8, 1818

To Miss Eliza Crombie, Crombie Hill, New Hampshire

My dearest sister Eliza,

We rest today, and I shall use the opportunity to write this letter. It has been very cold so far and this means the runners that Uz and Papa made for the wagon have let the wagon slide easy and Papa says we have made very good progress. We are already past Keene and almost to the river. Along the way we stopped where we could see Monadnock. Do you remember that time in the summer when we all went near there to visit the other cousins and we fixed a plan to climb up to the top but then we did not after all on account of the bear? Papa says for the Indians it was a special place, but they are all gone now.

Hester and Artemesia do not walk very fast but they seem content pulling us along and sometimes all three of us can ride and sometimes Papa or Uz will walk, and sometimes they let me drive the team. When we go up a hill all three of us walk with them to lessen the load and the steam comes off their haunches. It has not snowed very much but there is plenty of old snow laid down and that makes a good surface. I wonder in Ohio if the snow will be less. Papa says when Uncle Nathan came back to get Aunt Eleanor, he said that there are hills but not mountains there, and forest that goes on forever, and a lake that goes on forever, and be careful of wolves and snakes. He did not speak of snow.

I have made up my mind that I will write a letter to you every Sunday. Please read it to Mama. We are traveling every day but Papa says we will rest on Sundays and so that is when I will write a letter, because I tell you I did try to write a letter while I was riding and you would not be able to tell it was writing. When I write down these words for you, I feel as if we are all together. Because we share the words on the paper, because we touch the same paper and see the same writing. That's what it seems like to me.

Papa says the river should be just over the next hill and we will cross it on the new bridge that was built after the first one washed away. He came out to Brattleboro before and the bridge did not look very substantial but he saw some heavy wagons full of timbers going across so he thinks it will be sufficient to carry us into Vermont with three persons, two mules, and one wagon full of food and tools to build us a saw mill and a cabin. And if we do fall into the Connecticut, well it ain't too deep, according to Uz, and we all learned to swim in Quartz Pond anyway, except for Papa. I do like how even though I'm a girl and not even twelve-year old, Uz thinks I can handle myself in a situation. Papa just snorts like he does. Did he do that sound when he was a little boy, do you imagine?

I never wrote a letter before, but I am trying to do like Miss Chapman taught us. Everybody I would ever say anything to just lives close by us, or we see them sometime anyway, so tell me if I am doing it wrong. Papa says he does not know when we might be able to post my letters, so even though I aim to write one every Sunday, we might have to keep them safe until we can find a Postman. Sometimes the hotels or the jail might have one, but I don't want to go to the jail. Also, I have never seen a hotel.

We travel by Daylight. Uz wakes up and crawls outside and we usually do not make a big fire in the morning but just enough to boil water for tea and porridge. Then we travel all day scarcely stopping until sunset time, when we make camp and light a big fire and then get inside the wagon to sleep before it gets too cold. But it is cold anyhow. It is a natural thing to wish for the warmer times, except that Papa says we prefer snow to mud for our traveling, so we will be happy with our shivers.

So in order to take our mind off that cold, we talk all day, and Papa and Uz have a long talk that will not ever end about everything everybody did back in the war days. I was not born then, Uz neither, and Papa was just a baby right near then end of it and so he probably did not fight much, but even so it seems like they have plenty of opinions. I will tell you some of that later because now the sun is starting to get low and I will to go help gather some dry firewood.

Your loving sister,

Emma Too

31.

6-29-88

*Peterborough/Wilton/Lyndeborough/Keene/Brattleboro/
home. Writing this at the kitchen table. Kinda full circle—
think I wrote my first note for this project right here too. With
Mom sitting across from me, just like now. Having a coffee,
just like now. Is anything different? No, yeah.*

*Didn't write notes on last night in Brattleboro. Intended
to on bus to Springfield, but stared out the window. Intended to on the long train ride. Didn't. Intended to right after
getting home, or next day, or next. Didn't, didn't, didn't. I
don't need notes about any of that, not like I won't remember.
Slides got back, that finally got the journal out/pencil in my
hand. All way dark under-exposed as expected, but I could
still tell what they were—Ax and Grandma and me, us at PA
state park, us at Wales bridge, one Ax took of me in tent with
my shirt off so dark you couldn't see much, one I took of him
at picnic table, K in green jersey (Pboro not campsite), photo*

of stinky clammy bra I left hanging on a twig by big boulder morning after last night camping because I couldn't bear to wear again (maybe if anybody ever finds it they'll make up a story of how it got there), a white house on a hill, white house on hill, w house on h, whoh, whoh, whoh, etc. But key points? A/K, excitement/shame, white house on hill, anticipation, sadness, frustration, perseverance, resignation. Landscape as setting for history but in books and personal. History inseparable from landscape/from personality/human shit. No offense to hist. but for me maybe a new direction. Future looking forward not back. Bye bye hist. hello lit. Go with that. This is so legible, must be something wrong with me.

Long before the sun came up, I briefly opened my eyes, not sure if I had really slept. The whole night had been a hallucinatory repeating movie: riding along the curves and undulations, I focused on each rise ahead, propelling myself over to only to see another curve, another hill crest. Sweat dripped, lungs drew air, muscles powered motion. I was me yet not me. My heart raced not just from exertion but from anticipation at what might be just around the corner, if I only kept going. I followed churning hips, took my turns to lead, mesmerized always by the beckoning road ahead until, after a final surging effort, coasting freely down. When I caught my breath, I pulled aside to see that I was alone.

When I woke again, this time from a blank silent sleep, it was light. So much for the early start. I unzipped the tent and retrieved my bike clothes. I pulled on the dew-damp lycra things. A half-hour of riding would dry those out. In ten minutes, the tent and bag were packed, a muffin eaten, the sky brightening above the hill.

I set out knowing full well that I had very likely already found out as much as I was going to on this trip, that yesterday's time with Edgar Toomey had painted such a rich picture for me of the time and place from which Emma had come, I was unlikely to get anything better. But there was one little thing in the back of my mind: maybe I would come across a little white house on the edge of a hill against some woods. Maybe I would find the house in the painting from Aunt Cordelia's house. It was a preposterous long-shot, I knew. And it wasn't helped by the fact that I was going by my memory of the painting, having not brought a picture of it with me. And who knew if it depicted an actual place anyway. But still . . . I kept pedaling.

The ride was uneventful through Wilton, but once I found my way out of that town and up a narrow, part-dirt road toward Lyndeborough, things started to feel right. About 20 minutes up that road, I spotted a small white house on a hill ahead. I got a little closer and decided it might be the one—of course with an additional 170 years on it. I positioned myself as closely as I could to replicate the perspective of the painting as I remembered it, and took a photo. Then I wrote down the address from the mailbox (no family name, unfortunately, though the likelihood of the owner still being a Crombie would be nil), replaced the camera at the top of the pannier where I could get at it easily, and resumed riding.

Ten minutes later, I came across another small white house at the crest of a hill against a wood. This one was slightly taller proportionately, and not so close to the trees. But still a possibility. I positioned myself to replicate the perspective. These roads were gorgeous: narrow, stone-lined every one of them, following creek beds, then climbing and descending ridges to find other creek beds, with small farms here and there, large gracious houses painted white with black shutters from time to time and, every once in a while, a more recent and less permanent-looking home incongruously stuck into a little rectangle of grass cleared out of the woods.

I wished Axel were along for this part. After all those hundreds of miles of dealing with cars and trucks whizzing by at 60 miles an hour, this was the payoff. He would love this. Maybe, if he hadn't hurt himself, and that break hadn't presented such a clear point of departure, maybe we could have ridden along here and talked things out better. Maybe we'd still be "together," whatever that means. I had to stop for a minute to wipe my eyes, then set off again. I should quit feeling sorry for myself. Come on, Ellie, get it together.

On the other hand, maybe he was right. The reasoning played through my head again, as it had all day yesterday and last night. I would almost certainly be going off to grad school next year, and he was not on that kind of path. That could set up an uncomfortable sort of unequal status relationship, where my priorities were more important. How many relationships survived that kind of transition? It's my natural thing to set my course and just put my head down and barrel along, to assume that everyone supports me in that admirable focus and determination, but perhaps pausing to look around and evaluate things more intentionally is a good idea. It's not like you couldn't put your head back down and get up to speed again. Maybe it was smarter, wiser, to separate now, get our bearings independently, and then see if we would find each other again. How am I supposed to know the right thing to do at 20 years old? How is he? I mean I know as much as I have ever known, but I feel so completely unsure. Ahead, through a blur, I spotted a small white house on a hillside, woods behind.

I imagined Emma and her family living here, perhaps spending their days with other family members in that red house I had passed a minute ago: working the farms, the children attending school when it wasn't planting or harvest time, meeting for big family meals on Sunday afternoons. That vision was probably unrealistically idyllic: also shouting at each other, one brother resenting how the other brother had unilaterally decided to spend too much money on a certain crop, the sisters measuring themselves unfavorably against each other, bully kids beating up on vulnerable kids, or worse, adults abusing their own power over the children. Things finally getting to such a boiling point that some of them would just take off for the west and leave it all behind. Or try to. It could follow them. I positioned myself to replicate the perspective.

By the time I left Hancock, I had used up the roll of film: well over 20 small white houses on hillsides against woods. When I rewound the roll and removed it, I realized with annoyance that all this time I had been shooting Kodachrome color slide film, ASA 25, but I had the camera's light meter set for much faster film, Tri-X black-and-white print film, 400 ASA. This would mean that every photo I had shot would be severely underexposed. That would explain why the back of my mind had been telling me that some of those evening campsite photos should have required slower shutter speeds and/or wider apertures than the meter had been telling me. I chided myself for not noticing, reset the meter for 25, and figured I would add a special note when I had the film processed to ask them to push it as much as they could get away with since the whole roll would be uniformly underexposed by about three stops. That might be a futile request because Kodachrome film specifically has to go to the special Kodak lab anyway, but worth a try. Worst case, the slides would be very dark but I could still see enough to match to the painting.

All the picture stops had also slowed my progress, so I packed up the camera and began to focus on making good time to Keene, which was only about 20 miles from Brattleboro. If I could make Keene by 4:00 or 5:00, that should put me in good shape to get to Brattleboro before too late.

That's really the end of this story: anticlimactic, I know. But yet, I would submit, this story-without-an-end (which I guess in this case means without a beginning) is in many ways quintessentially American. From the most extreme case of slaves whose previous family histories were deliberately erased and disconnected by their enslavers, to Holocaust survivors whose families perished in concentration camps, taking with them knowledge of with their own history, to the seemingly innocuous case of the college student who was adopted and will likely never know the history of his "blood" family, many Americans know only that they are here now. They have only one direction to look: ahead.

For a young woman with colonial ancestry, the fruitless search for a specific place may indicate that the place never existed, or simply that it is gone, taken back by a forest that is profoundly unconcerned with human pedigrees. Or it may be a real place, but she just couldn't find it. Ran out of time. Ran out of reasons. Does it matter?

In old English villages or remote French hamlets, the residents may trace their connection to the particular rocks and mud and hills and rivers where they live hundreds of years into the past, a thousand even. Back to long before the current nations of which they are citizens even existed. In America, only the Indians, the Native Americans, might have that kind of connection—except that in nearly every case, the European settlers and the nation they founded have systematically pushed the natives off their ancestral lands. It is as if the Europeans, being aware of and in some way disturbed by their own lack of permanent connection to the land of this continent, have sought to make sure no one else has it either. Land is just empty space to build suburbs on, a blank slate for the expressions of the human ego. An economic and psychological resource that's there to be expended. It has no further meaning.

And yet, if this journey reveals anything about this nation's relationship to the earth and rocks and water and trees that have been the stage set for our famous (and not entirely accurately named) democratic experiment, it is that Americans do feel strong connection to the land. Why else create a beautiful state park overlooking a Great Lake? Why else name obscure little towns after famed cities back in the Old Country—Barcelona, Warsaw, Geneva? Why shoot Hatfields if you're a McCoy? Why honor the Native American names of places after the Native Americans have been forced to leave those places—Cuyahoga, Geauga, Erie, Seneca, Monadnock? Why build a sauna in the woods next to a go-kart track on what used to be an interminable stage coach path across New York? Why root for the Indians or the Yankees? The particular route taken between New Hampshire and Ohio is marked by countless little places that carry meaning, both for those who live there and for those who pass through. The river crossing where a young man named Uz died in an icy flood. Another river crossing where two young bicyclists—college students coming from a world of learning and privilege encountered a small tribe from another world of different assumptions and expectations. A place someone once called Crombie Hill, if only to have a name and an image with which to try to conjure where they had come from not only geographically but in every other way. American places, all of them.

I called the shop from Keene. Kelly answered and estimated they'd see me in a little over an hour because it was downhill most of the way and that's how long it had taken her. We had more pizza that evening and Kelly flirted a little and offered to stay the night, and other Steve laughed, and I politely refused. I half expected her to show up in the night, but no. They got me to the bus in the morning. I bought a train ticket in Springfield and still had some dollars left, after which I remembered the envelope my dad had handed me and opened it to find a credit card, including a note describing how to use it to make phone calls. I used it to call them and ask for a train pick-up at 3:30 in the morning in downtown Cleveland. No, just me, Axel was on another schedule. When the train went through Rochester that night, I wistfully thought how my roll of Kodachrome would probably be there getting processed in a week or so. When I did get the slides back, they were all very dark; the lab had included a note apologizing that Kodachrome could not be "push processed" but thank you for trusting Eastman Kodak. I set aside the three slides that included Axel and me, then compared all the white house slides to the white house painting. They all fit but none of them matched.

# # #

My deepest thanks to the following for their invaluable support in carrying out this honors project: My parents Steven and Gretchen Webster, my grandmother Jesse Webster, everyone we met who helped along the way, and especially Alexander King.

32.

Wed, Apr 18, 2018, 8:42 p.m.
To: ewebster@hdt.edu
From: Axel_1357@gmail.com
Sent from my iPhone
Dear Ellie, I hope this is you. I fished around a little on face-book and I figured out you are teaching at Hadentown, and it wasn't too hard to guess their staff email format. Seems like you are still Webster. You won't believe this but I just read your account about Emma Crombie. For the first time. Before yesterday, I did not know it existed. I could explain why but I would rather do that in person. Let's just say I keep telling myself, "do not yell at your mother, do not yell at your mother, do not yell at your mother." If I have reached the right person, please get back to me. If not, apologies for the errant shot.

Cheers,
Axel King

Thu, Apr 19, 2018, 9:07 a.m.
To: Axel_1357@gmail.com
From: ewebster@hdt.edu
Wow, that's a ghost from the past! Yes, you've reached the right person. Where are you? I would be glad to get together for a coffee. Campus is about a half-hour outside Nashville, but I live in town and could meet you in the city. Or a phone call or facetime if you prefer.

Yours,
Ellie

Thu, Apr 19, 2018, 9:15 a.m.
To: ewebster@hdt.edu
From: Axel_1357@gmail.com
Sent from my iPhone
I am based in Boulder these days but I travel for work and I could easily arrange Nashville first week of May and visit some clients. I will rent a car and you can tell me some place to meet. Let me know when/where and I'll be there.

Ax

Thu, Apr 19, 2018, 10:03 a.m.
To: Axel_1357@gmail.com
From: ewebster@hdt.edu
Dear Axel,
Okay, deal. Let's do Bent Note Bistro, in Five Points Nash-ville. I don't teach on Wednesdays, so how about 10:00 for a late breakfast, Wednesday, May 2?

Yours,
Ellie

Thu, Apr 19, 2018, 10:17 a.m.
To: ewebster@hdt.edu
From: Axel_1357@gmail.com
Sent from my iPhone

Thumbs up emoji. See you there.

Ax

33.

Axel rented a Hyundai Elantra at the airport. No need for anything too big, but the bike case had to fit in the back, and the way the seats fold down in the Elantra works great and you can't even see the bike from outside the car. The newer models have the GPS and map stuff built right into the little TV screen, so it was quick and easy to find the place, in a neighborhood up on top of a hill across the river from downtown Nashville. It seemed to him like a pretty laid-back neighborhood—older buildings maybe from the 1850s up to the 1920s, most everything one or two stories, lot of trees around. The parking spaces right in front of the place were filled up so he parked around the corner and walked back. It was a warm, breezy day, clouds and sun.

He was already half up the steps before he remembered that almost 30 years had passed and not only did he not look the same—mostly that was all the gone hair—but he didn't really know how different Ellie looked. Her Facebook pictures were of places and other people, not of her, and the profile pic was a cat. There was one of her in a group, but she was wearing a hat and sunglasses. Still, it was enough for him to be fairly confident it was her. It seemed that she might be married, too, or at least with somebody, but that was hard to tell. And he hadn't felt right snooping around very much, so he hadn't kept looking.

He stood in the doorway and scanned the booths along the windows and the stools at the counter, but no woman was sitting alone seeming to be waiting for someone, and no one else was standing near the entrance, so he stepped back outside and checked the outdoor tables. He was a little early and didn't know what kind of car she drove, or even if she would drive, so he got his phone out and sent a text to the shop he was going to visit this afternoon that he was safely in town and was planning to keep the arranged 2:00 appointment.

He looked up and saw a tallish woman walking toward him from about a block away. Could be. He got ready to step down off the landing, but then she turned and walked up the steps to a house. "Axel?" came a voice from behind him. He turned.

"Hey Ellie," he smiled. "Snuck up on me!" Her smile wrinkles had deepened and the hair was shorter and even more unruly, though it looked suspiciously free of any hint of gray. "Wow, so good to see you!"

"Likewise," she leaned in and gave him a quick, light hug, then motioned to one of the outdoor tables, positioned in the far corner. "My regular spot."

The two sat with their backs to the railing that was around the seating area. They were facing the building, the round table between them.

"Coffee for Ellie. And you, sir?" The waiter brushed a cottonwood fluff off his tattooed forearm.

"Please," Axel nodded. "Something dark?"

"You got it." The waiter went back to the steps and into the building.

"So," she said, and paused. "You're looking great."

Axel took off his hat and buffed his smooth scalp. "Nice and shiny," he said.

"I mean you're in great shape. Your skin looks good. All that."

"A bit weather-worn, but yeah. I'm feeling good." He gave her a theatrical up-and-down. "You yourself seem to have kept the she-beast thing going. What, are you a cross-fit ninja champion?"

"Yeah, that's right."

"And teaching agrees with you, I guess."

She laughed. "Agrees with me? We have a truce, let's say. You? What are you up to?"

"In the bike biz still, believe it or not. National R&D for 1357. Bike company. That's why I get to travel a lot."

"Impressive. Finish school?"

"Nope."

She laughed and shook her head. "Guess you didn't need it."

"Guess not," he shook his head. "Family?"

"Husband and a 21-year-old son. You?"

"Daughters 23 and 20. Their mom passed away 15 years ago."

"I'm so sorry. Wow, we've really got some catching up to do."

"We do. Starting with a big apology from me." The waiter delivered their coffees just as Axel was beginning. He took a fortifying sip. "Look, this is no excuse, because I never should have just disappeared and not tried to contact you, but I had a crazy idea that you didn't want to hear from me. That is, until a couple weeks ago when I went to my parents' old house, where my mom had lived for some months after the split, and then which was owned by my dad but used by him only now and then for decades after that. My dad is moving to Colorado soon to be closer to the grandkids—now that they're both ready to move away probably, timing is everything, right?—and he finally made up his mind to sell the place. He's been living on one floor in the downstairs for the last few years because his knees are too shot to go to the second floor or the basement. It's creepy, but they left my room alone. It still looks pretty much like it did about six weeks after I last saw you, after I cleared most of my stuff out and went to spend the next four years basically living out of my car and racing bikes.

"My, my," she said.

"Anyway," he continued after another sip of coffee. "My mom was staying there at the time because my dad had moved out to live with his soulmate Shari—and that lasted all of five months, in case you were wondering. After I left, she put all the mail I received in a drawer in the side table text to my bed, but she never told me that. I even asked, but since my collar bone healed up in about six weeks and then I was on the road most of the time, I hardly ever visited the house, and when I did, I looked for mail on the kitchen counter, where it would usually have been. I would ask her and she would just say, "if you were here at home, you wouldn't miss anything. You know I can't keep track of it all." And then after six months or so, she moved out and my dad moved back in. During that time, I visited the house maybe twice, and since that year I've been back in there only half a dozen times. I stopped looking for new mail for me, of course. I figured you had taken me up on my offer for you to get on with your own life and not get back in touch with me.

"Then two weeks ago, I flew into Cleveland to start to get the house ready for dad's move, and I am up in the shrine room, and I open the side table, and there's this stack of mail. Letters from the college, credit card offers, USCF bike racing junk mail, and a big envelope from you. I don't cry very often but my eyes welled up before I even opened it because it took me right back to that time, and worse, it made me suddenly aware that you HAD reached out to me, and you had heard nothing back.

"So, I chilled for a half an hour to calm down and then called my mom. Why hadn't she told me about this? 'Oh, didn't you know?' she said. 'I was punishing you.' And I say 'Punishing me? How could it be punishing me if I didn't even know it was there?' And she said, 'You kept going over to see your father and that woman. And besides,' she said, 'how would I know what was in that envelope? And then later I forgot.' And I said 'I only saw them twice, and you knew perfectly well this was from Ellie and that it would make her feel like I was shutting her out if I didn't get it and respond to her,' and she said 'So I guess that was an effective punishment, wasn't it?' And rather than do what I wanted to do which was scream at her 'Well, you ought to be ashamed of yourself, doing that to anybody. Grow up already!' or something like that, and then throw the phone across the street, I just said, 'Okay, Mom. Bye.' And I pushed end call before I said anything worse."

He took a breath.

"So, long story short," he continued, "I'm really sorry. If I hadn't been avoiding my parents so much back then, I probably would have seen it and read it then, and taken it as a message from you that you wanted contact, and then I wouldn't have just shut myself off and buried myself in bike racing and lived in my car for four years. I don't know if we'd have gotten together and stayed together, but at least there wouldn't have been this big stupid blank place between us. Also, there's information in there that I didn't know, sort of reading behind the lines, like that I was your first, you know—"

"Well I was embarrassed. I was 20 years old, a college senior, a grown and worldly woman . . . I wasn't going to say I'd never—"

"Hey it was the same for me."

"What?"

"Nobody before you."

"Did we ever actually talk about anything?"

"I thought we did."

She shook her head. "Well I expect part of why I wrote it was to say stuff I'd never said out loud. Better at typing than talking."

"Yeah. And then the other thing I wanted to say is it's really good. You can see in there the seeds of the novelist. I mean I know I'm in it and that might make me a little biased, but I think it's a really good story. Not that I'm a legit judge or anything. I hope you got honors for it."

"Wow," Ellie said, shaking her head. "Seeds of the novelist? Well, I spent the whole rest of the summer and the fall working on it. I was going to blow them away—it was three times longer than it needed to be and probably not much like any other honors project they'd seen. You know, because I was going to reinvent how history is told. But in the back of my mind I suspected my advisor was not that likely to approve it, so it was really an act of defiance as much as anything. I knew perfectly well it wasn't really a history paper anymore, if it ever had been. Even more to the point, after I'd written it and read it over I came to comprehend how extremely personal a lot of it was—even though through most of it I'd been holding back, trying to keep it academic, but at the end I think I kind of gave in and just got it all in there. You know, tastefully."

"You got a lot in there," he said.

"And it was personal not only about me," she continued, "but also about you and other people. That was the real problem. At the last minute I decided there was no way I was ever going to let that prick Hendriskson read it, and that meant I resigned myself to graduating without honors. Frankly, as a college professor now, I probably would not grant honors for that project, either, unless it was supposed to be a highly personal memoir for English or creative writing—there's not really enough analysis and context to call it history. That was really the revelation for me—I was and still am very interested in history, but that project in effect forced me to realize I had to change lanes, toward creative writing and literature. It was more of a historically inspired writing project than a history project. And I also have to say that graduating with or without honors didn't seem to have any effect on getting into grad school, because I got into a few. In all honesty I wrote it for you. I mean you were the audience I had in mind. It had to pass your muster. So as I was walking down the hall to that grand corner office of the history department, envelope in hand, all that kind of hit me at once and I stopped. I just stood there for a few seconds, then I turned around and walked a few steps back, and then I turned left and went out the side exit, crossed the quad to the post office, and mailed it to you." She turned away for a few seconds and then looked back at him. Her eyes were red. "This is too fucking sad," she said.

"No, it's good," he said. "What would have been too fucking sad would be if I had never read it, never gotten back in touch with you, never sat here today. And also if the internet hadn't been invented by Al Gore and if I hadn't gotten curious and gone looking to solve unsolved mysteries and found out that there is a Crombie family burial ground near Weare, New Hampshire."

"What?" she said.

"I said that after reading in your story about how the Peterborough library was working with the universities to develop a big database of grave sites but it wouldn't be ready for 15 years, I went looking. And goddamn if they didn't do it. So that got me thinking: I want to go finish the trip."

"Whoa, wait a minute, I'm not sure I can handle this," she said. "I mean, first of all, I had long ago written off the idea that Crombie Hill was any real place or even that half of those characters in the letters had ever existed. I'd come to the conclusion that it was an aborted creative writing project of one of my long-lost aunts. Maybe Cordelia herself. And second, you have to admit this is a bizarre situation—old lovers who are now happy and fulfilled in their current lives considering reprising a trip they took together. It seems like asking for trouble. I've written enough to guess where that plot line might go."

"Not putting you on the spot, sorry," he said. "I'm going to visit a shop in Brentwood this afternoon, then heading down to Chattanooga and Atlanta, and I'll fly home from there."

He handed her a business card. "I didn't want to put my cell number in an email, but it's on here. Weird paranoid thing. Paper can't be hacked. Just think about it for a while and then maybe something works out. My girls have never been to New England and I think I could entice them to go. Maybe hike up Mount Washington or something. Or Monadnock at least. We live in Boulder, so we have to be sporty. No choice. Though in fairness, one of them is a hard-core athlete and the other is more of an academic type, though she can carry off the sporty wardrobe if she has to. Anyway, do you have a copy of it?"

"Yeah, I think I still have the one I was intending to mail to you before I changed course and sent you the original. The one I have still might even my original notes stuffed into it. Those might be interesting, by which I mean embarrassing— what I was really thinking, not what I wrote in the paper. I'll see if I can find that." She wrote her cell number on the back of another of his cards, as well as her address. "Right around the corner here," she pointed over her shoulder.

"What's your boy like? What's your husband do?"

"He's a dork. Actually, they're both dorks," she laughed. "The older dork is a civil engineer, the younger one just grad-uated with an industrial design major last spring and he's, let's say, between professional opportunities and—you won't believe this—racing bikes."

"No way! I couldn't brainwash either of my girls into that. Did you keep racing bikes? I never saw you."

"I was afraid, so I stopped racing."

"It's pretty dangerous when you allow yourself to think about the reality of it."

She snorted. "Not that reality, that doesn't faze me. I was afraid I would see you."

34.

Ellie closed the front door behind her and went upstairs to the study. That old manuscript would be filed away somewhere. Why she had kept anything from college days was less a matter of need than inertia—it would take more effort to go through all the old papers and decide which ones to keep than it took to just keep an extra box around. But the question now was, where was that box?

She suspected it was one of the ones tucked into the storage nooks under the hip of the roof, so she slid the upholstered chair out of the way and opened the low wooden door. Of course most of the boxes weren't labeled, but she could get an idea of the vintage from the box itself: official looking file boxes that might even have a description of contents scribbled in the allotted blank space were from early teaching days; recycled liquor boxes were from grad school because the booze store had been around the corner from her apartment and they gave away free boxes; and she had an idea that the box of college papers might actually be an old milk crate with some hanging files and manila folders stuffed into it. Sure enough, back in the left corner, under a stack of posters and flyers that she remembered placing there to act as a kind of lid to keep the dust off, was the orange milk crate. Weighing down the stack of posters was Emma's box of letters and another bag with maps and notes and a few scribbled addresses and phone numbers.

There were only two copies of "Primary Sources: Retracing an American Journey;" the one she'd mailed to Axel, and this one. She could see a couple of errors that she had caught and fixed with Wite-out and repeated overtyping. You weren't supposed to submit a copy, but she had decided the original looked too blotched up with corrections. So she decided to turn in the copy because it looked cleaner (and also, probably, she later observed, as an additional act of defiant self-destruction), but instead had sent the photocopy to Axel. This original version, as she had recalled, had handwritten sheets of notes inserted throughout, pages from her original journal that she had torn out and placed in the narrative roughly where she had been on their journey as she had written them. Then as now, her cursive looked like her hand was too impatient for the words to come out. She lifted a sheet and read.

6-15-88 morning

As I write this, we're sitting around Natalie's table getting a quick bite before Ax and I head off. Her giant boobs are wobbling around like crazy and stretching out the word Geneseo and I'm trying not to laugh and also watching Ax try keep his eyes elsewhere. Yesterday too, bursting out all over the place.

One thing I became concerned about while she was going through the cemetery files was the lack of any record of Uz ever being buried here. Emma's account made it seem like a big deal, described the stone, a lot of people at the funeral, everything—yet no record. This seems like one more gap, one more thing that can't be verified, one more reason to suspect that Hendrickson's [illegible] some "coed" in the 1950s might not be so wrong. Not as late as 1950, probably, but maybe in the mid-1800s. Maybe recreating a real journey [illegible] details wrong because the author was making shit up. Fake record of a real trip?

Last night I crawled into the tent, got half undressed, forgot sleeping bag still hanging on line outside. [illegible] out half-dressed, I decided to wait for Axel to return from his shower so he could get it for me. Meantime, guess I fell asleep. I had some weird dreams about a river and a flood, cold muddy water flowing around a hill with a huge tree in the middle, and standing under the tree were my parents and all my grandparents, Axel and his parents, Natalie, about a dozen other people dressed up like Indians and colonials, and Richard Pryor. They were motioning at me to paddle faster, but I was being pulled away by the current and like often [illegible] I realized at some point that I was naked. But it was hard to cover myself because I was trying to paddle as well, but Ax said don't worry about it and smiled but I didn't know which thing he meant not to worry about.

When I woke up I was in my bag and covered up so I thought that meant he must have gotten me into it, so I asked him and he said Don't you remember? You were a wild woman, and I said What? and he said Joking, joking, but then he said You sure looked damn hot, I was proud of myself for not taking advantage of you and I said You should have, that's what I had in mind if I could have stayed awake and he just nodded.

Well, she thought. That adds another dimension, doesn't it? Since Axel's copy did not have these notes inserted, she decided she'd copy those pages and send them to him as well, especially given the decades-old communication glitch. Full disclosure. Besides, she thought as she deciphered (mostly) a few other notes, these make the story a lot more interesting, and the contrast with what made it into the official document is amusing. But would there be any hope that anyone else could read these scribbles? These days, it occurred to her, she could scan printed text with her OCR software and have all the text back in editable form within an hour. But this handwriting would be hopeless. She would transcribe them and send it to him by email with indications of where to insert each one page-wise.

The pages weren't numbered but she guessed it was around 150, double-spaced. Quite an opus.

She laughed at herself for employing the device of going through Emma's letters in reverse-time order, interspersed with her own account of the ride. So 1980s. But she got into it and stopped only at the terse and down-spirited ending. There was a little bit of embarrassingly personal stuff in there, but nothing too rude, at least in the official manuscript. Reading it reconstituted the feelings she'd had at the time: adventure, excitement, risk, resignation, loss, regret at turns not taken, imagined regret at not having taken the turns that were taken, empty satisfaction at having done a lot but not completed the task, the value of perseverance for its own sake, the value of walking away from pointless compulsions, the value of moving on to the next thing, the value of remembering the previous things, deep ambivalence about wanting or needing some kind of rooted identity. And beyond assessing her own internal state, she felt a persistent, low-level sense of having come near to understanding some things about her country without being able to conclude anything. Ongoing themes. Also her connection with Axel. Her unresolved feelings for this young man who had accompanied her, and what she could perceive in her narrative of his feelings for her. The distance made it clearer.

She could see why Axel had needed to contact her. She felt terrible for him, for the pain he had felt back then, for his recent shock at realizing that she too had felt pain that he might have been able to mitigate had he known she had tried to reach him. It's crazy how a small event or non-event, like whether or not someone receives a package, can be such a critical turning point. If it was a critical juncture at all. Maybe everything still would have evolved as it had. That was the other funny thought: things had turned out very well: she had a great husband and son, a fulfilling job, a lovely life all-around; and Axel, too, seemed to love what he was doing and to be very close to his daughters, despite the loss of their mother. It wasn't like there was anything missing from her life. You end up thinking of your life as a single course that ended up being traced among thousands of possible branches: no value judgment needed about which was the best path, the God-given path, the inevitable path. You end up having followed exactly one of them and no more than one, that's it. Here you are.

One of the possibilities now, one of the many branches that could be followed, would be to go back to New Hampshire and find that burial ground. And maybe go back to Madison, too. She resolved to ask David and Ethan about it, and felt pretty confident they would be on board with the idea, though it was a little weird to go on a trip based on completing a task your wife/mom and her former boyfriend from 30 years ago had failed to conclude. But since it did have a connection to her heritage and Ethan's, and since David always loved a project-based adventure, they would probably like the idea.

What was more of a mystery was why Axel was interested. He had no family connection, no personal heritage motivation. Was it guilt? Maybe he still had feelings for her, or maybe reliving the trip had rekindled feelings. She did not get that kind of vibe from him, though. There was still a connection, to be sure, no denying that. People don't get together in the first place unless there's something there. But everybody has a past, and the reason they call it a past is that it has passed. It seemed more like it just bugged him not to have completed the task, not to have made the finish line. She could empathize with that. That's just basic bike racer stuff.

So, she set aside the manuscript copy, and got out the box of Emma's letters and Aunt Cordelia's map and the New York and New Hampshire road maps from 1988. She brought them

downstairs and placed them on the kitchen table, the box top-
ping the stack. Then she spent another couple of hours tran-
scribing her pencil-scribbled notes from 30 years ago. Where
she was completely stumped, she just inserted [illegible] in the
running text. She found that amusing, too. Maybe a device to
use in a novel or story someday. Any professor of creative writing needs to have, for credibility's sake, a few publications of
fiction, preferably a couple novels and a bunch of short stories,
and she had those: novels *The Woodworker's Manual, Pentimenti,*
and *Margaret and the Red Wing Blackbird,* short stories collected in
a volume called *Collected Stories.* It was fortunate that the credibility could come without any significant sales. As she briefly
reviewed in her mind this published creative output, she came
to understand that the narrative of her quest with Axel to try
to find Crombie Hill was in many ways the origin story for
her writing career. All the themes were there (aimless ambition, perseverance and momentum and inertia, the essential
unknowableness of others inextricable from the vital need for
others, the major questions that prove unresolvable), regret at
things done or left undone, even the tone that could unexpectedly slide from jokey to melancholy and back. These thoughts
formed as she typed the last of the transcribed notes, which
she saved as a Word document and emailed to Axel with a
cover note: "Hey Ax, my version of this had my original handwritten notes interspersed. I could barely read them myself,
but I was able to transcribe most. I think these notes are a big
part of the story, so I'd suggest printing out the attached and
sticking the sheets in where the page numbers are indicated.
I'm okay with others reading it, would prefer reading it that
way actually. The notes explain a lot. " Then she hit "send."
Then she spent a couple of hours grading papers.

35.

Marianne looked up from the table when Axel walked in. "Hey, Dad. Good trip?"

He wheeled the bike case in the door and parked it against the wall. "Yeah, a fruitful one, thanks. You in good shape for commencement?"

"I think so," she shook her head. "Finally."

"You didn't have to get two B.A.s and a Masters."

"Yes I did." She closed her laptop and pushed her straight black hair away from her face. "Anna called."

"She still due in tomorrow from that training camp?"

"Yeah, three-something. Want me to get her?"

"If you could, that would be great," he said. "A little catching up to do. But if you can't, I can swing out there."

"I can pick her up, no problem."

"Thank you. I'm starving."

"You're always starving. You and Anna both."

"Not literally." He opened the cabinet next to the fridge. "Gorp." He poured some in a bowl and grabbed a handful.

"Can you pour me a little too?"

He handed her a bowl. "Hey I want to run something by you."

"Shoot."

"You know how when I was visiting Grandpa a couple weeks ago and I came back with that typed manuscript that my friend Ellie had written back in college about the bike ride we took from Ohio to New Hampshire?"

"The one where you didn't quite make it to New Hampshire?"

"Yeah. Though I did get within a few hundred feet." He chewed another handful. "Well anyway, I saw Ellie on this trip."

"You just happened to see her in Tennessee or Georgia or wherever?"

"No, I saw her on purpose," he said. "I needed to apologize for not getting back to her when she first sent that story."

"Okay, but wasn't that a long time ago?"

"Yeah, very long. But like I said, I didn't know she had sent it until a couple weeks ago."

"Awkward."

"Very. But it went okay. I think she understood what happened, how it happened."

"Nice."

"But anyway," he continued, "I suggested we go finish the trip. Based on some research I did online, I think we could actually find the spot we were trying to find in New Hampshire."

"Well good for you," said Marianne. "You should go."

"I was thinking you two might come along. See a bit of New England. Do some hiking."

"Why not just you and her? It's your project."

"Cause I want to share that part of the country with you. You've never seen it. If it all works out, she'd bring her husband and son."

"She's married?" Marianne pushed her hair back again.

"Yeah, sure. Lots of people are married."

"Okay, Dad." She gave him a skeptical squint.

"Oh, come on. It's not a romantic thing. Or I guess it is, but in the broad sense of wanting a satisfying ending to this story."

"Uh-huh."

"Look, if you read the story then you'll know what I mean. Don't say no until you read it, okay?"

"Okay, that's fair."

"And if the idea seems okay with you after you read it, then could you bring up the idea with Anna when you're on the way back from Denver tomorrow? She'd probably be more receptive if she heard it from you, you know?"

"Yeah, I know."

He went into the next room and returned with the manuscript, placing it on the table next to Marianne's laptop. "Thanks a million. Also I'm printing out some notes she emailed me, transcriptions of her written notes from back then—I'll stick them where they go in the manuscript. There's a couple parts that get a little intimate, but don't mind that. Remember it's a couple 20-year-olds. As soon as I print this, I'm going to unpack the bike and go take a shower."

"This is thick," she said. "I'm going to read all this by tomorrow?"

"It's one side, typed double-spaced. Old school. Won't take that long. A couple hours, maybe three." He handed her the printout of the notes Ellie had sent. "Actually, could you just insert these at the page number printed on the top, since you're reading anyway?"

"That's a lot of paper."

"A 30-year-old floppy disk would have died by now. And if the disk somehow still worked and you had an old computer that could read it, the file would be in some obsolete format you couldn't open."

"So ink on paper is the bold new future?"

"What's old is new again, right?"

36.

David walked into the kitchen and lay the manuscript on the counter. "I kind of wish you hadn't shared that with me, honey. You were totally in love with that guy."

"It wasn't that serious," Ellie said. "We just spent a lot of time together."

"You teach writing and literature, and I'm always hearing you say 'Show, don't tell,' and that manuscript is a stellar example of how to show that somebody is in love without ever saying it. The end was so depressing it almost made me cry."

"You should have heard the part after the ending," she mumbled.

"Hmmm?"

"Well, okay, I did have feelings and I guess it just showed in the writing. That's how it's supposed to work. But it was 30 years ago. Everybody has their early romance. You had Teresa, and you even lived with Kat."

"Yeah, yeah, you're right." He sat on the stool next to her. "And I suppose those, um, scenes of interpersonal intimacy in the notes—even those are pretty tasteful considering there was no reason they had to be written that way."

"The author is just inherently tasteful, I guess. I know those weren't in the official final manuscript, but I feel like, with a few decades of perspective, that material offers insight to the narrator's state of mind. Helps the story."

"Yeah, okay, but the narrator is you, not some made-up character. And then the guy the narrator is in love with comes by for coffee this morning?"

"I told you two weeks ago I was going to meet him today. And loved, past tense."

"But flying from Boulder to Nashville just for a coffee?"

"And for work—he made some appointments in Brentwood and down in Chattanooga and Atlanta. But yeah, he came mostly to see me, I think. It's a crazy story, but he had not received the package until a couple weeks ago."

"Thirty years later?"

"There was a very messy divorce and his psychotic mother hid it from him and then, she says, forgot about it. Which created the impression that he was blowing me off back then, which was not his intention. So he just wanted to try to make it right. Even though we've all moved on with our lives and everything's fine now."

"Yeah, okay." He tugged at his goatee. "But I don't know about all of us going back to New Hampshire to look for this graveyard."

"I don't either. And driving to Madison, Ohio from there."

"What?"

"Also driving from New Hampshire to Madison. Retracing Emma's migration in the forward direction."

"I mean, I'd do that with you, or you and Ethan, for sure."

"Would you?"

"Yeah, sure. It sounds like a cool adventure. And I'd go with Axel and his girls, too. It just sounds a little contrived."

"It's totally contrived," she said. "Wanna fuck?"

37.

"Dad?" Marianne knocked on the door to his office.

Axel looked up from the couch. "Hi."

"No way. You cannot go on this trip with her. It would be insane. You two were obviously totally in love with each other."

"Really?"

"Yes, really."

"But it was 30 years ago."

"And?"

"And since then, your mom and I met and we fell in love and had two lovely daughters whom I love very much and I wouldn't trade this life for anything. Except for having her here with us also."

"Well, that's good to hear anyway. Plus some of that intimate stuff—I mean it's kinda weird to read that."

"Yeah, I get it. Look, I just feel like it's unfinished business. It would be easy to make a trip back east and kind of close that loop, and at the same time give you two a little mini-tour of that area. I spent a lot of time around there back when I was racing. Lots of cool things to see, and I've come to understand how that area, those landscapes and everything that happened there, that was all really formative for me."

"If you're so familiar with those places, then haven't you already finished the business anyway?"

"Except for that cemetery. Plus, I've felt bad ever since for leaving Ellie on her own."

"Well, one, she handled herself just fine alone, and two, from reading the story I don't think it would have made any difference if there had been two of you. Or ten of you even."

"You know what I mean. I just hate unfinished business."

"Maybe that's not the only way to finish it," Marianne said after a pause. "I mean we could still take a trip out there, just the three of us. And you already told Ellie about the burying grounds, so she could go find that if she wants to."

"This is why you're getting two B.A.s and a Masters—that ability to see the obvious solution that isn't obvious to anyone else."

"Or not obvious to you, anyway!" she laughed.

"Touché." He rolled his eyes. "At least I can take half credit for your genes." He stood up and woke up his laptop. "Anyway, have a look at this." He zoomed in the map to the northeastern US." Here's Lake Erie and Lake Ontario northeast of it. Here's the Finger Lakes. Here's the Hudson River, then the Connecticut River. Boston is over here, Cape Cod out there, and up north of there and inland a bit are the White Mountains in New Hampshire, starting just above these lakes here. They're not anywhere near as tall as the Rockies out here—much older mountains, worn away by a few hundred million years of erosion—but they are pretty rugged, and the tree line is low, only around 4,000 feet, so once you get up high, you can generally see pretty far. It's lovely country. And south of the Whites but north of the Mass border is where this Emma Crombie would have started out." He zoomed in much closer.

"I'm guessing this burial ground is up in here someplace, northeast of Peterborough. Ellie probably got quite close to it 30 years ago, but of course without knowing it was there." He zoomed back out a bit.

"So what I figured we could do was fly into Manchester. Southwest has cheap flights from Denver. Rent a car there. If you want, we can go up north for a couple days and maybe hike Mount Washington or go a bit west of there where I always heard there were great hikes in Franconia Notch. Everything is within an hour or two drive. That's one nice thing about New England compared to out here—it's all pretty compact. Then we go down south and find the cemetery. There's another nice shorter hike in that general area, up Mount Monadnock. It's not tall, but there's nothing around it, so you can see forever. Emma even mentioned that in her letters. I did races all around there—Putney and Fitchburg and Sunapee and a couple things in the Berkshires—but I never did that hike.

"Then from there we go west, cross the Connecticut at Brattleboro and go across Vermont, cross the Hudson and get around Albany somehow, then follow routes 20 and 20A to the west, same roads but opposite direction of what we did on bikes 30 years ago. Stop in or near Geneseo. There's a state park with a deep canyon and supposedly some great hiking that's within an hour of Geneseo, Letchworth State Park. Grand Canyon of the East, they call it, ha ha. Then the next day, drive the rest of the way west. Go through Madison on the way to Cleveland, spend a couple days helping Grandpa sort and pack stuff up, then drop the car off at the airport, and fly back home. We could do the whole thing in as few as three days, or take a week and give ourselves a little wiggle time."

"Wow," said Marianne, "You have the whole plot worked out. Do we get to meet those Finnish guys and have a sauna? My legs would be sore for sure."

"That part isn't written yet," he laughed. "I hadn't gotten to the point of thinking about whether some of the people we met would still be there, but that adds a whole new dimension! Even better!"

"You actually are serious."

"Yes. And you're brilliant. It doesn't need to be a big joint excursion. I will just send Ellie the info on the burial ground and let her know that you girls and I are planning a trip east at some point and we'll let her know how it goes. And if she ever gets up there and explores the burial ground, she can let me know. And, of course if she's ever in Boulder or we're in Nashville, give a call, have a coffee."

"What's her son's name?" She pushed her hair back.

"I don't know. Not the husband's either. And I don't think I mentioned your names, either, only that you exist."

"Worse than I am. How can you have the job you have and not remember anybody's name?"

"That's what business cards are for," he picked one up from the holder on his desk. "So you'll bring this up with Anna?"

"Yeah. And I don't know about you, but thinking about her schedule and my schedule, sometime pretty soon—like late July or early August this summer—might be the time to do it. Who knows what my life will be like next year, and she'll be graduated by then, too."

"Now you're scaring me," he flipped down the laptop. "But you're right. Before long you'll both be off doing whatever you do and there may not be a better opportunity to do anything like this with the three of us. I'll start blocking out those couple of weeks on my schedule and we'll see what Anna wants to do."

38.

"It looks like this dude Ethan Wylie has a shit-ton of Instagram followers," Anna said. She had the same long black hair as Marianne, but where her older sister was of medium height and solidly built, like her dad, Marianne was smaller-boned and taller, like their mother Su-Yun had been. "Pictures of bike races. There, I followed him. See if he follows back."

Marianne looked over Anna's shoulder at the phone. "Bing, yep. Hey, tag me too."

"He must a have a GoPro," said Anna. "Look at some of this stuff. Yeeks." She scrolled down. "Oh, here we have some normal people pictures."

"Well, he's certainly a dashing fellow," Marianne said. "Got a little chin dimple. And those legs. Jeez."

"What, is this guy going to turn you straight?"

"I can appreciate beauty when I see it."

"Oh, look, some drawings of cars."

"And lawn furniture."

"Oh, I see. Industrial design major," Anna said. "So that's school stuff. You're right, he's pretty fucking cute, in a doofy kind of way. Too bad I'll never meet him."

"Dad would like this guy. That's ironic, huh?"

"You think he's doing okay?"

"Dad? Yeah, I do. At first this business with Ellie was setting off alarms, but we talked it through and I think it's just his need to have things wrapped up, you know? Like you don't mow 95% of the lawn, then stop. I would like him to find somebody, though. It's been a long time."

"But it's not her. She's happily married and all."

"Right. I don't think he was ever in 'get-back-with-her' mode. He just wanted to set things right. Some story, wasn't it?"

"Yeah," said Anna. "Actually, I'm really grateful to get the chance to read that. It's like it gives me this fresh view of my dad, more or less at the age I am now. It helps me understand him better. And I'm intrigued about her, honestly. She wrote that when she was our age too. She really kinda lays it out there toward the end. And her notes, geez. I guess all 20-year olds are horn-dogs. I'm kinda surprised he included those for us to read, but I guess it makes sense—full disclosure."

"Dad's a very nice and noble person and also a tough SOB who's not too inclined to share his feelings, even back then, that's what I get," said Marianne. "Though you can tell he felt for her, and not just because of the sex."

"Maybe in spite of the sex, almost. He was definitely in go-slow mode with her, way more than I would have been. Thank god for birth control. And I didn't expect to see that he was so affected by his parents' divorce, that it messed up his school and everything. He never blames them or even talks about that really. It's just like, 'this happened, then this happened.' Like Wednesday was sunny, Thursday partly cloudy."

"No point in getting mad at the weather."

"Yeah, but I still do!" Anna laughed.

"So you're cool with this trip? I think that first week of August would be good for me."

"Yeah, I'm in for sure. Maybe we scope out some rock climbing."

"Always trying to trick me into rock climbing. Just nice, boring walking on the non-vertical ground for me. Maybe splash in a lake. I know that's not very Boulder of me, but I haven't been a jock so far and I'm not likely to turn into one. And having been a lifeguard for two summers doesn't count—that was just sitting on my butt and blowing a whistle. Anyway, let's do it. Dad will be happy."

39.

"Hey I got a note from Axel," Ellie said, flopping a stack of papers onto the kitchen counter.

"And?" said David.

"He sent all the info he'd found out about the Crombie burial grounds."

"Helpful."

"Also says he and his daughters will make a trip to New England at some point, but they told him he'd be crazy to go with his now-married girlfriend from 30 years ago," she laughed.

"A prudent analysis," said David.

"And he agrees with them that there's really no need to all do the thing together. The main reason he had reached out was to set everything straight about the manuscript and the long delay and everything. But if we're ever in Boulder, drop a note and we'll have a coffee or something. And they'll do the same if they find themselves around these parts."

"Oh," said David. "Okay. Well, do you still want to go?"

"Yeah, I do. What did Ethan say?"

"I sent him a text talking about the idea and he said 'In.' I think that means yes. Though he'd miss some racing."

"Only a week or so," Ellie replied. "You have to build in a break or two anyway for recovery."

"Okay, well let's the three of us sit down and look at some dates."

"You want to drive or fly?"

"Cleveland's only 8 hours but it's probably a solid two days up to New Hampshire. Still, plane tickets times three, plus all the airport waiting . . ."

"I hear you. We drive."

40.

Ethan downed the last dribbles of the Arizona lemon tea and returned to scanning through the GoPro. It was kind of hard to see what the best pictures were on the tiny screen, but it was always good to get one or two up immediately after the race, so he'd plug into the car charger and pick a couple. The rest he would do later this evening at home.

Today, he'd mounted it on the seat post facing back, and that perspective often got some great shots of whoever was on his wheel as they went around corners. He pre-set it to take one picture every three seconds from the moment he pressed the shutter until the battery was dead. In practice that was just under an hour, depending on temperature and other more mysterious factors, so he'd reach down and hit the button when he figured the race was about 54 minutes from the end. It required more fiddling than one could do during a race to switch it from still to video mode and back, so he always decided ahead of time if it would be a still day or a video day.

The decision wasn't hard today. First, the crash on turn three at about lap 40, that was sweet. Rider expressions captured in mid-air: priceless. The second had been taken after he'd gotten in the breakaway with four other guys—a few laps after the break got away, two more riders bridged up from the main field, and one shot captured them red-lining it for those last few meters to get into the draft of the breakaway. He didn't know who any of the people in the shots were this time—it was an out-of-town race and of the half-dozen guys he knew here, two were up here in the break with him and the others had been buried back there somewhere in the main group, evidently not pursuing too hard.

He sent those two over to his phone and posted them on Instagram. #gonnahurt #500watts? Two of the first hearts came from moverachiever and annalog, whoever they were. Lots of people like bike racing pictures. Even realdonaldtrump had liked one once, as if he ever touched a bicycle. He did get his name on a stage race decades ago, though rumor had it he stiffed a bunch of people and never paid them.

This Friday-evening criterium would be the last race before the family trip up north, leaving tomorrow. That would be fun, a nice change of pace. Maybe he would read that whole story mom had written, maybe not. Dad had explained what it was about. Plus Mom said there was stuff in there she'd be embarrassed for her son to read, but so be it—it was out there. He pulled the compression sleeves onto his calves. Time for a rest week anyway and then build up for those September road races. After that, maybe look for a real job.

He was grateful that his parents seemed cool with his taking what amounted to a gap year, except it was after college instead of before. But he also knew there might be limits to that patience. At least he had gone to Hadentown, which meant tuition was free because his mom taught there and he'd lived at home, which meant he didn't have to fit loan repayments into his slim budget. Seeing what a lot of his friends had needed to do just to be able to start paying those loans back gave him a strong appreciation for his good fortune. It made him wonder if it was a misuse of the English language to call it a "financial aid package" when all it was doing was encouraging you to get into more debt than any bank would lend you as a regular customer after college. In bike racing terms, it was a little like luring gullible racers into burning up way too much energy way to soon so they wouldn't have anything left when it really mattered. Save your powder, man.

He pulled out of the lot, tooted the horn at a couple of his buddies, including his teammate who had gotten second place out of the breakaway thanks in part to Ethan's horsepower, and headed back toward Nashville, the sun still a couple hours from setting.

41.

Considering how convoluted and distance-inefficient many multi-stop flights were there days, the flight from Denver to Manchester seemed like something out of a movie: take off, look down at the Mississippi, eat some sugary peanuts, peek at Franconia Notch and the Presidential Range as you come in to land.

Anna untangled her lanky limbs from her sister's lap and roused Marianne awake. Axel, seated the row ahead, looked back. "Ready to go meet some presidents?"

Axel himself had never climbed Mount Washington except once on a bicycle for the annual event for which one had to enter a lottery. Back in the 19th century, entrepreneurs built a stone hotel on top of the northeast's tallest mountain, and had built both a carriage road, which would later become an auto road, and a cog railway to the top. The hotel was long gone, but the road and railway remained, as did an extensive network of hiking trails, also dating to the 19th century. Unlike many low-elevation trails that followed Indian routes, these paths up to the tops of mountains were cut by people of European descent who had settled in the area, not initially by Native Americans, who regarded many peaks as sacred and generally did not attempt to stand atop them. These trails carried the names, often, of the men who had cut them: Davis, Crawford, Jewell, Raymond; or of the named topological features they scaled or traversed: Tuckerman Ravine, Great Gulf, Dry River, Nelson Crag.

Nicknamed the "Rockpile," Mount Washington from a distance is an imposing hulk; up close, it is literally a pile of extremely hard, rough rocks, all that is left after millions of years of water and harsh winters washing everything else away. The mountain is situated such that it sticks up into the prevailing jet stream winds from the northwest, and it experiences notoriously fickle weather. This is tracked by a bunkered weather station at the summit, where a stiff breeze of 231 mph, the highest surface wind speed ever observed by humans on planet earth, was recorded in April of 1934, while spring was sweetly springing down in the valleys. Probably the reason there are no taller mountains in the northeastern United States is that the tops of all of them got blown away.

But on a nice summer day, the mountain can be an idyllic setting for a hike. When Axel had completed the Mount Washington Hill Climb in the early 1990s, the skies were clear, though the wind nearly blew him off his bike at the last switchback before the finish. You were allowed to ride your bike up the auto road on this one day (if you had one of the coveted lottery tickets), but no one was allowed to ride down: the steep grades, sharp turns, and oncoming traffic were more than a set of brake shoes could handle. You had to ride the choo-choo or take a shuttle van. For their planned hike, Axel and Marianne had devised a scheme where they would leave the rental car at the Pinkham Notch visitor center, just to the east of the mountain, then ride a hiker shuttle around to its western flank so they could hike up the Ammonoosuc Ravine trail on one side, visit the summit with all the tourists who drove or rode the cog railway to the top, then climb back down the east side to Pinkham Notch via the Tuckerman Ravine trail. It should be do-able in one long day.

The Ford Eco-Sport "or similar" Axel had reserved was in fact a Ford Eco-Sport, in black. Like all "sport-utility" vehicles, the space inside was much less than it looked like it should be, so they flipped half of the back seats down in order to pack in the three people and their luggage. Marianne crawled into the resulting cozy nest behind the passenger seat and promptly fell back asleep. They left Manchester and made their way over to the eastern edge of the state and up north to the Airbnb Axel had reserved in North Conway. Sunday and Monday nights there, then they'd head down to the southern part of the state and see if they could find that Crombie burying ground. Then drive east retracing the bike trip as best he could remember, guided by Ellie's account. In Cleveland by Thursday or Friday, they'd spend a day or two helping his dad get things organized for the move, then fly home on Sunday. If the girls discovered some places they really loved, they could always arrange to come back for a longer visit later.

"She's beat," said Anna. "Good timing on the vacation."

"Yeah," said Axel. "Though we're not exactly going to be lounging at the beach. M does tend to kind of load herself up, doesn't she?"

"Wonder where she gets that?" Anna patted him on the shoulder.

"Can't have good luck unless you're ready to push when the window opens."

"That's a weird metaphor. Wouldn't you just fall out the window?"

"Okay, I'll work on that one. Don't be an annoying English major."

"Can't help it. You raised me right. Properly, I mean."

"I guess," he said. "Unintended consequences."

Anna looked around and out the back windows. "Not that craggy around here. Very pretty, though."

"The mountains are higher up north," he said. "But still not like Colorado. Different kind of mountains, old and rugged, not sharp and new."

"I hope it's enough to get a good workout."

"You'll be okay with that, I think."

"Hey Dad," she looked over at him. "Thanks for bringing us out here. I meant to say that earlier."

"I should be thanking you," he said. "It's my lark."

"Your what?"

"Lark. Never mind."

"I'm pulling your chain. It's a kind of Buick, I know."

"I know it's strange, though, going on a trip that traces the history of a family that isn't even mine. And even if it was my history, I was adopted anyway, so what would that mean?"

"Were my history. Nature/nurture thing, right?" Anna said. "I mean, we could go looking for your ancestors. You can get those DNA tests, you know."

"Yeah, I did. Couple years back."

"You're kidding! Why didn't you say anything?"

"I guess because it didn't really reveal anything."

"Well, what did it reveal?"

"What would you guess?"

"I'm not gonna guess. It doesn't matter anyway. We're just American."

"Exactly. Although some people would look at you and your sister and think otherwise."

"They do, I know. But I know better."

"Thirty percent northern European, twenty-ish east Asian, probably Korea, some Native American in there, a bit of Mediterranean, a bit of West African. I'm a mutt."

"And mom was all Taiwanese, right?"

"Think so, but you never know. They didn't have the tests yet. And besides, she was born in California, and so were her parents. I think her grandparents got out of there as kids during Japanese rule, maybe in the teens or twenties. So she was as American as anybody else you know."

"Not as American as Emma Crombie. Her family got here in the 1600s, right?"

"Yeah, but remember they weren't the first ones here either."

"Hey, that's right. If we have native American blood, maybe we're actually more American than any of them."

"Except what does that mean, that the first person who wanders onto some piece of land owns it? All these people started off in Africa and started walking . . . some turned right after the Red Sea and some went straight north. Then they all end up here arguing about who owns it."

"So who does?"

"You know," said Axel. "I feel like these conversations never really go anywhere. What's the point? Maybe I'm the King of Siam, but there is no more Siam. It's all made up."

"So a person's heritage doesn't matter at all?"

"It's not the hand you're dealt but how you play it. That's what this country is about."

"So maybe this trip could be a way to understand that about ourselves," Anna said. "I mean, you were saying how these places and everything that happened in them were formative for you, so if you're talking about origin stories and you're talking about what you make of your experiences, then in fact you are retracing your roots."

"That seems about as American as it gets."

"How come mom went by Su-Yun and not some more typical American name, then?"

"She decided that was her American name. No less so than naming a kid Ian after some English ancestor. She could be a little contrary, you may recall."

"Not really. I wish I remembered more of that shit."

"Well, you're definitely your mother's daughter, let's just say that. For example your, ah, salty tongue."

"Nature or nurture? M. knows all that shit. but I don't want to wake her up."

"I rest my case."

42.

At 86 years of age, Edgar Toomey was still a few years out from
the average life expectancy for men in his family. He had retired from the Peterborough library years ago, but still liked
to volunteer for a few hours every week at the Monadnock
history center. They let him pick and choose among the questions that were submitted through the online portal, and he
had figured out that if he came in Sunday afternoon, he could
skim off all the best ones that arrived over the weekend before
the regular staff would get to them on Monday. On this particular Sunday afternoon, one online inquiry had caught his
attention. A woman was asking about the precise location of
a Crombie burial grounds somewhere up around Weare. This
rang the faintest of bells.

He checked the record and found the reference, but no
specific address—only Crombie Road. And Crombie Road itself seemed to have been renamed or abandoned in portions.
In any case, it was a tiny, out-of-the-way road, tucked away
on the back side of something labeled Poor Farm Land. On

the map it dead-ended where it came to the edge of a rocky slope in the forest. Someone at some point it time believed the Crombie Family Burial Grounds were here on Crombie Road and had noted that location in the database, but Edgar's further exploration found it listed as "unlocated." He checked the google satellite views and saw nothing that looked conspicuously like a burial ground, but there were a couple of sites that could possibly have been established as graveyards and subsequently forgotten and overgrown. These family grounds especially tended to be on private property, and if subsequent owners were not of that family, it was not unusual for the forest to reclaim its own. It didn't take long for things to grow over, and in the case of this patron, she said at least some of the family had left for Ohio 200 years ago.

Wait a minute. Wasn't that young lady in the bicycling gear from Ohio? It had been decades ago, but it's not too often that someone walks in dressed like that, and if they do it's to get some water and use the bathroom, not to conduct research on colonial-era settlements. He could not recall the specifics of her question, but he remembered she had some primary source materials that he had been able to copy and accession into the archives. That's right, letters, written by a child—and they had referenced a town that didn't exist, and he had suggested that it might have been an informal place name. Crombie was the name, he was sure. Crombie something. It had to be the same woman. At least this communication meant that she had survived that night. He recalled having been concerned about a single young lady out alone like that.

It did not take him long to find the records and the copies of the letters, which he re-read. He remembered now from having read them the first time that the young author seemed mature beyond the typical 11- or 12-year-old of this day, and wondered again if the letters were a later reconstruction, perhaps recreated by the same girl as a woman some years later. On the other hand, the Puritan religious tradition viewed children as small adults, expected them to read scripture, and gave them what we would consider adult responsibility at a young age. He came to the same inconclusive conclusion he had 30 years prior: probably they were written contemporaneously with the journey, or nearly as likely they were re-created or re-written sometime later and the author took that opportunity to clean up some of the 12-year-old's verbiage while replicating the original letter format.

He took a look at other records and found quite a few Crombies buried in nearby cemeteries around that same time period. He also found a lot of evidence of Crombies living in southcentral New Hampshire for 10 or 20 years, then moving elsewhere, sometimes back east to the coast, but more often to Vermont or Ohio or Michigan. By the 20th century, a few had ended up in Utah, though not, apparently, because of any affiliation with the Mormon faith. In fact, Edgar Toomey had come to the conclusion now, after so many decades of studying the history of these people, that Puritans had comprised two general groups: the most powerful were the true believers, a small minority intent on establishing their own society based on the strictures to which they subscribed; but a much larger group was motivated by a desperation to get out from under the oppressive authority of church and king and immutable social order, and who attached themselves to the Puritans not so much because they passionately followed that particular brand of Calvinist extremism, but because riding with the Puritans was their ticket out. It did not take too long for this latter group, once they had gained their footing on the rocky American soil, to decide they could not abide the oppressive authority of the Puritans either. So they would set out again for some remote place where nobody could tell them what to do. Either set up their own church or do without. Live free or die.

Dear Ms. Webster,

Thank you for your inquiry. I am afraid I must report that the locality of, or even the continued existence of the Crombie

Burial Grounds is an awfully uncertain thing. However, other cemeteries in the southwestern portions of Hillsboro County do contain quite a few Crombie graves. Hillside Cemetery, for example, has at least a dozen. Very many more are on the coast at Hampton and Hampton Falls, and these may well be your family ancestors as well, but about a century to 150 years earlier.

In subsequent years and centuries to the time period referenced in your communication, between 1800 and 1830, many of the Crombie surname who had lived in this area for one or two generations seem to have moved on to other places. Among the documented destinations: Ohio, Michigan, and Utah. Some others stayed; Crombies continued to be buried in Hillside Cemetery long after.

If I were you and making a trip to the area anyway, I would drive out to Crombie Road and see what I might find. It is quite possible that the reason this burial ground is listed as unlocated is that no one has gone out there to try to locate it. The situation is awfully remote and toward the ends of a number of dead-end roads and at the far, unpopulated corners of three townships; not many people will likely just happen across the place on the way to anywhere else. If you do venture there and find anything, please let me know so that we may update the information in the database.

One final note: I suspect that you and I may have spoken in person perhaps three decades ago. I recall a young woman in bicycling garb coming into the library one afternoon with a stack of letters that had been written by an ancestor whose name I believe was Crombie. If my memory is accurate, then allow me to say that it is awfully nice to talk to you again, and I hope we may help answer your questions a bit more promptly this time around.

Yours,
Edgar Toomey, Historian and Archivist Emeritus,
Peterborough Town Library

He proofread the text three or four times, top to bottom, bottom to top, then clicked on the "send" button. As soon as he hit it, he remembered exactly what it was for which she had been searching: a place called Crombie Hill. He checked the google map again: no place with that name, through Crombie Road did seem, as implied by the terrain markings on the map and the shadows on the satellite image, to climb a hill as it skirted behind the poor farm property.

<h1 style="text-align:center">43.</h1>

"Hey M," Anna said. "Look, it's a non-bike-race post."

"Wow, look at that," she paused eating her oatmeal to look at Anna's phone. "The mom and dad and the kid all standing in front of a river."

"Hashtag family vacation. WTF?"

"Hurry up, we've got to get going to catch that shuttle," Axel said. "I'd almost suggest leaving the phones here, but I know that's a non-starter."

"As if," said Anna. "Isn't that what they said on TV when you were a kid?"

"I don't know, I didn't watch much TV," he replied. "As if." He filled the three water bladders and set two on the counter. The third he slid into the hydration sleeve in his daypack.

Marianne stuffed one into her daypack and another into Anna's. "I'll put my boots on in the car."

"As will I." Anna took her last bite and rinsed out the three bowls, leaving them in the dish drainer.

Axel had his boots on already, but grabbed a pair of slip-on shoes to leave in the car so he could put them on after the hike. If it was anything like Colorado, his feet would be pretty beat up after a couple hours of descending, and it would be good to get the boots off.

"You don't have to drive all the time," Marianne said as they pulled on to Route 16 headed north.

"I think I do," he said. "Rental car contract. It would have been an extra couple hundred to add another driver, plus they make you jump through extra hoops for kids under 25."

"Kids? Even a kid with good grades? Figures."

"But thanks. At least today it's only 15 minutes."

They walked into the Pinkham Notch visitor center long enough to use the bathroom one more time, then went back out just as the big white hiker shuttle van was pulling up. Even at seven in the morning, there were already another six hikers lined up, some who were obviously embarking on multi-day excursions, judging from their enormous packs. Axel was glad he'd made an advance reservation for their shuttle space. It was chilly, maybe in the mid-50s, and damp and misty—a typical eastern mountain summer morning. It was a lot drier in Colorado. He bounced in place to try to keep warm.

Inside the shuttle, it warmed up plenty, and the added smells of various breakfasts and a dozen minimally bathed hikers prompted the opening of a couple of window vents in the back. It was too misty to see anything up high, but he knew they had started out at the base of Tuckerman Ravine, a huge glacial cirque that was as famous among later-winter DIY skiers as it was among hikers. He'd never done it, but you'd strap your downhill skies on your back, hike up three hours to the crest of the ravine, then spend five minutes skiing down—hopefully not setting off an avalanche or getting into a boulder field that wasn't sufficiently buried in snow. Almost every year, somebody slipped, either skiing down or hiking up, and started sliding and didn't stop until they hit something.

This was New Hampshire: it said "Live Free or Die" right on the license plate. Maybe both.

The long uphill grind would be Crawford Notch, as he recalled from racing his bicycle up it decades before. Your body doesn't ever forget how it feels to go up a hill really fast, even if it couldn't quite do the same now. That made him smile.

The van labored over the steep crest of the notch and began going down the other side, then turned onto a side road that branched to the right. The trailhead for the Ammonoosuc Ravine trail was adjacent to the parking lot at the base of the cog railway. There wasn't any particular reason that the trains had to be steam-powered other than nostalgia for the past days of rampant air pollution, but they were, so one got to hear the distinctive steam-engine chugging sounds and also see the black coal smoke billowing out of the smokestacks. The entire length of the railway included two rails and a toothed track down the middle, to which the train remained firmly attached so that it never could, in theory, roll free down the precipitously steep grade. Even so, to many hikers, taking your chances climbing up exposed rock ledges seemed a saner option. This particular trail paralleled the tracks but at some distance, so there would be an occasional glimpse of the cars laboring up and down the next ridge over, and the occasional sound of a steam whistle, but for the most part it was a quiet hike undisturbed by that 19th-century version of advanced human technology.

With a quick thanks to the driver, they stepped down, double-checked that they had all their stuff, and started walking. All the other hikers stayed on the shuttle, evidently bound for other trailheads further to the north. The cog railway parking lot was empty. According to the schedule board, the first trains would not depart until 9:00. Some of them were biodiesel-powered now, Axel noted with amusement. Whatever the market demands. They left behind the trailhead and followed the pine-rooted trail alongside the rocky Ammonoosuc River, calmed by the soft white noise of the water tumbling past them from up the mountain ahead.

44.

Ellie read the email from Edgar Toomey with resigned amusement. Of course, they would come all the way here only to find nothing. It had happened before, so why not again? To get so close—very close this time, maybe within a mile, maybe within a few hundred feet . . . but of what? What would a gravestone tell her? But it was wonderfully serendipitous that the same person to whom she had spoken 30 years ago was still working at the library. She'd still had his contact information from that visit, but hadn't even occurred to her to try to reach him directly. She had assumed he'd be long gone.

"Hey David," she handed her phone to him. "Have a look."

David found his reading glasses in a jacket pocket and picked up the phone, his other hand scratching his scalp through thick brown hair. His reaction was completely different than hers. "That's marvelous—we do a little investigative project, hit a couple cemeteries, maybe see if we can interview the neighbors on this Crombie Road. Let's eat something and go."

Ethan leaned over David's shoulder. "Ha! Dude remembers you! That's so cool!"

She shrugged. "They should be serving breakfast by now." She sent a quick thank-you-we'll-go-exploring note to Edgar Toomey and set the phone in her purse and stood up. "Let me get some real clothes on." She ducked in the bedroom and swapped the sweatpants for jeans and pulled a fleece on over her t-shirt.

In the breakfast room, David planned the day's exploration using his iPad. They had driven up by way of Interstate 81 and then jogged over on I-84 to Hartford to pick up I-91, even though it was probably about 90 minutes longer overall than the more western route via I-71 and I-90, because they would be returning home by that latter route and wanted to avoid the redundancy. In addition, David had figured out that the 81-84-91 route avoided all big cities except for Hartford and also avoided tolls, except for one bridge over the Hudson River. By any route, it was a solid two days of driving. After an overnight stop near Hagerstown, Maryland overlooking the Potomac, they'd made it to the B&B in Keene, New Hampshire late Sunday afternoon.

From here they could get over to the search area in about an hour, he estimated. Maybe less. They had this place booked for another night, so they'd just end up back here tonight. Tomorrow, if the weather cooperated, go climb Monadnock in the morning, then head west. Ellie came back with coffee refills. Ethan was taking a selfie by the toaster.

45.

They took a break after fording the river at Gem Pool. The walk had been lovely, steadily but not steeply uphill, the path not wide and smooth like those out west, but rocky and tangled with roots and often wet, all of which required a bit more attention underfoot. Anna had taken one little spill, scuffing her leg through her black leggings without actually tearing them. The air still hadn't warmed up much, though the sky was brightening a bit.

Marianne sat on a rock and gazed up at where the little waterfall emerged from the mist above. The topo hiking map indicated they'd be heading that way momentarily, that the gradual part of the climbing was over.

Anna sat next to her. "#toasted," she laughed, showing Marianne the Instagram post from ethanwylie.

"Not already?" Axel said from his perch on another rock a few feet away.

"Not me," Anna laughed. "Wanna keep going?" She slid the phone back into her pack. "Wait," she pulled it back out.

"This is a pretty spot—let's get a photo of the three of us." They squeezed together on a single boulder as Anna held the phone at her long arm's length. "Hmm, no service here all the sudden. I'll try to post it later from up higher. Meanwhile, airplane mode so I don't kill the battery."

"Good idea," Marianne pulled her phone out of her jacket pocket.

"I turned mine off completely before we started," Axel said. "It's fully charged, though. Insurance phone."

They resumed hiking. The trail ascended steeply via rock steps and ledges alongside the cascade. It was quite slippery in spots, and Marianne's boots in particular seemed to have soles made of some compound that did not grip very well here. On her second slip, she tore a little hole in the knee of her dark blue tights and drew a little blood from the skin below. "Trail rash," she quipped, and kept climbing.

Within ten minutes, the vertical effort had elevated them out of the mist and also elevated their body temperatures. It was no longer just walking, but scrambling from rock to rock, climbing up from ledge to ledge. The trails were well marked, and some serious heavy lifting of rocks had been done by trail crews to make sections passable, but in many places there wasn't much of a path, technically: just a sequence of strategically placed blazes of paint that showed the best way to get up a rugged granite incline and presumably kept one from getting off to one side or another where a bad fall might easily happen.

The trail emerged onto an open ledge and crossed the rushing stream. The tall pines that had surrounded Gem Pool had given way to low, scrubby vegetation, small gnarled trees, azaleas, other low bushes. To the left, the rest of the mountain loomed overhead; to the right, the water disappeared over a precipice a few feet away, on its way down to Gem Pool below. The path traversed about five feet of water a couple inches deep, sheeting over the smooth rock. Not wanting to test the suspect adhesive properties of her boot soles with so little margin for error, Marianne made her way up to the left and climbed across a couple of dry boulders under and around which the stream flowed.

All soaked with sweat now, they stopped a few minutes later on a broad ledge that looked out to the west. The first of the day's cog railway trains was beginning to chug up a ridge below and to the right. Anna stuffed her windbreaker into her pack. "Guess my question is answered about whether I need to worry about maintaining my fitness," she laughed. She fished through her pack and pulled out an energy bar.

Marianne unfolded the trail map. "So, we're looking at Mount Lafayette over there, and the Franconia Ridge. This big green part between here and there is the Pemigewassett Wilderness. Crawford Notch would be right down there to the left—can't quite see it behind those trees, I guess. And it looks like we're about here. Maybe halfway up to these Lakes of the Clouds and the hut right next to them."

Axel nodded, his mouth full of energy bar.

"It's kind of funny," Marianne continued. "You have half of these places sounding like Indian names, the other half obviously named after Europeans who came here. Washington, Lafayette, Pemigewassett, Ammonoosuc. I wonder who decided all that?"

"Whoever wrote it down first, right?" Anna offered, then pointed toward Axel's left arm. "Shit dad, you dinged yourself there."

Axel looked down and noticed the scrape on his forearm that hadn't bled at first was now dripping blood off the end of his elbow. He dabbed it dry with his napkin.

46.

Hillside Cemetery lived up to its moniker, stretching across an east-facing slope on the north side of Deering Center Road. Ellie's heart was beating a little faster than usual as she turned into the drive. There were a couple of pull-off spots just inside the entrance, so she parked the Subaru there and they began to walk uphill. Ethan immediately went straight up the steepest part of the hill amid the gravestones and left them behind, calling back, "anything Crombie, right?" David's extra thirty pounds, by contrast, suggested to him a more gradual path skirting the slope. Ellie stuck to the paved lane, which proved to be a middle road between the two men.

After a few minutes, David called out. "Over here!" Ellie and Ethan trotted down to where David was and they gathered around the Crombie stones, of which there were over a dozen.

"These dates seem to start with people born just after the Revolution and go for a couple generations after that," Ellie said. "So people Emma's age, a generation older, and a generation younger."

"That means some of the family stayed back here," David said, "at least assuming all these Crombies were related to each other."

"Well, they're all buried together," Ethan said. "That should be a clue."

"I still don't have any idea who any of these people are," Ellie said.

"How are they related to us again?" Ethan asked.

"They're not related to Dad of course," Ellie said, "but on my side, Emma Crombie was my grandma's great-grandmother I think. But there hasn't been anyone named Crombie in the family since Emma got married, and that would have been around 1830. It all traces down through the wives, so the names get lost unless somebody makes sure to keep it alive by naming their kids after somebody."

"So, am I named after his Ethan?" He pointed at a stone that read Ethan Crombie, Died October 12, 1838, AE 55.

"Yes, of course," David laughed. "Just like I'm named after this David. Oh, man . . . this guy died in 1862 at 18, Bull Run, Virginia."

"Damn," Ethan said. "That's dark."

"Oh my god," Ellie whispered. "This one says Seven Children of Mehitabel Lynde Crombie, died 1832, age 31. All under age 11, all on one stone. No dates."

"It was a different life then," David said. "You know that in the abstract just from reading your history books and watching Ken Burns shows on TV, but this really brings it home."

"Severely," Ethan said.

"The thing is," Ellie said, "There should be one or two generations before these people. Based on what Edgar told me, way back when, people would have first settled this area in the 1760s to 70s. That would have included the ones who fought in the Revolution, the three generations of patriot soldiers grandma told me about. Where are they?"

"I guess maybe in that Crombie burying grounds that has yet to be found," said David. "We could do a lot more research online, starting with these names, but I don't want to get the iPad out and do that now. Let's take photos of these stones and then we can dig around later when we get home." He looked at another group of stones adjacent, broken, knocked down, no names visible. "And these? Just in case?"

"What?" Ellie looked over, then shrugged and nodded. She was feeling nervous and distracted, for no reason she could identify.

"Let's get them all on one phone to make it easier later," said Ethan. "I have mega storage." He crouched down before each Crombie stone until he had photographed all of them. "All these Crombies, and I have never met anyone named Crombie in my whole life!"

"Neither have I," Ellie laughed. "Except I am one and so are you."

"Well," said David, "let's go see if we can find that burying ground."

47.

Marianne noted that the vegetation steadily got lower to the ground as they continued their steep uphill scramble. These plants had a distinct smell—a little bit piney, a little bit sweet. The blazes had moved away from the stream onto a slight ridge now and the rocks were dry, providing much better footing. Ahead of her, Anna used her long limbs to great advantage, spanning her legs from rock to rock and using her hands for balance as her legs did most of the work. She looked to be in a comfortable rhythm. Marianne couldn't match Anna's leg-span but employed her reasonably strong occasional-swimmer's arms and shoulders to hoist herself up higher; she, too, felt in a good rhythm. She could hear her dad behind, keeping pace, whistling some unidentifiable tune.

Presently they passed a sign indicating that they were entering the alpine zone. In Colorado, the tree line was higher than 11,000 feet. Here they were already above the trees at 4,000, more than a vertical mile lower. The sun had warmed considerably, but at the same time the wind had picked up as they emerged from the trees. The landscape had simplified to two elements: endless rocks and whatever little plants could manage to survive in and among the rocks. The trail was marked not only with paint blazes but with cairns of piled rocks, as tall as a person, every 15 or 20 feet.

They crested a small ridge and suddenly the summit of Mount Washington was visible above, its distinctive radio tower sticking up into the sky. Much closer was a small wooden building.

"That will be Lakes of the Clouds hut," Axel called from behind. "Good place for a break, get some water, use the bathroom, have a bite." He checked his watch. About two and a half hours to get up here. Pretty fast, ahead of the "book time" estimate in the White Mountain Guide. He had been a little worried that if they got too delayed along the way, they might run out of daylight before they got all the way back down to the car, but they'd be more than fine if they kept up this pace. They had headlamps and compasses and all that, but still better not to need them.

After a stop in the hut to avail themselves of its water and leftover breakfast coffee cake and composting toilets, they went out and sat on rocks beside one of the lakes for which the hut was named.

"So hikers stay overnight there?" Marianne asked.

"Yeah," Axel replied, "I never did it, but I think you make a reservation and pay your money, and you get a bunk and dinner and breakfast. There's a bunch of these huts and it's set up so you can hike from one to another in a day. The Appalachian Trail comes through here."

"Yeah, I saw a sign," Marianne said.

Anna was able to get a signal and posted the photo from Gem Pool. She thought it would be funny to tag it #familyvacation.

"I'm going to hit the bathroom one more time," Axel said, "then if you're ready we can climb up to the summit and say hi to all the motor-tourists."

"Sounds like a plan," Anna said as he walked off. "Hey M," she held the phone over to Marianne. "They're fucking visiting graveyards now." Ethan's post showed a bucolic view of a cemetery stretching across a steep hill, tagged #familyreunion, #familyvacation.

Marianne laughed. "Most normal people would go to Disneyland!"

Anna put the phone back in airplane mode and packed it away.

48.

The road changed to something creek road, then to Crombie Road, then back to Mountain Road. It didn't match the satellite map on David's iPad exactly, but it was close. Why you would bother to call anything a mountain road around here? He wondered. Like calling something Pine Tree Road or Piece of Granite Road. They slowed to a crawl, Ellie driving, Ethan scanning the woods, David following the iPad and the car's GPS. David looked up ahead. "Let's try that level place up there."

Ellie pulled the Outback as far to the edge of the dirt road as she dared. They climbed out. On the other side of the roadside ditch was a stone wall at the edge of the woods, in fact partially disassembled by the woods. Beyond the wall was open forest. Random rocks and boulders were interspersed among the trees in the level area that extended into the forest from the road, but there appeared nothing man-made. They got back in and crept ahead.

There were a few houses on Crombie Road, most of them looking like they had been built in the past 40 years, but a couple much older. It was Ethan who thought of looking alongside these older houses on the theory that a family plot might be located near one of these older homes. Ellie of course kept in the back of her mind the painting of the little house on the hill. And this time she had it not only in her mind, but on her phone, having taken a picture of it where it had hung on her study wall ever since they'd moved into the Nashville house.

Another promising-looking site proved nothing but some rocks, then Ethan spotted not a house, but a row of daffodils back in the woods. Likely evidence of some human intervention on that spot. Ellie pulled over again. Indeed, there had been something there—they found a stone perimeter marking the foundation of a house long-gone—but that was all.

David had imagined that some local residents might be out doing yard work or something, and they could impose upon such a person to share if they knew of any burial ground along this road, but they had yet to see a soul. Not even another car. Perhaps midday Monday was not the best time to run into people out here.

They passed a few more newer houses and turned left and uphill to follow the Crombie Road sign onto an even narrower dirt track, this one labeled No Outlet. After three more houses, all relatively recent, one with a good-sized fishing boat parked next to it, the road took a right turn and then petered out. Ellie figured they might as well get out of the car here and look around, since this was—figuratively and literally—the end of the road.

David and Ethan stood shoulder to shoulder, looking into the woods where the hill steepened beyond the where the trees closed in and blocked the way to all but those on foot. "Wanna walk up there?" David called back to Ellie and pointed into the woods where it looked like the road had once persisted for another few hundred feet. He assessed that these trees were not that old, as if the whole area had been clearcut at some point. There were mature trees, but no really old trees. Maybe this area at the end of the road had never had any structures on it. Maybe it had been a timber lot.

They followed what looked like it might be an overgrown road grade further up until it definitively ended in a cluster of large boulders that one might reasonably deduce had come tumbling from the rocky cliffs above to the right and blocked a road that used to continue, maybe still did on the other side.

"So do think this is it?" David turned to Ellie.

"The end of the road, you mean?"

"Crombie Hill."

"There is no Crombie Hill," Ellie said. "It was just an idea, a name for something that had no name—a way to conjure an image to evoke where you think you came from so you don't feel completely lost in the world."

"Are you sure? I mean this is a hill, and the road does say Crombie. Hill plus Crombie equals—"

"—Hill Crombie," she interjected. "I mean, what would this place mean to Axel, or you, or anyone other than the dozen or two dozen people might have ever lived on this little slope and left before it could even get a name permanently stuck to it?"

"Maybe you're right," he said. "Maybe it's just a way to give a name to something not really nameable, that would mean something different to every person. Maybe Axel's Crombie Hill wouldn't be this place at all. Maybe it would be the first home he remembers, or where he imagined his birth parents grew up. Maybe it was a bike ride ostensibly to find a departure point of someone's history but really to find something else."

She rolled her eyes. "That's reading a lot into it, don't you think?" She began walking. "Let's go."

Heading back down, David wasn't sure they were on a road grade at all. This might just be a natural drainage wash. Yet, on the left just before they emerged back onto the road, there was a row of daffodils, well past bloom, uphill about 100 feet from the road. They walked up for a closer look. It was hard to tell, but possible, that long ago, a small building had been here.

If so, some rocks had rolled in since from the hillside above. He looked more closely at those rocks without stepping closer. "Hey, careful," he said. "Looks like a rattlesnake curled up over there."

"What, where?" Ellie asked.

David pointed. "We have enough of those out in the woods in Tennessee that I think I know what one looks like. But I didn't think they were up here."

"No, me neither," said Ellie. "Though I hadn't thought they were in Ohio either, but I guess they were. And come to think of it, Emma Too did mention something about the town trying to burn out a bunch of rattlesnakes."

"Cool." Ethan walked a bit closer and zoomed in his phone camera. "Gives us real wilderness adventure cred."

The snake didn't move, apparently content to rest in the dappled sun.

"Well," Ellie said after a time. "I think we're done here." She began walking back toward the car, watching a bit more carefully underfoot. They gathered at the end of the dirt lane and looked up into the woods one more time. Ellie heard a scuffing sound behind. A white-haired man in jeans and a tan shirt was walking bowlegged up toward them.

"Morning," he said without stopping. "I wonder if I might help you."

"I don't think so," Ellie said. "Just looking for a long-lost grave site and not finding it."

"I know," he said. "I had a call this morning from Mr. Toomey down there in Peterborough. I might have something for you."

"You're kidding," she said. "What?"

"Well, he said that some folks might be coming out this way, and he got my name from talking to the selectman in town, who knew I been living out here for a good piece of time, might know something." He cleared his throat. "Don't know much, but when Mr. Toomey mentioned a burial ground with a name Crombie on it, I thought there isn't any such thing, or rather I heard of it but somebody told somebody told somebody that maybe some old graves that might have been someplace might have got moved up to Hillside many decades back when the old farm was sold off and subdivided. But there would still be the one stone out behind my old barn."

"What do you mean?" Ellie asked. Her neck tingled.

"Come see. Just around the corner. Might be interesting to you, might not. Bring your car on down and leave it in my driveway. I'll walk back and meet you on the road about a hundred yards this way from the drive. It's the one with the boat."

They got in the car, turned it around in a series of back-and-forths, and left it in the drive as instructed.

"I'm sorry," Ellie said as they met him next to a narrow lane that led into the woods, "I didn't catch your name."

"That's because I didn't say it," he said. "Peaslee. John Peaslee."

"Ellie Webster," she said.

"Not Crombie? Mr. Toomey said you're looking for Crombies. Not that there's any Websters here either."

"We are," she said. "Long time ago and descended all through the women."

"Can't say I've heard of anybody named Crombie living around here since I've been alive, and that 77 years," he said. "All they left is the name on the road."

They approached an ancient shed with heavy rough-cut timber walls and a slate roof. John Peaslee walked around behind the structure and pointed down. "And this one stone."

Emma Balch Crombie

1775–1817

Baby boy

d. 1817

49.

Axel finished typing and shut his phone down as Marianne and Anna returned from the restrooms in the big tourist building at the Mount Washington summit. The place was thronged. People were actually waiting in line to walk up the last 50 feet of rock to the actual summit of the mountain. Since it was lunchtime, he and the girls had decided to kill a little time eating and using the facilities before getting in the summit queue. His turn to go in now while they stayed with the packs.

Anna pulled a sandwich from her pack and began eating it, checking her phone with the other hand. "Good signal up here. We might have to switch to your phone later. I'm at about 60%."

"Yeah, it's been in airplane mode all day, should be good whenever we need it," Marianne replied.

"Holy shit," said Anna. "A fucking snake. What the hell kind of family vacation is this?"

Marianne leaned in. "What's the other one?"

Anna scrolled down to an image of a small gravestone. She zoomed in. "Oh, man."

Marianne sat back. "They're here."

"That's hilarious," Anna laughed. "What was the chance of that?"

"Pretty high, I guess," Marianne replied. "Well, they aren't right here. Where that burial ground would have been was in the southern part of New Hampshire, right? No more than a couple hours from here anyway."

"I guess so. It's not like they're in line over there to stand on the summit. Hey M, Dad's coming back."

Axel joined them on the bench. "Hey did you know this is one of the top three deadliest mountains in the U.S.? I read it up there. More than 100 fatalities since the 1800s. Just in case," he said, "I bought two more topo hiking maps so we each have one." He handed one to each daughter.

"Weather looks clear for the afternoon, just a few clouds here and there," Anna said. "Kind of convenient having the weather station a hundred feet from your phone."

"Yep," he said. "I checked the board they have inside. We should be good. I hear you don't really want to go down Tuckerman's in the pouring rain."

"Or down that thing we just came up," Marianne said. "You could easily find yourself taking the express to the bottom."

"Ouchy," said Anna.

A steam whistle announced the arrival of the next cog railway train.

"Hey we better go get in line before that train lets out," Axel said, standing up. "We don't want to climb all the way up here and not make the top because of a traffic jam."

They lined up with all the folks in street shoes and flip flops and summer dresses and casual slacks and the line slowly transported them to where a well-worn wooden sign marked the highest point in the northeast. Everyone who got there seemed to pose for a picture, with the people next in line doing the photography honors using the subjects' phone, so they did the same. Anna handed her phone to a teenage girl wearing shorts and a shirt from her Natick, Massachusetts high school swim team. "Hey would you mind taking our picture?"

"Sure," said the girl. "You hiked up here?"

Anna nodded.

"How long did it take?"

"What, maybe 4 hours, not counting stops?" Anna turned to her dad.

"Roughly that," Axel said.

"Jealous," the girl said, rolling her eyes out of sight of her parents behind her. "Cheese!"

"Hey can you do one vertical and one horizontal?" Anna asked.

"Okay, done." The girl handed back the phone.

They thanked the girl and her family and wished them a great day walked back down to the edge of the parking lot and found the sign for the Tuckerman Ravine trail. "Right here's where I almost got blown off my bike," Axel pointed out as they walked along the outer perimeter of the very steep final switchback in the auto road.

"I'm gonna quick post this before we head down, since I know we have signal up here," Anna said. "I'll catch up to you." She picked the horizontal picture because they all looked fairly Olympian, cropped it to a square, and tagged it #hardway. Then she shut down the phone, spotted Marianne's purple backpack and blue tights bobbing and weaving up ahead, and began down the trail. The sky overhead was clear, but off to the right and below she could see one thick cloud drifting its way up over the ridge.

If the summit area had been a strangely incongruous mix of families who had paid their $40 to drive up the auto road, people who had bought cog railway tickets to ride up, and mixed in among them a few grungy hikers who had arrived on foot, then the open slopes above Tuckerman Ravine were another kind of surreal. A few casual tourists ventured down from the parking area and train station, but within five minutes, the only other people were geared-up hikers. There were no trails per se, but rather a network of crisscrossing sequences of cairns and paint blazes punctuating the moonscape. As one followed one sequence, the cairns tracing the other nearby sequences shifted and sometimes lined up to imply trails that were not really there—which was why it was important to also follow the blazes and cross-reference your position against a topographical hiking map.

The air was cool but the sun had been on the rocks for long enough that they radiated some heat and Anna found them warm to the touch as she steadied herself against a cairn to make a big step down. She could see why people used those hiking poles out here. Marianne's purple backpack was now only maybe 20 seconds ahead of her. She wasn't hurrying, just steadily reeling them in. Farther ahead, Anna could see a sort of rim, beyond which was nothing but cloud. That would be the ravine.

Within seconds, the same cloud rose over the edge and enveloped them. Marianne looked back and gave her a little wave just before disappearing completely. Anna slowed down. Not only could she not see Marianne, she couldn't even see the next cairn. She waited for her eyes to adjust to the lower light. It had been right up there. She took a few steps, also looking for a white paint blaze. There it was—the faint shape of a cairn; then another. There was a white blaze. She kept moving. If a cairn was not in sight as she stood at one, she would venture carefully in the direction she thought the next would be until she saw something.

"Hey Anna!" She heard Marianne's voice from a ways off. "We're gonna stay put by this cairn until you catch us. Extra tall one, white quartz rock on top."

"Okay M," she shouted. "I'm good." She made out the next cairn and picked her way across the abrasive rocks. At that cairn she peered around for another. To her left there was something. She inched that way and then spotted a paint blaze, blue. "Hey M, can you hear me?"

"Yes!"

"What color are your blazes?"

"White!"

"Oops! Hold on a sec! I'm gonna put my headlamp on." She donned and turned on the headlamp and pulled out the map. Maybe she had gotten off Tuckerman and was on the Lion Head trail. Or some other trail. She thought for a few seconds. "Hey M!"

"What?"

"Marco!" Anna yelled.

"Polo!" Marianne replied.

Anna reversed direction and headed toward the voice. "Marco!"

"Polo!" This must have sounded extra surreal to all the other hikers within earshot, Marianne thought, but it seemed to be working. And surely they would understand. In fact, she could hear a few other raised voices out there somewhere. The wind had subsided in the cloud, but it was getting colder quickly also.

"Marco!"

"Polo!"

Now she was quite close. "Marco," she said.

"Right here," said M. The tall cairn and two headlamp glows now loomed out of the gray-white opacity.

"Hi," said Anna. "Well, that was unexpected."

"As expected," said Axel. "They say."

"It didn't look like that big of a cloud," Anna said. "Should we just camp out here and wait it out?"

"Up to you," said Axel. "Want to give it five or ten and if it doesn't break, then just keep close together but start moving? I think when we get down into the ravine it should be easier to follow, at least that's what the book says."

They hadn't sat for a minute before the cloud dissipated as quickly as it had come up. Anna looked back up the trail and could easily see what she had done. Then she looked the other way down the steep slope to the ravine edge and saw how getting off trail down there might be a more serious matter. No more "You go ahead, I'll catch up," at least not up here.

A number of marked paths converged at a place marked Tuckerman Junction, from which they continued a steady descent to a junction with the Alpine Garden trail, after which the Tuckerman Ravine trail dipped over the rim and plummeted quite steeply alongside a small cascade. Numerous signs warned DANGER: STAY ON TRAIL. They stayed on the trail.

50.

Mon, Aug 6, 2018, 12:57 p.m.
To: ewebster@hdt.edu
From: researchinquiry@monadnockcenter.edu

Dear Ms. Webster,

I am awfully gratified that Mr. Peaslee was able to show you the gravestone, and thank you for sending the photo thereof. I will add this to the archive.

There is scant information on ancestry.com about this family, or at least this specific branch, but I suspect the Monadnock Center will be the more fruitful source—records of defunct churches, land transfers, and so on that are not yet digitized. The added information of the woman's given name and maiden name Balch could open up some pathways as well, and we may be able to match the birth and death dates with Hillsboro county records.

This afternoon I will visit the archives and see what I can discover.

Yours,
Edgar Toomey, Historian and Archivist Emeritus, Peterborough Town Library

Mon, Aug 6, 2018, 1:05 p.m.
To: researchinquiry@monadnockcenter.edu
From: ewebster@hdt.edu
Sent from my iphone

Dear Mr. Toomey,
I cannot thank you enough for all your help. Even if this person turns out to have no connection to me, this project is a fascinating window into the world from which my ancestors came.
Thank you again.

Yours,
Ellie Webster

Mon, Aug 6, 2018, 1:08 p.m.
To: ewebster@hdt.edu
From: researchinquiry@monadnockcenter.edu

On the contrary, I am grateful to you for the opportunity to muck about in the archives with more purpose than usual.
Yours,
Edgar Toomey, Historian and Archivist Emeritus, Peterborough Town Library

51.

Ethan noticed the quick response again from annalog. This time there wasn't just a heart, but also a comment. "Welcome to New Hampshire." He checked to see if he had geotagging turned on and he didn't, so how did annalog know he was in New Hampshire? He looked closely at the images again for clues, but there was nothing there that said New Hampshire. In fact, a rattlesnake would say not New Hampshire to most people. And the gravestone . . . that was just a name, no way to know the place. He became more curious about annalog.

The most recent post was from this morning. Two young women and an older guy, presumably their dad, posed in front of a waterfall. It was tagged #familyvacation. They looked Asian, or Asian-ish. Cute. A long-limbed one who looked even more so with the black leggings, and a shorter more compact one. The guy looked pretty fit, too. Gnarly legs like an old bike racer. His eyes went back to the taller woman and zoomed in.

He went back to some earlier posts and determined that the taller one was probably annalog. He wondered if the other was moverachiever, since that name was tagged in many of annalog's posts, and because as he went back through his posts, it seemed annalog and moverachiever often liked his posts at the same time. The most recent post of moverachiever had been just an hour or so ago, and it pictured the same three people as the waterfall shot from annalog. He looked more closely and zoomed in to try to read the wooden sign in the picture. Goddamn, they were on Mount Washington. "Ha!" He said aloud.

David turned back from the front seat. "What?"

"Nothing," Ethan said. "Friends messing around." He liked both posts and repeated the comment "Welcome to New Hampshire."

"You guys wanna get a bite somewhere?" Ellie asked. "All this walking around with the dead people is making me hungry."

"Yeah, sweet," Ethan said. "Starving."

He could easily know from their picture that they were in New Hampshire, but how could they know he was here?

"Maybe we can find a place that serves rattlesnake," David said.

"McRattlers," Ethan said. Maybe something about the gravestone. Maybe the name was found only around here. What a coincidence that they had tagged their posts #familyvacation just as he had. Or maybe they did that on purpose. Did they actually know him? He wracked his memory but could not recall ever having met either one of them. And he would have remembered that for sure.

"There was a Friendly's back in town there," said Ellie. "Milkshake rhymes with rattlesnake."

"Poetic," said David.

"Tastes like chicken," said Ethan. They hadn't responded to his comments, either one of them. But up in the mountains they might be out of range or have the phones off. Funny how you could get so used to being instantly connected all the time. Made him think of how he and his parents had been talking his mom's bike ride in '88, and how they had just made one or two phone calls that whole time—collect calls, however that worked. They'd go days or weeks without hearing anything. And then the wagon girl, she's writing those letters and who knows when they will ever get delivered? A message could be on the way to you for a month and you would never know. Wait a minute. Bike racer legs, two girls, no mom. Crap, it must be them. They would know a photo was from New Hampshire by the gravestone with Crombie on it.

He hadn't actually read most of his mom's story yet, but he recalled one thing she had talked about and typed one more comment. "Did you find a little white house?"

52.

Mon, Aug 6, 2018, 3:37 p.m.
To: ewebster@hdt.edu
From: researchinquiry@monadnockcenter.edu

Dear Ms. Webster,

Interesting news here. I've found some old church files and other records that have some bearing. It's awfully complicated because it appears some of our characters were expelled from one church and joined another, and others did not particularly follow any church except for the requisite ceremonies, if even for those. Some were antipedobaptists, which means no one was baptized as a child, so you might have a birth record, if they reported it to the county, but no baptismal record until they were much older. It also appears there was a lot of shared caregiving among a few families and it's not exactly clear who was whose child or whether references such as "aunt" and "uncle" were to be taken literally.

All of that said, I can report the following:

The person on the gravestone, Emma Balch Crombie, was born nearby as Emma Balch, and baptized at age 14. I hope you do not find it scandalous for me to say so, but I believe she had a child not one year later, Elizabeth. It appears the father of said child was one Thomas Crombie, one year older than Eleanor. They were married after he attained majority at age 18. This was not uncommon, and such a marriage could legitimize the earlier birth. The son Uz was born about two years after the marriage, and the daughter Emma ten years later. The gap is so long there that there may well have been stillbirths, of which I can find no record. The gravestone of which you sent the photo affirms a church record that the mother and child died together in childbirth in 1817, when the mother would have been 41 or 42 years old. Also, sadly, not an uncommon scenario.

It appears that the father, along with son Uz and daughter Emma, departed the following spring for Ohio. The oldest daughter Eliza did not accompany them, and in fact is recorded as having been married in the spring of 1818 to Ezekiel Dow. According to a narrative in the antipedobaptist church records—written, in fact, as that church itself was being dissolved—this couple, along with the former Miss Crombie's grandmother and Mr. Dow's brother Robert, left the area for Ohio in the spring of 1819. If I had to venture a guess, it would be that the older daughter Elizabeth had stayed back to help care for the grandparents and perhaps to cultivate her attachment to the aforementioned Mr. Dow, and that they all made a planned move west in the spring of 1819 after, presumably, the advance party who had made the trip the previous year could have prepared lodgings and cleared a farm. Elizabeth would seem to be the person referred to as "Eliza Crombie" in the letters of young Emma.

As a particularly poignant note, it appears that the young girl's appeals to Eliza to pass along news to mama might be envisioned as visits to the same grave of which you have sent the photograph.

Because of the difficulties with church affiliation and lord knows what other difficulties, it is not hard to understand why these families might have resolved to move west to Ohio. The land would be more fertile and forgiving, and there may have been some attraction to the idea of starting from scratch from a social and religious perspective.

I thank you again for the opportunity to explore this material, and I wish you the best in all your endeavors.

Yours,
Edgar Toomey, Historian and Archivist Emeritus,
Peterborough Town Library

53.

Axel lowered himself over a slippery ledge and turned around to be a spotter for Anna, then Marianne. He was trying not to be dad-protector, but it was hard not to automatically assume that role. By any objective measure, they should be his protectors—two fit and experienced college-age people used to the outdoors, versus his 50-something battle-worn athlete a couple decades past his physical prime. He hoped at least that he wasn't being too obvious.

Anna had been off-trail in the cloud for only a few minutes, and she had handled the situation in a calm and level-headed manner, but the episode had spooked him severely. He was glad Marianne had done the talking, not only because it meant that he had not immediately done the step-in-and-take-charge thing, but also because he was sure they'd both have heard the fear in his voice. Not what the situation called for.

The thought that this "lark" of an adventure could put either or both of his girls in real peril caught him up short.

They were both adults, yes, and both capable people, but he couldn't shake the queasy feeling that he'd led them into danger. His heart was still racing, and not from effort. Maybe talking would break him out of his mental dread-loop. "Everybody good?"

"Yeah, I'm good." Marianne turned and looked at him after getting her feet to the ground.

"Yep," Anna.

"Good," he said. "Me too."

"You look a little pale," Marianne said. "You all right?"

"Yeah," he said. "Sacred the shit out of me up there. No good reason, but it just hit me."

Anna resumed walking, taking the lead. "Well," she stepped down another ledge. "It was legit scary. I mean there's not a lot of room for error."

"No," he said.

"You don't realize how much you count on your eyes until suddenly you can't see anything," Marianne said.

"But it was fun to play Marco Polo with M again," said Anna. "Been a while."

"I gotta say," Axel followed Anna down the ledge. "You both handled that exactly the way you should have. The only mistake we made was getting that separated in the first place."

"I'm not even sure that's a mistake," Marianne said. "Sometimes shit just happens."

"Mom's favorite phrase," he laughed.

"I wondered where I picked that up," Marianne said. "It's like it's always in the back of my mind. And very often applicable."

"I guess I got the potty-mouth gene from Mom," Anna said. "Though I'm not a scientist like you are."

"Definitely in the DNA," said Marianne. "Seventh chromosome."

They proceeded in silence for some minutes, following Anna's steps in the ever-adjusting rhythm of descending a rocky trail.

"She would love this," Marianne said.

"She would," Axel replied. "I think the last hike we did was Flattop in RMNP."

"These trails are way harder than any of the ones we've done in the Rockies," Anna said. "Compared to this, you could practically drive a golf cart down one of those."

"Yeah, it's not really accurate to call this walking," Marianne noted as she lowered herself between two boulders.

Axel followed. He could picture walking behind Su-Yun, Anna in the pack on her back, while he carried the exhausted Marianne. That must have been almost 20 years ago, maybe when they went to Zion. He smiled. "Do you remember that Flattop hike, M?"

"Yeah," she said. "I remember it being one of those endless drudgery ones."

"Probably so," he laughed. "There are a lot of those."

"So why the hell do we keep doing it?" Anna replied.

"Why do women keep having babies? Marianne countered.

"False equivalency, that's my fancy English-major term for that," said Anna. "I remember that hike, too, I think."

"You were pretty little," Axel said, "But I guess you might."

"Was there a burro down at the bottom?" she asked.

"There was," Marianne said. "Only time we ever saw one except at the Grand Canyon."

"I had forgotten that," Axel said, "but yeah, I think you're right. It was that same hike. The ranger said they were using the burro to haul some trail-work tools up because they didn't want to do a helicopter drop. I think you would have been four, almost five, Anna."

"And then the car crash was that winter?" Marianne asked.

"That's right. If Anna hadn't been in the back because she wanted to play with her beanie babies . . ."

"You always say that," said Anna.

"I know," Axel said.

"I still don't think it's fair," Marianne said. "Why did they get hit at all? It's too random, I can't handle it."

"I'll never be able to handle it," Axel said. "But I can be grateful that I have you two here right now." His mind went back to before the crash, to Anna's birth, to Marianne's—he smiled at recalling how both of them came out with shocks of black hair—then to the delightful (in a different way) years just with Su-Yun, to the unsettled time before Su-Yun, then back to a bicycle adventure with Ellie and the quest for Crombie Hill and battling with himself not to fall in love with her and losing. He winced.

Anna stopped in a brief flat place and stood off to the side. As Marianne began to walk past, her sister stuck out her arm and diverted her into a hug, which Axel joined a second later. The water continued to splash down the mountain, as it had since the glacier melted 10,000 years before.

54.

David set down the iPad next to his breakfast and called up the map. There were a few ways to get to the Monadnock summit, trails leading there from various entrances. On the theory that the most crowded routes would be the southern entrances, because those were nearer to Boston, he zeroed in on the Gilson Pond entrance, which would also be the closest one to their B&B. The up-and-back hike from there was supposed to be about 6 hours, so if they got there around 9:00, they could have lunch on the summit and get back down and still get over to the hotel in Bennington by late dinnertime. That timetable would require leaving here in about an hour.

He wasn't in bad physical condition, but he knew Ethan and Ellie were both in great shape and would probably like the longer hike from Gilson, compared to the shorter, 4-hour round-trip from the main park entrance a couple miles down the road. And he figured that strolling up this small mountain, barely over 3,000 feet, would be within his own fitness level as well. The walk would do Ellie good for sure. He could tell she was dealing with some stuff inside. Her novel characters always did that too—held stuff in, or thought they were holding it in—until either they sprung a leak or managed to bury it somehow until they were dead and it didn't matter.

Ellie walked in and David traced the driving route to the trailhead, then zoomed in on the hiking trails. "Looks good to me," she said. "A little steep there toward the top."

"If it's too much, I'll skip the summit and just camp out and have my lunch along the way, and you two can pick me up on the way back down," he said. "It's an up-and-back on the same trail."

"Where's Ethan?" she asked.

"I thought he was with you."

"Maybe he's out on that patio." She walked over to the window and pulled aside the curtain. "Nope."

"Well, let's give him ten minutes before sending out a search party," said David. "We need to leave pretty soon, but we're not late yet. Meanwhile, that gives me time to send a quick email."

Ellie filled a coffee and sat down to eat a muffin and some yogurt with fresh blueberries whose nonuniform appearance and intense flavor suggested a local source. "Did you have any of these berries?" She put the spoon down and stared into her coffee, her heart thumping.

"Yeah, delicious," he replied. "There, sent."

Ellie caught his hand. "David, I'm in trouble."

He scanned her face and nodded. "Was this a bad idea?"

"I don't know. Of course it was a bad idea. I feel like if this stuff was inside me, it probably would have come out anyway, but maybe not. Maybe it was safely sequestered and would have been contained beyond a human lifetime."

"So what's going on? Is it Axel, do you still—"

"I love him. I love you. I don't fucking know what to do. I'm such an idiot. Anybody could have predicted this would happen. I thought I was fine, everything was cool, and then I saw that gravestone and I just—I was back on the road again, riding by myself, mad at him for calling a pause, and crying my eyes out for having abandoned him so I could go look for this goddamn hill and these fucking ancestors, and then giving up on the whole thing because how could it possibly matter to anyone anyway? Why should it matter? It's gone. Past. You have to live forward."

"It's not surprising it would come back like that."

"What would come back like what?"

"That if you found yourself kind of transported to that time, that you would feel the way you did then."

"But that's the problem—I feel that way now. It's not back then."

"Well isn't you back then part of you now? Isn't everybody's life like that, all these tributaries that converge into your current life?"

"Good joke, 'current.' I see what you did there. You're not going to distract me with jokes, David."

"Accidental joke, but I'll take it."

"But maybe you're right, maybe I'm more re-living then than living now."

"To take the river analogy a bit further, your relationship with Axel in that time was a tributary that is a part of who you are now—like, say, my old relationship with Kat way back when is part of me now. But instead of that all being able to flow naturally and blend in with everything else leading up to now, it's as if a dam was erected and it's been containing that tributary except for a little spillway."

"Goddamn civil engineer."

"Thank you."

"And now that dam has collapsed or the gates were opened or whatever analogy you want to use, and all that stuff comes roaring down all at once."

"Yeah," said David. "It's overwhelming for a while, even dangerous, but eventually it flows through and the levels come back down and you look around and see if there's any damage you need to repair."

"How far are you going to carry this analogy?"

"From the source to the delta," he said. "I can't help it. So now you find yourself in a place where the River Ellie has doubled back on itself and it ends up really close to that old tributary, and you're startled by how close it is and the obvious question is whether to cut a channel between the two, except the only problem there is that water doesn't flow uphill, at least not for long. Any civil engineer could tell you that."

"Sure, I get it. Time flows downhill like water," Ellie said. "How poetic."

"Goddamn literature professor."

"And also that analogy doesn't make any sense with the dam and the floodgates thing," she offered. "I mean, you could be digging the channel from the river to the tributary, and meanwhile the dam lets loose and the flood goes by behind you and you don't even notice."

"Well, you're noticing this, sweetheart."

She sat up. "Thanks for trying to help, David, but this clusterfuck is my own creation. Mine and Axel's. I'm not sure if you can do anything."

"It's pretty intense." David paused and clutched her hand tighter. "I don't know what the right wise words are."

"There are no wise words," she said. "I fucked everything up. Twice now."

"It might be good material for a novel." He said the honest thing that popped into his head that also let him get a little distance from the emotion. But definitely not the right wise words, he thought as soon as they came out.

"Fuck you," she growled. Then she wiped a tear and said it again. "Fuck you David," and she started to laugh. Then she couldn't stop laughing and he put his arm around her and he couldn't stop laughing either. She leaned into him.

On the park bench behind the building, Ethan set down the Mount Monadnock coffee mug he'd gotten and filled up in the breakfast room and checked the phone again. The B&B's WiFi was squirrelly, but the cell signal out here seemed fine.

The women had not posted anything yesterday afternoon, but he hadn't checked after dinner. He had assumed they turned off the phones to save battery during their hike and he had meant to check later that day, but had fallen asleep instead. One thing was for sure, whenever he was done with this post-college interlude and got himself a real job, his daily schedule would be in for a shock. He took a picture of his coffee mug and posted it, #mountainfuel.

There was one new image, from moverachiever last night, showing three pairs of bare feet half-submerged in a stream, #aaaaaah. He checked to see if there had been any reaction to his question about the little white house, but it looked like annalog had not been back online yet. Maybe her phone had died and was still sitting on a charger. He pocketed his phone and walked around to the breakfast room to refill the coffee and get a bite.

Over Ellie's shoulder, David saw Ethan walk past the window. "Hey, there you are Ethan. You set to leave in a half-hour or so?"

"Sure. Just had to do my morning Instagram to appease my rabid fanbase."

Ellie stood up from her embrace with David, gave him a kiss, and started to leave. "All those screaming teenage girls. Want to use my bowl? Those blueberries are to die for. I'm going to go finish packing up."

"I'm packed," said Ethan. "Mostly because I didn't bring anything." He took the bowl and put it in the bus pan. "Just more coffee for me."

"They really are good," David said.

"What?" said Ethan.

"The blueberries. They're really good. Local I think."

Ethan spooned a handful into his palm and ate a couple. "No joke. Yum."

The entryway to the Gilson Pond parking area and their trailhead was across the road from a public beach on a lake. More than two of the people in the car considered an alternative scenario where instead of walking to the top of a nearby small mountain, they would instead spread out a few towels on said beach and sleep all morning. These private and unspoken visions, however, proved to be fleeting, and before they knew it, they were walking westward on the Birchtoft trail toward Mt. Monadnock.

The first section steadily climbed up a steady grade through piney woods, but soon enough it took the form of a typical New Hampshire trail: a steep incline of jumbled rocks a few feet wide. When said pathway emerged from the woods onto the fire-scoured summit ridge, the pathway became a sequence of paint blazes and cairns across the barren rock. David, as he had expected, moved at a more labored pace than his compatriots, but the day was cool and misty and he managed to clear the steepest portions and get onto the open ridge without overheating or running low on water. Ellie and Ethan, for their parts, moved at a moderate pace and stopped frequently to admire small plants and other highlights along the way.

Thus it was that the three of them arrived together at the summit of Mount Monadnock with its 360-degree views of the nearby mist, at a little after noon. They found a convenient vacant rock and unpacked their sandwiches. Approximately 250 other people had come up with the same idea, and so the atmosphere at the summit was somewhat like a college cafeteria, which is to say, something they were already used to. Ethan made his peanut butter-and-jelly into a smiley face and took a selfie with the smiley next to his own face. The signal was good up here, so he posted it, #frnds4ever.

55.

Anna zoomed in more on the image and gave a little nudge to Marianne. "Oh shit," she whispered and pointed up in the corner of the picture behind the bent sandwich, where two female figures with long black hair, one with a blue top and purple daypack, the other in a rust-colored top with a black pack, were seated on a rock, turned three-quarters away from the camera facing a man in a ball cap. "That's us. Like three fucking minutes ago."

Marianne slowly turned to look over her shoulder. "Damn, you're right. We gotta move." She scanned the scene for a vacant rock that would be out of sight, and spotted a small ledge about 30 feet away, near the trail where they had come up from the visitor center.

She stood up and motioned toward it. "Hey Dad. We're freezing. Let's go down there and get out of the wind." She started walking and Anna jumped up to follow.

Axel shrugged and walked down after his daughters. "I'm not sure this is a whole lot warmer," he said, sitting down beside Anna and facing back toward the summit. Plus, it wasn't actually cold up there in the first place."

"We must have gotten sweaty and chilled," Anna offered.

"Wow," Marianne said. "Look at that view over there." She pointed down the trail, away from the summit, into the mist.

"Inspiring," said Anna. "Wow. Nature."

Axel turned around. "Mmmm-hmmm. Hey, I'm sorry we came up here and it's all socked in, but it's still pretty."

"It's awesome," Anna said. "No shit. Just not your typical post card view, that's all. In fact, I'm gonna post a picture." She put her phone in panorama mode and stood up between Axel and the mountaintop and slowly stepped around one full circle.

"Don't you want to go to the top to do that?" he asked.

"No, it's all foggy, nothing to see far away. More interesting this way because you get some of the rocks and people and stuff." Anna waited for the camera to process the image, then posted it with the tag #mightaswellenjoytheview.

"Well, I'm going to go stand on the top before we head back down," said Axel, getting up. "You two can stay here in your warm cozy place for a couple minutes until I come back."

"No wait, we'll go with you," Marianne sprang up. "You're right, it's crazy not to go all the way up there. I mean we stood in line for Mount Washington, didn't we? At least all these people actually walked up here."

They boxed him in, one ahead, one behind. There was a dangerous ten seconds when they passed within 20 feet of Ethan and David and Ellie, who fortunately were facing away from them. When they got to the United States Geographical Survey's metal emblem marking the summit, Marianne positioned them so they were facing away from the clump of shrubs behind which the other party was seated. To keep her dad's attention directed in the safer direction, she enlisted a young man to take a family photo of the three of them. "Great day, huh?" the kid sarcastically commented.

"Beautiful," Axel said without irony. "Just a little bit subtle."

The boy returned Marianne's camera. "Hey, would you take one of us?"

"Of course," she said, and before she knew it a family of five were standing where they had been so Marianne could take the photo, and now she and Anna and their dad were facing the dangerous clump of shrubs. She could see that Ethan had stood up, but was still facing the other direction. "Thanks, gotta go, have a great one!" She handed the camera back to the presumed mom of the family, then quickly turned to walk down from the summit away from where Ethan was standing.

"Isn't this the wrong direction?" Axel asked.

"Oh yeah," said Anna. "Hey M, this is the wrong trail." We should head over that way." She pointed down and to the right, where it looked to her like a bank of rocks and bushes might mask them somewhat. Anna forged ahead, Axel behind her, Marianne following. "Here it is!" Anna announced. "Back down we go!" Anna and Marianne could not believe their good fortune at having managed to avoid actually encountering the other three, but they didn't know if those three might also be following back down the same path, so they made very good time all the way down to the car.

"I'm going to stop in here before we go," Axel said, ducking into one of the latrines at the trailhead.

"Good idea," Anna said, and both women went into the other.

Sound clearly traveled freely between the adjacent facilities, so they didn't talk. Marianne silently checked her phone while Anna peed, then they traded places. Anna then pointed out that a few random people had liked the panoramic photo, and so had ethanwylie. Uh-oh. She switched to the camera roll. The boy had taken two pictures of the three of them standing at the summit. The first one was framed a little better but it looked like her dad's eyes might be closed, so she zoomed in. Sure enough, eyes closed. She scrolled over to

the second one and that was great except that you could see
Ethan Wylie waving in the background. She posted that one,
#photobomb?

On the other side of a wooden wall, Axel stood in front of
the sink beside the urinal and slowly shook his head into the
mirror; finally he threw up his hands in a gesture of resignation and walked toward the door.

56.

The old wooden frame building that had housed Green Mountain Velo was no longer there, replaced by a newish brick and glass structure housing a bank on the first floor and medical offices above. Ellie hadn't had any luck trying to track down scruffy guy Steve or Kelly, mostly for lack of real or full names. The old shop phone number was now in the name of a private citizen. She knew it was a long shot that the store would still be there, especially since she couldn't find any mention of it on the internet and it didn't seem from the google satellite image or street view that it was still there, though she had no idea what the actual street address had been. Still, it seemed worth a quick detour through Brattleboro just to see. Though, if reconnecting with Axel was proving to be complicated, seeing Kelly again might be weird too. On the other hand, who cared now what two young women did or didn't do 30 years ago?

She double-checked the view, looking southward down the street where she had watched the morning sun lighting up the buildings decades earlier. "No, it's gone," she said. "Progress marches on. Let's go."

Ethan drove now, as they continued a rotation that had begun on the long trip up Interstate 81. "We go to Bennington, right?" he asked.

"Correct," David affirmed from the passenger seat. "Shouldn't be more than an hour to that hotel."

"Wait, pull over there!" Ellie called from the back seat. "Let's get a cookie." She was surprised that the country store was still there, on the south side of Route 9 just past I-91, and she couldn't resist the opportunity to compare today's cookie with the cookie of her memory. Ethan found a break in the oncoming traffic and darted into an open parking space right in front.

"Y'all want to drive or sit here and chow?" Ethan asked as they came back out.

"Plenty of time," David replied. "Let's sit. Okay with you El?"

She nodded, mouth full of oatmeal cookie. They took one of the tables out front and looked back down the hill over Brattleboro. The river was just visible in one or two places. "Well, that's as far as Axel got, way back when," she said.

"You okay?" David asked.

"Yeah, a little nostalgic," she said. "To have the freedom to just take off and do a trip like that. No house, no job, just go."

He nodded. "That's all the stuff we set out to acquire, then once we have it, it's like, okay, now what?"

Ellie sipped her tall iced tea. "I wouldn't trade it, though. I mean, look, we're able to just up and take this trip—even with the house and jobs and everything."

"And a kid," Ethan added.

"Oh yeah, that too," she laughed. "He's low-maintenance, though. And also not a kid anymore."

"Is that bike still around—does Grandma have it?" Ethan asked. "The International?"

"It's probably in their basement. Was last time I saw it."

"Sweet. I don't remember ever seeing that. When we get to Ohio I'm going to look."

"You can also just go visit them yourself, you know," David said.

"True dat," said Ethan.

"I'm not sure which cookie is better," Ellie said, breaking the last portion into bites for the other two. "Recent memory cookie or long-term memory cookie."

"What was that dude like?" Ethan asked.

"What dude, Axel?" Ellie replied.

"Yeah, if it's not too awkward."

"It's awkward but not too awkward," she laughed, bracing herself internally. "Everybody's a grown-up here."

"I'm not," said David in a mock English accent.

"Except for him," Ellie added.

"Right, I knew that," said Ethan.

"Well, I wouldn't have ridden bikes all that way with somebody who wasn't a good person," she said. "And I got to care about him a lot. It was mutual. You'd like him. In fact, you're a bit like him in some ways, not just the bike thing."

"Yeah, how so?"

"The march to your own beat thing. It turned out he never finished college, for one thing, and yet over the years he managed to build up this interesting career. I don't know if getting off the conventional path was intentional or just forced by circumstances, but for him it worked out."

"So is that like you saying it's cool with you if I kinda wing it for a while?"

"You're doing it anyway," David replied with a chuckle.

"But seriously," Ellie said, "he knows tons about bike racing and he knows the business and a lot of the science that's going on, and he'd be a natural sort of person for you to talk to if you were interested in learning more about that world career-wise."

"Not just as a racer," David said. "As a designer too."

"Huh," said Ethan.

"The ginger cookie is really good," said David, handing a piece each to Ellie and Ethan.

"The chocolate chip is gone," said Ethan. "Sorry."

"That's okay, we got two," David said, breaking the final cookie into three. Ellie seemed to him a little more peaceful, gazing out over the valley as she chewed. Caught his eye and smiled.

The afternoon sun was peeking through the thinning clouds now, and the patio was blissfully warm. Ethan slid his chair back to rest on the painted wall of the store and checked his phone. Among the new Instagram posts was one from annalog just minutes earlier, tagged #somebodyelsesancestor.

Emma Balch Crombie

1775–1817

Baby boy

d. 1817

The angle of the light on the stone was different from when he had taken his photo yesterday morning, this time brightening the inside edges of the carved letters with a warm afternoon glow that added an air of melancholy. As if it needed any more of that.

57.

Rob Orford cleared off the kitchen table and stacked the blankets at one end of the couch. He wiped down the grubby woodwork where the dogs brushed against the white paint. It would be great to see Axel again. Twenty years, maybe more, since they'd hung out at least once a year when Ax was in town to do the Putney road race or Stowe or Killington or Sunapee or something else nearby, and would stay with him, and then they'd see each other even more frequently when Axel was starting out as a sales rep for Nara Tech Imports. He'd met the older daughter once, when she was a toddler and the other one wasn't born yet, and he'd always liked Su-Yun. What a tragedy that was. Poor guy. Poor everybody. It was the least he could do to put them up, for old times' sake.

But Axel had sounded great on the phone a few weeks ago and seemed to have everything together. Life goes on. As they had arranged, Axel had sent a text when they got to the river, and they ought to be rolling up any minute now. Rob laughed at the old days when he had needed to give detailed and counterintuitive directions to find this out-of-the way house the first time Axel had stayed over, where now you could just plug in the address and your phone or your car would guide you to the spot. He heard tires on the gravel drive.

"Hey Axel, you're looking so shiny!" Rob stepped down off the front porch.

Anna and Marianna followed behind their dad. "Steve!" Axel called out. "You're looking scruffy!"

They embraced.

"Rob," Axel said, "This is Marianne, who you met when she was little, and Anna."

Rob extended his hand. "Rob Orford. Come on in. You got bags?"

"We'll get them later," Axel said. "Here, I smuggled some beer across state lines."

"What's this?" Rob held up the six-pack.

"I don't know. Grabbed it over by North Conway. It said Tuckerman on it."

"It's probably warm enough to sit on the porch if you want," Rob said. "So have a seat and I'll get you all something to drink. Beer? Wine? I got a couple sodas, too, and of course water."

"A beer sounds great," Marianne said.

"I'm not 21," Anna said.

"Private home," Rob said. "Have what you want."

"Beer for me, too, then," said Anna.

"Me three," said Axel.

"You want one of these Tuckerman deals or the Vermont equivalent?"

"Vermont," said Axel. Anna and Marianne nodded.

"Back shortly," Rob said.

"So that's the bike store Steve from the story?" Marianne asked.

"Yeah," said Axel. "His name isn't really Steve."

"I got that."

"Funny how a name will stick, huh M?" Anna said.

Rob came back out with a bowl of pretzels, then four beer bottles.

"Where's the other Steve?" Anna asked.

"I sent Kelly a note. She moved back to Maine a long time ago, then I think out west someplace and got married, then they all came back to Maine and we reconnected. Living over in Yarmouth, with three kids, I think, probably high school/college age. Long story short, she sends her regrets and best wishes."

"No kidding, married with kids? That's a transformation," Axel said. "I figured redhead woman Steve was long gone. It also occurs to me just now that I should have sent your contact information on to Ellie in case she's ever up this way. Although she may have gotten it back when."

"No, haven't heard from her. As you know, the shop closed a couple years later because the bank owned the property and wanted to build there, and probably all Ellie had was the shop card since that had the phone number. Just calling Brattleboro and asking for Steve probably wouldn't work, even with the redhead description. Though this is a pretty small town. And I wouldn't have put it past Kelly to try to track her down. She kinda had a thing for Ellie. More than kinda. The morning after that day we put you on the train and the ladies rode off together, Kelly rode into work in the same bike duds she had on the day before, changed into civilian attire here. I didn't pry. Guess she got over Ellie eventually, though!"

"I remember the shop closing, "Axel said. "You still doing okay selling real estate?"

"It's up and down, of course, but yeah. Endless supply of New Yorkers who want the quiet life, so they come up here and make it noisy. And how's Boulder?"

"I think it was a good place for the girls to grow up. It's a good home base, lots of fun stuff to do outside and the Denver airport gives good access around the country. Works great for my job."

"Which is?"

"More or less evolved from when I joined Nara Tech. There was a design and engineering spinoff and that merged with this Boulder company to create 1357, and that's who I work for now. I manage a lot of product testing in different environments around the country, different kinds of riders. Try to get a sense of what people will be aspiring to do two years from now and have a product ready to lead them into that."

"So, what's that now?"

"Trade secret, man."

"I'm not in the biz anymore."

"Gravel bikes that are really just road racing bikes with disk brakes and lots of clearance for fat tires. Plus indoor training intersecting role playing games and social media. And e-bikes."

"Okay, I won't tell anybody," Rob gestured sealing his lips. "And now, speaking of the future, you're backwards-tracing your bike ride from 30 years ago?"

"It's really just a way to show my daughters a bit of New England. We did a one-day Mount Washington crossover yesterday, then a quick run up Monadnock today."

"Nice. Been busy."

"Also, my dad is getting ready to sell his house south of Cleveland and move out to Boulder, so we're going to drive out there, give him a hand moving stuff around for a day or two, then fly back home. We haven't visited him there for a long time."

"And retrace the old bike ride along the way."

"Yeah, more or less."

"Paint by numbers," Rob said.

"Or connect the dots," Axel replied. "Anyway, it's great of you to put us up. I was hoping just to say hi, have dinner or get a drink."

"My pleasure. I think the last time I saw you was before you moved out west, you and Su-Yun and your older daughter here."

"Marianne," said Marianne. "Thanks for the beer. Hits the spot."

"Sure thing. You ladies are both so much an interesting mix of your mom and dad, though you look a little more like him and your sister a little more like your mom," Rob said to Marianne.

"But they say M's personality is like mom and I'm more like dad," said Anna.

"Mysteries of genetics," said Marianne.

"Or not," said Anna.

"Now you're channeling you mother," said Axel.

"She was a lovely person," Rob said. "Glad I knew her at least a little bit."

"Thanks," Anna said. "It's nice to hear that."

"In the early days before Su-Yun, I used to have to convince your dad to sleep in the house. He was so used to sleeping in the car."

"With his bike?" Marianne asked.

"Yep. All he wanted was to have a shower and use the bathroom."

"Damn, that's hard core," said Anna.

"I have more civilized habits now," Axel said.

"Although that's pretty much what they did riding in those wagons to get out west, right?" said Marianne.

"Maybe that's where I got the idea," Axel said. "Also, I already had the station wagon, and I was not interested in living with either of my parents, and I was broke."

"How did you live, what did you eat?" Marianne asked.

"If you got on a team with some sponsorship, that could keep you in good shape equipment-wise and clothing-wise, and they would help a little with travel expenses. If the team was reasonably successful, you'd split all the winnings, and then some of the teams had a couple riders who had access to some what you might call philanthropic support—which is to say mom and dad might throw a little money at the project to help the riders buy food and maybe a cheap hotel every couple days so you could get cleaned up. Then if you sleep on people's floors and in your car, and figure out some way to make a little money over the winter, you could survive for a while. Saying you're a pro bike racer sounds glamorous as long as you don't have to release the tax returns and everybody sees that because of all the in-kind compensation you actually made seven thousand dollars in reportable income over four years."

"Oh, harsh," Anna said.

"On the other hand," Axel continued, "those years are what gave me the base of experience and the connections to start doing what I'm still doing now, so another way to look at it was that it was like four years of graduate school and at the end of it I didn't have any debt."

"That's a close-to-the-bone life, though," Rob said. "You can do it when you're 25 but not much beyond that."

"One time," Axel said, "I faked a crash in a race because you'd have medical insurance through the cycling federation to cover you if you had to go to the hospital because of something that happened during a sanctioned race. I didn't have any insurance of my own at the time, and I took a spill while I was out training on a Thursday and I was pretty sure I broke my wrist, but I didn't want to go to the doctor without insurance. So, I toughed it out for two days until Saturday—fortunately it was cold so I could wear long sleeves and nobody would see my black-and-blue arm. I took a little soft fall about ten minutes in, then went around to the medical tent and they said I should get a ride to the hospital unless I wanted to use the ambulance, but that might not be covered by the insurance for an injury like this, so I got the official insurance certificate from the medical tent and drove myself to the hospital one-handed just like I had driven to the race in the first place, and they asked me if I had just done this or if it happened earlier, and I said I fell a couple days ago and thought it was okay, but then I fell again today and made it worse, and they looked at me kind of sideways, but then they x-rayed it and confirmed a fracture and soft-splinted it and told me to take it easy. So, I didn't race the next weekend, but the one after that was just a time trial, and those are pretty safe."

"So," Marianne said, "do as I say, not as I do, pretty much."

"Pretty much," Axel said. "And anyway, you're both on my insurance to age 26."

"What, so you don't trust us to make it on our own like you did?" Marianne replied.

"Uh, let's just say I don't want to you have to be as lucky as I was to get away with that." He paused. "But yes, you should make it on your own. You have so far."

"Not really. You paid for college."

"You earned lots of scholarships and grants and also worked side jobs, and you chose to go to a state school so you wouldn't get buried in debt. I just did the regular stuff every parent signs up for."

"I don't know, Dad," Anna chimed in, "M has all these super-employable science credentials, but I'm just a shitty English major who does some sports."

"I'm not worried about you," Axel said.

"Well, I am," said Anna. "What am I going to do?"

"You have that versatile liberal arts education. You'll be fine," Axel said. "You can analyze and communicate."

"This coming from the guy who didn't finish college," Anna replied.

"Look," he paused. "My life was pretty much in chaos at that time, with my parents splitting up and me not even sure what to study. It's not like there's only one good pathway for each person. Things could have turned out a lot of different ways given different circumstances—even slightly different circumstances."

"So it's just luck?" Anna pressed. "I thought you said we shouldn't count on good luck."

"There's a lot of luck," he said. "Good luck and bad luck. And also just randomness. But if I can fall back on a lame bike racing analogy, if you try to put yourself in position to minimize the potential impact of bad luck, and be ready to capitalize on good luck, and to improvise based on all the random shit that happens, and be there to help your friends, then that all adds up to better odds that you'll do alright."

"I'm going to step away from the motivational speech and order some pizza," Rob said.

58.

"Okay, see that house there on the left with the lot in front? Pull in there," Ellie pointed. She noticed that her arm was trembling. Did anyone else see that? Come on Ellie, get it together.

David slowed the car and turned into the empty gravel parking lot. About half of the paint had peeled from the building. Adjacent and leading slightly up the hill to the left was the paved serpentine track, long-neglected. Grass grew high around it and weeds had forced their way through cracks in the pavement. Saplings and a few medium-sized trees were filling in from the edges of the former open field.

"Wow," said Ellie. "Well, they stopped running the track in 1997, I think that's what Mikko said."

David looked back toward the road. "Another 20 years you'll be driving by some young woods and not even know anything was ever here."

"Can we go check it out?" Ethan opened the door.

"He said it would be fine to do that," said Ellie.

They opened the doors and got out. Ellie glanced to the right as they walked past the building. The patio was still there, tables and chairs pushed up against the back wall under the overhang, a tarp draped over them and weighted down with a few rocks. A path still led into the woods up to the right. They continued up the hill to the left. Three deer leapt up from the tall grass and bounded off toward the sapling woods as they approached. The air was dead still, and hot, and full of grasshopper sounds. Ellie checked her watch. It was about 12:30. Breathe steady.

Ethan located the start/finish straightaway and looked ahead and behind. "Not much room for a wind-up." He began walking along the track in the slightly uphill direction. Ellie and David followed. The pavement jogged a little bit to the right and Ethan cut right up against the right edge, setting up for the big left-hand hairpin. A minute later, he began the turn, angling across the track toward the inside of the curve, but not all the way in because with the banking of the track it would be possible to carry a lot of speed right down the middle without getting thrown to the outside. He kicked a branch out of the way just at the apex and began walking back down.

Ellie and David followed along the whole way. When they came to the dodgy place in the track where she and Axel had both bobbled, it came back to her and she called ahead. "Watch it here."

Ethan nodded. "A little whoop-de-do." Safely past that danger spot, they successfully navigated the rest of the turns and came back onto the finishing straight. "One-two-three, all on the podium!" Ethan yelled and thrust both arms into the air.

Ellie stepped beside him. "Almost got you at the line."

David stopped the timer on his phone. "Eight minutes and twenty-four seconds. A new track record!"

"For slowest," said Ellie. The exertion and deep breathing had calmed her down a little bit. She turned and looked back down toward the road. A tractor pulling a wagon loaded with hay bales rolled by. "Want to do another lap and see if we can beat it?"

This time she led the way, taking a higher line on the big hairpin. "This way you can really swoop down."

"But it's slower," Ethan said.

"Right, we're trying to break the record," said Ellie.

Ethan made a show of trying to catch Ellie at the finish line, bumped her shoulder, then did a slow-motion summersault. "Boom!"

David swerved around the crash and checked the stopwatch. "Eight thirty-nine!"

"Woo-hoo!" Ethan suggested that his mom re-enact her victory salute for his Instagram feed. He showed her the image for her review before he posted it. Disheveled hair, sporty sunglasses, big smile, raised arms with flexed biceps and pit stains in her maroon t-shirt. It looked legit. Approved. #finishline!

Another car appeared on the road below, downshifting as it slowed and pulled into the lot. Ellie began walking down and raised her hand. The slim figure that emerged from the car returned the wave and began walking toward them, limping slightly. David and Ethan followed Ellie. "Mikko!" she called.

"Doctor Webster!" he replied.

"You really didn't have to come all the way up here," Ellie said as they embraced. "So nice of you. This is my husband David, and our son Ethan." They shook hands.

"It is very good to meet you in person. Ellie has told me about you every time we would see each other."

"So, are you officially retired now?" Ellie asked.

"I suppose so. Let us say I am on a glide path to full retirement, teaching one or two classes fall semester only for the past three years," he motioned them over toward the patio. "I gave up tenure, but it's a good arrangement for me."

"How is Pekka?"

"He is still in the Russian prison recovering from the incident with the nerve agent," Mikko replied, shaking his head resignedly.

"Whoa," Ethan said.

"They are still mad at him for smuggling all those defectors?" Ellie asked.

"No, I think it was the Boris and Natasha video."

"Sad." Ellie replied.

Ethan smiled, now that he remembered his mom's account of the running joke the two Finns had about being pursued by the Russians.

Mikko caught Ethan's smile. "They are still quite well, running the small hotel in Kuopio. I just visited last summer. We went kayaking, drank too much beer with too much tax on it!"

"Have they let her become a citizen yet?"

"She is working through the bureaucratic process. Maybe another 20 or 30 years."

"Hasn't it already been 20 years?" Ellie followed Mikko's lead and began removing rocks from the tarp. The four of them pulled the two tables out and positioned all the chairs.

"They have been back there for 20 years, but I don't think she began the citizenship process until perhaps 12 years ago," he said. "So it's moving quite briskly."

"I'll get the sandwiches," David said.

"You can put them in the refrigerator with the beer," Mikko said. He unlocked the back door. "I will start the fire."

"Fire?" Ethan asked.

"You could go with him and help with the wood maybe," Ellie said.

Ethan shrugged and followed Mikko up the path into the woods.

"I have not been here since the spring," Mikko said. "It's harder to get a group together without Pekka here, and I am not coming by myself. I put a small electric sauna in my house near the college, and that serves my needs." He crested the hill and walked down toward the lake and the wooden building beside it. "But there is nothing like the outdoor wood-fired sauna with a natural lake." He and Ethan removed a dozen logs from the pile behind the building and Mikko stacked five or six in a metal-lined cavity built into the building, directly under the metal chimney. He retrieved some matches and a couple of wax fire starters from behind a small wooden door and soon a fire was crackling along vigorously. He put two more logs on, then walked up onto the little porch and opened the door and looked around.

"No birds, no snakes, not too many bugs," said Mikko. "Good." He grabbed a broom from the corner and opened the door to the next room, quickly sweeping it out and reclosing the door. Then he swept the foyer. "Now after sweeping, no more shoes inside. Would you please take this bucket and fill with water from the lake?"

Ethan walked down the dock and dunked the bucket. When he returned to the porch, Mikko thanked him and handed him another empty bucket. "And this one as well, thank you."

Ellie and David appeared on the pathway, Ellie in a black one-piece swimsuit, David wearing plaid board shorts. Ethan carried the second bucket onto the porch, where Mikko took it from him. "And two more logs on the fire, if you please, then everyone can take shoes off and come in."

"Um," Ethan said, "it seems like y'all already had a plan here."

"Very astute," said Ellie. "You can run and grab your bathing suit if you want. That's not the official way, but I brought mine."

"Me too," David said.

"Okay, thank God," Ethan replied. "I'll be back in a few."

59.

Anna reached her phone up from the back seat to Marianne's right so she could see the post from ethanwylie. Marianne shrugged and handed it back. There was nothing much to suggest where it had been taken, so Anna zoomed in on the corners to look for any clues in the background. Grass, trees, a little bit of what looked like an overgrown parking lot or something. That was definitely Ethan's mom Ellie, though. He had her tangly not-quite-blond hair and the quick-tanning skin. She wondered what his voice sounded like. They'd all passed so close together yesterday, maybe she even heard it without knowing. Though that had been a big crowd up there, lots of voices.

The terrain outside was a series of broad valleys and ridges. The car would climb one, reveal the view of the next valley, then coast down to the bottom before beginning the next ascent. It had been this kind of patchwork of woods and fields since they'd left Albany and then Schenectady behind. It was a greener, gentler landscape than Colorado, where those brown tumbleweed plains just sort of tilted steadily up to the west across half the state until they ran into the first mountains, the Front Range, where Boulder was. She imagined what it would be like if you had started out here, rolled through this welcoming countryside, then kept going west as the green gradually turned yellow and pale and dry, crossed a couple huge rivers and then at some point spotted those first peaks rising up on the horizon. When you got closer and looked up at those daunting mountains from just below them, maybe you'd say, hey, maybe we ought to stop right here. Let's call it Boulder, because I see one over there.

She felt the car slowing and she looked ahead. They were turning into a gravel lot where two cars were already parked, and beside one of them, Ethan Wylie had turned to see who was pulling in. Axel stopped the car and climbed out. "Hi, Ethan right?"

"Uh, yeah," Ethan replied. " . . . what's up?"

"Sauna reservation. Everybody here?"

"Everybody?"

"Your parents and Mikko."

"Yeah." Ethan dropped the black running shorts he'd use for a bathing suit and bent down to pick them up.

"Hey," Axel said, "so this is Marianne in the front seat, and Anna in the back. They're getting their suits and joining us."

"Hi," Ethan said, leaning down to car-window level.

Axel retrieved his suit from the back. "David just texted me and said they're just going in now. You can change either there at the sauna or inside the house. Back door's open. I'm gonna change and I'll come back and lock the car when you guys are all out of there." He walked off toward the house.

Anna closed the back door. "I think maybe we been punked."

"It would seem so," Marianne said.

"You know what?" Anna said. "Dad kept insisting we bring bathing suits even though this was a hiking trip and there was no reason to bring a bathing suit. Those fuckers planned this thing all along."

"And pretended like they didn't know we were all in New Hampshire, right?" Ethan said.

"Right," said Anna, and started laughing. Ethan was adorable. She got flustered. "Geez. Now, where's my suit? Dad of course already had his where he could grab it easily."

"Can you get mine while you're there?" Marianne asked. "I think it's in the side compartment of that black duffel. My pink and purple reversible one-piece."

Axel returned in his red swim trunks as Anna was closing the back. "One more thing." He grabbed a cooler bag. "Okay, let's go." He beeped the car lock.

As they walked past the house, Ethan veered across the patio in back. "Gotta pee. I'll catch up to y'all."

"So you leave your shoes on the porch," Axel said. "Come inside and take off your street clothes, then wipe down using this bucket over here and put on your suit, then grab a couple towels and come in the sauna room and close the door fast so the heat doesn't get out. See you in a minute." He finished wiping himself down and ducked through the door into a cloud of steam. "Hi Ellie," they heard him say, "Mikko. And you must be David, great to meet in person." The door closed.

Aware that Ethan would be arriving soon, they removed their street clothes quickly, wiped down, and grabbed towels. Marianne pulled on her suit with the purple side out, then opened the door and stepped into the steam. Anna looked again to confirm that in each of her hands was a stylish black bikini top. The two equally stylish bottoms, therefore, were in a drawer back in Colorado. She draped a towel over her front and leaned in after Marianne.

"Welcome," Mikko said. "Mikko Toivonen. You will be Marianne and Anna, I think?"

"Hi," said Marianne and Anna in near unison.

"Which one is who? Where is the young man? This is his fire."

"I'm Marianne, that's Anna," Marianne said. "The young man will be right in."

"Um," said Anna, raising her hands to show the two bikini tops while holding the towel under her chin. "This is what happens when you pack in the dark. So, uh . . ."

Marianne took a moment to grasp Anna's predicament, then laughed. "Just grab us a few more towels." Anna blinked at her uncomprehendingly, but turned to retrieve more towels and handed them in. "Look," Marianne said, "it's just like at the gym. Sit on one towel, cover up with a couple more towels. It's not like you're going to wear a swimsuit in the shower anyway. Come on, have a seat, sister solidarity."

Anna shrugged and closed the door. She reappeared fully swathed about 20 seconds later. "Um, Ethan is here now."

Marianne slid the straps off her shoulders, wrapped the towel around, stepped out of her suit without undoing the towel, and took a seat. "Hi," she said, turning around, "you must be Ellie and David."

Seated on the middle tier next to David, Ellie had been leaning back with her eyes closed, in her mind disappearing into the steam as she steadied her breathing, tried to imagine and yet not think about how this all would go. "Yes, right, I'm sorry," she said as she opened her eyes. "Nice to meet you . . ."

"Marianne," she reached her hand back and Ellie grasped it. "Heard a lot about you."

"Really?" said Ellie.

"Well, kind of . . . I feel like I know you a bit from reading your thing. And I went and found one of your novels."

"Oh damn," Ellie said. "Well, thank you, I think. Sorry, I feel kind of awkward."

"Don't," said Marianne. "We're all cool with it."

"All?" said Ellie. "You all read it?"

Anna and Marianne nodded.

"Can I just disappear?" Ellie asked.

"I have never read this thing," said Mikko. "What are they talking about?"

"Okay, if I can't disappear, how about get me a beer?"

Mikko opened a cooler and handed a can back, opening it first. "It's embarrassing?"

"Yes," said Ellie. "It is. I wrote an account of our bike ride—Axel's and mine—and it goes into some . . . uncomfortable details in our current context."

"Ah," said Mikko. "Well I hope it is no surprise to anyone, but Pekka and I, we could tell you two were . . ."

"I know, I know," Ellie broke in. "I know."

"But it was beautiful," said Mikko. "And everything looks beautiful now. So just let it be."

"We just," she paused. "It just never got resolved. Part of me is stuck back there and I didn't know it. It snuck up on me. Just like the first time. I'm focused ahead and I don't know what's coming up on me."

"I'm sorry," said Axel. "I never should have contacted you in the first place."

"It's my own fault," said Ellie.

"No it isn't," said Axel. "Why is anything your fault? If anything it's my fault."

"Excuse me," said David. "As an interested party here, might I suggest that fault isn't the issue, if there is any fault at all. The issue is you two have a little bit of business from 30 years ago that you never wrapped up, and I'm confident that as two fine and decent people, both demonstrably functioning adults, you could probably figure it out. We just need to give you a little time together to do that." He stood up. "Let's give them some privacy."

"David, no," Ellie said. "You don't have to do this."

"I know," he said. "See you in a bit."

"Ten minutes," said Axel. "Thank you."

Mikko stood at the door, "You know, I probably told you before. The sauna is where all the problems of the world are solved."

"Yes, I remember," said Axel. "I hope you're right, because we don't have bicycles in here."

Ethan put the phone among his clothes, picked up two towels, and opened the door. "Wooo," he said, just as everyone but Axel and Ellie filed out the door. "Well," said Ethan. "Let me guess—I follow them?"

Ellie looked up, crying, and nodded.

Ethan paused. "Really? You good Mom?"

She waved him off. "Yes. Please."

The door to the dock closed behind Ethan.

"Well," said Axel.

"Yeah," said Ellie.

Outside, Ethan arrived where the others had paused near the ladder and gestured behind him with his thumb. "Y'all sure that's a good idea?"

"No," said David. "You got a better one?"

The few seconds that followed were audibly marked only by faint distant bird calls and insects buzzing.

"Best idea," Mikko said finally, "is swim. Get in while still warm from the sauna. Clean the pores." He folded his towel and stepped off the dock into the water. Resurfacing, he motioned to David and Ethan. "Just look away, ladies can get in."

David and Ethan looked up at the sky while Marianne and Anna jumped in. The three in the water looked up at the two men. "I don't know why we bothered with that, Ethan already saw my naked ass anyway," Anna said. "Right?"

Ethan nodded. "Cannot tell a lie," he said. "So y'all's turn to turn around now." They did, and Ethan removed his trunks and jumped in.

"And what am I supposed to do?" David called after them.

"Whatever you like," said Mikko. "But get in."

David kept his trunks on and climbed down the ladder.

"So the deal is," said Ellie. "The deal is that I love you. I never said it, and now I'm saying it, and it's a fucking disaster."

"Could be," said Axel. "I never told you either, but I did. Do."

"Do what"?

"Love you, Ellie. There, I said it too. Thirty years late."

"What does that mean?" Ellie looked over. "I love you?"

"Well, they're not going to come back in here and find us fucking."

"No," she laughed. "They're not."

"So that's a start," he said.

"What will they find us doing?"

"Not fucking."

She smiled and shrugged. "Why not?"

"Well, besides the obvious reason that it would be ridiculous and we're 50 instead of 20," he paused. "Maybe just respect? For all of them, for each other, for ourselves. Plus there's more than one flavor of love, right?"

"Meaning what? Fifty-year olds have sex."

"Meaning if we were lovers thirty years ago and we didn't even know or admit we were in love, then we could love each other thirty years later and not be lovers."

"That sounds dangerous, don't you think?"

"What isn't dangerous?" he replied.

"Why haven't you remarried, found someone else?"

"I guess that follows."

"Yes, it does."

"I just haven't. No real intention about it. Busy with work and the girls. No longer girls."

"Somebody deserves you. It's not fair for no one to have you."

"Not fair?"

"To the world, the universe. To you."

"That's nice of you to say. Really. But I just left you cold out there. I had what I thought were good reasons but now I'm inclined to think it was mostly just fear of future rejection."

"Did you think, when you found that manuscript and read it, that I might still be out there, unattached?"

"The thought crossed my mind. But then—it wasn't that it would have been too much to ask, but that it wouldn't have been you. You weren't going to wait around."

"But I did. For a long time."

"Damn, I'm so sorry Ellie. I was just blind."

"I'm not mad. I never was. Well, I was for a while—mad at you for unilaterally deciding to break it off. But also mad at myself for not accompanying you back, just as a friend. I abandoned my best friend. Anyway, there was a while there after that trip—a couple years—when I just wasn't interested."

"While I was feeling the same."

"You know what Kelly said?" Ellie stood up and ladled some more water onto the coals.

"What?"

"That it was a hero thing."

"A hero thing?"

"When I finally told her that you and I had split and explained the circumstances, she said it sounded like you were trying to set it up so you were the bad guy so I wouldn't have to leave you later when I realized you would never be my intellectual peer, and that way I wouldn't have the guilt of being the one who left you, and you could take all the pain and guilt on yourself so I wouldn't have to feel any."

He started at her for a second. "Sounds ridiculous, but she wasn't too far off. Part arrogant, part naive. What a winning combo." He shook his head. "The hero thing. When did she tell you that?"

"Night after I put you on that train."

"Don't know how, but she sure read that situation. Maybe she'd seen it before. So she ended up with you that night?"

"Oh," Ellie paused. "Yeah, well, I was feeling sad and vulnerable and she offered to stay with me, so . . ."

"You kind of left that out of your story."

"No, it's not even in the notes, really, I realized. I mean I kind of hinted at it. And it's there in the official version, just in, shall we say, metaphorical language. It seemed important somehow but I was torn between disclosing it and being discreet, so I went into full creative-writing mode. You could call that arrogant and naive as well. Maybe that comes with being

20. I felt incredibly guilty about it—not what we did, but the feeling that I was doing it for the wrong reasons—personal weakness, or a kind of rebound after splitting with you, or being mad at you, or missing you, or even just so I'd be assured of a place to sleep the next night. All of it mixed up together. You were gone and here was someone who wanted me in what seemed like a very uncomplicated way. It wasn't fair to her. What if she really had feelings?"

"Yeah, that could hurt," he said.

"Anyway," Ellie said, "how do we go forward from here? I'm not going to bail out this time."

He nodded and looked up. "Well, think about a month or two ago. Things were cool, right? To me, things are cooler now. We got a chance to fix a few old wounds. Maybe open them first and that's a lot to deal with, but then begin to heal them. That has to be a good thing. So how about we just go on with our lives? This doesn't have to stop everything."

"You mean it's like there are all these tributaries that flow into our lives, and this one happened to have been dammed up for a long time and then everything got released all at once and it's really intense but after a while things will settle down again and we'll realize that we can just go on, that it's okay, that everybody's life is like this?"

"I hadn't thought of it that way, but . . . " he paused. "Let me tell you about Su-Yun. Would that be okay?"

She caught her breath and looked up at him wide-eyed. "Yes. Yes, of course."

"First of all," he said, smiling, "you would have loved her. Maybe in a slightly competitive way. Not because of both having a connection to me, but because you're both just kind of like that. Always pushing a bit. Other people, they just have to deal with that. That's just what bulldozers do. Me, I'm not so much a bulldoze-my-own-path kind of person, but rather look around and evaluate the situation and always be ready and know when to chill and when to put the hammer down. So we were a good match in that way.

"When she was pregnant with Marianne, she wasn't going to take any drugs, or go into any hospitals. It was just going to be her and her baby and me, making our own way. You're probably expecting me to say that the pregnancy ran into complications and she had to give up on that fantasy, but the funny thing is, no—we were living in a little cottage out in the woods, and we got her into the bathtub and she delivered M just fine and I cleaned her up and cut the cord and then the next day (because it was at about 3:00 in the morning), the next day after the sun came up we called her folks and everybody and they all said Oh wonderful, what room is she in at what hospital, and I'd say 'She's in the kitchen. Come on over.' So we got to show everybody. And M was such a beautiful baby. I know I'm biased, but she just had this kind of inner calm that radiated out through her beautiful skin. Still has it. Look at her for a few minutes when you get a chance. It's a glow.

"Anna, on the other hand, she was always moving, walked very early, always trying to catch up to Marianne and pretty soon she did, but partially because M was fine with being caught. She just never cared about that, whereas Anna always wanted to win every race. By that time Su-Yun had made her point about how she was going to have her baby and nobody was going to tell her otherwise, and Anna ended up being just a regular birth in a hospital. We'd moved by then, out west to Boulder, so maybe that was part of the difference, too. People came by the kitchen and I had to tell them she was in the hospital and they would look all worried.

"What was a little tough, ironically, was when M began to send signals about what would become her sexual preference. This was maybe when she was 7 or 8, not long before Su-Yun died. I would say something like, 'You know, I wonder if she likes girls, I mean will grow up to be attracted to other women,' and Su-Yun would just shut out that idea. 'No, I don't think so.' I think she was scared not of homosexuality, but that her daughter would feel pain. As if you can keep your kids from feeling pain. We found that out in a very intense way not too much later."

"I'm so sorry," said Ellie. "If anything I could say would make it better . . ."

"Thank you," said Axel. "It hurts like a motherfucker, I'll tell you that. And no matter what you do, you can't make it right. It's real and there forever. But the thing is, it's not the slightest bit unusual as a human experience. I mean just wander through a cemetery from a hundred or two hundred years ago and see how many died so young—moms, dads, and so many kids. Well, you know that just from trying to find those Crombies. People used to lose the people close to them all the time. I mean *all* the time. Even the commonplace can be almost unbearable. But if humans teach you anything, it's that it's amazing what ends up being bearable."

"How did you all get through it?"

"It's not something you really put behind you—I mean people talk about loss that way and you can try to think of it that way so you can get on with things, but it's not really behind you. It's still there. On the other hand, as your life goes on, that certainly won't be the only loss you experience, and it certainly doesn't weigh down the joys, the satisfaction of accomplishing things or even just living day-to-day in a manner that seems worthy of the privilege of being a human being. So you say, 'okay, that's part of me too,' and you keep going. Because there's so much to do, and the person you lost would want you to do it. Does that make any sense?"

"Of course. I mean especially because her death does not seem—I don't mean to be callous—but it does not seem to be the one defining event of your adult lives."

"No, it's a big one for sure, but she wouldn't like that anyway, looking backwards so much."

"I have to say that's one thing that ended up really bugging me about trying to find Crombie Hill and all that—I wanted to go forward but it was almost like the idea of Crombie Hill wouldn't let me. Until I decided that most of the story was made up. That freed me up, and in a weird way allowed me to let the idea of you go as well. Then I find out decades later that it was true after all. Which is part of why I've been so confused about you. What I feel about you. What's now, what's past, whether there's a distinction. What I feel about David is not so confused. He's the best thing that ever happened to me, and I think I'd be safe to say I'm the best thing that ever happened to him. And Ethan is the best thing that ever happened to us both. So that's a lot of bests. But amid all that, I know in my heart that you were a best thing also. I didn't have any context at the time to understand what our time together meant, but I think I get it now. It was love, for sure, and that love is still in me in the way that tributary feeds the river. There's a sweet note in the water, a taste of the earth of those landscapes we crossed together. It's part of me, which means you're a part of me. I'm not so scared of that now. It seems okay."

"You need to tell me more about them, about David and Ethan."

"I was getting to that. I just need to make sure you knew you're part of my origin story, and I don't take it for granted. I regret that it was so painful for a while, but there's nothing I can do to make that pain go away. It's there in the water with everything else.

"So I met David because I was pissed off. I went to a town council meeting where they were discussing some proposed changes to a park that abuts the college campus—I had been at Hadentown for a year—and I was there to protest the changes, which involved some renovations to the landscaping that would be undertaken to conceal a storm water-management system that somebody said needed to be built into a particular hillside. The somebody was David, who worked for an engineering firm that had been hired to study a problem of periodic increasingly catastrophic floods. He had this unassuming personality and a pretty disheveled presentation of himself that, over the course of a 20-minute discussion, essentially got everybody to admit that the amount of paved surface that they had all demanded so that they could park conveniently close to each of the seven places they wanted to go each day meant that for each person there was enough pavement to park eight cars (counting the parking space they had at home) and water would naturally flow off these impervious surfaces (that's their engineer term), which amounted to about a quarter of a football field per person, and if everyone would be willing to make do with three of those spaces instead of eight, then the need to manage stormwater runoff would be much less. This was not an engineer telling us what needed to be done. It was our own collective choices dictating what needed to be done, and the engineer was there to try to make it work. Damn, this is sounding a little bit too relevant. Anyway he and I got to talking. Over the next weeks and months, we got to eating together, walking together, then sleeping together, then living together, then getting married. It seemed perfectly casual and natural, but I've always suspected that he actually engineered the whole thing in some way.

"Anyway, you talk about contrasting styles between you and Su-Yun, well with David and me, we have a draftsman and a bulldozer, or a planner and a builder if you will. There's a time for each, but they are at their very best when they work together. I can get things done. He can discern what needs to be done and how to get there. That's the practical part, and of course it doesn't hurt to have your comfortable roles. But what I really love about David is the part he doesn't really show. I don't think he conceals it on purpose. It just doesn't come out. He really, really cares. And he will work really hard in complete anonymity to get things to work out all right. After I knew him better, I figured this out, and I figured out how it could drain him, how it was always draining him, and how I could be what he needed, too. A bulldozer on his side. A quiet, loving bulldozer who would put away her bulldozer costume and just be a generous lover and a good and faithful friend, and even sometimes quietly plan things so he didn't have to. In turn, sometimes he puts down the drafting pencil and gets out the hammer or the chainsaw. We have a secret pact." She laughed. "And you'd never guess how good he is in bed. Not that you'd even think of that. Sorry, TMI."

"True, I was not thinking about that."

"Our kids would like each other, too, don't you think?"

"Interesting segue, Ellie. Yeah, I think they've been doing a little pre-screening via internet. Your Ethan seems to have that 'gol dang' persona worked out pretty well. I can tell they find it very endearing. Anna is smitten."

"He's pretty genuine. I mean there's a lot of authentic 'gol dang' in there. I think he's aware he'll be taken a certain way because of it and he just doesn't give a flying fuck as long as people get excited about the things he gets excited about—which lately is mainly design and materials stuff related to bicycles. The designer in him is glad to be underestimated—then he can surprise people with unexpected genius, right? But I'm not sure how good a strategy being underestimated is for getting a job, you know? There are times when you don't want to be underestimated."

"Yeah. Though I'd say in general great work will reveal itself, right? Better to focus on the best design first then the marketing rather than the other way around. Still, corporate America may disagree. Seems easier to sell what sold before than to get behind a better product that's too different."

"Sequel syndrome," she said.

"Is this a sequel?" Axel stood up. "I'm getting hot. Is this version 2 or version 3 of the trek across New York thing?"

"I don't think so. It's all one back-and-forth story," Ellie said. "And I agree, I'm boiling. Let's go get in the lake."

Axel followed her out the door.

Ellie stopped at the ladder and looked out. Mikko was farthest away, chatting with David who had his back to the dock. Marianne and Anna and Ethan were treading water in loose triangle to the left. None of them looked up until

Marianne noticed Ellie and gave a little wave. The other two turned around and waved as well. Then they turned back toward each other and resumed their conversation.

Axel counted the heads bobbing and the suits on the dock and observed, "I think we're the only ones not naked. Isn't that ironic, you know, metaphorically speaking?"

"See," Ellie replied. "You could have been an English major."

"I was, for a while. And you could have been a bike racer."

"Mmmm-hmmm," she said. "I was that for a while."

"Aren't you getting in?" David called. "Think about your pores."

Ellie dived in and, somewhat to her surprise, she was not immediately transported to 30 years before. That took a few seconds. She scissor-kicked on her back and glided over to David and Mikko, looking back up at the dock where Axel watched for a moment, then dived in and swam toward his daughters and Ethan. Shortly thereafter Marianne and Anna declared they were cold and wanted to go back into the sauna.

Ethan stayed. "Everything cool?" He asked quietly without actually looking at Axel.

"I think so, yeah," Axel replied.

"Some weird shit, y'all have to admit."

"Just you wait," said Axel.

"For what?" Ethan turned toward him, alarmed.

"For when you're 50," Axel laughed. "You'll see."

The steam swirled lazily in the room. Ellie watched droplets beginning to form on her skin. Maybe five more minutes, then go jump in the cool lake again. "This is so nice of you to come open the place up for a bunch of strangers," she said. It's totally above and beyond."

"It really is my pleasure," Mikko said without opening his eyes. "As I was saying to your son, since Pekka moved back to Kuopio, there have not been so many occasions to do this. So I welcome the chance. And also it is good to see old friends and meet new ones, though everyone knows we Finns are taciturn and antisocial."

"Is that when the track shut down, when Pekka left?" David asked.

"Two years before he left. There were some very small accidents and the insurance rates got too high for a weekend hobby. And certainly even despite that matter, once I was only one left, I was not going to run it all by myself. So now it serves only as a false front for the sauna. A ghost track, like a stage set for a Hollywood movie."

"And that's why they left?" Ellie followed.

"No, no. Our parents had the hotel in Kuopio and they wanted to retire, that's all. I think he would have preferred to stay here, but they have made the most of it. Kuopio is a pretty place, and more people go there now than it used to be."

"I have never been to Finland," Axel said.

Silence.

"Well, since it seems none of you have been, when you go," Mikko said, "you know there is at least one hotel you must visit." He ladled water onto the stones. "And you already know how to enjoy the sauna." Steam filled the room.

Ellie stood up and exited the dock door. She walked out to the ladder, put down her towels, removed her black suit, and hopped into the lake. After she'd been treading water for a few minutes, Marianne walked out. She put down her towels and dove splashlessly in.

"So, you guys worked out a little conspiracy, huh?" said Marianne after she resurfaced.

"Conspiracy? No, we just thought it would be fun come back up to this area and try to finish the project and see what people were still around. You kids all flipped out so much that we just sort of left out the part about meeting here."

"Oops, one little detail."

"Really it was that once I called Mikko and he said he'd love to come fire up the sauna and mentioned he'd just spoken to your dad about the same thing, then it didn't make sense to ask him to do that twice on two different days, so from that point we each began scheduling around ending up here this afternoon."

"Okay, I guess that makes sense," Marianne said. "Although if I was either one of you I would have been pretty apprehensive."

"You got that right. We're idiots, your dad and I. Although it was hilarious yesterday trying to avoid running into you on Monadnock. We really didn't know we were all planning to do that hike at the same time on the same day."

"You saw us?"

"Well, I saw Ethan playing with his phone a lot, so I figured something was up. I took a look around and saw you guys walking down. Nice-looking family."

"We practically ran down because we thought you might be behind us."

"That's funny. We went down a different trail."

"Did Dad see you?"

"Oh yeah, right away when you first walked up and were looking for a place to sit down. But he played it cool."

"He does that."

"What?"

"Plays it cool."

"Always did."

"He'll err on the side of not telling you what he's thinking."

"Considerate, but also tactical."

Marianne smiled. That seemed about right. "Well, it's good to meet you. You seem nice. I read your story and I was a little worried."

"Worried?"

"Not like you were a bad person, but you know, it was weird to see that my dad and somebody else were in a relationship like that before my mom came along."

"Yeah. I know. I don't want to make you guys uncomfortable. I hope it's okay."

"It's okay." Marianne paused. "You know, also, when I read that part with the woman Kelly, I thought you handled that well. The interaction and the writing."

"You've got to be kidding. I've always felt shitty about that. Like I used her."

"Look, I'm a woman, a queer woman specifically, and I thought you were both kind to each other. Respectful. It didn't need to be any more than that."

"Well, I never would have expected that reaction. I've wondered occasionally what happened to her."

"Married with grown kids in Yarmouth, Maine. We stopped and saw Rob—the other Steve."

"No fucking way. Well, to quote Kelly, people are flexible sometimes." She paused. "I just—"

"What?" Ellie's face was turned away, and when she turned back, Marianne saw she was trying not to cry. "Are you okay?"

"I just wish—" said Ellie, "I just wish I could have told Axel at that time what I felt about him then. I didn't understand it until he'd left. So much unnecessary pain."

"Both ways, I think."

"Yeah, we both got hurt, but I caused the whole thing."

"You didn't cause it. He didn't cause it either. Circumstances caused it. It's just a cluster-fuck. Shit happens for no good reason. Believe me, I know." Now her eyes were red.

"Oh, sweetie, I'm sorry." Ellie put her hand on Marianne's shoulder but swimming meant it was only for a second. "A botched communication three decades ago is nothing compared to what you three have gone through with your mom. I just can't imagine. I've been so lucky, really, in so many ways."

"We're really lucky too. One tragedy, yes, but it doesn't cancel everything good."

"No, that's right. When I think of the lives of all those people I was trying to trace, there was just one terrible loss after another. So many babies never made it to adulthood. Moms died giving birth all the time. A brother and son killed within months of the loss of a wife and mother and an infant. It just rips you up to think about it. But that was everybody's life."

"They probably even had their versions of you and my dad."

"The possibility of alternate realities sounds like a wild sci-fi idea until you see it in your own life, and I have to say it's pretty startling. So that's the other 'what if' I can't get out of my head: what if Ax had received the package back then, what if we had gotten back together, what if our life courses had been altered—maybe that means no Ethan and no you and no Anna. I can't get my head around that at all. The world is better for having you three in it. So despite all the 'what ifs,' I still wouldn't trade what we have today, know what I mean? None of us would."

Marianne didn't have words, just looked at Ellie and nodded.

"The longer you live, the more of a past you have," Ellie laughed. "How's that for profound? I think my brain is slowing down. Time to go get warm again." She climbed up the ladder and grabbed her suit and the two closest towels.

When she re-entered the sauna, beers had been taken from the cooler and opened and David was telling Mikko about the Smoky Mountains and the Blue Ridge and the Cumberland Plateau—all his favorite places in North Carolina and Tennessee, and Axel was chiming in with accounts of epic bike races he'd done in that region—the Tour de Moore in North Carolina in the spring, the twilight criteriums in June, and also in New England—races at Putney, Stowe, Killington, Boston, Fitchburg, New Bedford. Mikko in turn regaled them with tales of insane rally drivers in Finland. Ethan was dripping in sweat but also completely enthralled, and Anna was drowsing in her upper corner, grinning with eyes closed as Ethan said something particularly Ethanesque.

Ellie closed the door behind her and went to sit up on the top tier near Anna. She leaned back and closed her eyes. She could still conjure up the feeling of that first blissful swim after that first sauna. Maybe they should get a cabin back home and build one of these things. Somewhere kind of sheltered where it wouldn't matter if you wore a bathing suit. Somewhere kind of like this.

"I guess it's silly to keep this suit on," Axel said quietly to Mikko, removing his shorts to the notice of no one.

"Best way," said Mikko without opening his eyes.

Soon, the four men finally resolved to go outside and passed Marianne going the other way on the dock. "I had just given up on anybody else ever coming out there," she said as she closed the door behind her.

"What?" said Anna, her eyes startling open. She looked around blankly for a few seconds, then said "Oh. Right. That's so weird, I never doze off like that."

"While you're still up, could you please grab us each a beer out of that blue cooler," Ellie said. "I can't move."

Marianne retrieved three cans and sat at Anna's feet, placing the cans on the bench above.

"Where did all the men go?" Anna opened a can.

Nobody answered, but she didn't mind. The question had been more of an observation.

Marianne reached over and ladled some water onto the stones and steam filled the space.

The men collectively elected to return to the sauna. Mikko made a detour on the way back in to put the last three logs on the fire, then entered and re-took the hottest seat front and center. "Did they tell you we will start a new company?" he said.

"New company?" Ellie asked.

"Yeah," David said. "Reconfigure the United States for bicycles. I can engineer the infrastructure, Axel can develop and test the products, Ethan can be the designer slash guinea pig, and Mikko can brainwash all the young impressionable students."

"Do the women get to do anything or is this a boys' club?" Anna asked without opening her eyes.

"You didn't start your own company yet while we were out swimming?" Axel said. "Usually you two would have dreamed up something by now."

"It's called Sit in the Sauna and Drink Beer, Inc.," said Marianne. "It's part of the service industry."

"It's the future," said Anna.

"It's also the past," said Ellie.

"Solid business model," said Axel. "Let's go get some venture capital."

"Speaking of swimming," said Anna. "I need to go back out there." She stood and wrapped herself.

"The heat will last perhaps another 30 minutes," Mikko said.

"Time for a couple more rounds," said Ellie, standing.

She and Anna and David exited.

In the water, David released a loud sigh. "I don't know whose idea this was originally, but they are to be commended."

"Mikko's, really," said Ellie.

"He seems like an interesting guy," said Anna. "He's a teacher?"

"Yeah, at Mount Pleasant College near Ithaca. Semi-retired," Ellie replied.

"He doesn't look old enough," Anna said.

"Healthy living, right?" said David. "Amazing that you and he end up knowing each other for all these years after a chance meeting on a bicycle trip."

"After I finished grad school, I applied for a position there at Mount Pleasant, and I thought I remembered that one of those Finnish brothers we met had taught there, so I went and found my old baggie from the ride full of slips of paper with contact info scribbled on them, and I called him up to see if I could learn anything about working there. Didn't get the job, but we'd see each other at publishing conferences later on and we just kept up the connection."

"And you're a professor in Nashville, is that right?" asked Anna.

"Mmmm-hmmm, at Hadentown College," Ellie said. "Little liberal arts school, maybe like Colorado College near you. Couple thousand students. And David is based in Nashville but travels around a lot consulting on big important stuff like bridges and waterfront developments."

"I can't claim credit for this waterfront development," David said, "but I might steal ideas from it."

"I've got one year left at Colorado State," Anna said.

"Major?" Ellie asked.

"English," said Anna. "Useless."

"Hey, watch it," said Ellie.

"Oh, that's what you teach?"

"Mmmm-hmmm. Maybe you've been listening to too many STEM-heads."

"Yeah, those fuckers are everywhere."

"And they want everybody to adhere to their world view because that would give them more clout. Is your dad pushing you that way?"

"Dad? Oh, no way. He's all for the English major, but then he's comfortable improvising."

"You're not?"

"Well, I guess I am," said Anna. It's just that you hear the message over and over again that you're a loser if you don't go into math and sciences. Kinda wears on you."

"It's like they forget the whole point of the liberal arts. But you know they say that actually the right brain is the master and the left brain is the emissary."

"Who said that?"

"I don't remember. Google it."

"I'm getting tired of treading water," said David.

"You're not treading water, you have a great career even if it is excessively STEM-oriented," said Ellie.

"Ha ha," said David, climbing up the ladder.

Ethan passed him walking out. "Hey Dad." He fist-bumped David, dropped his towel, and jumped in. Ellie climbed out and followed David back inside. Marianne appeared before the door closed and walked out and joined her sister and Ethan. "Am I interrupting?"

"Interrupting what?" Anna flashed her sister a look.

"Just being sure," Marianne winked. "I know my sister."

Anna smiled and rolled her eyes.

"So," Ethan said, spinning in the water to face them.

After a few seconds, Anna responded. "So?"

"I mean, here we are," he said.

Marianne turned to Anna. "Well, he's got that part down. No thoughts about being casually naked with our long-ago-lovers parents and their grown offspring?"

"Baby steps," said Anna.

"More of a question," he said. "Why are we here? This is great but the whole thing seems kinda sketch."

"Like we're pawns in someone else's chess game," said Marianne.

"But they aren't very good at chess," said Anna.

"Check," said Ethan. Anna decided his voice sounded a more like his father's: soft and high and a little bit hoarse, while his mom's was more resonant and gravelly like Miley Cyrus. There wasn't any particular accent, but he did habitually say "y'all" for the second-person plural, and that provided some geo-location.

Mikko walked out. "Almost out of fire," he said. He unwrapped his towel, and climbed down the ladder.

"Do we still have time for another round?" Marianne asked.

"Yes, sure," said Mikko. "Just go soon."

She took a few strokes to the ladder and hoisted herself out of the water. Anna followed her. Axel and David passed them on the dock.

"One more reheat," said Ethan, climbing out.

"I'm going back to my comfy corner," Anna said as Ethan came trotting up behind her.

"I like that plan." He closed the door quickly. Marianne was already sitting on the lower bench with his mom, so Ethan climbed up and propped himself in the opposite corner from Anna. "Dangerously comfy," he said.

Ellie generated a new steam cloud. "It's cooling off a little," she said.

"I know where the wood is," said Ethan.

"It's tempting," Ellie said. "But I guess we all still have to get to Geneseo tonight. That's another few hours."

"You're going there, too?" Marianne asked.

"Mmmm-hmmm. Looking for a grave we might have missed. I guess that's what we're doing. I don't really know anymore."

"Oh, the brother who got caught in the flood?"

"Yes. Uz. Interesting name."

"And wasn't there the rollerblade lady in that same town? Did you keep in touch with her?" Marianne reached for the ladle. "I have to do this one time." Steam billowed.

"No," said Ellie. "At least I didn't. I think Axel said he used to see her in his racing days. Always looking for a couch to crash on."

"Hmm, a likely story," Marianne said.

"Are we all staying in the same place tonight?" Ethan asked.

"Yeah, all of us in Natalie's back yard," said Ellie. "Did you bring the tarp?"

The door opened and David and Axel walked in. "Okay, your turn in the lake," said the latter.

"Not yet," said Anna. "Just a few more minutes."

Mikko entered. "It's just embers now, so maybe five or ten more minutes of good heat."

"Tragic," said Ethan.

"You can stay longer," Mikko said. "Just get the logs on while the embers are still good."

"That sounds great, but I think we told the apartment host we'd be there by about 7:00," said Axel," which means hitting the road in about an hour, and we haven't eaten those sandwiches yet."

"Two more logs and eat in the car," David said.

No one could think of a reasonable objection to that. Mikko ducked back outside for minute and the heat increased almost immediately. Anna was snoring lightly in her corner.

"You know what's been missing from this trip?" David asked.

"A rollercoaster?" Axel offered.

"Traffic jams?" said Marianne.

"Grading papers that should have been finished before we left?" said Ellie.

"Black people," David said. "I don't think I have seen a single African American. What's up with that?"

"You're probably right, but what made you think of it?" Ellie said.

"I don't know. It's not like our part of Nashville is a model of progressive integration or anything, but at least you run into folks of different colors throughout your day. But I was just reviewing our trip in my head and comparing the people we've met to the folks I usually interact with at home, and it just seems like there's nothing but white people out here. No offense to Mikko."

"A college town is different because it draws students from far away," Mikko said, "and the cities like Rochester and Syracuse all have African American population, but you are right—out here in the rural places and the small towns, it's white people whose ancestors moved from the east coast. And from Finland of course."

"And the only reason the white people could freely settle here," said Axel, "was that the Indians were gone. And the way that happened was not pretty."

"Did you worry when you were riding across here?" Marianne asked.

"Me? Because my skin is a little dark?" Axel laughed. "No, but maybe I should have. Do you girls feel uncomfortable? I'm sorry, not girls."

"A little," Marianne said. "I don't feel in danger or anything, but I feel like the people around here probably wouldn't think I'm a real American. Or the folks in New Hampshire. All those centuries-old graves stones with English names on them."

"Well, you have an English surname and so do I," Axel said. "King is about as Anglo as it gets."

"Like Martin Luther King, right?" said Anna.

"Well, there's an appalling story there, right?" Ellie said. "All the slaves being cut off from their heritage and getting the names of their English purchasers attached to them."

"Wylie. Webster. English names, too." David said.

"Toivonen is not English," Mikko said.

"No," David agreed.

"And I bet no families of former slaves have the name Toivonen," said Anna.

"So who is American?" Mikko asked. "What is an American? I passed the test decades ago, I am a citizen. Or are you all the real Americans even though you never passed a citizenship test?"

"Or is Ellie the most American because her ancestors were here longest ago?" David asked.

"Either her or African slaves," Anna said. "Slaves got here from the 1600s to the mid-1800s."

"Or the Indians," Axel said.

"Yeah, Dad has some Native American genes, so we win," said Anna.

"I'm no English major," said Marianne, "but maybe the right word isn't 'or' but 'and.'"

"Are you sure we should have put those logs on the fire? It got all serious in here," Ethan said.

"It's stuff we have to think about," David said, "especially with politics like it is today."

"I'd rather not," Ethan said. He stretched back into the corner and folded his arms.

"Okay, how about this," Anna said. "Change of subject. We're all going to the same place tonight, right?"

"Different hotels, but same town, yeah," Axel said. "Good old Geneseo."

"And tomorrow it's go to a history museum and maybe a cemetery and that park with the big gorge, right?"

"Yeah," said Axel.

"So let's mix up the cars," she said. "Not that I'm sick of you guys."

"Okay, I'm going with Mikko," said Marianne. "I'm going to need a job soon."

Mikko laughed. "That didn't work for Dr. Webster."

"I was thinking more like Cornell," she said.

"Oh yeah, that'll be easier," Ellie laughed.

"They have programs in my field and I could get a lab job and then work on a PhD. at the same time."

"M, darling, you're doing those super-Asian stereotypes again," Anna said.

"But seriously," Ellie said. "That's a nice idea. Why not shuffle up the passengers for a few hours?"

"Fine by me," Axel said. "I'm the only driver on the paperwork for our rental, so I guess I'm stuck, but everybody else could move around. Plus we can only fit three total."

"Each person think of a number between one and ten," Mikko said. "Ready? Hold up that number of fingers." He turned around and scanned everyone's hands. "The two numbers closest to Axel's number ride with him, so that is . . . Ethan and Marianne."

"But I've been riding with him for days," Marianne said. "Who wants to trade, Ellie or David?"

"You go," David said. "We don't want girl car and boy car, right?"

Ellie shrugged.

They all sat motionless and silent until Mikko poured one last ladle of water over the stones. "Go now before steam clears," he suggested, "best memory." They filed down the dock and dropped into the lake one-by-one.

60.

Mikko stacked the towels in back and closed the hatch. "One machine washing a year, whether they need it or not." He walked back around.

"I'm so glad to see you again and to see you looking so well," he said, shaking Axel's hand and clapping him on the shoulder with his free hand. "And your daughters. Most impressive and lovely. You must be a proud papa." He shook their hands as well as they thanked him for the hospitality.

Ellie leaned in for a kiss. "This was just wonderful, Mikko. Thank you again. Highlight of my trip. Kind of like the last time." She thought of a few way to elaborate, but didn't.

Mikko nodded and reached over to shake David's hand, then Ethan's. "So good at last to meet you both."

He stepped away. "Safe travels, everyone, and thank you for providing me the excuse to come here and share the sauna!" He started up the red Mazda and, with a flash of the headlights, headed back in the direction from which he had come.

"You ride in front, Ethan," Ellie said. "I'll draft behind you guys." She climbed in the back.

"She'll sit back there all the way then jump us at the end," Ethan said.

"A winning strategy," Axel said.

David toyed with the thought of asking if either Marianne or Anna wanted to drive, partially because he was already tired from having driven much of the morning, but he decided that might be too stressful for them—or for him, depending what kind of driver the chosen one might prove to be.

Between Ellie and Axel they had the directions to both apartments, which looked to be a couple blocks apart, so the rental car pulled out first. It's not like there would be much to it: go west on Route 20, turn left on 20A, turn right as they came into Geneseo—just backtracking the route they had ridden 30 years ago but covering the distance in two or three hours instead of one very long day.

"Do you think you remember how to get to Geneseo?" Ellie called up to the front.

"Yeah, sure," Axel said. "I've been there since. Not in 25 years, but it was enough to remember. But no intention to go Natalie's today!"

"That good, huh?"

"Let's say it was good at first . . ."

"Wait, you two really had a thing going on? I was just kidding."

"Yeah, for a little while. A couple races were nearby—Olean and some other one—and one time I called her up because I still had her number from our trip—this was probably three or four years later-- to see if she wanted to get a beer or something."

"And of course she invited you to stay over."

"Of course."

"Free hotel."

"Yeah, but we had a nice time together too."

"What, were you attracted to her right from the start?"

"Well, she was an attractive, interesting person, sure, but no—I was with someone else at the time, you may recall."

"I guess you were," Ellie paused. "I wasn't quite sure at the time."

"Everybody says it was obvious, right?" Axel laughed. "Despite our best efforts."

"Best efforts?" Ellie replied.

"Trying to pretend to myself and anyone who was looking that I wasn't getting serious about you. But the harder I tried, the deeper in I got."

"You knew then? I guess I knew, in some part of me, but it wasn't till you left . . ."

"You could be pretty, ahh, focused back then."

"Yeah. Like I said, things can sneak up on me. Well anyway, what happened? Why didn't it work out with her?"

"Weeeeeeeell," Axel said, "I don't feel like it's right to blame the other person, but she just started getting kinda nuts if you ask me."

"What, were you living there?"

"For a couple months after the end of one season. I got a job at a ski area close by there, and I stayed in her place and kicked in some groceries and paying the utilities and stuff. It hadn't gotten really weird yet but it was heading that way. And I think it was probably my fault too, because truth be told I was not in a mental place to make a real commitment. So I came up with an excuse that my team needed me in North Carolina for the winter to run a training camp. It was no hard feelings, I think. I hope. I used to drop her a note from time to time, and we did just have a beer once."

"You just made up a training camp to get out of there?"

"No, not exactly. I went to North Carolina and found some guys and we started a training camp. And then that's actually where I met Su-Yun, strangely enough."

"She came to your training camp?"

"No, she was in grad school in Chapel Hill."

"So what got weird?"

"With Natalie? Just some of her ideas, things about the government and the secret big money behind everything . . . I guess it's not that surprising when you consider how she lived, you know, in retrospect."

"What if we run into her? That would be awkward!"

"Not likely," Axel said.

"Very small town. Can't bet against it."

"That is a point," Axel said. "But who knows if she even still lives there? Even we did run into her, it wouldn't be the first awkward moment of this trip, right?"

"Are you sure you don't want to sit in the front, Mom?" Ethan turned around.

"Sorry, honey," Ellie said. "I'm monopolizing. Which is dumb because I thought one of the fun things about riding together would be that you and Ax could talk about bikes and racing."

"Yeah, we could," Ethan said. "But if you have more to catch up on, that's cool. I'm enjoying this, too."

"Ah, probably good to change the subject anyway," Axel said. "So you're a Cat 2, I hear, rampaging throughout the southeast and midwest?"

"I don't know about rampaging," said Ethan, "but I've been trying to give it a go for a year or two. Then maybe use my degree and go be a designer some place."

"Not a bad plan," said Axel. "Easier now than when you're 30, at least."

"For what it's worth," Ellie said, "his parents concur with this plan. No student debt, thank god."

"Yeah that kind of frees a person up, doesn't it?" Axel said.

"I guess so," said Ethan. "Thanks for your faculty discount, Mom. Anyway, one problem is the road scene has been kinda drying up. There just aren't that many races, even compared to a couple years ago. I'm gonna have to get a gravel bike and do that."

"Not the same, though," Axel said.

"No. So when you were racing it was lots of crits, right?"

"Yeah, kind of a golden age for criterium racing. All these different cities would close off a few blocks downtown, crank up the music, and make an all-day festival out of it. They would drum up lots of sponsors so the prize money was pretty good, too, so you really could spend the season racing and actually come out ahead. You know, provided you slept on people's floors and ate nothing but frozen burritos."

"What was a typical bike for that?"

"Component-wise, most people used Campagnolo until Shimano came along with index shifting that actually worked. Then everybody followed suit. A few years later came STI type shifters built into the brake levers, and that became the standard after about five minutes. Clipless pedals were standard by the end of the 80s. You could just have a good road bike and do everything, but the schedule was so heavy with criteriums that most of the serious racers had more of a crit bike. Super tight, short wheelbase, crazy stiff. Tough enough to survive getting dumped a few times every year. They were pretty heavy, actually, by today's standards. Overbuilt steel frames. Followed by overbuilt aluminum frames."

"Not like a gravel bike?"

"The opposite of a gravel bike. More like a track bike with gears."

"Not comfortable on a long ride over bumpy country roads?"

"Not at all."

"So would you have a different bike for training?"

"I never did. Just put up with the beating, you know? I was pretty broke, so I had a cheap backup bike, but it was set up the same way so I could swap wheels if needed. Since I stopped really racing," he laughed, "I have much nicer bikes."

"Like what?"

"Top-secret prototypes, man. That's my job, working with the designers to develop prototypes for what we think will be in demand in a couple years. Then I test those myself and take them around and have my stable of trusted guinea pigs test them. You ought to come out to Boulder. I could show you around the facilities."

"I'd like that. Do you need an all-rounder guinea-pig, 6-1, 170 with a decent sprint and pretty good power?"

"What's your FTP?"

"About 320 last I time did the test."

"Nice, that's getting close to go-to-Europe watts. Have you worked on power specifically, or is that more of a baseline?"

"Baseline, I'd say. Nothing against data and science, but I kinda prefer racing to training. And I love just riding."

"Yeah, no offense to all the data science, but long-term I'm more interested in the design. What are you riding?"

"Felt. Long top tube, handles great. But I'd be riding it anyway since those are the team bikes."

"Well designed bikes, though. You wear gloves?"

"Not usually, why?"

"Just curious. Informal poll. Some people just want to feel every little bit of the road, bumps and all."

"That's me."

"Me too," said Ellie. "I never liked gloves either."

"I always had to wear them," Axel said. "My hands would go numb. I think maybe taller folks who have longer limbs end up absorbing a lot of shock with their arms and legs. And they don't have as much weight on the handlebars proportionately. But sprinter-basher types like me usually wear them."

"How much did you race, mom?" Ethan turned around.

"Three full seasons and part of another, mostly just in college. I started with the collegiate team and then did some on my own on the side. But pretty much stopped senior year, though."

"School stuff?"

"Sure, you could say that," Ellie replied.

"You still have that red Eddy in the basement, right?"

"Yeah. I'm sure it's completely obsolete now, but it's still a beautiful thing to look at," she said. "Which is all I do with it."

"We should get you on a modern bike," Axel said. "You'd be amazed."

"I'm sure I would," she laughed. "You know, though, despite the fact that I stopped a long time ago, I feel like I learned things from racing that have served me ever since."

"Follow wheels but avoid crashes, right?" Axel said.

"That's a good metaphor for something, I'm sure," she said. "But also that everyone has strengths and weaknesses, and it's possible to get so obsessed by working on the weaknesses that your strengths kind of wither—and of course it's also possible to focus so much on the strengths that the weaknesses end up killing you. So the sweet spot is work on the weaknesses enough so they don't sink you, but really try to maximize where you already have strengths."

"Yeah," said Axel, "there are lots of stories about riders who could have won the Tour de France but they weren't quite good enough in the mountains, or they could drop everyone on the climbs, but they would give it all back in the time trials. The ones who figured out how to shore up the weakness without compromising the strengths end up winning the thing."

"It taught me things I didn't realize I was learning," Ellie said, "like how these group dynamics work when everyone's in competition to win, but there are also big benefits to working together. You can't imaging how useful that ends up being in academia!"

"You should hear her going off on those folks at the dinner table," Ethan laughed. "Even makes me blush sometimes."

"Also, the bike teaches you how tough you are," Ellie continued. "How hard can you push for how long? How much pain can you endure? Can you bounce up from a crash? And part of that is learning how to gage your efforts, so that if you do decide to throw in an all-out push, you do it strategically so it's most likely to pay off."

"And then to do that dozens of times and it doesn't pay off," said Axel, "but then you try it again because this is still the best time to try it."

"Yeah, that sounds familiar," Ethan said. "So did riding loaded touring bikes across upstate New York teach you anything? That's a whole different kind of thing, right? Still a pretty serious effort, though."

"You know, I've been wondering that," Ellie said. This conversation was having an unexpected effect on her—she had climbed into the car with some trepidation that the next hours would be tense and awkward, but instead it was as if Ethan was quietly guiding her—guiding her and Axel both—through what could have been a perilous passage toward a place of peace and clarity. "I'm not sure what I learned. I literally and figuratively just filed it away decades ago. Until Axel sent me an email. And that kind of stirred up this idea that I hadn't properly finished something."

"Again, sorry," Axel said.

"No, as you said before, it's been a bit overwhelming, but I'm also grateful for the opportunity to catch things up, make things right. I feel like we've kind of run the rapids and come out the other side okay. The thing is," she said, "now that I've had a chance to kind of retrace it all, I'm not sure it ever mattered that it didn't feel finished. What would that finish line look like?"

"Is it better having located that gravestone?" Axel said. "You have to admit, that was a real long-shot."

"Yes," she said. "But on the other hand, we already knew they had started out there, and where they went, so oddly I didn't feel much different having found a precise place where Crombies had lived. And discovering that I had gotten so close thirty years ago. But meanwhile, seeing the stone with those few tragic, matter-of-fact words chiseled in, that added such meaning to Emma's letters, knowing that she was writing them to be read to her dead mother—whether she wrote them as they traveled or after they got to Ohio matters less to me now. She's heartbroken and hopeful, both. So, in one way what I found out was that the thing I assumed would be important, like knowing the exact plot of land where someone had lived and from which a wagon had departed in a previous century, that ends up not mattering so much to me."

"What mattered was that a girl had wanted to share her experience with someone who wasn't there anymore," said Axel. "She knew that, but she did it anyway."

"Damn, that's pretty sad," Ethan said. His phone told him of a new instant message.

"You know," Axel said, "I didn't expect it but I was comforted in a way to see that stone—and thanks to David, by the way, for sending such good directions since we didn't have anything to Google. Not because it provided any kind of closure—I mean it's not even my family—but because it reminded me of how universal this experience is, and always has been, and always . . ." he stopped, and after a few seconds resumed. "Maybe you leave a trace, maybe you don't. People just persevere. That's how we all got here."

Ethan called up the message, which included the text "gotta pee" and an image of Anna cross-eyed. "Hey, I think they want to find a bathroom." Ethan held up the phone over toward the driver's seat.

Axel glanced over. "That's my girls," he laughed. They were just coming into a town, so he pulled in at the first gas station. The Subaru behind the SUV followed and parked directly behind. Axel watched the doors fly open and the occupants head for the convenience store. "No need for gas just yet. Anybody here want to go in?"

"I'm good," Ellie said.

"Guess I'll go," said Ethan, closing the door.

Seeing that David was walking up, Axel rolled down the window.

"I'm a little sleepy," David said when he got up there. "Marianne's going to drive for a bit."

"Cool," said Axel. "She can drive a stick. Everything good?"

"Yeah, all good. All good El?"

"Mmmm-hmmm. Boys talking bikes."

"The young ladies were recounting their recent Mount Washington adventure," David replied. "Sounds like something we ought do so sometime—be an excuse to get myself in better shape."

"It was a beautiful hike," Axel said. "Weird with all the tourists who drive or take the train. We got lucky with the weather, I think."

"They said there was some excitement with a cloud bank," David said.

"Scared the shit out of me," said Axel, laughing. "Gotta be careful up there. It's sneaky dangerous."

"They also described how they slowly figured out from Ethan's Instagrams that we were all in the same place, and then got panicked that we would have some kind of confrontation on Monadnock."

The three were still laughing as Marianne and Anna walked up to the SUV.

"Hey dad, is there any trick to getting to this place?" Marianne asked.

"Nothing much to it until some little streets at the end," Axel replied. "Should be a right turn then a few blocks once we get to the town. When we get close, just follow us or text if we get separated. And thanks for driving."

"Glad to. Here comes Ethan. That's all of us."

David climbed in the passenger seat, Anna behind him. Marianne slid the driver's seat forward. "Let's see, reverse is on the other side here but everything else is the same." She started it up and adjusted the mirrors. The little black SUV ahead of them pulled out. She put it into gear, lifted the clutch to feel where it engaged, and rolled off. At the road, she looked over her left shoulder and noted she'd have enough time to pull out before the approaching cars arrived if she did so briskly, so she kept rolling and shifted quickly through the gears and settled in a few seconds behind the rental car. This thing wasn't as zippy as the VW back home, but it was fine.

"Thanks for letting me drive," she said. "Lets me feel use-ful, and the rental places cut it off at age 25 apparently."

"No, thank you. It's a big help. You're 23, 24?"

"23."

"And your sister?"

"20."

"So how do you like Boulder? You grew up there I take it?"

"Yeah. Nice enough town. A lot of sporty-granola types, some random fake cowboys, the usual soccer moms."

"Sounds like Nashville," David said. "And your mom passed away some time ago, is that right?"

"Yes, in 2003. Car accident."

"I'm so sorry. That must have been rough, and hard for your dad being left on his own to raise you two."

"Thanks, I appreciate that. He's a tough guy, fortunately."

"Nobody's that tough. I just can't imagine."

"My grandparents moved in with us for a few years. I think that helped a lot."

"Your mom's parents?"

"Yeah. My Dad's are kinda dysfunctional."

"Had they already lived in town?"

"No, California. But they were able to sell their place there for enough for our grandma to retire a little early, and my grandpa worked for a bank that had Denver offices, so he was able to transfer. Our mom was their only kid and Anna was in the car with her. I think they didn't want to take any chances."

"She was in the same accident?"

"Yeah, in the back seat. An oncoming driver turned left in front of them."

"Oh my god, how horrible."

"I could have been with them and I probably would have been sitting in the front, so that was lucky for me."

"What was your mom's name?"

"Su-Yun."

"Pretty. Is that Chinese? Korean?"

"Chinese. Taiwanese, really. Her grandparents came from there."

"Where are you from?" Anna called from the back.

"I grew up in Raleigh," David said. "Faculty brat."

"Really? Mom went to grad school at UNC Chapel Hill," Anna said.

"NC State for us, both my parents worked there."

"Was that a good place to grow up?"

"Yes, nice enough city. Plus, you could get to the mountains in a couple hours and to the beach in four."

"Maybe I should apply for a lab job there," Marianne said. "Bunch of universities in that area, right?"

"Yep. Hot and humid in the summer, though, not like Colorado. What did your mom do? What was her graduate degree?"

"She was a physical therapist, sports medicine," said Marianne. "That's how she met dad. He had some kind of little boo-boo."

"I think he said he screwed up his shoulder," Anna said.

"Anyway," Marianne said, "he kept racing bikes a lot in the summers for a couple more years after that and she would travel with him sometimes. Then he scaled back the racing and settled into the 'real job' thing, and they got married and started looking for good places to live that would probably have plenty of injured sporty people so she could set up shop. With dad's work, he could live anywhere that was kind of centrally located and had good air service."

"And Boulder was that magical place with all the breaks and sprains," David suggested.

"Yep, and I guess it also turned out to be a good place to base the new 1357 company," Marianne said.

"Does that refer to something, 1357?" David asked. "Just odd numbers?"

"Well, yes and no. It was supposed to be the first four prime numbers," Marianne said. "But then after they were incorporated someone pointed out that the number 1 is not a prime number and the number 2 is a prime number. So, uh, now they don't mention the prime number thing."

"Is 1357 prime?" David asked.

"Nope, 401st semiprime. 23 times 59," said Marianne. "I calculated that off the top of my head. Or maybe I looked it up one day when I was bored."

"I think they just wanted something that sounded techie and unique," said Anna. "And the numbers look cool on the side of a bike frame."

"And that couldn't be divided up easily, you know, as a metaphor for the durability of the company?" David offered.

"I hadn't thought of that, but you may be onto something!" Marianne laughed. "And you are an engineer, I think, is that right?"

"A civil engineer, to be precise. We do exciting stuff like making sure your sewers work properly, keeping parking decks from sliding down hillsides, damming up rivers, building bridges over the rivers we dammed up."

"That could be interesting," she replied.

"If you find red tape interesting, it's a source of endless fascination," he said. "But I should be more grateful. It is a job where you really get to do something useful."

"So which one of you does Ethan take after?" Anna asked.

"Ethan takes after Ethan," David said.

61.

Axel slowed and turned on the right turn signal as the car coasted past the cemetery after they entered Geneseo, then he remembered he wasn't going to Natalie's house. Amazing the things that stick in your brain, he thought as he turned the signal off and continued on. After a minute, there was a sign to downtown pointing right, and he put the signal back on. Marianne saw it, though a couple of cars had gotten between them at a traffic light, and did the same. He waited 30 seconds after turning off, then resumed once the other car was just behind.

They stopped in front of the place Ellie and David and Ethan had rented, a block and a half beyond where the others were staying. There was a large front yard with a couple of picnic tables with umbrella covers.

"Get settled and grab a bite?" Axel said as they gathered on the sidewalk.

"Did you see anyplace? David responded. "I wasn't looking."

"I saw Chinese," Marianne said. "That would be fast."

David turned around. "Get take-out and some drinks and set up out here?" He pointed at the tables.

Axel and his daughters ordered food while Ellie went and got beverages. "No Genny pounders to be seen," Ellie said on her return. "So I got a hodge-podge of craft brews from around here and fizzy water and a bottle of genuine Finger Lakes Riesling."

There was a passing discussion about how to store the leftovers, but soon enough all the hot-sour soup and Hunan vegetables and curry chicken and country style tofu and garlic beef and bok choy and spring rolls were gone and all that remained was most of the alcohol. So they set to work.

"Oh, one thing," Anna said. "Szechuan Paradise had this flyer for the farmers market tomorrow. Seven to two with lots of stands, and they even got a sign-up to do a shooting range. I need practice." She put the flyer on the table.

"I'm in for that," Ethan said.

"Duh," said Marianne.

"Three plans for me tomorrow," said Ellie. "Hit the market for a little while. Drop in the history center and maybe the cemetery to see if I can find Uz Crombie. Then go with David up to Letchworth State Park and see that gorge. Should be possible to do all three, but I'll need to get going early. We have two cars, so it's not like anybody needs to follow my schedule."

"I'll go with you ma," Ethan said. "Just when is that shooting thing?"

Anna checked the schedule. "One."

"The gorge is only maybe 20 minutes away," David said. "We'd have time to run up there either before or after, depending how long we take at the market."

"Okay, deal," said Axel.

"Look at this," Marianne said, pointing at the schedule and taking in from Anna. "Says tonight there's supposed to be a ceremonial planting of a new Big Tree, just at dusk.

That would be pretty soon now. Too bad, that would be fun. It doesn't look far from here. There's a little map."

"That's to replace the Big Tree that got washed away way back when?" Ellie asked. "I remember that. I think we saw what was left of its big old trunk in the museum last time we were here."

"'Near the site of the original Big Tree,' that's what it says," Marianne replied.

"Gotta be," said Axel. "I remember that too."

"In fact," said Marianne, "this farmers market is a regular thing, but this is some kind of bigger festival organized around some historic date for something, though I can't find anywhere what that something is." She turned the sheet over and back over again. "Just a festive festival I guess, celebrating the forgotten events that must have probably happened on this date."

"I bet somebody blew something up on this date in history," Anna said.

"That's a safe bet," said Axel.

"I mean, you know, patriotically."

A rumble of thunder emphasized Anna's thought.

"Hmm, better drink up," David said. "We can save the extra stuff in the little mini fridge in our place."

A brilliant flash lit up the sky, followed a second later by a violent thunderclap.

"Okay," Axel said. "Catch you all tomorrow morning. Want to say 8:00, right here? I think the market setup will be kind of behind us, a couple blocks."

"Perfect," Ellie said, gathering bottles as a few heavy raindrops began to fall.

62.

Ellie was up early and worked her way via side streets over to the market area. Vendors were just beginning to set up, so she wandered back and stopped in a small park, where she sat on a bench. She looked out over the adjacent parking lot, which seemed to be where market vendors parked their vehicles. A couple pickups, a few panel vans, an old gray Volvo station wagon, a hatchback or two. Axel texted that they were just leaving their b&b and should be there in five or ten minutes. Ellie texted back with a thumbs-up and walked back to meet everyone.

As Ellie led the way back toward the market, retracing her steps from half an hour earlier, she did a small detour and pointed out the gray Volvo to Axel. "What do you think?"

"Hmm, maybe," he said. "What's with all the fertilizer?" He pointed.

"Oh, I hadn't gotten close enough to see that," she said. In the back, partially obscured by a brown plastic tarp, were stacks of bags marked "Ammonium Nitrate Fertilizer." She stepped back. "Well, it is a farmers' market. Lots of farmers use fertilizer, right?"

"And drive 45-year-old Volvos?" Axel stepped away from the car also. "I told you she was kinda wack."

The farmers market was set up around a main intersection downtown, with vendors setting out their spreads on folding tables on the deep sidewalks and some parking spaces blocked off for the purpose. The six began a slow circuit.

Axel looked around. "Well, I guess we just play it cool and see what happens. I mean, she wouldn't recognize anybody but you and me, right? And I look a bit different."

"Not with that hat on you don't," said Ellie.

"Well you look exactly the same," Axel replied. "So maybe keep those sunglasses on."

"And also this." She picked up a purple baseball cap from the adjacent stand. "Could I please buy this Geneseo hat? Sunnier than I thought it would be," she said.

"Yeah after those rains last night, who could blame you? Twelve," said the vendor, a round and ruddy-faced young man with a spotty blond beard.

"Thanks." She handed him a ten and two singles and put the hat on.

After the hats and t-shirts vendor came one selling local pottery, then a farm stand with some greens and early corn. Axel heard a loud laugh from across the street and cautiously turned. "I think she's over there," he said.

Ellie picked up an ear of corn and pretended to hold it up to the light. Assuming that was Natalie, Ellie was pretty sure she was wearing, if not the same outfit as 30 years ago, a current version of the same cutoff shorts and tank top, in the same size, though the plumpness of the person had increased. The reddish-brown hair, now shoulder-length, had one shock of silver down the middle. "Yeah for sure," Ellie said. "Well, what do you want to do?"

"Keep walking around," he said.

David leaned in. "Is that your old acquaintance?"

"We're pretty sure," Ellie said. "Trying to decide what to do."

"Well, you gotta go talk to her," David replied. "If for no other reason than to see if she recognizes you. Plus if you didn't, you know you'd wish you did."

"I guess you're right," she said. "Let's just make our way around like nothing's out of the ordinary."

They quickly perceived that one side of the street was lavishly adorned with large Trump signs and a Betsy Ross-era American flag painted on a piece of plywood, while the other side, the side where they were now, featured a Black Lives Matter banner and an assortment of Democratic-leaning messages.

"I wonder," Axel said as they waited for a walk light, "if there's a DMZ." He looked over toward Natalie at her stand on the right side near the plywood flag. She was facing the other way at the moment. The six visitors took a very leisurely tour of the three stands before hers, but soon enough, they were there.

"Welcome, folks," Natalie said. "Have a look around."

A man in a red ball cap looked up from a bin of tomatoes. "Anything good?" he asked.

"All of it, of course," Natalie replied. "Those are the first tomatoes of the season right there. Those are okay but the next ones will be better. Some berries—super ripe already so eat 'em right away. The best corn will be a little later. These early varieties aren't quite so sweet."

The man nodded.

"Plus you have to get the secret booster sauce out there, right?" Axel mumbled.

"What was that" Natalie looked back at Axel.

"Oh, sorry, I was talking to her," he gestured with his thumb toward Marianne, who was standing next to him.

Natalie glanced at Marianne and then fixed eyes back on Axel. "Folks in town visiting? First time here?"

"First time for me," Marianne said. "We're from out west."

Axel moved around the corner.

"Where abouts?" Natalie asked.

"Colorado. Boulder."

"I heard of that," Natalie said. "Never been there, o'course. Been planted here my whole life. What brings you all this way?"

"Vacation," Marianne said.

"To Geneseo New York from Colorado? Tell me another one!" Natalie exclaimed. A few heads turned their way.

"Well, it's a change of scenery, right?" Marianne replied. "Staying here a couple nights on the way from one place to another. And this seems like a nice town."

"Yeah, but scratch the surface . . ." Natalie said. "I mean you ever seen *Twin Peaks?*"

"I've seen Pike's Peak. Where's Twin Peaks?"

"Kids these days," Natalie shook her head, then looked up and scanned the group. "So, this is your family?"

"Partially," said Marianne. "My dad and my sis." She gestured with her elbow at Anna beside her.

"Hi," said Anna.

"And those other folks?"

"Friends we just met," said Anna. "Partially."

"And that's your dad over there, carefully inspecting the cauliflower?"

"Yup," said Anna.

"I mean," Natalie walked over to Axel, "What's there to inspect? It's a cauliflower. Does it pass your muster?"

"It's a classic cauliflower," Axel said, putting it down. "How much?"

"Nothing better than a big head of raw cauliflower for a car snack, right?" Anna joked.

"Four bucks," Natalie said. "But she's right. You sure you don't want some cherry tomatoes instead?"

"Maybe that's a better idea," Axel replied. "I should just let the kids decide everything."

She turned toward Ellie. "And you ma'am?"

That caught Ellie off-guard, and without thinking about it, she politely removed her sunglasses to reply. "Mmmmm, lettuce?"

"Lettuce." Natalie said. "Which kind of lettuce?"

"Uh, what's that one there?" Ellie pointed.

"That's beet greens, honey."

"Oh yeah," Ellie laughed "There's beets attached to one end. Pretty good clue."

Natalie looked at Ellie, and back at Axel, then back at Ellie, then at Ethan next to Ellie. Then back at Ellie. "Hmmm," she said.

"Busted," Ethan mumbled.

"How much for the beets?" Ellie asked.

"Beets in the car. That's even better than cauliflower." Natalie shook her head. "Gimme a sec." She stepped back.

"Okay," Ellie said, her back tensing.

"Wait, I don't need a sec," Natalie pointed right at Ellie, then at Axel. "That's bike racer Axel, and you're . . . I can't remember your name."

"Me neither, half the time," Ellie said.

"She's not lying," David chimed in. "I'm married to her."

"Crombie!" Natalie cried out. "Somebody Crombie!"

Ellie softened and chuckled. "Hi Natalie. It's good to see you again."

"Damn, I knew it!" Natalie said. "Eleanor. Eleanor Crombie! You know how I remembered that? Because years after you were here, I was up in the Temple Hill Cemetery giving a little tour for the history center, and I saw a name on a stone. A real unusual name. Uz."

"You're kidding me," Ellie said.

"There's no record anywhere," Natalie replied. "I guess the official ledgers all come from parish rolls from the churches, and he was here so early and not a member of any church here, but the stone is up there, near the high corner, north west. Saw it with my own eyes. But of course I couldn't find you. I tried but you're not listed anywheres."

"Well I am a Crombie," Ellie laughed, "but my name isn't Crombie. Webster. Ellie Webster."

"Tickle my ass with a feather!" Natalie laughed. Heads turned.

"In fact," Ellie said, "the main reason we stopped over in Geneseo was so I could make one last try to see if Uz Crombie was ever really here. I'm sorry, I should have tried to reach you. That would have been kinda obvious."

"Well, why would I still be here?" Natalie replied. "Right? Nobody else has stuck around."

"Sometimes people stay put," Ellie said. "Never assume one way or the other, that's my lesson."

"Well anyways, you're here now," said Natalie. "Where you staying at?"

"Couple air b&bs over that way," she pointed.

"Yeah, I know those, there's a few of 'em over there. So introduce me! Who is everybody?"

Ellie pointed past Ethan. "That's David, my husband. This is our son Ethan. Axel you know. And Axel's daughters Marianne and Anna. And all of you, this is Natalie."

They gathered closer and took turns reaching across the stand to shake Natalie's hand.

"So," said Ellie, "what have you been up to that has kept you here in Geneseo New York?"

"Same old same old," Natalie replied. "Me and the historical society didn't quite see eye to eye on a few issues, so I haven't been volunteering there in a good while, but the little farm project I got started grew into pretty much of a full-time gig, just not any kind of regular nine-to-five full time."

"Farm project?" Axel asked.

"Yeah, got part of the old estate carved off as a local organic deal, sell at the farmers' market and a few local groceries. Lets the family feel like they're responsible citizens, you know?"

"That's nice," said Ellie.

"That why there's all that fertilizer in the car?" Axel asked.

"No, that's a big secret," Natalie replied in a low voice.

"Planning to blow something up?" David joked.

"The farm is supposed to be all organic," Natalie said. "If anybody found out there's a little ammonium nitrate boost every once in a while, that wouldn't go over so well. That's why it's not stored out at the farm."

"It's a natural compound," Marianne said. "Chemicals aren't unnatural."

"Plus, it really could be dangerous," David said. "We use that stuff sometimes in demolition and blasting. You have enough in the back of that car to blow up a bridge."

"How about a dam?" Natalie replied.

"Well, that would depend," David said. "How big of a dam?"

"Oh, like Mount Morris," she chuckled. "Put the valley back the way it was before we 'settlers' came and ruined it."

"The one in Letchworth State Park?" David replied. "Yeah, I know that dam. And the history of floods before it was built in the late 40s. Rochester used to get creamed pretty frequently. But in any case it would be a long shot; you'd need more explosives than that."

"Oh, cut it out—I'm JOKING," Natalie replied. "So, what are you, some kind of dam expert?"

"Civil engineer," he said, grinning. "But people have referred to me as 'that damn expert.' Especially when I tell them how much something will cost!"

"All you gotta do is tax and spend, right?" Axel said.

"Everybody loves infrastructure but nobody wants to pay for it," said David.

"Hey Dad," Anna leaned across Ethan. "Speaking of putting people to work, we could use extra hands to move stuff in Grandpa's house and plus you want to give Ethan a tour of 1357 and he needs to get his ass in gear career-wise anyway, and so wouldn't it be smart for him to ride with us to Cleveland and then fly out to Boulder and stay with us for a little bit before he goes back home?"

Axel looked at Anna, then Ethan, then back again. "This didn't occur to you just this second, did it?"

"Conspiracy afoot," Natalie said. "I can smell one of those a mile away."

"Uh, maybe we might have discussed the general proposal a little bit," Ethan said.

"I mean, it's a very sensible idea," Anna replied.

"That's my Anna, always sensible," said Axel. "Well it's fine with me. Should we suggest the idea to David and Ellie?"

"They're cool with it," Ethan said. "If you are."

Axel glanced over to where David and Ellie had been watching and listening. David chuckled and Ellie shrugged sheepishly.

Ethan followed up. "I don't have a race on the docket until the last weekend in August, so I got the time and it looks like I can get a ticket on y'all's same plane pretty cheap, so if it's cool with you I'll go ahead and book it."

Axel nodded at Ethan then Anna and gave a thumbs-up.

"So wait a minute," Natalie said, "her kid's a bike racer and yours aren't?"

Axel shrugged. "I tried but it didn't take."

The sound of a rumbling motor arose from one end of the street, and a motorcycle rolled slowly up the middle.

"Oh, that'll be Nigel," Natalie said.

The black bike was ridden by a tall, weatherbeaten man in black motorcycle leathers. Long, straight gray hair brushed his shoulders and an extended Lemmy-style mustache dipped around the sides of his mouth and ran up to his sideburns. "Hey, mates," he nodded as he took his feet off the rests and walked the bike into the space beside Natalie's stand, engine still idling. He rocked the bike up onto its kickstand and cut off the motor. "What've we got here?"

"Old pals," said Natalie. "And their new families."

Nigel scanned the group. "Pals from when?"

"Remember I told you about those two bikers, bicycle bikers I mean, who came through and stayed a night with me back in the '80s? They were biking from Ohio to New Hampshire? That's them." She pointed at Axel, then Ellie.

"Much respect," said Nigel. "Anything with two wheels. And I've ridden it all, so I know you scaled some hills."

"Mmmm-hmmm," Ellie said. "With my own two legs and my own two lungs."

"A little bit easier on a Harley, right?" Ethan offered.

"A Harley?" Nigel replied. "I wouldn't know. I'm a Triumph man. Ain't got the belly for a Harley-Davidson."

"Oh, burn," Anna said.

Nigel laughed. "Can't say which comes first, the belly or the bike, but they go together, don't they? Never see one without t' other."

"You can show correlation," Marianne said, "but causation is much harder to prove."

"Am I cool because I ride a Triumph," Nigel asked, "or did I choose a Triumph because I'm cool? Dunno. But cool and Triumph go together."

"Exactly," Marianne agreed. She finally placed where she thought she'd heard his voice before: the lovable cockney thugs who steal the puppies in *101 Dalmations*.

"Works out nice you's all here for the Big Tree festival," Nigel said. "Got rained out last night, but trying again this evening."

"He's talking about the tree," Natalie said. "We have a new tree to plant where the original Big Tree was. It got canceled last night because of the rain, but we'll try again tonight."

"Dunno if nobody will show up," Nigel said. "But too bad for them. I've a little surprise in store for that." He stepped back and looked up and down the street. "Any fun today?"

"Fun?" said Axel. "Sure, it's been nice."

"The farmers market, I mean," Nigel replied. "It's usually a lively political discourse, you might say. The pro-Americans, the anti-Americans, the greenies, the NRAs, the BLMs."

"Oh, well that's interesting," Ellie said. "Who decides who's pro-American and anti-American?"

"Everybody!" Natalie proclaimed. "You have eyes!"

"Point taken," Ellie said. "It's pretty hard not to take sides."

"Plus you know, those aren't the only lives that matter," Nigel said.

"Yeah, but you know what they mean," Ellie said. "Black people have been getting the shaft for hundreds of years."

"The War Between the States ended a long time ago," Nigel said.

"Even after the civil rights stuff in the 60s, there's still plenty to do," Ellie replied.

"Like what? I don't get any special treatment. Everybody has the same opportunity now."

"Not if you ask black people."

"Well, they just don't appreciate the opportunity they have."

"I don't know about that," David said. "Not true for the people I know."

"You know special people, then."

"For example, I don't know a single black man who hasn't been pulled over many times."

"Don't break the law, then. That's simple, isn't it?"

"No, I mean pulled over for nothing. Pulled over because a lot of cops think any black man is suspicious."

"Look, I'm no friend of the cops. Most of 'em just get a badge so they can play the bully, give people like me a hard time just for existing."

"I have only been pulled over twice in the last 20 years and I was speeding a lot both times," David said. "It just doesn't add up."

"That's because you're driving a family wagon. Put yourself on a Triumph in some leathers and long hair, then see what happens."

"But you have a choice to ride that and wear that and have that hair," David replied. "A black guy can't just change his skin. And shouldn't have to."

"Freedom," Nigel said. "I'm going to ride down the wrong side of the road if I damn well want to. You know what man stands for that!"

"Isn't that just because you're British, the riding on the other side?" David offered.

"British?" Nigel replied. "I'm from Virginia."

"Virginia?" David laughed. "No, where are you from originally?"

"Lorton, next to Alexandria," Nigel said.

"Where's the accent from, then? Are your parents British?"

"What accent?"

"Good set-up," Ethan laughed. "I gotta try that one."

"What do you mean by that?" Nigel raised his voice.

"Hey!" Natalie yelled. "Let it go Nigel. These are guests."

"Fair enough, luv, fair enough," Nigel said. "I'm going to tend to some commitments. See you all up at the tree setting, I hope."

"When is it this time?" Natalie asked.

"We decided 5:00, to allow time for a storm to pass before dark. Learnt our lesson from last night. Cheers." He hobbled stiff-legged down in the direction from which the six visitors had initially come.

"Hey," David said. "I want to scope out the rest of the market. Meet back here at 10:30?" He and Ellie and Ethan continued down the line.

"I never would have pegged Natalie for turning into a Trumper," Ellie said once they were a few stands away. "She seemed way more lefty than that three decades ago."

"Well, the far-left and the far-right kind of run into each other out there, right?" David said, "they agree on boundless freedom for me and personal responsibility for everybody else."

"And entitlement. Like other people don't deserve America as much as they do."

"They do have a point, though," Ethan said, "about the rules and regulations. I mean there's a lot of stupid rules."

"Welcome to my world," said David.

"The government just wants to control every little part of your life, it seems like. Why can't they just trust you to handle it yourself?"

"Yeah, like telling women what they can do with their bodies, right?" Ellie said.

"This may sound off-script, but every regulation is a response to something that went wrong where somebody got hurt," David said. "They don't come out of thin air."

"Like those stupid fork ends on bikes that keep the front wheel from falling out if you're too dumb to put it in right but that also prevent you from making a quick wheel change," Ethan said. "Totally defeats the purpose of having a quick-release wheel."

"It doesn't totally defeat it," Ellie said. "You can still change a wheel without needing a wrench, right?"

"Yeah, but still. It's dumb in a bike race."

"It's a classic blunt instrument situation," David said. "Try to come up with one general rule that will solve most of the problems without relying on human judgment in that moment, but it doesn't solve any particular problem very well."

Yeah, so why take human judgment out of it?" Ethan said. "Isn't that what leaders are supposed to do?"

"Absolutely," David replied. "But then look at how black people were treated by the supposed leaders before the civil rights era, or look at how workers were trampled in the Gilded Age, or how polluters used to get away with poisoning people. You could make a case that regulations are the rational response to failed leadership."

"Axel talks like a Republican sometimes," Ellie said.

"I don't know," said David. "It was more like he was coming from that place a lot of athletes come from, where you're skeptical of handouts. You want a level playing field, and people should get ahead based on their own hard work and talent. It's not that they're against people getting help, but they worry that at some point the help may be a disincentive to work."

"Why is that Republican?" Ethan asked.

"It's not," said Ellie. "But sometimes if you have that kind of attitude and you've managed to get ahead, it can be hard to see what advantages you might have had, even harder to see somebody else's disadvantage. Off the playing field, so to speak. But that's not Axel, he sees it."

"Well, I don't win bike races because of anything being handed to me," Ethan said. "When I win—if I win—it's because of hard work and smart tactics. And some luck."

"Yeah, true," Ellie said. "And your superior genes."

Axel and Marianne and Anna lingered a few stands away at the sign-up for the shooting range.

"Was Natalie like that when you first met her?" Marianne asked.

"Like what?" Axel replied.

"You know, so uh . . . so much energy, so undirected."

"Yeah, I suppose so."

"And that guy, he wasn't around then, was he?"

"Not that I knew about. He's a piece of work, huh?" Axel laughed. "Though I guess we should be careful yapping about him."

"Nice that we're all staying here one more night." Anna said as they began walking.

"That was the plan, though because our next stop is Grandpa's house and it's only about five hours away, we could grab Ethan and skip staying here tonight and head that way sooner if we run out of things to do here."

"Yeah, thanks for having Ethan come along with us. Nice of you. We can use the help and it should be good for him to see some of how your world words?"

"And by coincidence, your world, too, eh?" Axel chuckled.

"Yeah, whatever that is. Go ahead and tease me, I deserve it. He's just so adorable. I mean not just that, but, you know. Where did they go anyway?" Anna looked behind her.

"I like that guy Mikko," Marianne said.

"Me too," said Anna. "Really nice of him to come do the sauna for us."

"Yes, it was," Axel said. "He and his brother Pekka did the same for us on the bike ride."

"I know, I remember reading it," Anna said. "Very similar except you didn't even try to wear bathing suits that time!" She laughed.

"That's the right way to do it, they said," Axel replied. "I wouldn't disagree. Plus, we had very limited clothes and didn't want to get stuff wet."

"A likely story," said Marianne. "You were just forced to go skinny-dipping with your girlfriend."

"And two thirty-ish Finnish guys," he laughed. "One of them gay, though he didn't exactly say so at the time. He was all discretion, when I think about it. And I was pretty clueless anyway. It wasn't quite so easy to be out back then. Not to suggest that it's a walk in the park now, but things have improved a bit." They were back at Natalie's stand now. "Hey Natalie, as long as we get going by mid morning tomorrow, we're fine," Axel said. "So I expect we'll be there for the tree thing this evening. Besides, I found out I have some Native American ancestors, so it would be like visiting the old family neighborhood, right?"

"I pegged you for Seneca 30 years ago, didn't I?"

"I don't know about Seneca, and it's only 4 percent, but hey, I'll take it!"

"So that still leaves 2 percent for us," Marianne said. "Unless Mom had some too."

"Doubtful," Axel said.

"All the Native Americans walked across the land bridge from Asia to get here in the first place, so that would make it 52 percent," said Anna. "Pretty good math for an English major, huh?"

"But they got to Asia from Africa and so did the Europeans," said Marianne. "So just make it simple: everybody is 100 percent African."

A guy in a red hat nearby raised his head slightly and looked from Anna to Marianne and back, then placed a box of raspberries on the table in front of Natalie. David and Ellie joined them at the stand.

"If I don't see you before then," Natalie said, "just park down at the end of Big Tree lane off 63. There's a path along the river, pretty obvious." Then she turned to guy in the hat. "Just the berries? Two bucks, and thank you."

"I'll take some of those berries, too," David said, handing Natalie two dollars. "So the kids over by the Black Lives Matter sign, are they from this town too?"

"I don't know," Natalie said. "Never talked to them. They don't come over here."

"And you don't go over there?" Axel asked.

"Got my stand to watch, you know."

"We'll go over there and bring back a report," said Ellie. "We're just dumb outsiders who don't know you're not allowed to cross the street."

She started straight across, David following.

"I think I'll watch from here," said Axel.

"Well, we're going with her," Anna said. "Come on, M."

"Where's Ethan?" Axel asked. Only Natalie remained to answer the question, and she just shrugged.

They watched as the four visitors greeted the people at the Black Lives Matter table, who appeared from this distance to be two young ladies, one white and one black. They chatted for a few minutes. Axel could not see from here if there was any produce to buy or other merchandise. He looked up and down the tables on that side and determined that they mostly were offering merchandise—used books, earth-toned t-shirts, small framed pictures of flowers—along with one selling preserves and honey and maple syrup and another selling herb mixes.

Vendors on this side included two other farm stands, someone selling Make America Great Again merchandise, and another with a Confederate flag theme. "Hmmph," Axel said aloud.

"What?" said Natalie.

"Wasn't upstate New York on the Union side?"

She looked down where he was looking. "Oh, that. It's rebel thing."

"Couldn't there be a better way to show your rebel cred?"

"What, too politically incorrect for you?"

"No, just seems like hitching your wagon to a rotting horse corpse. What is that supposed to actually mean?"

"There's some things the liberals just won't ever understand."

Axel laughed. "What's your definition of a liberal?"

"Simple answer? Those people over there," she pointed across the street.

"Well, I'm standing here. I am a registered independent, and I don't buy your party line. I don't buy any party line. I make my own decisions. And I just can't see how I would ever decide to display a Confederate flag in 2018."

"How about a BLM flag?"

"Probably not. But at least I know what they're talking about."

"Which is? Don't all lives matter?"

"Yeah, but if you've been singled out for mistreatment for generation after generation, then you might get fed up and say it's time to single me out in a better way."

"Same with folks who show the Confederate battle flag."

"I don't see that, sorry."

"Poor white folks have been downtrodden and trashed on even worse than blacks."

"I don't deny poor white folks are trashed on—like all poor folks are trashed on in this great country—but to say they've had it worse than blacks, that's ridiculous."

"So you're on their side?"

"Side? Who made up these sides? It's bullshit. Make your own decisions. You don't have to pick a restaurant and swallow its whole menu."

"Well you know if I made a sign that said White Lives Matter, that would piss you off more than the BLM sign does."

"Yeah, because white people start off with advantages over black people and I tend to root for the underdog. I'm never going to root for the Yankees over the Indians."

Natalie harumphed loudly. "Chief Wahoo! Now we're talking politically incorrect!"

"Touché!" Axel laughed. "You know," he said, "there already is a White Lives Matter sign."

She gave him a skeptical squint.

"Your Confederate battle flag over there. That's what it means, isn't it? Why else would anyone display it north of the Mason-Dixon?"

"Hey look, buddy," Natalie paused. "Are you going to buy anything or just take up all my time?"

"The tomatoes look great. Will they hold a couple days in a warm car?"

"Just keep the air flowing around them."

"Okay, two containers."

"Six. For you, five."

Ethan appeared at Axel's side. "Is this a trusted seller?"

"Five stars," Axel said.

"I was just learning all about the Second Amendment," Ethan said.

"Just when you thought you were out of school," said Axel.

"Mom came over there and I was pretty sure she was going to start a fight with the one guy who was doing most of the talking," Ethan said. "Especially when he looked at Marianne and Anna and said maybe they should go back where they came from."

An angry shadow flashed across Axel's brow and he looked up the row. "Where?"

"No worries, man. Anna goes, 'Yeah, we're going back home to Colorado on Sunday' and then M goes 'But we've really been enjoying our trip to America,' and they just walk away. Fucking classic. Pardon me."

Natalie shook her head. "I have to live with these people, you know."

"Where are your folks?" Axel turned to Ethan.

"Oh, they've been having their fun," she said. "Just quietly. So far."

Axel scanned the street. "Where are they now? They didn't come with you?"

"Nah, they're on like a diplomatic mission. Taking messages back and forth between the BLM girls and one of the NRA guys. They're all saying that they want to learn how to shoot."

"My girls?" Axel said.

"Yeah, them and the BLM girls, all of them. He invited them to sign up for the firing range. They're going to close up their table a little early—just let it be self-serve."

Axel leaned over and whispered into Ethan's ear.

"Oh . . ." Ethan paused and chuckled. "I get it."

"What?" Natalie asked.

"Should I tell her?" Ethan looked at Axel, who nodded.

Ethan leaned over and whispered in Natalie's ear. She paused for a second, then let out a single, loud "ha!"

63.

There was enough time before the firing range appointment to visit the cemetery or the state park but not both, so they split into two groups. Ethan accompanied Ellie to the cemetery, and Axel drove the rest of them up to Letchworth State Park to see the famous dam and the gorge of the Genessee River.

Approached from this direction, the first feature encountered was the dam and the wide, open space upstream of the dam that would fill during rain or thaw events, with the water released gradually after—thus sparing Geneseo and Rochester and other towns downstream along the Genessee from the devastating floods that had been a periodic occurrence for centuries prior. David scanned the scene. Not far away, just beyond a bend to the left, the river emerged from this gorge in the highlands into a wide, flat floodplain that continued north all the way to Lake Ontario. It had been like that for the past 10 or 12 thousand years, since the glaciers had retreated, with the river habitually jumping its banks until only a few decades ago when the dam was built. But that had been too late for the

Big Tree. Too late for Uz. Then again, that repeated flooding was part of what made the valley so fertile. Without those historic patterns, maybe no Big Tree in the first place, no town of Geneseo at all.

They climbed back in the car and went further upstream in the park, to where the river had eroded its way through layers of soft shale that now formed vertical walls that were, in some places, hundreds of feet high.

They walked up to an edge and Axel pointed across. "That rock is so soft, the trees are constantly slipping off the top edges. Compare it to New Hampshire or Colorado. This was a lake bed not too long ago, and all those layers of mud and silt are just sort of stacked up here, like a crumbly pie crust. In the Rockies and the Whites, you have hundreds of millions of years of pressure that have cooked everything into granite, much harder. There's stuff like this around Cleveland, too. I think the whole Great Lakes basin was a big inland sea, and none of it has gotten cooked yet. Scoured by glaciers, but not pressed and heated."

"Tennessee has some of each," David replied. "Everything from the ancient Appalachians at one end to Mississippi flood plain at the other. And a range of barbecue styles to match."

"Let's go," said Axel.

"Mister healthy," said Marianne.

"I only eat barbecue if I need to protein-load," said Anna. "Which is frequently. Does New York have barbecue?"

"I'm sure," David said. "Just not its own." He laughed. "I'm going to walk up and check out that bridge. Back in a minute."

"I'll come with you," Marianne said.

Axel gave them a little wave and sat on a nearby bench. Anna started to follow, but then rejoined her father. He scooted over and smiled at her, then looked back out over the river. "Can't believe I never came here," he said. "So close."

"Yeah, it's pretty." She patted him on the knee. "Nice family, Ellie and David and Ethan. Thanks for introducing us. I know it must be a little weird."

"A little," he said. "Then again, life is weird."

"I like Ethan a lot."

"You didn't have to tell me that," he laughed. "It's great to see. I guess I'm not in any position to, uh, advise you."

"I'll ask. Really, I will. So you're handling it okay, this old stuff with Ellie? From the outside it seems okay."

"It will take a while to stop replaying everything I did wrong back then. But I think it was the right thing to do to reconnect. At least I hope it was."

"Here's where I'm not in any position to advise you. Except I will say one thing, you have—you both have—really tried to be kind and fair about the whole thing. You can't regret that."

"No."

"And you have to give David a lot of credit. He's somehow managed to really walk a fine line on this thing."

"I know. I'd like to thank him for that, but how? What do I thank him for? Still working on that."

"I can see what you saw in her. She's got some kind of wild spark going in there. And she's so pretty in that uncon-scious disheveled kind of way of people who seem like the less they try to look pretty the more pretty they are."

"Yeah, maybe I go for that."

"Mom, too?"

He nodded. "And she passed it along to both her daugh-ters in different flavors. The spark thing and the pretty thing."

"Well, we've got a lot of you in us, too, you know. You can't put it all on somebody who isn't here to defend herself!"

He laughed. "Like what?"

"Like not needing to say out loud every single thing that comes into your head. Like picking yourself up of the ground and keeping on going. Like being fair to everybody even if they don't deserve it."

"You mean that potty mouth of yours is *after* editing?"

"Now see, just now I was going to say 'Fuck yeah!' but I didn't."

"Very demure of you." He put his arm around her. "Hey, seriously. Thanks for checking up on me. I know I'm not the most transparent person. I appreciate it. I do think I'm okay, and Ellie, too. And if you and Ethan really do hit it off and make a go of it, well that would be one more weird thing in this world. But wonderful too. Sort of cosmically right somehow. You have my full support, to the extent that you can use it. I'll try not to, uuh, push. Or pull. I'll try not to fuck it up. How's that? Love you, Anna."

Ellie closed the driver's door and got her bearings. The stone should be somewhere in this area, in the northwest corner of the cemetery, according to Natalie's description.

Ethan joined her. "Just start combing row by row?"

"Suppose so," she said. "Maybe I start here and work that way, and you start at the far corner of this patch and we work toward each other?"

"Cool," he said. He walked along the gravel drive and around the perimeter until the drive met another.

Ellie watched him until he turned around, then remembered what she was here to do and began walking. The stones varied a lot in size, in polish, in the kind of stone. Some at first seemed clearly older, but she began to suspect they had just been made of softer stone to begin with. A close examination of some dates confirmed the suspicion. The stone Emma Too's father had used must have been pretty hard if Natalie could still read it today. She got to the end of the row and turned 180 degrees to walk down the next one. A few of these names were also street names in town, she noticed. More evidence that it was the oldest part of the cemetery.

One caught her eye, a small stone, clearly very old. Ursula Ward, 1816–1823. Not too many first names begin with U. A very large obelisk stone with the name Walker on it, surrounded by small flat stones of given names: Robert, Jane, Hillaire, Henry, Henry, Henry, Margaret. Some stones had just the name, others included a phrase echoing a different world: Thomas Baily, b. 1788, Left the Form July 24, 1844. "Left the Form" sounded amusingly like "Bought the Farm" to her, but she didn't laugh out loud. Stop, turn, next row.

"Here he is," Ethan called out. "Taken by a freshet."

Ellie walked over and stood beside her son as they regarded the grave of a great, great, many times great uncle.

Uz Crombie

1797–1818

Taken by a freshet

Just about Ethan's age. Marianne's age. Anna's age. Her own age when she had first come to this place. And Axel's. The world ahead of them. Ellie trembled, holding Ethan's arm. The father had carved the words into the stone, the name of his own son. The year his son was born. The year his son died. The buried young man's own father carved the words, she kept thinking. While Emma Too watched, maybe for hours. Every letter, every number, laboriously chiseled by his own father into the hardest stone he could find.

David looked up at the bridge, then took out his phone to photograph it. "Another one for my collection."

"A bridge collector?" Marianne asked.

"Bridges, tunnels, dams, embankments, terraces, harbors, castles, moats—the human equivalents of spider webs and bird nests and gopher holes."

"And snail trails and beaver dams and termite mounds and conch shells and coral reefs and cat piss on the bedpost."

"Poetic," he said. "You and Ellie."

'I'm in good company, then," Marianne smiled and flipper her hair back from her face. "She's quite a woman."

"Yes, quite," he said. "Glad you've had a chance to spend some time together."

"Me too. We had some good talks."

"She told me."

"I hope I didn't lay too much on her."

"She hoped she didn't lay too much on you," David laughed.

"But you," Marianne looked at him. "You're the unsung hero here. None of this healing happens without you."

"Oh, I don't know about that. I'm just trying not to put my foot in it."

"Far from it. I don't want to embarrass you in public, so I won't say it in public, but thank you. It's hard to imagine a better husband or friend. Not just nice, but smart. You would have had every right to shut my dad out completely."

"That wouldn't have solved anything."

"That's what I mean," she said.

"He's a fine man," said David. "You and Anna are lucky to have him."

"I know. Well, likewise, Ethan and Ellie are lucky to have you. I'm glad it seems like—well like everybody has gotten or is getting through this potentially disastrous situation un-scathed."

"I wouldn't say unscathed. Maybe scathed but better for it, if there is such a thing."

"I don't know, my sister's the writer. And Ellie. We'll have to consult the grammar experts."

"It's a good thing our families seem to, uh, get along to-gether. We might be seeing more of each other."

"It does appear to be heading in that direction. But I tell you what. Anna talks a sassy game but she hasn't really been in a serious relationship, and if Ethan doesn't treat her right, I will beat the shit out of him. Or at least try. Though she could probably do a better job of it herself."

"That's so sweet, I'm telling Ellie. She already loves you and that will put her right over the edge."

"Thanks," said Marianne. "I'm not naturally good at it, but I try to be charming."

"Will you protect Ethan, too, if Anna is mean to him?"

"She won't be," Marianne said. "But yes."

64.

The firing range wasn't a formal facility, but an arrangement of tree stumps at the back edge of Lester Springer's property a few blocks from the farmer's market. A pockmarked grassy hill rose just behind the stumps. Targets were painted on the stumps, which were arranged to be different distances from the firing position, but most of the paint had been chipped away, so Lester walked out and stapled a paper target to each of them. On the far left was a larger stump with no target. To the right of the stumps was a wooden fence with assorted cans and bottles and plastic animal figurines arranged along top of it.

"Now these are just single-shot .22 rifles," Lester said. "Just like what you use in Boy Scout camp." He went over basic safety protocols, then illustrated how to load a round into the chamber. He walked up to a split rail fence that served to define the firing position. "You want to stand like so, with your left shoulder forward toward the target and the butt of the rifle snug against your right shoulder so you can get your eye to the sight. Don't cock the rifle until just before you're going to shoot. That reduces the chance of any accidental discharge. Line up the sight with the target, exhale, and squeeze the trigger real steady." He fired into the big stump. "We use the big one here to practice before we start shooting at the targets. Then we'll rotate through them, 25, 50, and 100 yards. Don't worry about missing—that's what the big hill is for."

As Anna had guessed, their instructor assumed none of them had ever so much as touched a firearm, much less been a collegiate biathlon champion, so she played it cool. This was the proper way for him to approach it: conservatively, to make sure no one got into any danger. She offered to go first so she could be the model good student and give the two BLM girls a solid example to follow. Marianne already knew how to shoot also, but she'd always preferred skeet.

Anna allowed Lester to position her shoulders, advise her how to place her feet, suggest which eye to use. She fired and watched a few wood chips fly from the big stump.

"Good," he said. "All right, next up." Marianne followed the instructions and also hit the stump. "Real nice," he said. "I'm sorry, I should have got your names."

"I'm Marianne," she said, "and that's Anna."

"Sisters, I might guess?"

"Yep. That gnarly guy over there with the bike hat is our dad Axel. And our friend David with him. And you're Mr. Springer, is that right?" Marianne asked.

"Just Lester is fine." He turned to the other two. "And who have we got next?"

"I'm Debra," said the darker-skinned woman, "and that's Carrie."

"Down from Rochester?" Lester asked.

"I grew up here," Carrie said. "Deb's my roommate at SUNY. From Ithaca."

"Serves me right for guessing," he said. "Okay Debra, your turn."

As Anna had hoped, Debra had been watching carefully and, though it was clear she was not already familiar with shooting, she had picked up enough not to be totally at sea. "After you cock it, make sure to brace it tight on your shoulder, although this is only a .22 so you're not going to bruise yourself with the recoil," Lester said. "There, good, like that. Okay, aim, then squeeze." She hit the edge of the stump. "First try, good job."

Carrie stepped up. "See if I remember anything from shooting cans with my brothers," she said.

"BB gun?" he asked.

"Yeah. Also went skeet shooting a couple times, that was a shotgun."

"Well this will be kind of between those two," Lester said. She hit the stump as well.

Lester led them down the fence line. "Okay now comes the hard part. We're going to have each of you at one of these marks on the fence. They are color coded, red, green, blue with the paint on top of the stump. You fire at the target straight out from you, then when everyone has shot that round, we rotate. Since we got four of you and just three distances, after the 100, you sit one out. So let's have Marianne sit out the first round, then follow. Sorry Anna, you get to start with 100, the blue one."

Anna was beginning to feel a little bit bad about the ruse, and though she wasn't completely confident that she could hit the 100-yard target with an unfamiliar rifle she'd only fired once, her biathlon gun was also a .22 and the one shot had felt pretty similar, and this target was bigger than they used at 50 meters in the biathlon. She decided that if she hit the 100-yard target on the first try, she would come clean.

"Okay," Lester said, "let's start with Carrie, give it ten seconds, then move on to Debra, and so on. Carrie, whenever you are ready, you may fire."

She cocked the rifle, lifted it, steadied her aim for a few seconds, then fired, hitting the outer edge of the black circle. "Nice," said Lester. "Try to calm that breathing and don't take quite so long aiming and you'll find it even easier. Okay, Debra."

She spent even longer aiming, then missed altogether. "Don't worry about it," he said. "Keep working at it, it will come. Did you see how Carrie braced her leg and fired quickly after aiming? Do things like that and you'll be successful."

Axel could hear himself saying more or less the same thing when he had first taken them to the firing range when they were teenagers. He watched as Lester gave Anna the go-ahead and she raised, aimed, and fired the rifle in one clean motion. He couldn't see from where he stood whether the bullet had hit the target 100 yards away, but Anna's body language suggested so.

"Damn," Lester said, lowering his binoculars.

"I'm sorry," Anna said.

"Sorry?" Lester said. "One inch off-center at 100 yards?"

Marianne laughed. "No, this is what she's sorry about." She held up her phone so Lester could see. The photo showed Anna with her skis and rifle, standing on the middle step of a podium above two other women, snow swirling around them.

"Oh," he laughed. "A ringer. You set me up!"

"That's why I said I was sorry. Want me to help?"

"Are you a certified instructor?"

"No, but is this a certified venue?"

"Guess that's a point," he said. "Just a little afternoon fun among friends, right?"

Anna nodded. "If it's okay with you. We ought to pay you for all these rounds, though."

"Forget about it. Fair trade if you tell me about the biathlon. I got a 16-year-old son who's turning into a pretty good middle-distance runner, and this might be something we could share. I know they do it around here, up north at least."

"Is he a good skier? No offense, but it's easier to teach a great skier to shoot than the other way around."

"Not on a team or anything, but he enjoys going out with his buddies."

"I'm sure you would guess," said Anna, "that the hard part about it is you've got to go from all-out skiing at close to max heart rate, then settle down and squeeze off five shots fast. Always 50 meters, and the rifle is a .22. Then ski again. Every miss you have to do a lap of a penalty circuit, 150 meters. Lowest time wins."

"I'd like to see that," he said.

"Well," she looked down to verify that she was as usual already wearing running shoes and shorts. "How about we rest the rifle over there by the duckies. Set five of them up at 50 yards, meters, whatever. I'll run half a mile or so and end up there and see how many I can hit."

"Show-off," said Marianne.

"I know," she said. "Maybe I'm like Ethan with his bike racing instagrams. Where are they, anyway?"

"Not back from the cemetery, I guess," Axel said. "They'll be along."

"Their loss," Anna said. "Coulda seen me get all sweaty and miss all the ducks."

"I have nothing with a multi-shot magazine," Lester said. "What if we line up five rifles?"

"Ooh, extra challenge," Anna said. "Yeah, if you load 'em, I'll cock 'em." She looked around. "How about if I run over by the barn, down that lane, and loop back up here? The uphill ought to get the heart rate up pretty well. For any miss, I run to the barn and back one time. If you all want to keep shooting, I'll be behind you anyway. Glad I didn't wear flip-flops today."

Lester retrieved one more rifle from inside, loaded it, and leaned all five on the fence. Anna took off her t-shirt and draped it next to the rifles. The spectators stood about 20 yards back from the improvised start/finish at the edge of the fence. Lester gave her a ten-second countdown on his watch and yelled "go!"

Anna took off toward the barn, the red shorts and black sport top easy to track against the pale green grass. Ellie and

Ethan saw her approaching as they rounded the barn. "Hey!" Ethan yelled.

"Can't stop!" Anna called as she turned past the barn began to run down the hill on the lane, which curved along the edge of the woods. She left the lane and ran up the grassy slope and was back at the starting point in about two and a half minutes. She ran directly to the rifles just as Ellie and Ethan joined the others.

"Pop!" One duck fell. "Pop!" Another. "Pop!" This duck wavered, but didn't tumble. "Pop!" Duck fell. "Pop!" Duck fell. She tore off to the barn, touched the wall, and ran back to the start/finish.

"Four minutes and three seconds," Lester said, shaking his head. The crowd of seven went wild.

"There," said Anna, hands on knees, still panting. "That gives you the idea. Now add snow and skis and longer distance and more shooting both standing and prone."

"Whoa," Ethan said. "Can I try that?"

"First dibs to our existing customers," Lester said.

"No thanks," Marianne said. "But I will finish our rounds of shooting, if that's okay."

"Sorry," Anna said. "I don't mean to hijack this thing." Marianne smiled and shrugged.

"You ladies?" Lester asked.

"Same as her," Debra said. Carrie nodded.

"Okay, let's give the boy his run around and we'll get back to our instruction in five minutes. Do you need a rifle lesson?"

"Is that just a regular .22 like at the firing ranges?"

"Yes it is," Lester said.

"Well, I've done that a few times," Ethan said. How about one practice shot, then I go?"

Lester loaded a rifle and handed it to him. "The green one is 50 yards. All clear!" Ethan stepped up to the fence, cocked the rifle, sighted, and fired.

"Second ring," Lester said. "And your form looks good enough. So let's go."

They set up 5 ducks, a few of them getting a little worse for the wear, and loaded and placed the five rifles. Ten, nine, eight . . . Ethan tore off toward the barn.

"He's gonna be 20 or 30 seconds faster on the run," Anna said as Ethan descended the hill on the lane.

"Can't shoot like you, though," said Lester.

"Nope," said Anna. "We'll see."

Ethan dashed up to the rifles. Miss, hit, hit, miss, miss. He did his three wind sprints to the barn and back and did them very quickly, but did not make up the time.

"Four forty-seven," said Lester. "Looks like you could afford only one miss more than her."

Ethan collapsed on his back on the ground. "Much respect, ma'am."

"Thanks," she said, pulling her t-shirt back on.

"How do you get so still with your heart racing?" Ethan sat up. "My arms were spazzing all over the place."

"That's my secret—everybody's secret who's good at this. You're fast on skis but maybe not the fastest, but you're the fastest who can chill out enough to shoot."

"And how did you discover this sport?" Lester asked.

"I was watching the Olympics on TV when I was in ninth grade. They interviewed somebody and she said she got into it one, because she had both the big motor and the steady hand, but also because there was so much competition to get on the more popular teams and this sort was a little bit overlooked sometimes. Which is to say she could actually get on the team. Then she worked really hard and got to be one of the best. I thought that was like trying out for the school band—everybody wanted to play flute or trumpet, so you could improve your odds by picking up the piccolo."

"An English major ought to be able to come up with a better analogy than that," Marianne said. "It's really that she has the horsepower to race a gazelle and the fine motor skills to perform brain surgery."

"How about ski fast and shoot a gun?" Axel offered.

"Thanks, Mr. Literal," Marianne said.

"No prob," Axel said.

They resumed the rotation and Anna stood aside. No one else was able to hit the 100-yard target, but Debra hit the others, which she attributed to calming techniques learned in her yoga classes. Ethan took Anna's place in the rotation and was preparing to try for the 100 when Natalie came jogging up, out of breath.

"It's gone!" she panted. "The car is gone."

65.

Natalie explained to the officer again that she always left the car unlocked in a corner of the lot behind the funeral home because that was the most convenient place to load up from for the farmers market and she's been doing it that way for 20 years at least, and that the reason she left it unlocked was that all the door locks had long since frozen up and you couldn't get a key in there anyway, and fortunately the 1973 Volvo wagon was old enough that it didn't have automatic locks and that's why Natalie never locked herself out, besides if you couldn't leave your car unlocked, then what was this world coming to, and also besides, most of the key had broken off in the ignition a long time ago but you could still start it up by sticking the broken stub in there and so she just left the broken key attached to a fob sitting on the seat because if she lost it she could never start the car because there wasn't another key and she wasn't about to go get fleeced at a Volvo dealer to get new keys made because they would probably make her put in new ignition and replace all the door locks too and that was just too much.

Was there anything of value in the car? No, not really. And she stopped short of saying about the fertilizer on account of how the farm was supposed to be chemical free and all that. All the valuable produce she had over at the tables and it was when she was going to get the car to load up the unsold vegetables because the market was closing up for the day that she found out the car was gone. At first she thought it was probably those BLM folks, but then they were here with Lester so that couldn't be.

Also, did she ever think of just sticking a screwdriver into the ignition, because that had worked for the officer's brother-in-law for years on his old Newport, because the ignition looked normal and no one would guess you could just stick a screwdriver in it, and that would have gotten around the problem of leaving a key fob sitting on the seat all the time, which would be a fairly obvious security risk if you asked that officer.

Yes, but she needed the screwdriver in the house to get the toaster to pop up before it started a fire like had happened a number of times.

Okay ma'am so we have a gray 73 Volvo wagon, and what was the plate on that? You don't recall? It might of fell off? Yes it's just a short distance but you still need plates to be legal on the road. No I guess if it was a wagon and you pulled it with a horse then maybe it would not need a plate. But were you pulling it with a horse? No, well then that's really not material to our current situation. If you took the motor out, yes, that would make it even clearer that it's a wagon and not a vehicle, but I expect it did have a motor in it when you drove it down here this morning. Yes, thank you for confirming that. Now we will be keeping an eye out for this vehicle. I can't recall as I've seen another one like it, so if she's on the open road, I expect we'll find her. You just sit tight. I have your land line. No cell, is that correct? Okay. Has any of you got a cell number where I might call if we find out something and there's nobody to get the land line? Now do you need a ride someplace?

Ellie offered that she had room in the Subaru and could give Natalie a ride back to her house.

The officer thanked them all and set off.

"Well," said Lester. "At least you have a sharp-shooter with you if it comes down to that."

"What, you're coming with us?" Natalie replied. "We gotta find Nigel."

"No, not me. This young lady here can shoot the beak off a chickadee."

"I would never do that," Anna said.

"Why do you gotta find Nigel?" Lester asked.

"I just got a bad feeling," Natalie said.

"Do you want to go back to your house?" Ellie asked.

"First I got to pack up the produce and run it back over to the farm," she said. "Then we could go back there. But of course I don't have the car."

"I expect between our two, we could fit everything," Axel said, glancing at Ellie for confirmation. She nodded. "We're both parked back in that direction, so let's go." Axel took a step, then turned. "And thank you, Mr. Springer. You ended up giving us a good chunk of your afternoon."

"Just Lester," he said. "It was my pleasure, folks, and I'm interested to learn more about this biathlon."

"There's a national website," Anna said, "usbiathlon.org. They ought to have the local chapters listed, if your son wants to get into it. Also when the season gets going I post a lot of stuff on Instagram—training and competition stuff that might be interesting. annalog, my name plus log. What's his name,? I'll watch for him."

"Michael," he said. "He does Instagram, too. mboing Get it? I even do it, but I'm not so creative. justlester."

"Great. Actually, even better . . . if you've got a cell number I'll text you links when I get home."

"Absolutely," he said. They exchanged texts.

"Nice to meet you, Lester, and thanks for sharing so much of your time with a bunch of strangers."

"Strangers no more," Lester said. "You take care, folks. And if any of you all want to come practice, you know where to find me. Always welcome. I'll keep my eye out for Nat's car." He waved and walked toward the back of the house.

Natalie led the way back downtown, half walking, half jogging. David and Ethan lingered behind at a more moderate pace. They rounded a corner one block from the market area and she stopped short. "Damn, I was afraid of that." The tables had all been pushed up for storage under the awnings against the storefronts. The tomatoes and berries and other produce was gone. On the other side of the street, the Black Lives Matter table was also up against the wall, but the banner was folded on top, weighted down by the two boxes of literature they had been distributing.

Debra and Carrie walked over and retrieved those materials. "Thanks for the interesting afternoon," Carrie said.

"Good luck on the car. Sorry that happened to you," Debra said.

Natalie nodded. "Thanks. You be careful, girls."

They carried the boxes around behind the building.

"Well," Natalie said, "I guess there's not much reason to go back to the farm now."

"Where did everything go?" Ellie asked.

"They probably gave it away or took it home when they put the tables back," Natalie said. "Can't just leave fresh produce sitting out unattended. Critters come after it."

"That seems weird," Ellie replied. "Who is 'they?'"

"The city," Natalie grunted. "Always looking out for my best interest."

"I don't know, they left the BLM stuff alone; somebody even folded up the banner," Axel said.

"Just showing their bias." Natalie looked up and down the street. "Gimme a second, be right back." She walked between two buildings, reemerging a short time later just as David and Ethan arrived. "That's what I was afraid of. Nigel's bike is still back there. I bet he has the car."

"What's wrong with that?" David asked. "Does he drive on the wrong side or something?"

"You don't know Nigel," she said. "He's a good man, but he gets passionate about his ideas. I'm afraid he's up to something."

"For instance?" said David.

"For instance, something a little bit extreme that he might be sorry about later. Dammit. What time is it?"

"Almost 5:00," he replied.

"Damn," she said. "I gotta get down to the river and set up for the Big Tree. My schedule is shot. Would you mind, could we run down there?"

David looked over at Axel and Ellie, both of whom shrugged and nodded. They loaded up the two cars and Natalie led them through city streets, then out of town to the west.

Natalie instructed Ellie to where to pull off then had her park at a road siding. Axel tucked the other car in behind. She led them down a path for a few minutes until they emerged from the low, scrubby woods onto a peninsula created by a bend in the river. "Oh good," she said. "The shovels and the tiki torches already made it down here. Could you all help set these up? We want a semicircle facing the river. The tree's coming downriver by raft and we'll slide it up on the plastic sheet here. We dug the hole a few days ago, so it will just be a matter of sliding the root ball over here, dropping it in, straightening it, and shoveling in the extra dirt around it. The river meanders a lot down here, so we can't put it exactly where the old tree was. It'll be on the inside of this bend over here."

"It just shows up on a raft by itself?" Ellie asked as Marianne and Anna and Ethan began placing the tiki torches, the ends of which were gathered in knotted Wal-Mart bags. Marianne noticed the torches were stamped "Made in Malaysia."

"It will be tied between two canoes guided by Seneca and colonial re-enactors."

"What are they re-enacting?" Ellie asked. "Was the original Big Tree planted that way?"

"Of course not, it was just there. That's how the whole place got its name," Natalie said.

"Okay . . ." said Ellie.

Three people emerged from the woods on the opposite shore, followed by four more. "Here come the spectators," Natalie said. "It's easier for some folks to just park on River Road over there and walk down from that side, you know instead of driving all the friggin way around to get to the next bridge. Where the hell is Nigel? We have ten minutes. He has a lighter. Does anyone have matches or a lighter?" They all looked at each other shaking heads to indicate the negative. "Hey, anybody over there got some matches or a lighter?" She yelled across the river. One man fished in his jacket pocket and waved his hand in the air.

After a minute he yelled back. "In a bag with a rock. Incoming!" He heaved a blue plastic package, which landed upstream a few feet from the water. Ethan, who was closest, retrieved and opened it.

They lit the tiki torches. Now there were about 20 people on the opposite shore. A rumble filled the muggy air and Natalie looked up and to the left. A bank of clouds was building up above the trees, sunlit billowy tops and charcoal gray below. "Thunderstorm. That's just what we need."

"Good thing there's a dam up there," said David.

"Oh shit," Natalie muttered.

"What now?" said Ellie, standing next to her.

"The dam."

"The dam?" Ellie replied.

"I just figured it out. My sweet lunatic Nigel is going to blow up the dam!"

Ellie's mind immediately conjured a low rumbling sound and visions of tumbling blocks pushed downstream by a rush of muddy water. She pictured herself being pulled away from the others as the water rose and blocks crashed past. It was right here—all of it with Uz had happened right here. The thunder got closer and she saw a flash of lightning.

"He's going to what?" David replied. "That was a lot of work, building that thing."

"Government work," Natalie said. "What a dramatic and symbolic act that would be. Save America from itself."

"It's not far," David said. "We could go head him off."

"You have a rifle? Take sharpshooter girl with you," Natalie pointed at Anna.

Anna shook her head. "Back at home, no rifle here. And I'm not going to shoot the guy. He's your boyfriend, for one thing. And what if I shoot him and it turns out he wasn't going to blow up the dam?"

"Shoot the fertilizer," Natalie. "Blow it up!"

"I don't think shooting the fertilizer would blow it up, David said. "Maybe on TV."

"Then what the hell do we do?" Natalie threw up her arms, a gesture perfectly timed with another flash of lightning followed a second later by a crackling clap.

Thunder echoed across the valley and a few large raindrops began to dot the river surface. Just as the treetops began to sway as the wind picked up, a boisterous call of "huzzah!" came from upstream. They turned to look as a canoe emerged around the bend, followed by a raft, followed by a second canoe. In the center of the raft was a tree about ten feet tall, including the substantial root ball. Standing beside the tree and steadying it was a tall man dressed in colonial garb. The silver undersides of the leaves seemed to wave in celebration as the wind swirled overhead. "Huzzah!" cried the man and the four canoeists. The tall man thrust his arm into the air and in the process tilted the raft, which tilted the tree, which pulled the rope attached to one canoe, which threw the two Seneca re-enactors who were in that canoe into the river, which caused the tall man to bellow "Fuck all!" as he tried to regain his balance, which pulled the rope to the other canoe, which the occupants of said canoe had already had the presence of mind not to tie to a thwart but simply to hold by hand, and which now they promptly released, thus avoiding their own capsize. "Bollocks!" yelled the tall man as the raft spun past the peninsula. He leaned back against the weight of the tree but slowly the leverage of his height took over and the tree tipped itself over and dunked him into the Genessee. The clouds let loose with a pummeling downpour.

"Nigel" Natalie yelled. "Get him, he doesn't swim!"

Marianne was in the water by the word "swim" and quickly applied her lifeguard training to clobber the flailing victim into submission so she could get her arm under his chin and haul him face-up toward the shore. Ellie and Natalie, who were closest by, quickly waded in and helped drag him up unto the mud. The two dunked re-enactors climbed to safety on the other side, while the two who remained aboard their craft, having determined that everyone was safe, had taken off through sheets of rain in pursuit of the raft and its tree, loose ropes dragging in the water behind. Relieved of its counterweight, the tree had flipped itself back up and was now rocking steadily side to side. The pursuers got close before the next bend, but the current increased there as the river narrowed and the raft and its upright occupant disappeared around the corner, bound for Rochester. The re-enactors began paddling laboriously back upstream, fighting not only the current but the gusty winds that accompanied the passing storm.

Nigel sat in the mud and watched the tree go. "I'm sorry, luv."

"Oh my god!" Natalie cried. "I was so worried."

"It's not so deep," he said. "Might've been able to save me own neck. Might've not." He nodded at Marianne.

Beside him, Marianne stood and brushed the mud off her knees. "Just doing my job," she said. "My former job."

Natalie shook her head. "First the car gets stolen, then you disappear, then I suddenly realize you're probably going to try to blow up the dam."

"Blow up the dam?" Nigel looked at her incredulously.

"Like we were joking about earlier. With all the fertilizer in the back of the car, add a flame and it's basically a bomb.

Oklahoma City all over again. You said you had a big surprise for the ceremony."

"The surprise was me dressing up like Paul Revere and riding 'round with the tree. The falling in the river bit was improvised. What's this about blowing things up? We didn't discuss nothing like that"

"Maybe that was before you got there," she reconsidered.

"And the car," Nigel said. "Nobody stole the car. It's back in the lot, like we planned."

"Planned?"

"We did. I picked it up from the market, like we planned, to get the tree over to the raft launch place—and that looked something special, I'll tell you, a ten-foot tree tied down to the roof—and then I go back to the market. Seeing you was gone, I assume you're entertaining the guests and I goes ahead and takes the produce back to the farm, then take the car back and park it, and ride my bike over here. Fraid there's some dirt and scuffs on the roof, luv. Could buff it out, I expect."

"So the car is back behind the funeral home now?"

"Of course it is."

Natalie paused for a few moments. "Well . . . good. That's good isn't it?" She looked at Ellie for some reason.

"Yes," Ellie said. "That's good."

The rain eased up. The conversation ceased for a few minutes while their attention was taken by what was going on across the river. The two re-enactors who were still in their canoe gave up fighting the current, made their way to the riverbank, and climbed out, then began walking the canoe back upstream. The other canoe had lodged itself under an overhanging branch. Its crew waded downstream and freed it. One of the two paddles was deemed lost, but the other crew came across it while negotiating their way up the shoreline. With both canoes and their crews intact again, the re-enactors prepared to cross the river. When they arrived, Natalie thanked them for their participation and handed one of them a plastic baggie. "There's a check in there for each of you."

"Thanks, Miss," he said, "but the job isn't done. No tree planted."

"Don't worry about that," she replied. "We can reschedule again. If we managed to do without a Big Tree for 150 years, what difference does a few more weeks make, or even a couple of years?"

"Well, you keep us notified. We want to come back and finish the thing. No charge."

"You don't have to do that," she said. "But much appreciated." She eyed the clouds. "Looks like we get a little break here—best everybody gets home while the getting is good."

David looked beyond her. "Think we're done with storms for tonight?"

"If you believe the weather report," Natalie replied. "That's what it said—20 percent chance of a passing afternoon shower. So they were only 80 percent off. Seems like it's clearing out, though, sky looks bright west. Leave all this crap here. We'll get it in the morning."

She called out to the remaining members of the dwindling crowd. "All done for now. Thanks for coming out. We'll go get us another tree and try again in the near future. Be safe getting home!" Marianne noticed that Lester Springer was over there. She waved in case he was looking. He waved, either to her or in acknowledgment of Natalie's send-off. Then he turned around and walked into the woods. Natalie turned to Ellie and David, who were standing closest. "Listen, I gotta get my Nigel into dry clothes. He's fragiler than he looks. It has been great seeing you all and thanks for the help. I'd invite you over but my place is a wreck right now, half-remodeled for the past six years."

"We have a couple nice picnic tables in front of our b&b, Ellie said. "No worries. Couldn't find Genny pounders, though!"

"Ha! Okay, well if you're ever in town again—which I seriously doubt but I thought the same thing 30 years ago—call me up. Same land line, no cell phone. I'm in the book."

"There's still a book here?" said Ellie. "Long gone where we are."

"I kept my old phone book," Natalie said. "Since I got no computer."

"Oh, right," Ellie said, deciding not to fall into hole in Natalie's logic. "One more thing before you go. Thank you so much for the info about Uz and his grave. Ethan and I went there and saw it. For me it was . . . was unexpectedly moving. So thank you. Do take care." She leaned over and gave Natalie a quick hug. Nigel offered a general wave and the two of them walked back up into the woods.

Marianne, Ethan, and Anna were standing next to the hole that had been dug into high ground inside the bend in the river, looking at the phone pictures Ethan had gotten of Nigel on the raft before he fell into the river. "That was a white oak, right?" Marianne said, pointing at the sapling in the photo. "When it gets mature, if it doesn't have any other trees around it, the branches reach as much sideways as they do straight up and it will become one of those majestic half-dome trees you see standing out in the middle of fields. They can live a few hundred years."

"Yeah," Ethan said, "I think that's what Natalie said."

"Well," said Marianne, "I know my trees well enough from botany and forest-management classes to know that there are lots of white oak saplings along the path from the road to here. A few mature trees, too, but since they're in a forest they go up instead of out. They could well be descended from that original old tree. So I have an idea."

"I getcha," Anna said. "We move one."

"Hey you three," Axel called. "Ready to head out? We were thinking another picnic same place as last night would work out, assuming the rain is over."

"Hole's already dug, wouldn't take 20 minutes," Ethan said. He looked across the river. No one else here. "We have an idea," he called back.

"Uh-oh," said David.

"You want to leave it to us or be co-conspirators?"

"Hmm, tough one," Axel said.

"Surprise us!" Ellie called.

"Okay," Ethan called back. "Can I steal our car for about a half hour? That would give you time to get us some yummy dinner."

"Uh, sure," said David. "Here's my key." He fished in his pocket and tossed it to Ethan, who had walked closer.

"Okay, thanks," Ethan winked. "Off with you now or you won't be able to plead ignorance."

"We're leaving, we're leaving" Ellie said. They disappeared into the woods.

Marianne waited about 90 seconds, then walked briskly back up the path, Ethan and Anna grabbing two shovels along the way.

"There were half a dozen good saplings right at this bend," Marianne said, stepping off the path. "This one, maybe. Or that one over there's a little more in the open—it's already spreading a little."

"It's a good size already, too," said Anna. "Looks about like the one that got away, maybe a little bigger."

"Agreed?" Ethan looked at them and, not hearing a 'no,' began to dig. Anna joined in on the opposite side. In a few minutes they had encircled the tree and dug deep enough that they could, the three of them together, rock it back and forth until Ethan was able to chop the tap root.

"Now we just drag the motherfucker over there, right?" Anna said, leaping up to grab the thin trunk at a high place and tilt the top downward. The wet ground was a big help in that it had made the shoveling easier, but it also made the walking muddy and perilous, and each of them slipped and fell once or twice on the way. But soon they had hauled the tree to its destination and were able to position the root ball next to the dug hole. They rocked it into the hole. Among the three of them they were able to reposition the ball slightly to straighten the tree. Then they shoveled the extra loose dirt around it, put the shovels back where they had been leaning at the edge of the clearing, and trotted for the car.

Fortunately, as Ethan expected, there were a couple of towels in the back, a habit born of many trips with dogs and many side-detours to swimming holes. They wiped off most of the mud, then Anna and Marianne sat on one towel while Ethan sat on the other, in an attempt to keep the car clean. The new Big Tree was not visible except from the riverside, but Natalie would see it in the morning when she went to retrieve the shovels.

Ellie climbed out of the rear seat and closed the door. "I'll go in and bring out drinks. We'll see who gets here first, you or the offspring."

"Any requests?" David asked as he lowered the window.

"Thin crust if there's a choice. I wonder if you automatically get New York style out here or if they hate anything to do the big city?"

"Could be both," he said. She gave him a kiss through the window and they drove off. "Thanks for driving," he turned to Axel.

"No, thank you," Axel said, "for subjecting yourself to all this. I appreciate it. You didn't have to."

"I suppose not," David replied. "But I would have always felt weird about it if I'd squashed the idea. Also, maybe I was stupid, but I was pretty sure it would work out okay. You know, trusting people."

Axel nodded. "You didn't even know me. That's a lot of trust."

"But I know Ellie, and I felt like I knew you, too, from reading the account and talking to her, but you're right. There was a risk. Things could have changed."

"Things did change. Life went on. A lot happened. Here we are."

"Everything leads to this point, I guess," Davis said.

"I meant here we are at the pizza place," Axel laughed, "but you're not wrong. It seems like many things in my life have led to pizza."

"All roads lead to Rome."

"You ever been to Rome?" Axel turned off the car and climbed out.

"In college for a semester."

"Nice."

"You?"

"Bucket list." He paused by the door. "I'd rather not go alone, though. Maybe I can swing a trade show or something. Find an Italian client."

"Did you travel before, with the girls and your . . ."

"Su-Yun," Axel entered the pizzaria. "No, not much. That was for the future. Which turned out not to exist." Axel's chin was turned up toward the menu board above the counter but David could see his eyes were blank and unmoving. He put his hand on Axel's shoulder, but Axel shrugged it off. "Sorry," Axel said. "No offense. I'm just having a little moment here. Could you order? I'm gonna step outside for a second."

David momentarily considered following Axel, but decided to give him a minute alone. He stepped up to the counter. "Three larges, please. A pepperoni with black olives, a prosciutto and spinach, and mushroom and red onion and green pepper. That ought to cover it." The guy at the counter said fifteen minutes.

David went outside. Axel was standing by the car, facing the dramatic pre-sunset.

"Need some money?" Axel asked when David came up beside him.

"Nah," David said. "All good."

"Thanks," said Axel. "I didn't mean to bite your head off back there. This doesn't have anything to do with you, or Ellie even. It's me."

"Yeah I get it. But it's not just you. The future does exist, right? Keeps coming no matter what."

"I didn't mean for me, just for her. Just for Su-Yun. It's not fair that she can't be here."

"No," David agreed. "Not at all."

"I want her to know you, to know Ellie, to know Ethan. Hell, to know her own daughters, see who they've become."

"Even you."

"Even me. If I'm honest, especially me. I'm better than I was."

"Not everybody can say that," David said.

"I guess not. I think it's true. I hope it's true. I think my daughters, you know they kind of left me no choice."

"That goes both ways, Axel. I don't know if I've ever met two finer young women. That doesn't just happen out of nowhere. You have to take some credit for that."

"I just trusted them and stayed out of the way."

"Sure, maybe . . . but they've been paying attention to you, your example, and it shows."

"Okay, I'll take it. Thank you." He smiled and put his hand on David's shoulder. "Now we're even."

"I'm not usually very touchy-feely," David said.

"Me neither." Axel took his hand down.

"Thanks for taking Ethan along."

"My pleasure. Speaking of fine young people."

"He's more of an idiot than your two, though."

"Male of the species, as Marianne would explain." Axel laughed. "And it takes all of us to make the world go 'round. Idiots, future idiots, past idiots, and women."

Ethan parked the car in front of their b&b. Ellie was there at one of the picnic tables. "You got even more muddy," she observed.

"Yeah. Probably okay if we sit outside, right?" Ethan said. "I found towels in the back for us to sit on, so at least the car is okay."

"Cars should come with towels, at least Subarus should," said Ellie. "Towels and the coexist sticker."

"Standard equipment," said Anna.

"I've been left here to guard the tables. Boys went to get pizza," Ellie said. "I already got all the drinks from the mini-fridge in the little cooler here, if anybody wants anything." She popped open a beer can.

"I'll take you up on that," Marianne said. IPA in there?"

Ellie handed her a can.

"Left my phone in the car and I forgot I gotta do an Instagram post," Ethan said. "Back in a sec." He and Anna got up from the table.

"This will sound weird," Marianne said, "but I can't help imagining you 30 years ago, traveling with my dad, way before us or my mom or David or Ethan. A different world, almost."

"Part of me still feels like that 20-year-old" Ellie said. "Part of me is here and now. I also can't stop imagining Emma Too in this same place at that even more distant time. That heartbroken little girl, out here in a place she's never been, on her way to another place she's never been, with her equally heartbroken dad who has never been there either. But she persevered, and without her, there's no me. No Ethan. No lots of people. So much comes down to just continuing on."

"History is . . . strange," Marianne said.

"Have you got anybody? Ellie asked. "I mean like a relationship?"

"No," Marianne replied. "Not at the moment."

"Grad school can do that to you."

"It's not that, I don't think," she said. "It's more me."

"How so? You're personable, smart, et cetera, et cetera, et cetera. Not to mention cute."

"Guarded. I'm just very guarded. Guarding against what, I don't know. I mean I went through all the stress and anxiety of coming out and then what do I do? Nothing."

"Never?"

"Well, not much. I'm trying to be patient with myself."

Ellie smiled and reached out for Marianne's hand. "I hear you. Look, if I weren't heterosexual and married and your dad's old flame and three decades older than you, I'd date you in a second. Who wouldn't love you?"

"Um, thanks?" Marianne laughed. "My little sister, she's blessed with this naturally easy way with other people, completely unselfconscious. I envy her sometimes. Often."

"Marianne, I suspect that like most people who make something look effortless, she probably works hard at that. It's important to Anna to feel at ease, so she works at it."

"Who says I'm at ease?" Anna said as she and Ethan plopped down on the bench. "I'm freakin' flipping out."

"Sure you are," Marianne rolled her eyes.

"I mean, Ethan is going to come with us in our car, then stay with us at Grandpa's and fly with us to Colorado and stay with us there. There's no way I can keep this act up all that time. He's going to get to see the real me at some point. That's terrifying."

"He's sitting right next to you," Marianne noted.

"I'm sure he's just as terrified as you are, Anna," Ellie said, retrieving a couple of cans at random and placing them in front of Ethan and Anna.

"Roger that," said Ethan. "I'm going to be the guest of these people I've known in person only for a couple of days, and your dad and sister and even your grandpa will be there. Lots of ways for me to crash and burn. Major stress."

"Just do a little interstate bike ride together, that would be so much simpler," Ellie said. "Oh, wait, never mind . . ."

The black SUV pulled up and David emerged from the passenger seat with three pizza boxes.

"Two meat, one veggie," he placed the boxes on the table in front of Ethan.

"We're gonna run out of drinks," Ellie said. "Should have asked you to get more."

"There's water," David said. "Or somebody can run out."

"I'll go back out if we need it," Ethan said as he typed something into his phone. "Bring back a couple more pizzas, too. Freakin starving."

"Do you have your stuff together for tomorrow"? Ellie asked.

"All I brought was that daypack," Ethan replied. "So yeah, all good. I have some cash, too, and my card."

"Never looks prepared, but then he is," Ellie said. "Where have I heard that before?"

"You read it somewhere," Axel laughed.

"You ought to write up this part, too," Anna said. "Kind of complete the cycle. The same plot form comes back three times in three iterations. That would be properly literary."

"In that case, a third person should write it." Ellie looked pointedly at Anna.

"In the third person?" Anna replied.

"Ha-ha," said Ellie. "English major joke. That's why we're the only ones laughing."

"Dad smiled, I saw it."

Axel was still smiling. The sky had cleared and the low evening sun was intensifying all the colors against the long shadows. It was still full summer, he knew, but that angle of light foreshadowed a lower sun a month from now, then cooler air, then snow and dark, then the slow climb back toward spring. By then he might have both daughters at home, or he might have neither. And maybe his dad. Another year.

The sound of a motor arose from the direction of the main road. Half a minute later, Nigel's black Triumph rolled to a stop in front of them. Natalie was seated behind him. "We never gave you a proper send-off," she said. "And also I had to address the tragedy of you not finding any Genny pounders."

"Stay and sit a while," David stood up. "Plenty of space."

Natalie leaned forward and spoke into Nigel's ear. He nodded and she climbed off. He nudged the bike forward around the black SUV and parked it between it and the Subaru.

"Nice spot here," Natalie looked around. "When you said b&b with picnic tables over this way I knew exactly where it was. Farm's that way down this road." She pointed away from town.

Nigel placed a 12-pack of oversize green cans on the table with one hand, and added a grocery sack containing two large bags of chips with the other. "Partake," he said.

"Thanks much," Axel said. "We were going to have to go back out."

Nigel walked over to Marianne. "Felt like I never said a proper thank-you, miss."

"Marianne," she said.

"Marianne, I much appreciate you hoisting me out of the drink like that. I'm a lucky man you were there."

"Training kicked in. I didn't even think about it," she said. "I'm glad it was good training."

"Oh for God's sake," Ellie said. "Take a little credit."

"All right," Marianne smiled. "You're welcome. And I appreciate your making a point to thank me."

"Good person to have around, Marianne is," Ethan said, turning to Natalie. "Sorry the Big Tree thing didn't work out for you today. That was a cool project. I mean the idea that a tree like that could outlast all our lifetimes."

"Two times over," said Anna. "Three or four times over."

"Who knows what America would be by that time?" Ellie laughed.

"I'm not even sure what it is now," Ethan said. His phone signaled, and he glanced at it.

"That original Big Tree," Natalie said, "it washed out in the 1850s, and they say it was at least 300 years old then. That's almost back to Christopher Columbus. Way before the Pilgrims and the Mayflower. Only Indians around at that time, maybe a French fur trader now and then."

"So, Natalie," Ellie said, "you remember when we came back through here way back when, I don't know if I said it at the time but part of my idea besides trying to figure out where people had come from and how they got where they got, was to get a handle on the character of this country. And I gotta say that part ended up being totally inconclusive. All I got was a pretty wide variety of people I met who, if they considered the question at all, didn't agree on a whole lot what it meant to be an American."

"Yeah, that sounds right," Natalie said. "And you forgot one other thing: your traveling partner."

"Of course," Ellie said. "I kinda dragged Ax along, but it wasn't really his project."

"Well, you so sure about that?" Natalie asked. "Maybe he wasn't looking for what you were looking for, but he was looking for something. You don't just head out on the road for no reason at all, do you?"

"I went willingly," Axel said. "I thought it would be interesting to find out what Ellie wanted to find out. I thought the ride would be fun. I looked forward to spending the time with her, too, of course, although foolishly I thought I could do it without becoming, uh, emotionally entangled—you know, ride that fine white line. Then in the space of a week or two we both end up in the ditch."

"What I mean," said Natalie, "is that who you travel with is a big part of how you feel about the country you're traveling in, you get me? I mean you can choose who you want to be with now and in the future. But you can't choose your ancestors. I saw this over and over volunteering at the history center. You ever notice how people are always trying to find blue blood or claiming credit for what their ancestors did, or equal parts trying to get away from what their ancestors did? But really just think about somebody like Axel there—because he's adopted he probably won't ever know any of that, which makes you think about how much difference it really makes. Everybody has ancestors, but you're not traveling with them now. Good thing, too, sometimes. Maybe you dig and dig and dig and find out there's some motherfucker back there who thought it was fine to torture or kill people because it was his right as their owner, or maybe there's a priest who used the mantle of the church to abuse children, or maybe there's just one sorry fuck-up after another getting blind drunk every night and beating the shit out of their wife and kids. Know anybody with ancestors like that? Yes, you do. It's me. Who knows, maybe it's you too."

"I hope not," Ethan said, breaking the extended silence.

"Well I know you've got some old slave holders on my side, we've talked about that," David said. "Maybe they were the quote unquote good slaveholders, but still."

"No such thing as that," said Ellie. "Meanwhile I'm pretty sure there would have been some witch-burners back there among those old Puritan Crombies, torching anybody who they decided had blasphemed."

"Okay, okay," said Anna. "I get the hint."

"Don't mind me," Natalie said, "it's not my place to tell anybody how to talk. Plus I saw how you can shoot!"

"Come on," Anna said. "I'm just like anybody else. I have my act. You have yours, Nigel has his. We play our roles."

"Exactly," Natalie said. "We all live with other folks and if you're lucky enough like me you can end up with a soulmate. And you adjust to each other because you're traveling together and it beats traveling alone. College town folks act like college town folks. Big city folks like big city folks. Me, I live in a place where most everybody is descended from people who were heading west but stopped and put down roots here at least 150 years ago. Not a hell of a lot has changed since then, except everything all around us. So that's the main topic of conversation, it seems like. Hold back the flood."

"That's all real America," David said. "Big city, college town, this place right here. If you're trying to figure out America, you gotta come up with something that includes all three of those—plus the Arizona desert and Montana ranches and every city around the Great Lakes, and Memphis and Denver and the Blue Ridge mountains and Atlanta and Hawaii and Alaska and—I cringe to say it—even Florida."

"I been a lot of those places, before the bones got too brittle and I settled down here," Nigel said. "You're not wrong, that's a lot of different kinds of places with different kinds of people. But they do have one thing in common. Freedom, right? That's America, isn't it? What it's all about."

"In the first sentence of the Constitution," David said. "'promote the general Welfare' comes right before 'secure the Blessings of Liberty.' Those two things don't always work in the same direction—like in my job I might do a project like your Mount Morris dam. Classic general welfare. It costs a lot of money to build it but it works if you spread the cost out over a lot of people, then the general welfare is served because floods are prevented and people don't die and property isn't lost. But on the other hand, any big project like that is gonna cramp somebody's individual liberty. Anything from paying taxes you didn't want to pay to having your farm taken away."

"You don't need that dam," Nigel said, "if people just pay attention and don't build their house right in the flood plain."

"That's the calculation," David said. "What's worth what?"

"Uz would still be dead," said Ellie.

"Who's that?" Nigel asked.

"Uz Crombie. Long lost uncle," said Ellie. "Just one person who didn't make it."

"Lot of people didn't make it," said Nigel. "I almost didn't myself any number of times. In California once, in New Orleans. Lortnon, Virginia. But here I am."

"So you were like Uz," Ellie said. "Passing through someplace where whether you lived or died didn't have anything to do with if you decided to pay for a dam, because the dam you might have paid for would have been somewhere else. You're depending on the infrastructure of others, as my husband would say. You're a traveler, an outsider."

"I am," said Nigel. "I go my own way. No place owns me. This country lets me be that way."

"Not like in the old world where all our American settlers came from," Natalie said, "where the same families might have lived in the same towns for a thousand years. The longer you stay, the more the fibers creep up around you and bind you to the place, one strand at a time. Look at me, it's happening already, and for my family it's only been a couple hundred years at this river bend. And before them, just the Indians. Maybe that's why they had the good sense to keep moving. Stay in one place a while, and it doesn't take too long before you begin to feel a certain patch of land is mixed up in who you are and if you leave, you're gonna leave some of you behind."

"That's why people go, isn't it?" Nigel replied. "Leave yourself behind and make a new one."

Ethan nudged Anna to look at his phone. Marianne leaned over too. Ethan's Instagram post tagged "#littlebigtree" with one photo of Nigel standing on the raft in the river and another of the planted sapling had attracted a number of likes, including one from justlester that said "thanks annalog." Anna got out her phone and replied #busted #notsorry.

"I'm from a sporty little college town," Marianne said, "and like you say Natalie, certain kinds of people want to live in a place like that, and so I don't run into people like, say, your friend Lester Springer very often in my day-to-day life. And no doubt he probably doesn't hang out with too many lesbian academic biopsychologists. But he and I got on just fine. He's a good man and I'm glad I know him now. If I hadn't been traveling, if I'd just stayed in Boulder forever, I would never have met Lester. So you're right, birds of a feather do flock together. People evolved to form tribes. But I think we also evolved to cross tribes. To take a chance. To cross that mountain or valley and see who lives over there. Maybe end up throwing in our lots together with a new community. That way you keep mixing up the gene pools. Genetic diversity: it's good for the species. That's been happening since long before America, but maybe there's something about this country that has encouraged us, for better and worse, to keep trying to get over the horizon."

"I can imagine being that person," Anna said, "I know there are historical factors that drive migration and all that, but I keep coming back to the personal stories. The more you zoom in from the general history lesson of 'these are the cultural and economic forces that led the former Puritans to move west from New England blah blah blah' to the individual stories, the more you learn it's things like a letter somebody wrote, or personal grief, or too many rocks in the field, or a gigantic flood, or losing your religion, or finding religion, or restless ambition, or desperation to support a family, or somebody died, or somebody was born, or distress because your parents are splitting up, or prejudice or hate or fear, or maybe the strongest one—love. Those are the things that move people. So that must be how America got to be this way, right? All that shit."

"That's what led me out of history and into literature, all that shit," Ellie laughed. "All of that shit happened and keeps happening along this path we're on right now, just these few these roads between New Hampshire and Ohio, all criss-crossed with stories. More stories than you could know or imagine." Ellie paused. "You ever hear the one about the little white house on the hill at the edge of the woods?"

66.

When the families got together in the morning, Ellie suggested they just get on I-90 instead of retracing the small roads all the rest of the way back. "All we really want to do on the way to my parents' is stop by and have a look at the old house in Madison. I haven't been there since it was sold. My mom says they drove by a couple years ago and it looked like some recent owners had nicely restored it, took down the decrepit old trees that had grown up in front, let the woods fill in behind. Nice little bucolic scene from the nineteenth century. Miraculously not yet vinylized by suburban sprawl, as my husband would put it."

"I'd be fine with getting to my dad's a few hours earlier," Axel agreed. "And I don't feel any need to ever go to Wales Center again anyway," he laughed. Ellie shook her head to confirm that sentiment.

"Hey Mom," Ethan said, "tell Grandma and Grandpa I'm sorry to miss them this time but I'll make a special trip up in the fall, okay? Been too long."

She hugged him and kissed his cheek. "Mmm-hmm."

Approaching Lake Erie from the east in New York state, one often thinks about how this vista must have struck the earliest viewers upon seeing it for the first time: over the tops of the trees, a band of dark blue; or on a cloudy day, a tint of gray melding into another gray along an indeterminate assumed horizon. And then, after spending what would invariably seem like too long a time actually getting to the water, to discover that it is not what it appears to be, a vast new ocean, but rather an unfathomably large vessel of fresh water. Water, water everywhere, every drop to drink. Astonishing.

Only Axel saw it, and only Ellie, the two drivers. They thought of waking the others to show them, but decided to let them sleep as I-90 made its southwesterly way along the lake south of Buffalo. The highway follows the bluffs, a few hundred feet higher than the lake, land falling away to the water a mile or two away on the right, trees and fields bordering the left. For a hundred miles or so stretches an area of vineyards that produce a typical range of popular varietals, but the climate and soils find their happiest marriages with white wines that agree with the moisture and the winters and the clay soil. The region extends from New York state west of Lake Chautauqua, along Pennsylvania's short Lake Erie coastline, and finds its western limit in the Grand River valley around Madison, Ohio.

The drivers hadn't particularly intended to stay together all this way, but no other cars had come between them, so now, not long after the interstate crossed from Ashtabula County into Lake County, Ohio, Ellie put on the right turn signal. As she decelerated in the exit lane, the small black SUV pulled alongside momentarily. She glanced to the left. Axel smiled and looked over, lifting a few fingers in a gesture something like a salute. One of the daughters, probably Marianne since Anna would be in the back with Ethan, was asleep in the passenger seat, head leaning on the window, nothing visible but the black hair. Ellie smiled, too, and without thinking much about it, blew a kiss to the adjacent car.

When she stopped and turned right to cross the Grand River and find Middle Ridge Road, the change in motion aroused David. "Madison?" He asked.

"Mmmm-Hmmm," Ellie said. "Just need to find the house. Should come up pretty quick on the left. It's all fixed up now, I guess. Wonder if I'll even recognize it."

"Sort of like closing the circle, coming back here, isn't it? Of a 30-year journey."

"Longer than that, if you count Emma Too."

"Although is it a circle if you're just time-traveling back and forth along the same pathways?"

"Same path, new pavement, new trees, new paint on the houses, new travelers. Same plot, same landscape, new characters. How long could this go on?" She laughed. Then, as the car crested a rise and she looked up to the left, she felt a spark of recognition. "That might be it."

67.

Dear Grandma,

I've been meaning to write you for a while. I wanted to have a nice, neat end to the story, and I don't have that, but still there is a lot I want to tell you. I'm sorry it took so long.

One thing you will be glad to know is that Axel is doing very well. He has two lovely daughters, both grown, quite different from each other except in that they both embody a kind of independence of which you would very much approve. Their mother, Axel's wife Su-Yun (her grandparents came to California from Taiwan), was killed in a car accident many years ago, and I can tell they are all still sad about that and always will be. Still, they are well. Axel seems strong and quick on his feet but also a little bit melancholy. Maybe he was always that way.

David and I have had a wonderful 23 years in Nashville, our son Ethan with us 21 of those. You would like the neighborhood where we live. It's old and dusty and used to be formal but now is casual. Teaching is good for me these days, but I have my issues. My students come from such a variety of backgrounds that I get more and more interested in them and how their stories could inform my own writing that I kind of forget to teach, if you know what I mean.

The world of civil engineering, where David spends his days, has a little bit of that too—at least you're supposed to really try to understand how people are going to use and experience public works projects before you build them. Of course, so MANY people use a public works project that it's kind of hard to focus it down to an audience. Still, it seems noble: to try to make grand things that serve small needs. That's David—his great ambition in looking at a huge project is how can it provide small delights to regular people. It almost a subversive pleasure for him, to turn the vast and impersonal into something gentle, even funny. I think I'm just too selfish, too focused on individual expression, to think like that. I guess that's why we fit so well together, part of why I love him so much. I sorely wish you'd had a chance to meet him.

Ethan reminds me of no one so much as Axel, which makes no sense. But seeing Axel doing well sets my mind at ease a little bit about Ethan. He (Ethan) is big into bicycle racing for now, but educated as an industrial designer. I think his thought is to try to get into the design side of bicycles while he is still racing a lot, then plan a kind of transition. Oddly, this is a little bit like what Axel did. So I think he will be okay, though he seems a bit directionless. At the same time, I am well aware that Axel went through some difficult times to get where he is, and I surely don't wish for our own son to endure anything like that. So I don't know. You can't protect your kids from going through things. They have to. But still.

He and I (Axel I mean) never did find out that exact place where Emma came from—at least we didn't find it back in 1988. You wouldn't believe how many scenes I came across that look kind of like that picture from Aunt Cordelia's house—and not only in New Hampshire! It got to be almost comical. I ended up suspecting that it depicted a kind of place rather than an actual place, but who could know? I do know that we surely had an adventure chasing that image, trying to go backwards and figure out how we got to today. I spent months writing it up for my senior honors project and then decided I didn't want them to read it—I really wanted only Axel to read it. So I sent a copy to him, then filed my own copy away to be forgotten for 30 years. I guess it wasn't forgotten. But definitely filed away. You're not going to believe this, but poor Axel, his parents were splitting up just at that time, and through a series of reasons I don't need to go into here, he never received the manuscript. His mom had stowed it away in a place he never knew to look for it. That is until he was recently visiting that old house (where his dad lives now but doesn't go up the stairs because of his knees—told you it was complicated), and he found the envelope I had sent him way back then. He arranged a meeting so he could apologize, or I'm not exactly sure why, actually, and he came to Nashville and we had a coffee and talked about it. What I didn't say before was that we had kind of split up at the end of the bike ride, partly because he broke his collarbone (not even a bike accident, just tripping and falling in the dark in a stupid campsite!) and couldn't ride anymore but partly also because it seemed inevitable that our lives would soon go in different directions, with me headed for grad school and him not, etc., etc., etc. He saw that coming but I didn't really. But we agreed that if I wanted to get back together, I would send him some kind of message or call. This was the time before cell phones so I did call and talk to his mom a couple times because she was living at the house, but she was so knocked out by the divorce that I guess she never let him know. And he wasn't around much because he was racing full-time during the season, so you could see how the message might not get through. Funny how something like that could not so easily happen today, with smartphones and email and everything. And like I said I sent the manuscript and he never knew that either. So it ended up seeming to me—and I can say this honestly because I am me—that he did not want to see me anymore. It all made sense on paper, I guess, the reasons for parting ways, but it never felt right to me. And it hurt. Bad. Which kind of surprised me because I hadn't really thought we were that 'serious,' if you know what I mean. Then I find out 30 years later that he had (naturally enough) interpreted having not heard from me to mean that I didn't want to see him. I think he was looking at the breakup as a way for him to give me a graceful way out, but all the time hoping I wouldn't take it. And that hit him pretty hard. I mean, as bad as it hit me, I would say. I can still feel the pain right now and I don't know if it's mine or me thinking about his. Is that stupid or what? Neither one of us wanted out, but each thought the other did, or thought it was just the honorable thing to do, or something. It's like frigging Shakespeare or something.

Anyway, now what do you do? You have this unfinished story from decades ago, like you were reading a novel and lost the book before you could finish, and in the meantime, after looking around for the book for a long time and just hoping it would show up, you eventually just get on with things. Then all of a sudden decades later you find it again. So, it doesn't make any sense to not take it to the end and see how it works out. Right?

I still remember that night when you wished Axel and me a safe trip, and I remember your request to report to you what we discovered about America by retracing this ancestral migration. Knowing you, you might have been joking about that last part, but having your blessing was important to me, and to Axel, too, I think. It's very important to him to be trusted. As to what we discovered, I supposed that maybe 30 years of fermentation and aging would distill my impressions into some kind of coherent idea. What I have instead is the mental equivalent of what you might find in someone's attic: a baggie full of scribbled post-it notes, a stack of unlabeled pictures, maybe an old home movie or two. Possibly somebody once knew what it all meant, possibly never. The headstone of a mother who died and the child she lost at the same time. The letters written for that mother. David catching a tear.

The broad expanse of Lake Erie opening on the horizon. A rattlesnake curled benignly in a patch of sun in a place where rattlesnakes aren't thought to be. Neglected hotels at the edges of tired towns on an obsolete highway. A puff of dust on a distant paper target. Axel's quiet grin. A farmers' market in election season. Weeds winning on a race track. A sauna in the forest, and swimming naked in the water. Little League baseball. Lonely mountain trails and crowded mountain summits. Reading the words of tough young Emma and wondering about the woman she grew up to be. A dear grandmother griping with good humor about the family patriarchy; and entrusting me to a boy she had just gotten to know, and him to me; and being right in her judgment on both counts, I guess, in retrospect. A fearless young woman diving into a river; a close-up of her muscular arm clamped under a stubbled chin. Being mesmerized by the wheel in front of you at the end of a long day on the bicycle. Trees lost downstream. A sapling transplanted to the riverbank. Bad-ass Ethan blushing when Anna smiles at him. The land bearing everything on its shoulders, barely noticing, while people debate about who rightfully owns America. America the unresolved, like its people, unresolved but always searching, putting down markers, taking up markers, moving on, staying behind, telling stories, losing the thread. A small white house on a hill at the edge of a wood.

To be cherished . . . to be forgotten . . . to be continued . . .

Love,
Ellie

THANKS

My first acknowledgment goes backhandedly to COVID-19, which created circumstances that made it possible for me to write this novel—namely that I was able to step away from my 9-to-5 job and spend more concentrated time writing. It was also helpful that the pandemic had prompted my local public library to make its ancestry resources accessible remotely, which helped me discover that some of my mother's forbears had walked to northeastern Ohio from central New Hampshire in around 1820, even before the Erie Canal was dug. Intrigued, my wife EB and I took a road trip to retrace their likely route (roughly following Route 20 which followed wagon trails that followed earlier Indian paths north of New York's Finger Lakes). It's an interesting swath of America. I finished the first draft in the summer of 2021 and made significant revisions in 2023 thanks to very helpful comments from many people, including Donley family members Carol, Karen, Ted, EB, and Gwen; friends Richard Brink and Matt Berg; and members of the Proper Nouns writing group.

Crombie Hill
A novel
"A captivating blend of literary prose and historical fiction . . . lyrical and immersive . . . a timeless meditation on the connections that bind us together across generations."
—Goodreads/A Look Inside

"The emotions, human drama and intelligence kept me propelled through the whole thing."
—Goodreads

"Having traveled a similar route, it was enjoyable to read of places I've been through. Now I want to travel it again—with the areas highlighted in this delightful book. Very reflective and insightful read." —Goodreads

Also by G. M. Donley

The Virtues of Alignment
Stories and not stories

The Legend of Castle Cove
A novel

Night Music
Images from dark and noisy places in Cleveland
"Donley's images convey the visceral experience of being at a show in a small, closely packed room."
—Anastasia Pantsios, journalist and photographer.

A Small Book About Design Craft and Practice
"Such an easy and clear writing style. Made me want to really dig into the world of graphic design."
—Don Julien, filmmaker